Praise for the Abigail Adams Mysteries

The Ninth Daughter

"An exciting new mystery series set in revolutionary Boston. Abigail Adams could become my favorite historical sleuth."
—Sharon Kay Penman, author of *Prince of Darkness*

"[An] exceptional debut . . . While bringing to life such historical figures as Sam Adams and Paul Revere, Hamilton transports the reader to another time and place with close attention to matters like dress, menus, and the monumental task of doing laundry. Historical fans will eagerly look forward to the next in this promising series."
—*Publishers Weekly*

"Hamilton . . . has just the right touch to guide the intelligent Abigail through the dangerous shoals of being a patriot while seeing the good side of the colonies' English rulers. There are no missteps here in what should prove to be a captivating series for all historical fans."
—*Library Journal*

"The wry repartee between Abigail and John, together with the fact that this clandestine investigation of the murder of loose women would never have made the official record, make Hamilton's debut believable and gripping."
—*Kirkus Reviews*

"A deep historical mystery. Based on true activities of that time, Ms. Hamilton weaves a tale that could have actually taken place . . . [illegible] new-series story with a surprise [illegible] t comes next."
—[illegible] *Readers Connection*

"A super Revolutionary War–era . . . amateur sleuth."

—*Midwest Book Review*

"The story line provides a deep look at Boston as rebellion is in the air. Fans will want to join the tea party hosted by Ms. Hamilton with guests being a who's who of colonial Massachusetts." —*The Mystery Gazette*

A Marked Man

"Well-crafted . . . Hamilton once again brings to life colonial Boston on the brink of revolution, vividly portraying such noted patriots as Sam Adams, leader of the Sons of Liberty; silversmith Paul Revere; and Dr. Joseph Warren."

—*Publishers Weekly*

"Hamilton has faithfully re-created eighteenth-century Boston and its now-famous residents. She has taken a familiar time period and easily brought to life the historical figures who were key in the Revolution and in creating a new nation . . . This time period in American history, especially in the Boston area, is rife with secrecy and suspicion of others, making it a perfect setting for a complexly plotted mystery with many suspects and motives."

—*The Mystery Reader*

"The story line is fast-paced and the investigation super, but it is meeting the prime real persona and fictional characters representing the divided times in Boston in 1774 that makes *A Marked Man* a strong late-eighteenth-century thriller." —*Genre Go Round Reviews*

"A rather enjoyable read and was excellent in its presentation of historic Boston. The tensions between the two sides were described in such a way that the reader could feel it for themselves. It was a true historical fiction allowing the reader to see a glimpse of a world gone by while weaving a story to capture the imagination." —*BellaOnline*

"This is quickly becoming one of my favorite series. It can be difficult to use an historic figure in a work of fiction, but Ms. Hamilton makes Abigail Adams and other famous people such as John and Sam Adams and Paul Revere come alive on the page. All the sights, sounds, and smells of Boston in 1774 paint a vivid picture of life at that time. This is a thoroughly enjoyable sequel to Hamilton's first Abigail Adams mystery, *The Ninth Daughter*." —*Over My Dead Body*

Berkley Prime Crime titles by Barbara Hamilton

THE NINTH DAUGHTER

A MARKED MAN

SUP WITH THE DEVIL

The Ninth Daughter

Barbara Hamilton

BERKLEY PRIME CRIME, NEW YORK

THE BERKLEY PUBLISHING GROUP
Published by the Penguin Group
Penguin Group (USA) Inc.
375 Hudson Street, New York, New York 10014, USA
Penguin Group (Canada), 90 Eglinton Avenue East, Suite 700, Toronto, Ontario M4P 2Y3, Canada
(a division of Pearson Penguin Canada Inc.)
Penguin Books Ltd., 80 Strand, London WC2R 0RL, England
Penguin Group Ireland, 25 St. Stephen's Green, Dublin 2, Ireland (a division of Penguin Books Ltd.)
Penguin Group (Australia), 250 Camberwell Road, Camberwell, Victoria 3124, Australia
(a division of Pearson Australia Group Pty. Ltd.)
Penguin Books India Pvt. Ltd., 11 Community Centre, Panchsheel Park, New Delhi—110 017, India
Penguin Group (NZ), 67 Apollo Drive, Rosedale, Auckland 0632, New Zealand
(a division of Pearson New Zealand Ltd.)
Penguin Books (South Africa) (Pty.) Ltd., 24 Sturdee Avenue, Rosebank, Johannesburg 2196, South Africa

Penguin Books Ltd., Registered Offices: 80 Strand, London WC2R 0RL, England

THE NINTH DAUGHTER

A Berkley Prime Crime Book / published by arrangement with the author

PRINTING HISTORY
Berkley Prime Crime trade paperback edition / October 2009
Berkley Prime Crime mass-market edition / October 2011

Cover illustration by Griesbach & Martucci.
Cover design by Judith Lagerman.
Interior text design by Laura K. Corless.

ISBN: 978-0-425-24463-0

BERKLEY® PRIME CRIME
Berkley Prime Crime Books are published by The Berkley Publishing Group,
a division of Penguin Group (USA) Inc.,
375 Hudson Street, New York, New York 10014.
BERKLEY® PRIME CRIME and the PRIME CRIME logo are trademarks of Penguin Group (USA) Inc.

PRINTED IN THE UNITED STATES OF AMERICA

10 9 8 7 6 5 4 3 2 1

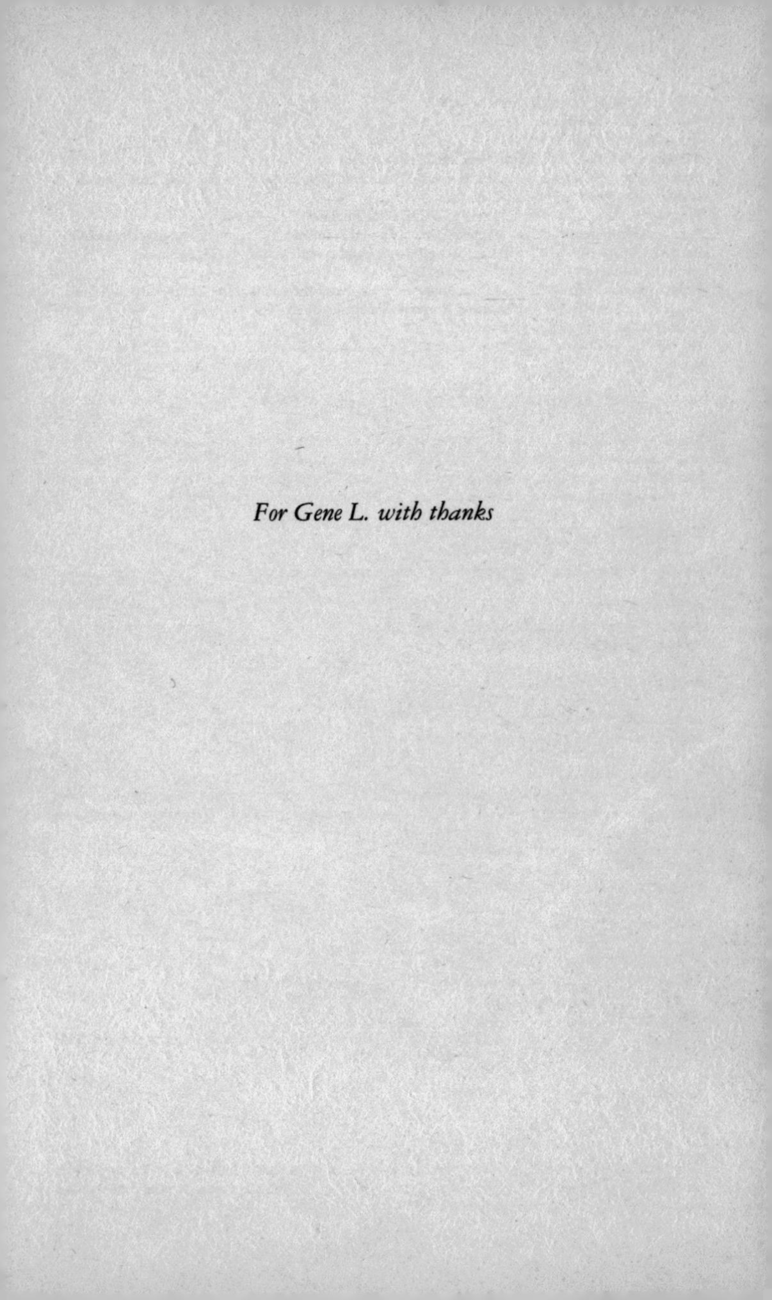

For Gene L. with thanks

One

Abigail Adams smelled the blood before she saw the door was open.

In November, Boston didn't reek the way it did in summer, especially down here in Fish Street. The coppery blood-stink cut the more prosaic pong of fish-heads and privies from the moment she stepped through the gate into Tillet's Yard, the way the single thread of gore seemed to shriek at her against the gray of the wet morning, trickling down Rebecca Malvern's doorstep.

For that first instant, Abigail thought: *One of the cats*.

Or maybe Nehemiah Tillet's cook had been clumsy, gutting a chicken.

Only then did she see the open door.

The British—

Her marketing basket slipped from her hands and she gathered her skirts, strode to the place, heart in her throat.

Rebecca—

It wasn't the first time blood had been shed in Boston. Before Abigail's eyes flashed the red-spattered snow of King Street, three and a half years ago now but alive in her mind as if it were yesterday. For an instant she heard again the shouting of the King's soldiers and the mob, smelled powder-smoke thick in the air.

Rebecca's broadsides against the King and the King's troops were absolutely scathing. *If someone told them who she was, and where she could be found—*

Abigail froze in the doorway, hand pressed to her mouth.

Her first impression was that the whole floor of the tiny kitchen had been flooded with blood. It pooled in the hollows of the worn bricks, overspilled the threshold. Yet it wasn't the first thing that slashed her mind, seized her eyes.

A woman lay facedown close to the overturned table. Gray dress, dark hair; skirt and petticoats turned up to her waist. Her bare buttocks and thighs were crisscrossed with knife slits. One shoe of fine green leather had been kicked off, lay on its side like a tiny wrecked boat against the irons of the hearth.

"Rebecca—"

Abigail's vision grayed.

The British—

Then against her will the words came to her mind—*or Charles Malvern?*

He wouldn't! She groped for the doorframe, thoughts momentarily frozen at even a mental accusation of such a thing. Charles Malvern was a pinchpenny, moneygrubbing Tory, violent of temper and outspoken in his opinion that the Crown had every right to kill traitors where they stood. Yet surely, *surely*, he would never do this to the woman who had walked out of his bed and house.

Would he?

Someone had.

Not Charles! Not Rebecca—!

Abigail took a deep breath, feeling as if her knees would give way. Stepped across the great pool of gore on the threshold, stumbled to the side of . . .

Not Rebecca. The words that had sprung to her mind as a frantic plea to God suddenly rearranged themselves, and she thought, with an odd calm, *No, in fact, it* isn't *Rebecca.*

Or at least, that isn't Rebecca's dress.

She dropped to her knees.

Dear God, forgive me for feeling relief. It was certainly some poor woman who had been used this way.

Hands shaking with reaction and guilt, she reached to

turn the woman over to see her face, then made herself draw back.

John—her beloved, self-important, irascible John, the hero of her heart, husband of her bosom, and occasional bane of her existence—was forever coming home from the colony courts fuming at the imbecility of police constables who dragged furniture about in burgled houses, who stepped on footprints left by thieves, who casually tossed out broken dishes or torn rags or any of a thousand things by which, he said, any reasonable man could reconstruct who, exactly, had broken into someone's barn or rifled someone's strong room. *Nincompoops!* (This observation was usually made at the top of his lungs and accompanied by hurling his wig against the kitchen wall.) *You'd think the lot of them were in the pay of horse thieves themselves!*

Abigail took a deep breath, folded her arms on her knees, and bent her body to try to see the woman's face.

She was obliged to straighten up again and swallow hard. Not only the woman's backside and thighs had been slashed, but her face, from what Abigail could see of it, had, too. It was difficult to be sure, because of the blood that covered it from her cut throat.

But the dress at least certainly wasn't Rebecca's. Her friend had, in truth, owned gowns as fine as that heavy gray silk with its sprigs of pink and green. But she had left them in her husband's house, when she had walked out of it for good in April of 1770. In the three and a half years since then, the frock Rebecca had worn when she left had gone the way of all flesh, replaced by whatever castoffs her friends, or the parents of the pupils she taught, cared to give her.

The dead woman's dress, and the layers of blood-boltered petticoats obscenely visible piled up on her back, were new.

And her hands were not Rebecca's hands.

Abigail had spent the first six months of Rebecca's new

freedom salving and binding cuts, blisters, burns, and scrapes while Rebecca learned to do her own cooking and her own washing, she who had never wielded anything more harsh than a quill pen in her pampered life. Rebecca's hands were short-fingered and covered with wrinkles, though she was over half a decade younger than Abigail's thirty years. These days, Rebecca's hands were perpetually stained with ink from the poetry and political pamphlets she wrote at night, and with chalk from teaching a dame school to earn enough to buy herself bread. This dead woman's hands were as Rebecca's hands once had been: soft and white, each nail pampered like those of a Spanish infanta.

Abigail sat back, and breathed again. Not Rebecca. Not her friend.

But in that case—?

Sick shock, as her eyes went to the door of the little parlor. *No—*

She made herself rise, and reached it in two steps. The little house that had been built behind Tillet the linendraper's shop had begun its life as a storage building, with the kitchen tacked onto one side and a bedroom and an attic added on top; Abigail liked to say that her daughter Nabby's dolls were more spaciously housed. The parlor was dim, its single window that looked onto the alleyway shuttered tight, but as she stepped into it Abigail's straining eyes could see nothing out of place, no humped dark shape in any corner.

She opened the casements inward and shot the bolt of the outer shutters, pushed them back in a sharp sprinkling of last night's raindrops; turned swiftly and saw—

Nothing out of the ordinary. The parlor looked as it always did. The door to the stairway above stood open. As Abigail crossed to it—two steps—she noticed the puddle of rainwater on the floor beneath the window. "Rebecca?"

Dear Heaven, what if he's still in the house?

He. The one who did that—

She went to the hearth, took up the poker, and noted as she did so the ashes heaped there, untidy, no sign of the fire having been banked for the night. *Too much wood burned*, she thought. *Why would she have sat up so late? Why the parlor, and not the warmer kitchen where she usually worked?* Every candle on the mantelpiece was burned short.

No smell of blood in the stairwell. Every tread creaked. *If he was here I'd have heard him . . .*

Still her hands were cold with fright as she came out into the minuscule upstairs hall. Barely a foyer between stairways, with the door of Rebecca's chamber to her left, open into shuttered darkness.

The attic trapdoor at the top of its ladder was shut. Abigail strode to the bedroom door, peered inside. "Rebecca?"

Narrow bed neatly made. Nothing—her mind evaded a specific. Nothing *untoward* on the floor. The attic's tiny window would be shuttered and there was no bedroom candle on the sewing table by the bed. After a moment's hesitation, Abigail climbed the attic ladder, opened the trap, and put her head through. "Rebecca!"

Mr. Tillet—or, more truly, Mrs. Tillet, who appeared to use her husband as a sort of hand puppet for the transaction of legal business—rented out this house behind the main premises, but reserved the attic for the storage of Tillet family property: boxes of old account books, crates of chipped and disused dishes, sheets that had been turned too many times to be of any use to anyone yet that Mrs. Tillet would not surrender to the ragbag. A set of carpenter's tools against which Mr. Tillet had lent one of his sons-in-law money, and had foreclosed upon. Only dark shapes in darkness as Abigail looked around her, yet the smell of dust was thick, and she saw no mark of hand or knee in the thin layer of it around the trap.

The Tillets, she thought as she descended. Yet the Tillet

house had been quiet. Even with the Tillets gone—*What had Rebecca said yesterday? A family wedding in Medford?*—surely Queenie the cook would have summoned the Watch, if Rebecca came beating on her door last night—

In the pouring rain? Would Queenie have heard her? The cook slept in the west attic of the big L-shaped house, Abigail recalled. *Would I have stood there, pounding the door and shouting, with the man who perpetrated this horror still in my house?*

Even the thought of doing so tightened her chest with panic.

Where, then? And—

She came through the door at the foot of the enclosed stairwell, saw—with the greater light in the parlor from the window unshuttered—a half dozen sheets of paper, littered on the floor. Abigail bent to pick them up, reflecting that John's admonitions notwithstanding, the sarcastic political broadsides that Rebecca wrote under names like *Cloetia* and *Mrs. Country Goodheart*, at least, should not be left here for the Watch to find.

Before I leave I'd best have a look around, to make sure I have them all. The last thing I need is for Rebecca to escape the madman who did murder in her house, only to be sought by the Crown Provost Marshal for fomenting sedition—

She looked at the paper as she moved to put it into the pocket of her skirt.

It wasn't a poem.

Her glance picked out John's name, close to the top of the list, and after it *Novanglus, Mohawk, Patriot* . . . the various pseudonyms under which he, like Rebecca, penned criticisms of Britain's rule of the Massachusetts Commonwealth. Other names on the list had similar pseudonyms appended, but many did not. She noted John Hancock's name, one of the wealthiest merchants in Boston and known throughout the colony as the man to go to if you wanted good quality tea without the added expense of the British excise tax. Below it was the name of her friend Paul Revere the silversmith, and young Dr. Warren—with his various noms de plume—and Rob Newman, sexton of the Old North Church. Billy Dawes the cobbler, Ben Edes the printer (with the names of all the various seditious pamphlets for which *he* was responsible, good Heavens!), even poor mad splendid Jamie Otis—

She knew the handwriting, too. It was the unmistakable, strong scrawl of John's wily cousin Sam: Sam who was the head of the secret society dedicated to organizing all who wished for the overthrow of the King's government in the colony. The Sons of Liberty.

Every name she recognized on the list—and there were a good many that she did not—was a man she knew as belonging to the Sons.

All of whom, if the list fell into the hands of the Governor, would certainly be jailed, and would quite possibly be hanged.

Two

Sam Adams lived in Purchase Street, in what was now called the South End: that portion of Boston which had been open fields and grazing land not very long ago. It was twenty minutes' walk along the waterfront—crowded and busy, even now on the threshold of the winter's storms—and twenty minutes back.

Too far.

From the brick steeples of Faneuil Hall, Old North Church, Old South, King's Chapel, all the bells were tolling eight.

Paul Revere would be at his shop by now, and it was only a few hundred yards to the head of Hancock's Wharf.

Hurriedly, Abigail looked around the parlor for more papers: two of Rebecca's mocking jingles and half a dozen sheets of the volume of sermons she was editing as yet another means of making enough to keep a roof over her head. With John's voice ringing in her mind, *Don't touch a thing, woman!* she gathered the broadsides, left the sermons where they were—

What else?

Skirts held gingerly high, she stepped into the kitchen again. She saw now that what had first appeared to be a battlefield of blood was in fact blood mixed with water. A costly brown cloak lay sodden with last night's rain between the body and the door. The water it had released had mingled with the single thick ribbon of blood that emerged from beneath the corpse.

The woman's dark hair was neatly coiffed: not even death had disarrayed it. What had to be diamonds glimmered in her earlobes. A love-bite a few days old darkened the waxy flesh of her bare shoulder, and there was another beside it, white and savage yet curiously bloodless-looking. Her legs lay spread obscenely. *I'm sorry*, Abigail whispered, fighting the urge to straighten the body, pull down the petticoats, cover her from the stares of the Watch that she knew would come. *To leave you thus will speed vengeance, on him who did this to you.*

What else?

Another of Rebecca's songs lay near the hearth, the punned names and descriptions of Boston merchants who claimed to be patriots while selling provisions to the British troops unmistakable. *I have my sources*, Rebecca would say to her, with her grin that made her round face look like a wicked kitten's. *I'll make them squirm.*

How long, before someone came?

Abigail put her head cautiously out the kitchen door. She'd heard Hap Flowers—the younger of Nehemiah Tillet's apprentices—in the yard a few minutes ago, taking advantage of Mrs. Tillet's absence to use the privy in peace. The linendraper's wife would watch and wait for the boys—and for the sullen little scullery girl—suspecting them of loitering to avoid work. Any other day at this hour, Abigail knew the cook herself would be in the kitchen starting the day's work at this time, but with any luck Queenie, too, would be taking advantage of her mistress's absence, and no one would be near the wide kitchen windows that looked onto the yard.

There was a shed across the yard, where the prentice-boys left packing crates to be broken up for kindling, sometimes for weeks. Abigail darted out, found a medium-sized one that neatly covered the line of blood across the back step, ducked back inside. With luck the boys—and Queenie, too—would think Rebecca herself had set it there, for purposes of her own.

In the parlor, a basket held spare slates and chalk, for such of Rebecca's little pupils as forgot to bring theirs from home. On one of the slates Abigail chalked, NO SCHOOL TODAY, and set it on top of the crate.

What else?

She kicked her feet back into her pattens, which she'd stepped out of—the movement automatic, without thinking—in the parlor, to climb the stairs. Slipped outside, closed the door, threaded the latchstring through its hole. She realized all this time she'd still been wearing her heavy green outdoor cloak, barely aware of it, so cold was the little house. The iron lifts of the pattens clanked on the yard's bricks as she hurried toward the gate, praying the Tillets had not left Medford until that morning. She recalled Rebecca saying, "Thursday," but didn't know whether that meant morning or evening: Medford lay a solid day's journey to the northwest for a wagon such as Tillet owned. Queenie the cook might prefer "resting her bones" and drinking her master's tea to making the slightest inquiry about her master's tenant, but upon her return Mrs. Tillet would be on Rebecca's doorstep before she'd changed out of her travel dress, to collect the sewing that she considered gratis, as a part of Rebecca's rent of the little house. If the wedding had been Tuesday—

"Morning, Mrs. Adams!"

Queenie's voice from the back door of the Tillet kitchen made Abigail startle like a deer. She turned, smiled, waved at the squat, pock-faced little woman in the doorway, and kept moving. She hoped Queenie didn't see her stoop in the gate and gather up her market basket as she passed through to the alley.

She tried not to run.

It was full daylight now, Thursday, the twenty-fourth of November, 1773. Gulls circled, crying, between the steeples and the gray of the overcast sky. The breeze came in from the harbor laden with salt and wildness. When she glanced to her right down those short streets that led to the waterfront Abigail could see the masts of vessels rocking at anchor, the surge and orderly confusion of stevedores and carters on the wharves. Coastal sloops and fishing-smacks at Burrell's Wharf and Clark's Wharf, unloading tobacco from the Virginia colony and the night's catch from the harbor. Ahead of her she could see tall vessels from England tied up at Hancock's Wharf, with all those things the mother country manufactured and the colonies were forbidden to produce.

Glass for windowpanes, porcelain dishes. Nails, scissors, bridle-bits, axheads, knives. Fabric—if one did not want to walk around in drab homespun or spend one's days and nights at a parlor loom—and the thread and needles to sew it with; ribbons, corset-strings, hats. Sugar that had to be imported from England even though it was manufactured on this side of the Atlantic, in Barbados and Jamaica. Salt for preserving meat; mustard and pepper. Stays and buttons and shoe buckles, coffee and tea.

The colony must support the mother country, the Tories said: timber and wheat, potash and salt fish. *Unnatural mother, who forbids her children to outgrow their leading-strings!* She could almost hear Rebecca saying it, on one of dozens of nights during the six months she'd lived with her and John after leaving Charles Malvern, sitting with them at the kitchen table at the white house on Brattle Street, while John "cooked up" his letters, articles, protests under a dozen different names. *What would you or any of your neighbors say of Abigail, sir, if she tried to keep Nabby or Johnny from learning to walk, to run, to one day take their place in the world of grown women and men?* And John had grinned at her and dipped his pen in the standish (that had been imported from England—the ink, too!) and had said, *That's good . . . I'll use that.*

Her mind chased the thought back. Rebecca, still with Charles then, had been in that same kitchen with her in

March of '70, when shots had rung out in the snowy twilight. It was Rebecca who'd stayed with the children—Johnny had been three at the time, Nabby almost five—when Abigail, great with another child, had gone to the end of Brattle Street, and had seen the dead of what had come to be called the "Boston Massacre," and the dark gouts of blood on the trampled snow.

Her second daughter—her poor, fragile Suky—had died, barely a year old, only the month before the Massacre. It was Rebecca who had comforted her, talked with her so many nights in that kitchen, when John was away at the distant courts or meeting with the Sons of Liberty—to Rebecca she had been able to say what she would not say to John for fear of opening the wounds of his own raw grief. When Charley was born at the end of that May after the Massacre, Rebecca had been there to care for the other two, and had stayed on until nearly October, before finding rooms of her own in the maze of crowded boardinghouses and tenements in the North End.

And now she had fled—*Where?* As she passed North Square Abigail almost turned her steps to Revere's house, knowing it was there that Rebecca would go, but if Rebecca for some reason had not, then Revere would be at his shop. In any case—

The shop windows were unshuttered. Smoke issued from the chimney, white and fluffy, a new-lit fire. For one instant, as she opened the shop door, Abigail's heart leaped, as she recognized wily cousin Sam, and Dr. Warren, standing by the counter. But as she crossed the threshold she heard Sam saying, "Not a man in ten cares about their damned tea monopoly. Not one in fifty cares that the King can declare a monopoly, and then give his friends the only rights in the colony to sell the stuff at whatever the market will—Abigail, my dear!" He had a beautiful voice, deep and convincing, and a way of speaking that could ignite the air even if all he was doing was gleefully relating the latest fight between the household cats. "To what do we owe this pleasure?"

"Has John returned from Salem?" asked Dr. Warren. "He said he'd—"

"There's a dead woman on the floor of Rebecca Malvern's kitchen," said Abigail quietly. "Her throat was cut. Rebecca is gone, and I found this"—she held out the list—"near the body."

Sam's pink face turned the color of bad cream.

Revere said, "I'll get my hat."

Dr. Warren said, "Good God!" and dropped to his knees beside the body.

"I left her as I found her," explained Abigail, as the young physician gently lifted back the jumble of petticoats, to reveal the extent of the slashing. Abigail had to turn her eyes away.

Sam called over his shoulder, "Who is she?" on his way into the parlor. Abigail heard him tapping and pushing at the paneling. Though she knew that time was short—anyone could come upon them and call the Watch with who knew what information still lying loose in corners—still she felt her ears get hot with anger, that he did not even pause in his stride.

Carefully, Warren turned the woman over. "Get some water, if you would, please, Mrs. Adams."

Abigail hesitated, but the sight of those distorted features under their darkening crimson mask sent her to the half-empty jar of clean water beside the hearth. They could do nothing until they'd identified her, after all. As she returned, carefully carrying the soaked rag wrapped in a dry one, she noted the marks of her own pattens on the bricks, where she'd trodden in the blood when first she'd entered that morning. There were a man's tracks, too, dark and nearly dried.

"What happened?" she whispered in horror, as Dr. Warren wiped the gore from the woman's cheeks and nose. "She wasn't—strangled . . . Why does she look like that?"

"She's been lying on her face." The young doctor's fingers brushed the yellowish shoulders, the stiffening curve of the neck, avoiding the gaping red slit that knife or razor had opened from ear to ear. "The blood will sink down through the flesh once the heartbeat ceases, like water oozing out of a sponge. All this"—he gestured toward the slashed legs, the cuts on the cheeks and breasts—"looks as if it were done after she was dead."

Abigail reached to draw up one of the chairs, then went over gingerly to it, and sat down on it where it stood. *Must not disturb anything . . .*

"Do you recognize her?" Sam reappeared in the parlor doorway.

Behind him, Revere said quietly, "I doubt her own husband would."

Only Revere, thought Abigail, *seems to have taken note of the broad gold wedding band on the woman's bloodless hand.* She said, "Her pockets should tell us something," and Dr. Warren—who was in truth very young—looked shocked at the suggestion.

As she came over to his side, her skirts firmly gathered up to avoid the blood, Abigail heard Revere ask Sam quietly, "Anything?"

"Not yet."

She looked up sharply at the pair of them, Revere dark and burly in the short rough jacket of a laborer, Sam looking like what he was—a slightly down-at-the-heels middle-aged gentleman, until you saw his eyes. It was his eyes—the way he glanced around the kitchen as if seeking something, concerned with something beyond the horror of this woman's death—that angered her. She said, a little tartly, "I take it Rebecca didn't simply write poems and broadsides to make fun of the British. Was she a Son—or a Daughter—of

Liberty?" The edge on her voice came not only from Sam's abstraction in the face of death: She, Abigail, would have been a Daughter of Liberty herself, had such an organization existed—and had she not been either carrying a child or nursing one for most of the preceding nine years (*thank you, John*). It was typical of Sam that he hadn't even thought to form such a group while organizing the men.

Sam cleared his throat, a little deprecatingly, and it was Revere who answered her question. "Mrs. Malvern handled the communication between our organization and the other Committees of Correspondence in other colonies."

"That explains, I suppose," said Abigail drily, "how Rebecca got her information about what passed in the British camp. As to this poor soul—"

Carefully, she worked her hand through the placket in the gray silk overskirt, the embroidered underskirt, and found the pockets—silk, too, by the feel of them—tied around her waist. One contained three keys, a handkerchief, an ivory set of housekeeping tablets with a pencil attached; the other, a single piece of paper folded in quarters.

"That's ours," said Dr. Warren, looking over Abigail's shoulder as she unfolded the paper. Written on it was simply, *The Linnet in the Oak Tree. Cloetia.* "One of our codes, I mean. Linnet is Wednesday. The Oak Tree is midnight."

"And Cloetia is one of the names Rebecca used, to sign her poems." Abigail turned the purse over in her fingers, opened it to dump five gold sovereigns and a few cut pieces of Spanish silver into her palm. "Did the Sons give Rebecca money for informers?"

"Patriots have no need for paid spies," declared Sam indignantly. "There are more than enough good Whigs—true patriots—who have their country's good at heart, to—"

"So she would not have had a sum of money in the house, for instance, that contributed to this—this *obscenity*?"

"Ah." Sam rubbed the side of his nose with his forefinger.

"We do pay for information sometimes," said Revere. "Though robbery doesn't seem to have been involved here. Nor, to judge by her earrings, does money seem to have been the reason this woman came here last night."

"We won't know what her reason was," said Abigail softly, clinking the coins in her hand, "until we know who she was, and what she may have brought with her besides what was in her pockets. For all we know, she was wearing a diamond crown, and the killer overlooked the earrings."

She got to her feet, looked down at the woman, now lying on her back. Her revulsion and horror had dissolved in her anger at Sam, and in the blood, the horrid wound on the throat, the flattened bulge of the engorged and darkened breasts she saw now only the mute plea for vengeance and for help. She handed the purse to Sam, slipped the folded paper into her own pocket.

"In any case you'd probably better see if any more money is in the house, since Rebecca never had a penny of her own to spare. And you might want to sift through the fireplace ashes, to see if anything was burned or half burned that might tell tales to the Watch. John says he's caught more than one plaintiff in a lie, by scraps he's found at the back of someone's hearth. I'm going upstairs to see what I can find."

Three

The light was stronger in the bedchamber now, as the sun strengthened somewhere beyond the overcast of the sky. The first thing Abigail saw by it as she stepped through the door was the slight depression in the worn pillows, and the stains of mud and wet on the faded green and white counterpane of the bed's daytime dress.

Someone had lain here. *Not Rebecca*, Abigail thought, shocked—Rebecca would no more lie down on a made-up bed with her shoes on—and, it looked like, a rain-wet skirt—than she'd have run down Fish Street naked. Yet when she stepped closer, she saw the single hair on the pillow that looked indeed like her friend's—dark, almost horsehair thick, with a springy curl to it that had been the despair of Rebecca's maid back in the days when she *had* a maid. Abigail pursed her lips with vexation that she hadn't brought her little ivory measuring tape with her, then turned to the sewing basket on the bedside table, heaped with its neat stacks of cut pieces of linen and calico: the unofficial corveé Mrs. Tillet demanded of her husband's tenant. That sewing, reflected Abigail, and the understanding that Rebecca would attend three services every Sunday with the family at the New Brick Meetinghouse, where Mr. Tillet was a deacon, *and* help Queenie in the kitchen on those days when one or the other of the Tillet daughters would come to dine with their husband and babies—

In the eighteen months that Rebecca had rented this little house, Abigail had heard everything there was to hear about its landlord and his grasping wife.

There was a measuring tape tucked in at a corner of the basket, and the measure, from hair to the muddy smudges, marked the height of the woman who had lain there at something just over five feet. Rebecca's height. And the dampness corresponded in extent to a woman's skirt: not wet as if she'd been soaked, but she'd definitely been out in last night's rain. As Abigail laid the tape-end to the pillow, she saw on the worn linen a red brown dot of blood.

Dense in its center, clouded at its edges as if diffused by hair. Damp in the center, dry at the edges, as if it soaked deep: an investigation of the pillow within the sham confirmed this.

A slow bleed, over a period of time.

How much time?

Abigail couldn't imagine how she would calculate it, but it was clear Rebecca had lain in one position for a long while. Dazed? Unconscious?

Bound?

Cold inside and breathless as she had been when first she'd entered the kitchen downstairs, Abigail looked around the room again, slowly, seeking anything out of the ordinary.

A simple bureau. A single cane-backed chair. No candle on the bedside table—she had not come up for the night, then, when she'd been brought up here, laid upon her bed—whose linen, thankfully, showed no sign of violence or struggle. The faint smudges of dirtied water—as if Rebecca had stepped briefly on her own doorstep after the rain had begun—were barely an inch long, in one place only.

Trembling, Abigail made herself draw a deep breath, and focus her mind: a discipline learned in the course of a year of dealing with a strong-willed and unwilling five-year-old boy in church when she was trying to concentrate on the sermon. The candle hadn't been brought up but the shutters had been closed and latched, probably when first the evening's cold had settled in. Rebecca had left her sewing by the bed, gone back downstairs to the kitchen where it was warm.

Rebecca's Sunday dress hung on its peg, her Sunday underskirt beside it. She had no shoes, but what she wore every day, and those, like her everyday dress, were missing. Abigail recalled the mustard yellow frock her friend had worn, trimmed and flounced in blue and edged with rich lace, when she'd appeared on Abigail's doorstep that night in April of 1770: *I have left him, I have left him, I won't go back . . .*

Too fine for a woman to wear to work about the house. Abigail had lent her her own second-best everyday bodice and skirt. Rebecca had sold the lace-trimmed dress, she remembered, and bought stockings and cloth for chemises with the money. Everything she had put on her body from that time had been castoffs, worn-out, turned, recut. Charles, Abigail recalled, had tried to sue Rebecca for the money he had spent on the dress.

The bed, the chair, the bureau were likewise castoffs, from friends, or members of Abigail's wide-ranging merchant family. The rag rug had come from the Brattle Street Meeting-House's parlor—

The rug. It had been thrust aside from its usual position between the bed and the door. Kneeling beside the door itself, Abigail saw three more blood droplets on the worn planks, just at the opening edge.

No trail of drips from the bed. The wound hadn't been bleeding freely, then. She'd remained beside the door—*doing what?* What *would* she have been doing, that the drops had fallen onto the floor and not her shoulder?

The door opened inward, without bolt or latch. Only wooden handles.

Abigail stepped into the tiny hall again.

Last week, her daughter Nabby had imprisoned six-year-old Johnny in the bedroom they shared by running a length of light rope washing-line through the door handle on the outside and tying it to the stair rail. Such a rail was indeed visible at the top of the staircase. Johnny, who had John's gunpowder temper, had wept himself almost sick with rage at his imprisonment, and the family had only the boy's innate caution to thank that he hadn't tried to liberate himself through the bedroom window.

Yes, Abigail thought, as the glint of metal caught her eye from a shadowed corner of the hall near the head of the stairs.

Scissors.

From the sewing basket by the bed.

He'd imprisoned her, then. Carried her up to the room, laid her on the bed—bound or unbound—and tied the door shut. She'd regained consciousness, gotten to the sewing basket, used the scissors to cut herself free, and managed to get the door open enough to get a hand through and saw with the blade at the rope. While downstairs—

Abigail shuddered. *Whoever he is, I will see him hang.*

She descended the stair to the parlor again, stopped on the threshold in fresh horror. "What are you *doing*?"

Dr. Warren straightened up from his knees, slopped the wad of pink-stained rags back into the bucket that stood on the floor at his side. In the dim gleam of light from the kitchen—the parlor shutters remained closed—the bare bricks glistened damply. "We trod in the blood," said Sam, sitting at the desk wiping his boot soles with another handful of dripping rags. "You, me, Paul . . . all of us. Watch her head," he added, as Revere came in from the kitchen, carrying the dead woman in his arms.

Abigail could only stare, openmouthed with outrage.

Acerbically, Sam added, "If the Tillets' cook saw you in the yard, there has to be a reason you didn't go to the Watch at once. It can only be that you didn't see her, or anything amiss in the kitchen. She's a little hard to miss."

"You *can't*—"

Abigail brushed past Revere and into the kitchen again, to see what the men had wrought in her absence. The floor was clean. The man's tracks in dried blood were gone. The overset chair, replaced at the table; the fireplaces cleared of ash.

John would have an apoplexy.

And the killer, whoever he was, would go free.

In the parlor behind her she heard Revere say, "She's starting to stiffen," as he maneuvered the awkward body into the stairwell.

"I found these." Sam came to her side, held out to her a handful of scribbled sheets. "She must have had them out last night. They aren't ours."

"Rebecca did other things for her living, besides write pamphlets for the Sons of Liberty." Abigail took them: more scrawled sermons, virulent with descriptions of Hell's fire and of devils *clinging like leeches to the corner of your mouth, to catch the smallest whisper of ill words—O Sinner, do you feel the prick of their claws*? "Orion Hazlitt is having her go over these, before he sets the type."

"Would she have gone to Hazlitt?"

Abigail heard in his voice something more than speculation about Rebecca's choice of refuge, and saw the glint of gossipy curiosity in his gray eye. She made her voice calmly flat. "'Tis a good ten minutes to Hanover Street. Farther than my house, which lies in the same direction."

Sam canted a suggestive eyebrow, which made Abigail want to snap at him that Rebecca's friendship with the young printer wasn't any of Sam's business.

Rebecca had endured enough glances of that kind from her husband's supporters—that assumption that any woman who lived by herself was a slut in her heart—without getting them from the Sons of Liberty as well.

"She was hurt," said Abigail tightly. "I found blood on her pillow. I think the killer must have struck her on the head. She managed to get out of here, but if he saw her—if he knew *she* saw *him*—"

"Hrm." Sam frowned. "It was dark as Erebus, remember, and raining oceans. She could have given him the slip, easily enough. She knew the neighborhood and he didn't—"

"And what makes you think he didn't?" retorted Abigail. "Any one of your North End toughs who thinks it's a good joke to tie a burning stick to a dog's tail—any one of the sailors from the docks who'd rather fight with the Watch than eat his dinner—"

"Now, a little rioting on Pope's Day isn't the same as this"—Sam nodded back toward the kitchen—"and you know it. Mrs. Malvern has to have gotten away because if she didn't, one of the neighbors would have found her body as soon as it grew light. They'd have brought word of it to me or to Paul or to the Watch . . . and none of those things happened. By the same token, if Mrs. Malvern was hurt as badly as you fear, and fell, at daybreak she'd have been found by a neighbor. Orion Hazlitt—"

The stairwell door opened: Revere and Dr. Warren emerged. Warren went to collect their coats from the chair beside the desk—*Of course,* Abigail noted wrathfully, *the puddle of rainwater beneath the window has been mopped away with everything else.* Revere moved to close up a hinged niche in the paneling that Abigail had not seen before, close to the fireplace in the room's darkest corner. A secret niche—empty now, but Abigail could see how a paper or two, dropped by someone standing before it, could easily whisk through the kitchen door.

Rebecca's hidey-hole for unwritten poems—and incriminating lists.

"When you first came in here," said Sam quietly, "you didn't take anything, did you? Other than the list that you brought me?"

Exasperated, Abigail replied, "John has always told me that if you want a hope of solving a crime, never remove or alter anything from its scene until you've had a chance to examine everything there."

"Well, the next time someone's murdered in the house of one of the Sons of Liberty," retorted Sam, "we'll have John talk to the Watch . . . *if* he deigns to be in town for the occasion. In the meantime, when you were here this morning, you didn't happen to see a brown ledger, about so big—" His hands sketched a quarto-sized rectangle, about half the size of the green-backed household ledger that still lay on the corner of Rebecca's desk. "It would have 'Household Expenses' written on the cover."

"And I collect," said Abigail, "it does not contain anything to do with the cost of candles and flour?"

There was another silence, as the men looked at one another. Then Sam nodded toward the niche as Paul fiddled shut its catch, and his heavy jaw set hard. "The rest of the papers in there had mostly to do with Rebecca's pamphleteering, and her sources of gossip within the British camp. But the brown ledger held the names of *our* men in the British camp—and the ciphers we use to communicate with them and with the Committees of Correspondence in Virginia and elsewhere. If those fall into the British commander's hands, we're all going to be in a great deal of trouble."

Four

"For Heaven's sake, woman, don't march out of here as if you were leading a troop of dragoons!"

Half past nine striking from Old South Meeting-House. Abigail—who had simply put her head out the rear door to ascertain whether Queenie was in the Tillet kitchen—could see no sign of activity in the house, but the sounds of passing footsteps, of sailors shouting to one another in Fish Street, of peddlers and stevedores along the wharves, came clearly to her. She drew back inside, where Sam, Revere, and Dr. Warren clustered nervously behind her.

"Give me the count of three hundred. That should give me time to go around to the shop, and ask the boys if Queenie or that scullery girl is there, and draw them out of the back of the house. You can empty the water and the rags into the outhouse as you go out, and I'll keep them talking for a while, before we come back here and find the body. I'll try to have Queenie with me when I—"

"No!" Sam's big hand flinched in a shushing gesture. "We go to Hazlitt's first. *Then* we call the Watch."

"You really think that mother of his would have let Mrs. Malvern through the door?" Revere asked, a few minutes later, as the four of them made their way along Middle Street trying to look like people out pursuing their lawful business.

"A woman crying for help, on a pitch-black night, in

the pouring rain?" By his disbelieving frown, Abigail deduced that Dr. Warren hadn't heard Lucretia Hazlitt on the subject of Babylonian harlots who deserted honest husbands in order to seduce *her* innocent son. "For that matter, why wouldn't Mrs. Malvern have simply run to the nearest watchman—?"

"Perhaps because it was pitch-black and pouring rain," replied Sam, "and the nearest watchman was huddled next to the common-room fire at the Sheep and Lamb—"

"At midnight?" protested Warren—who obviously thought that all taverns along the Boston waterfront obeyed the city ordinances about closing times.

Sam and Revere gave him glances that pitied his naïveté. They crossed the Mill Creek on its little bridge, the waters low now on the slack tide, though when the tide was running it could make a respectable enough torrent to turn the water mill that reared up to their right. Abigail couldn't keep herself from glancing down at the gray stream and tried to put from her mind what this street would be like on such a night as last night had been, with every house shuttered tight and the rain hammering down, no starlight, no moonlight, only the rush of the tidal flow in the stream to guide a woman groping in the darkness.

"Mother, I'm quite sure that Deacon Curtin has heard every one of the arguments for Mankind's Salvation by good works," Orion Hazlitt was saying as Sam and Abigail entered his tiny shop.

His mother neatly sidestepped the gentle hand that he put out, and planted herself before the customer, whose face was growing alarmingly red. "*Forgetting those things that are behind*, the Apostle says, *and reaching forth unto those things that are before, I press toward the mark.*" Still dazzlingly beautiful, for all the silvering of the raven hair beneath her house-cap, Lucretia Hazlitt shook a finger at the elderly man whom Abigail recognized as one of the Deacons of New South Church. "Now, if the truth revealed unto the Apostle had been, *I sit still, knowing that God hath already saved me without the slightest stir on my part toward salvation*, would he not have *said, I sit still, knowing—*"

"Please." Hazlitt took his mother's hand, began to lead her toward the shop's rear door, which led, Abigail knew, into an even tinier "keeping room." These little kitchen-cum-parlors backed most Boston shops whose upper floors housed the shopkeepers' families. His strained smile did nothing to change the outraged deacon's glare, but he tried anyway. "My mother doesn't always know what she is saying."

"So I should hope," retorted the man drily.

"I know without some hypocrite roarer to tell me, my son, that *Faith without Works is dead—*"

"Exactly so, Mrs. Hazlitt." Abigail stepped neatly to Mrs. Hazlitt's other side, and took her hand. "Yet, m'am, I have wanted for a long time to ask you, how do you reconcile what the Lord said to Ezekiel, about *my comeliness that I had put upon you . . .* ?" Though Abigail loved few things more than she loved a good discussion of well-reasoned theology, she knew she wasn't going to get one from Mrs. Hazlitt. She hoped, as the widow poured an excited torrent of Scripture, personal visions, and the revelations of her own favorite pastors over her, that Sam would conclude his questioning of Orion promptly and come to her rescue.

And the part of her mind that wasn't silently protesting the view of God the Eternal Tally-Keeper—silently, because Mrs. Hazlitt never permitted anyone to interrupt the flow of her revelations and opinion—raised a disbelieving eyebrow and asked, *Sam?*

"The Devil speaks through the mouths of sinners," proclaimed Mrs. Hazlitt, pacing back and forth before the unswept, ash-piled hearth. "The Devil sends them into the world to tempt and try us, and to argue us out of our faith!" Glancing around her at the uncleared table, the market basket still sitting empty on the sideboard, the empty woodbox, Abigail wondered if the latest in the line of "girls" hired to help the household had quit—or been released—or was simply more slack than most about her duties. Prior to his mother's arrival to share his house, Abigail knew that Orion Hazlitt had managed, on the slender proceeds of his printing and stationery shop, to pay an elderly housekeeper . . . an arrangement which had concluded within three days of Mrs. Hazlitt's appearance on the doorstep.

"The Devil sends tempters to call my poor son away from me, to take him from my side." The lovely widow stopped directly before Abigail, stared at her with tears suddenly brimming in her emerald eyes. "He wouldn't forsake me of his own volition, and I tremble for him, tremble at his sin! *Honor thy father and thy mother, that thy days may be long in the land that God hath given thee!*"

"Of course, m'am." It was no wonder, Abigail reflected, that for two years now the printing business had been in slow decline, and the shop, with its few books and boxes of stationery, wore a dusty and neglected look. Too many days Abigail had walked down Hanover Street and seen the shutters up while Orion, with superhuman patience, reasoned with this woman, or cleaned up the messy destruction that resulted from her moments of fury.

"Why would God have given Mankind Commandments, if as that—that deplorable and desolate Worldly-Man out there—has said, that some are saved from the beginnings of Time? *Honor thy father and thy mother*, and yet he thrusts me away from him! He leaves his own mother to be drowned in the Flood, while he chases after the Daughters of Babylon, the Daughters of Eve! The serpent, the harlot—"

"Now, Mother." To Abigail's infinite relief, the door through to the shop opened and Orion came in, trailed by

Sam. "Wasn't I there to hold your hand, the moment the rain began?"

Mrs. Hazlitt flinched at the word, and shivered. "*Fifteen cubits upward did the waters prevail*," she whispered, "*and the mountains were covered.*" Her long, slender hands clutched at her son's coat-facings, and she pressed her face to his breast. "*All flesh died, that moved upon the earth.*"

"Mrs. Adams," whispered Orion, with a nod in the direction of the cold fireplace. "Could you bring me that vial, there on the corner of the mantle . . . Just a drop, in a cup of water . . . *only* a drop . . . Mother," he said gently, in the voice of one trying to coax a much-loved child, "Mother, it's all right, I'm here. I've been here all the time. There's nothing to fear. Your little king is here."

Sam stood with folded arms in the doorway, watching with a combination of exasperation and pity. He wasn't insensitive, Abigail knew. Only swept, like a prophet, with a sense of his mission, and at the moment, his mission was to protect the cause of colonial liberties—the Sons of Liberty—from being absolutely undone by having the Watch come into Rebecca Malvern's house and somehow stumble upon the book of names that he hadn't been able to find. Orion looked fagged to death, as if he had had very little sleep, and if the state of his mother's mind at the mention of rain was anything to go by, the night must have been a trying one.

"*The waters prevailed*," she murmured, sinking down into her chair, "*and all the high hills under heaven were covered*. But you were there to save me and comfort me. Don't ever leave me, my son." She looked up at Abigail. "My son is a good son. A child of righteousness," she whispered, and transferred her grip to Orion's hands as he put the cup to her lips. "I pray every day that he will be delivered out of the snares of Evil, and find his way back to Salvation before it is too late. Save me and comfort me . . . How could a boy who is so good run after the ways of Sinners, and stuff himself in the trough of Hell?" She began to nod.

"What happened?" Orion asked over her head in a low voice. "Mr. Adams tells me you found a woman—dead—in-in—He said that Rebecca—that Mrs. Malvern," he corrected himself shakily, "—is-is gone, fled—"

"Did you see her yesterday?" asked Abigail.

"Yesterday evening, yes. That's what I was telling Mr. Adams. I went there just after eight, to pick up the proofs for the sermons she is correcting for me, and a broadside about the meeting Tuesday against the tea tax." Just about the only printing business that remained to him, Abigail knew, was that done for the Sons of Liberty. And even in that he was becoming less and less reliable, as he struggled to balance caring for his mother with making a living.

"Did Mrs. Malvern say anything about meeting someone there later?"

Hazlitt shook his head. "She said she had sewing yet to finish for that Tillet harpy, and after that was going to bed. I was ashamed to keep her up, waiting even that late for me. But that wretched witch Queenie spies on her. The Tillets would put her out, if they thought she was meeting a man. The woman you found—"

"We have no idea who she is. Clearly she's wealthy. She had on diamond earrings—"

"They threw her down from the window." Mrs. Hazlitt raised her head, blinked sleepily up at Abigail. "She tir'd her head, and painted her face, and called out to Jehu as he drove his chariot into the court. They threw her down from the window. Her blood was sprinkled on the wall and on the legs of the horses, and the horses trode her underfoot. When they came to bury her, there was naught left of Jezebel the Queen, save her skull, and her feet, and the palms of her hands." She tucked her son's hand a little more closely beneath her cheek, and drifted off again into her dreams.

Abigail looked around the little room again, at the messy hearth, and the candlesticks clotted with tallow and the few dishes containing nothing but bread crumbs and butter-smears. There was a stain on the whitewashed plaster of the wall, where food had been recently thrown. "Have you no one to look after her?" she asked. "Or yourself, for that matter—"

"The girl chose yesterday afternoon to go off and visit her family," sighed Hazlitt. "She should be back tomorrow. I shall manage. It isn't the first time."

Presumably, reflected Abigail, any girl willing to work for what Hazlitt could pay, and put up with Mrs. Hazlitt into the bargain, was not to be turned out no matter how flagrantly she took advantage of her employer.

"Have you called the Watch?" asked the printer.

"We're off to do that now." Sam glanced over his shoulder into the shop at the tinkle of the bell above the door. But it was only Revere and Dr. Warren, elaborately casual as a couple of Roman Senators pretending they didn't have daggers under their togas. "We needed to make sure what you knew, before we went stirring up any ponds and raising a stench. For all we knew, she'd come here to you—"

"Would to God she had!" Hazlitt looked desperately across at Abigail. "I would have thought she'd go to you, Mrs. Adams, if she couldn't wake that half-drunk slut of a cook . . . whom Judgment Day wouldn't wake, belike."

"I would have thought so, too," said Abigail quietly.

"It's early days yet." A trace of uneasiness stained Sam's rich voice. "Listen, Hazlitt. While you were in Mrs. Malvern's house, did you see a brown quarto-sized account book anywhere? It had 'Household Expenses' stamped on its front cover."

The printer shook his head. He was, Abigail guessed, thirty, and took after his mother's beauty. When Abigail had first met him back in '68, she'd marveled that, poor as he was, he had no wife. Had he married then, she wondered, would his mother have been able to move in with him as she had? Or would she have done so—quoting the

Fifth Commandment all the way—and driven the wife out, as she'd driven that poor housekeeper? Weariness and shock, instead of aging his face, seemed to make him appear younger, like a boy frightened and uncertain. She put out her hand, and touched his elbow, where his hand cradled his mother's cheek. "Forget the book," she said, and Sam opened his mouth in indignation. She went on, over his protest, "Did Rebecca ever speak to you of a woman friend—a wealthy woman—who might be sympathetic to the cause of our rights? Or, did she ever speak to you of someone who might wish her—Mrs. Malvern—ill herself?"

He lifted his head and his green eyes flashed sudden fire. "Other than that brute of a husband, you mean? The swine had the temerity to write to Tillet, threatening to bring him to law for 'harboring a harlot,' as he called her, and 'operating a house of ill fame.' If ever there was a case of God's hand being needed in mortal affairs—" He broke off, and turned his face away, his breath coming fast and a stain of angry crimson flushing his cheekbone.

"Without the hand of the Lord, no mortal affair can prosper." Mrs. Hazlitt raised her head, her fingers tightening around those of her son. "All our deeds are in vain, unless God guide us by his strong hand, and only through the hand of the Lord lies our salvation."

"Harlot or no harlot," said Revere, "I'd give much to be there when the Watch tells old Malvern his wife's gone missing. And under such circumstances as these."

"Good God, man," cried Warren, "you're not thinking Malvern had aught to do with—"

"I'm not thinking anything," retorted the silversmith lazily. "But after all the spite and venom he's poured forth to anyone who'll listen these past three years, I'd be curious to see how he takes it."

How indeed? Abigail followed the men back into the shop. Sam was still fretting about the missing "Household Expenses" book, demanding of Orion where Rebecca would have gone, if not to the Tillets or Revere, to the Adams house or the printshop—? *Little enough chance I'll have to even speak to him, once the Watch has given him the news . . .*

Great Heavens, surely they wouldn't detain him?

What is it John said, that of all murders done, the culprit is usually known to the victim? *Would the Watch be such fools as to think that—as the missing woman's estranged husband—Charles Malvern had had anything to do with such a crime?* She recalled the little merchant's anger-crimsoned face, when last she'd seen him, those cold eyes like gray buckshot . . .

"Are you coming, Mrs. Adams?" Sam opened the shop door for her. "We need you to discover the body, and summon the Watch."

Something in Sam's briskness—or perhaps only his preoccupation with his precious book of contacts—raised the hackles on her neck as it had in Rebecca's kitchen earlier. She stepped back from him, pulled her scarf more tightly around her throat. "Discover it yourself, Sam," she said briefly. "I think I need to pay a visit to Rebecca's husband, and tell him that his wife has vanished—and see if he has aught to say, about where she might have gone."

Five

He hounds me. Rebecca had wiped her eyes as she'd said it, on an evening in summer—the summer before last, one afternoon when Rebecca had crossed the bay to Braintree with some of Abigail's Smith cousins, and they'd spent the day in the summer tasks of threading leather-britches beans to dry, and bottling blackberries from the woods behind the orchard. Abigail had been heavy yet again with child—baby Tommy, old enough now to stagger sturdily about the kitchen. Walking swiftly through the market, thrusting guilt from her heart as she would have brushed falling rain from her face, Abigail earnestly hoped that Pattie—the fourteen-year-old farm-girl who'd lived with the family since their return to Boston a year ago—was keeping an eye on him . . . on Charley, too. There were simply too many things a pair of enterprising little boys could get into, in a kitchen on a freezing day.

He hounds me. He has always considered me his property, like his horses or the corn in his ships. He questions the servants about everything I do, he opens and reads my letters, he demands accounting of every penny I spend and he has imprisoned me under lock and key as if I were a disobedient child. Yet he has said, he will not let me go.

And Orion Hazlitt had cried: *If ever there was a case of God's hand being needed in mortal affairs—*

Abigail shook her head, her heart aching at the desperation in the young man's voice.

The clock in the brick turret of Faneuil Hall chimed ten

thirty. Abigail drew her skirts aside from barrows of country apples, wet from the rain. Pens of sheep blocked her way; crates of fish, drying now and several hours out of the sea: *By the time I can do my marketing they'll be stale, and the best will be gone . . .*

But her steps did not pause. *If I am to see him at all, I must see him first. Before the Watch.*

Her mind chased Rebecca's voice back along a corridor of memory.

They're spying on me. I know they're spying on me. All except Catherine—my maid—and he has the other servants spy on her. *I dread he'll send her away, and get some creature of his own, like that horrid Mrs. Jewkes in* Pamela. That had been earlier, before she'd left Charles Malvern's house: only weeks after she and Abigail had first met. When she'd wept then, the lace border of her handkerchief had been wider than the linen it surrounded.

I used to laugh at Pamela, *but I swear I feel like that wretched ninny these days.* Rebecca had never had much use for Abigail's favorite novel, or its saintly heroine. *He actually did lock me up, for nearly a week. He's said he will again, if he hears I've come here to see you. "I will not be defied in my own house," he says. The servants seemed to think nothing of it. And no one will help, because like* Pamela's *Mr. B, he can hurt them in their pocketbooks—*

And it was true, Abigail knew, that the innkeeper from whom Rebecca had first rented chambers in October of '70 had been nearly driven out of business by the prices Malvern and his network of merchant cronies had demanded of him for victuals and wood. The same thing had happened to the second room she had rented, early in the summer of '72. The Adamses had returned to Braintree by then and Abigail had asked her to move into the crowded little farmhouse, but again Rebecca had refused. *I can't live with you and John forever*, she'd said, but Abigail had been aware at the time that Charles Malvern's youngest child, four-year-old Nathan, had been ill. Though Rebecca was estranged from her little stepson's father, still she would not leave Boston. She had found the little house behind the Tillets'—who loathed Malvern over the politics of their respective congregations—but by what Orion had just told her, Malvern had not ceased his efforts to make his estranged wife's life as difficult as possible.

And then, thought Abigail, as she turned into the waterfront bustle of Merchants' Row, *there was the matter of Rebecca's father's will.*

It was the last occasion upon which she—or as far as she knew, Rebecca—had seen Charles Malvern, except to catch a glimpse of him across the sanctuary of the Brattle Street Meeting-House.

Abigail slowed her steps as she passed the Malvern countinghouse, at the head of his wharf. Not a grand wharf, like Hancock's, or the marvel of the Long Wharf that stretched half a mile out to sea, but big enough to serve either of Malvern's oceangoing brigs. The *Fair Althea* stood in port, named for the woman Abigail suspected its owner had never forgiven Rebecca for replacing. Malvern had rebuilt the countinghouse at the wharf's head, on the site of his grandfather's original modest structure: two and a half stories of solid Maine timber, with a warehouse behind it for muslins and calicoes, tool-steel and paint.

The tide was out. The sloping shingle below street level was dotted with heaped boxes, rough drays, coils of rope, and wet-dark cargo nets spread to dry. At the nearby Woodman's Wharf a vessel was loading with kegs of what smelled like potash, stevedores shouting to one another as they worked. Beyond lay the leafless forest of bobbing masts, and the cold air muttered with the creak of ropes, the endless soft knocking of pulley blocks against the mast-wood. The world smelled of seaweed and wet rope.

Wind smote her, but it was not colder than Charles Malvern's wrinkled angry countenance and pale eyes, when last she, and Rebecca, and John had stood before him.

"By the terms of James Woodruff's will, I am executor of that property." Malvern had spoken to John, not to Rebecca, his square brown hands folded ungivingly on his desk. The merchant was even shorter than John, and though now in his midfifties, and wiry in build, gave an impression of tremendous, almost threatening, physical strength. His merchant father had sent him to sea in his youth, and he retained the hardness of a man who has had to impose his will by force on other men in order to survive. "It was made over to me as Rebecca's husband—"

She heard the pause before her friend's name, heard in that harsh cracked voice the refusal to call her *Mrs. Malvern*. Mrs. Malvern was and forever would be the woman he had lost.

"—and she has but to give over her present mode of life, to regain its use. To hand property to a woman who has forsaken her husband to live upon the town would do neither her nor the community any service, and would provide the worst sort of example."

"To whom, sir?" demanded Abigail hotly. "To other wives who find it not to their taste to have communications with their families forbidden? Who don't care to be imprisoned like felons for weeks at a time or to have their books burned and rooms searched?"

"Precisely, Madame," Malvern had replied. "If my wife cannot tolerate my attempts to better her, but would flee the lesson like a fractious child, then shame upon her as well as upon myself. If I keep watch upon her it is because she has lied to me, both about her faith and about the conduct of my first wife's children, to whom she has shown nothing but dissembled hatred since first she entered my house. I defy the law, or any man of business, to fault me in separating her from her family, after she has robbed me and given the money to them—to purchase the property whose income she now claims as her own."

"That is not true!" Rebecca rose, stepped to the desk before which John already stood. It had been early December, as bleak as it was today, and with the smell of snow in the air. Abigail recalled, as much as the interview itself, how cramped and stuffy the little office had felt, and how intrusive had been the noise of the wharves and the street outside, after a year and a half of the farm's slow-paced peace. "That land was my father's," Rebecca said. "And his father's, before that—"

"Which would have been sold to pay your father's debts," responded Malvern, "had you not helped yourself to the household money entrusted to you, and pledged my good name in a loan, to salvage it. And if your client"—here he had turned his bitter pale eyes back to John—"wishes those facts to be aired at large before the General Court of the colony, along with her father's will, which clearly places the property in my hands in trust for her *as my wife*, I will certainly oblige her and you, Mr. Adams, by so doing. In the meantime she has but to return to my roof, to fulfill her own portion of a contract of which she is now in violation."

Tears glittering sharply in her brown eyes, Rebecca had said, "I would sooner take up my abode in Hell."

The following week, Abigail recalled, two clients—both merchants connected with Malvern—had withdrawn their business from John, even as John had lost half a dozen during the months that Rebecca had lived beneath their roof.

The Malvern house, like the countinghouse, was solid. Modest in its way, it had clearly been built to proclaim the extent to which God had favored the endeavors of the family. Three stories high, it was fashioned of both timber and bricks, and kept the old diamond-glass windows of an earlier day. As Abigail approached it a carriage was brought to its door, and the two surviving Malvern children emerged, followed by a black manservant and Miss Malvern's plump, giggling maid. *They lie about me to their father*, Rebecca had whispered desperately. *They carry tales—terrible things!—and he believes them . . .*

And what parent would take the word of a new young wife, before that of his own daughter and son?

Jeffrey must be twenty now. From the opposite side of King Street Abigail watched them. Rebecca had written to her that the young man had begun at Harvard. Taller than his father, he favored the first Mrs. Malvern's pale beauty, especially when he threw back his head and laughed at one of the maid's flirtatious sallies. Mistress Tamar Malvern tapped her brother sharply on the sleeve with her fan, but laughed as well. From a sharp-faced little vixen of eleven when her father had married Rebecca, she had grown into a lovely peaches-and-cream brunette, with the air of a girl who is quite aware that men swoon at her feet. Neither gave the manservant so much as a glance as he opened the carriage door for them. The servant stepped back sharply to avoid being splashed as the carriage pulled away.

"Mrs. Adams." He saw her across the street and smiled, teeth very white in a fine-boned ebony face. His name, Abigail recalled, was Scipio; he'd greet her with his sunny smile at the Brattle Street Meeting, if he was sure his master wasn't looking. Sure enough, he glanced back at the house as if to make sure he was unobserved before crossing to her. "Are you well, m'am? And Mrs. Malvern: Is all well with her?"

"No," said Abigail softly. "I am sorry to say a shocking thing has happened, and I was coming now, to let your master know of it. As far as I know she's all right," she added, seeing how the man's eyes widened with alarm. "It wouldn't be right to tell you details before I've spoken to him—"

"No, of course not." He collected himself quickly, hastened ahead of her, to open the house door. "I'll let him know you're here."

No fire burned in the grate of the book-room where he left her, though there were Turkey carpets on the brick floor. Charles Malvern was not a man to heat rooms when they were not in use. A portrait of the Fair Althea hung on the wall, very like Jeffrey but with kindliness rather than wit in her smile. Beside it hung a painting of Tamar, done recently, where once Rebecca's pen-sketch of little Nathan had been displayed: the child whose birth had cost his mother her life. Abigail remembered that Nathan had been fascinated with it, had sat, too, looking up at the likeness of the mother he had never seen. The sketch was gone. Abigail wondered whether Malvern had disposed of it when Rebecca had left, or after the boy had died.

"Mrs. Adams?" Scipio reappeared in the doorway, to usher her across the hall.

"Good day to you, m'am." Charles Malvern rose from his desk when the butler admitted her, came around himself to bring up a chair. His wide-skirted dark coat and plain Ramilles wig were not one shilling more costly than they had to be, to let others know of his consequence in the world of trade and business. Their former encounter and her championship of his estranged wife flickered like malign fire in his eyes, but he asked politely, "Will you take tea? 'Tis a raw morning."

"Thank you, no." Any number of Abigail's friends observed the boycott but made it a point to call on their less political friends for a cup of Hyson or Bohea in the course of a cold afternoon. That, in Abigail's opinion, was cheating.

He didn't offer the acceptable Whig alternative of coffee, but signed Scipio from the room. "To what do I owe this honor, m'am?"

"A shocking thing has happened." He was walking back

around his desk as she spoke, and Abigail couldn't keep herself from waiting until she had a good view of his face, to see how he would take the news. "There was a murder done last night, at the house where Mrs. Malvern is now living—"

He turned back, eyes flaring, as Scipio's had, and she saw in them for one second not just surprise, but apprehension and even fear. She went on swiftly, "A woman: We don't know who."

"Not Mrs. Malvern?" That first instant's horror—like the echo of her own cry, *Not Rebecca!*—disappeared and was replaced by suspicion: the wary anger of a man who has been cheated by a mountebank, and looks out lest he be cheated again.

"No. But Mrs. Malvern has disappeared—"

"Has she?" He settled back in his chair, and his voice was dry again. "I daresay she's run to that heretic printer my daughter tells me she's dallying with."

"If it is Mr. Hazlitt you mean," said Abigail, feeling the blood rising in her cheeks, "I have come from there just now." *Heretic*, in Charles Malvern's mental lexicon, meant, Abigail knew, anyone of less than stringently double-predestinarian Calvinist belief. Even a convert, like Orion Hazlitt, from a less doctrinaire sect was forever suspect, much less a former Catholic like Rebecca. "Inasmuch as she has assisted him with the text of the sermons he is printing—"

"Sermons forsooth!" He almost spit the words at her. "By whom? One of those lying unbelievers at the New Brick Meeting-House? What woman was killed? How did she come into the house, if not for ill purposes? And at night, you say? Was she another like my wife, who'd go about the town alone—?"

"We don't know," repeated Abigail, seeing the seamed little face opposite her darkening a dangerous crimson with rage. "She was found in Rebecca's"—she bit back the word *kitchen*, remembering that she was only supposed to have this from hearsay, and finished—"house this morning, slashed to death, and used most horribly."

"Then she had her deserving." Malvern almost shouted the words at her. "If she was one of Sam Adams's gang of traitors. A trollop, as they'd have Rebecca be, for their dirty sakes. Belike it was one of them that did the murder—"

"I don't think so." Abigail fought to keep her own temper under control. "I'm trying to find who she was—"

"Why ask me, then? That lying Papist turned her back on any decent females she knew when she left this house, and the truly decent ones turned their backs on her. Surely *you* would know, her dear good friend, her *almost-sister*, *her only true friend in the world . . ."*

He is jealous of you, Rebecca had said, on another of those occasions when she had sneaked from her husband's house, to take refuge in Abigail's kitchen. *Of my father, of the secrets I tell my maid. Even of little Nathan. He wants me to be his completely . . .*

"But, I do not," said Abigail, keeping her voice level with an effort. "And I doubt you would say this woman had her deserving, if you—" She bit off her words once more. *You weren't there . . .*

"If I what?" shouted Malvern. "If I were willing to wink at treason, at sedition, at the creatures your husband and his cousin play upon to get their way? Don't tell me she wasn't hand in glove with these Sons of Liberty—Sons of Belial, more like! You ask your husband, if you want to know who this bitch was that was murdered, or where my wife might have run off to. And so I'll tell the Watch, when they come—if they come, and this isn't all another of Sam Adams's lies. And as for you, Mrs. Adams, shame on you, a mother of children, and shame on your husband for permitting you to walk about the town like the harlot of the Scripture: *Now is she without, and now in the streets . . . her feet go down to hell.* To Hell is where you have led my wife, Mrs. Adams, in dragging her into the affairs of your so-called friends. And for that I will never forgive you, or them. Now get out of my house."

Scipio whispered, "What happened?" as he emerged from the book-room, to escort her to the door.

In the study, Malvern's voice bellowed, "Scipio!" and the butler flinched.

"Mrs. Malvern has disappeared," replied Abigail swiftly, softly—knowing the master's wrath would descend on the slave's head if Scipio were one moment late in answering, or if the merchant so much as suspected the butler had spoken with his dishonored guest. "Where would she go, if she sought refuge? To her maidservant? She left Boston, didn't she? Catherine, I mean—"

"She did—"

"Scipio, get in here, damn you!"

"She might. It's a long way, I don't know the name of the place but I'll—"

The study door slammed open. Impassive, Scipio opened the outer door for Abigail, held himself straight and correct as she passed through. Only when Abigail glanced back over her shoulder as the door was closing, did she see Charles Malvern seize his slave by the shoulder of his coat and thrust him back against the wall, and strike him with the back of his hand across the face.

Six

Inwardly shaking from her interview with Malvern—and possessed by what she knew was a fantasy that she would reach home to find a dripping-wet Rebecca huddled beside her kitchen fire—Abigail forced herself to stop in the market on her way back to Queen Street. As surely as she knew her own name, she knew that once she reached her own house, no marketing would get done. John (surely John was home by this time—it was nearly noon by the clock on Faneuil Hall) would demand a minute account of what she had seen in Rebecca's kitchen, and would also demand to know why she hadn't stopped Sam, as if anything less than a nine-pound gun could stop Sam once he got going. Poor Pattie would be struggling to finish her own chores and Abigail's neglected ones, and both Johnny and Nabby—usually at Rebecca's dame school at this time of the morning—would be underfoot, not to mention the two little ones . . .

Life on Queen Street was one continuous domestic crisis, with brief breaks for meals and church on Sunday.

So while her mind tugged and tested at where Rebecca could have taken refuge, at who the dead woman was and how the killer could have gotten into the house, she borrowed a basket from one of the farmwives she knew at the market—her own having been set down at some point in the morning she could no longer recall—and filled it with squash and corn and beans, pears and the best of the available remaining pumpkins, two chickens, and a lobster. She also paid a farthing for molasses candy, for the children and as an offering to Pattie for running off and leaving the poor girl with the whole house to clean *and* the ironing.

Not that Pattie was ever resentful or sulky, thank heavens. The girl would never set the world afire with her wits, but when King Solomon had set a good woman's value above mere rubies he'd clearly displayed his shortcomings as a housekeeper . . . *A reliable servant's is above the stars in the sky.*

Which is what comes of having kings write scripture and not housekeepers.

I must remember to bake extra tomorrow, and send something to Orion.

She turned the corner into Queen Street, and saw bright as the blood-stream on Rebecca's doorstep that morning the scarlet of soldiers' coats.

Not for a second did she doubt at whose door the men stood.

John. There was a list that we didn't find, and the Watch did . . .

Abigail went cold down to her toes.

Over a dozen neighborhood children milled around them, at a safe distance precisely calculated, like blue jays teasing a cat. "Bloody-backs, bloody-backs," chanted Shimrath Walton, and shied a knob of pig dung at the smaller of the men: not the first such missile, to judge by the state of the boy's hands and the man's uniform. The little soldier's face turned as red as his coat and he took a stride toward the offenders, but they scattered, shrieking with laughter, only to reform a few yards away. "Lobsters for sale!"

"Sure now, what'll your Ma say, you chuckin' your lunch about like that?" retorted the taller soldier, which got a laugh from the children in return.

"Shimrath," said Abigail sharply, "come here this moment. You, too, Jed," she added, picking out the leader of the little band, and before she could single out a third, her own Nabby and Johnny darted out of the alley that ran beside the house:

"Ma, the redcoats have come to arrest Papa—"

"We tried to stop them." Nabby flung plump arms around Abigail's waist and held her desperately tight. "We tried—"

"Are they still in there?"

Both children nodded. Nabby was a silent girl, even at eight years of age worrisomely withdrawn. Her composure shattered, she looked like she'd been weeping: She adored her father. All Johnny's blunt-spoken sarcasm seemed to have deserted him as well.

"Nabby." Abigail bent down to her daughter to whisper, "You run at once to Mr. Revere's shop—Johnny, you go with her"—Johnny would never tolerate seeing his sister dispatched on an errand if he were not given one as well, and never mind that he was barely out of dresses—"and tell Mr. Revere that soldiers are here—How many are there?"

"These two and an officer inside," reported Johnny promptly. "He's from the Provost Marshal." In addition to studying Latin and the beginnings of Greek under his father's eye, the pale, fair-haired boy had lately become the neighborhood expert on the facing-colors and insignia of the regiment stationed on Castle Island.

"Tell Mr. Revere that. He'll know what to do. Shimrath, run tell Mr. Sam Adams. He may be at his house again and he may still be at Mrs. Malvern's house in Tillet's Yard—Jed, you go to Tillet's Yard. I'll hold them here."

The children bolted in all directions. The shorter guard, not having been privy to Abigail's murmured instructions, grunted, "Thank you, m'am. Those brats are a nuisance, no error." The taller—a young man with a snub nose and wide-set blue eyes—regarded Abigail worriedly as she moved toward the mouth of the little alley that led to the yard behind.

"Sorry, m'am." He stepped in front of her. "Just but

family permitted in." His English was one step from Gaelic, and not much of a step at that. "Lieutenant'll be done in a minute—"

"I am Mrs. Adams." Abigail handed him her shopping basket and the pumpkin. "If you would be so good as to carry this in for me?"

The young man cast a disconcerted glance back over his shoulder, and the older one waved him impatiently, adding, "And keep hold of your damn musket!" when he would have set it against the wall.

"Yes, sorr. Sorry, sorr." With his weapon tucked awkwardly under one arm, the pumpkin under the other, and the heavy basket in both hands, he followed Abigail around to the yard and the kitchen door.

"Put it there." Abigail nodded toward the broad table of scrubbed oak in the center of the big room: kitchen, workroom, dining-hall, nursery, schoolroom, and stillroom combined, the warm heart of the house where everything of importance was accomplished. When the children were in bed it was here she and John would work on pamphlets, letters, reports to the Committees of Correspondence in other colonies, and it was here, upon occasion, that members of the small, unofficial committee that headed up the Sons of Liberty sometimes met as well.

At the moment Pattie, bless her faithful heart, was finishing with the lamps for the day, setting the cleaned tin triangles aside on their shelf—wicks neatly trimmed—to await the fall of night. This task she abandoned, face flooded with relief, at her mistress's entrance. "Oh, Mrs. Adams—!" At the same instant three-year-old Charley—ordinarily the household's most outspoken supporter of the Sons of Liberty and Death to King George—flung himself against Abigail's skirts and buried his face in her cloak, clearly not up to the task of fighting full-grown British soldiers after all. Tommy, sixteen months old and Charley's most loyal follower, wasn't far behind.

"Flogged them, have you?" Abigail pressed both fair little heads reassuringly, and regarded the abashed soldier with a chilly eye.

"M'am, I swear—"

"Never mind. Pattie, I abase myself with shame for having abandoned you so heartlessly; there's molasses candy in the basket which this nice young representative of His Majesty's government has so kindly carried in for me. It is for you and for them. Is that cider I smell heating? Please pour some out for—what is your name?—Please pour some out for Mr. Muldoon, and bring in three cups of it on a tray to the parlor: the good cups. *Don't* set your musket down there, young man, unless you want my son to shoot either himself or you with it—not on the table, either, if you please. We're going to prepare food there. Pattie, may I trespass upon your good nature still further and ask you to start getting the chickens ready to roast and the lobster to boil, and the pumpkin to cook with apples and corn? I shall be in to help you as soon as matters have been dealt with in the parlor. And fetch one of the clean rags and lay it on the sideboard for that fearsome piece of artillery. Charley, you and Tommy may help Pattie with that."

Having kicked off her pattens, hung up her cloak, removed her bonnet, straightened her day-cap, and donned a clean apron while she spoke, Abigail made her way through the door and into the parlor where John stood facing the representative of the British Army's military law.

"Mr. Adams," she greeted the short, chubby, round-faced little man beside the cold fireplace. "The house appears to be singularly well-protected today. To what do we owe the honor of this visitation?"

"Mrs. Adams." John took her hand. "Allow me to present Lieutenant Coldstone, of His Majesty's Provost Guard. Lieutenant, my wife."

"I am honored." Coldstone bowed.

He was well-named, Abigail reflected. His features had

the appearance of something carved from marble: delicate, icy, and rigidly composed. The snow-white powder of his wig somehow added to the colorlessness of his features, rather than showing them up pinker, as the (admittedly ill-powdered) Muldoon's did. His eyes were dark, and chilly as a well digger's backside.

"The Provost Marshal," said John, lifting from the mantelpiece a folded sheet of paper, "seems to believe I have some knowledge of the death of Mrs. Perdita Pentyre, if no worse involvement, and the disappearance of Mrs. Malvern, in whose house Mrs. Pentyre's body was found. Did you know anything about this?"

Perdita Pentyre! The name left Abigail momentarily breathless. She closed her mouth on a gasped demand, *Are you sure?* Because obviously both John and Lieutenant Coldstone were very sure. *Perdita—*

"I heard that a body had been found, yes." Abigail collected her thoughts, her heart sinking. "And that Mrs. Malvern had disappeared." *And still has not come forth . . .*

"From whom did you hear this," asked Coldstone, "and where?"

"In Fish Street, at about ten this morning when I was doing the marketing." And thank goodness that, like King Solomon, this impeccably uniformed young man knew nothing about housekeeping and would be unlikely to ask why a woman whose home was as neat as Abigail's would leave her marketing until so advanced an hour.

"Fish Street doesn't lie between here and the market," pointed out Coldstone.

Not so ignorant, after all. "Mrs. Malvern is a close friend. Situated as she is—obliged to teach a dame school, and without a servant—I went there to ask if there were anything I could obtain for her. Thank you, Pattie—"

The girl came in, laid the tray with its three tall beakers of cider on the parlor table, cast a glance at Coldstone as if she expected him to arrest her as well, and ducked from the room.

Coldstone ignored the cider. "Did Mrs. Malvern ever speak of Mrs. Pentyre? To your knowledge, were they acquainted?"

"They may have known one another by sight," responded Abigail, still trying to take it in, that the young and lovely wife of one of the richest merchants in Boston had known Rebecca well enough to have her throat cut in her kitchen. She stammered a little: "Mrs. Malvern had left her husband by the time Mrs. Pentyre—Miss Parke, as she was then—married Richard Pentyre. Coming as she did from Baltimore, and Mrs. Pentyre from New York, I doubt Mrs. Malvern would have known Mrs. Pentyre as a girl."

Perdita Pentyre!

The silk dress. The diamond earrings. It made sense. Richard Pentyre, every inch the picture of an English gentleman, was bosom-crony to Governor Hutchinson and recipient of every favor and perquisite available to a loyal friend of the King.

And why not? His young and lovely wife was mistress to Colonel Leslie, commander of the garrison on Castle Island.

Her hand did not move, but she could almost feel through the fabric of her pocket and petticoats the note she had taken from the woman's dishonored body. *The Linnet in the Oak Tree. Cloetia.*

One of ours, Dr. Warren had said.

Perdita Pentyre, an agent of the Sons of Liberty.

Who would have thought it?

"I beg your pardon." She was aware that Lieutenant Coldstone had said, *Mrs. Adams?* with a note of interrogation in his voice. "My mind was otherwhere. Mrs. Malvern is, as I said, a close friend to our family. She lived with us, when first she was obliged to leave her husband's house—"

"So she is close to both your husband and yourself."

His eyes were on John as he spoke, and Abigail, with a warning ringing oddly in her mind, like the smell of smoke in the night, glanced swiftly at John's face. He wore an expression of wariness, such as she'd seen on him when he played chess with an unfamiliar opponent. Only grimmer.

She answered, "Yes."

John added, quietly, "As I've told you."

"And she is not an intimate friend to Mrs. Pentyre, so far as you know?"

"Not so far as I know."

"Does she share your husband's political opinions?"

Abigail's glance went to John again, and this time the tension in him was unmistakable. Not a chess game. *A fencing-match*, she thought, *like the one in* Hamlet*: the rapiers unbuttoned, and one blade poisoned.* "We met at church," she said. "Like both of us, and many others, Mrs. Malvern believes that the colonies have the right to a voice in their own government, though what that has to do with such a crime being committed beneath her roof I am at a loss to imagine."

"Are you, m'am? At what time did your husband come in last night?"

"He did not," replied Abigail. "He has been pleading a case in Essex County since Monday. He was to have returned last night, but I presume was delayed until after the time that the gates are shut and the ferry closed down for the night. When I left for the market this morning he had not yet come in."

"As I told you also," added John, whose cheeks had developed red blotches of anger. "I expect my children will say the same, if you care to interrogate them."

"John," said Abigail sharply, "what does—?"

Coldstone held up a staying hand. "What time was that?"

Queenie saw me outside Rebecca's door. "Nearly half past seven. Daylight."

"And you have only just returned from your marketing?"

"I went first to Mrs. Malvern's house to see if there was anything I might get for her, and found a slate by her door, saying, No School. I thought she might have been ill, and walked on to return a book I had borrowed from a friend in the North End; I returned by way of Fish Street again, to see if she was awake and in need of anything. 'Twas then I heard that a woman had been found in her house, dead, and no one could say what had happened to Mrs. Malvern or where she might be. I have been seeking word of her."

"In preference to a reunion with your husband?"

"My dear Lieutenant," said John, with a half grin that did not reach his eyes, "Mrs. Adams is the original Eve for curiosity. She *knew* where she would be able to locate me, when she needed me."

Past the Lieutenant's shoulder, Abigail saw a man cross the window on the outside, a distorted shape in the uneven diamonds of glass. The fourth or fifth to do so, she thought, in five minutes—unusual for Queen Street at this time of a weekday morning.

"As I have told you already," John went on, "I spent last night at Purley's Tavern in Salem, my horse having strained a fetlock a number of miles from the ferry—"

"You could tell me you spent last night in Constantinople, and be away from Boston by the time I'd sent Sergeant Muldoon there to check your story."

"You can certainly send Sergeant Muldoon to check with the ferryman as to the time I crossed this morning."

"As a lawyer, Mr. Adams—and the cousin of the man who heads up the Sons of Liberty—you know quite well that there are other ways into this city than the Winnisimmet Ferry or the gate at the Neck . . . and other ways that a man might have to do with a woman's death, than wielding the knife himself. I—and Colonel Leslie—would prefer to have you where we know we can lay our hands on you."

With a shock Abigail realized that Johnny had not been exaggerating. The Provost Marshal's man was, indeed, here to arrest John—for the murder.

Cold panic flooded her, then hot rage. *Seditious* the Crown might well call him—as it called all its enemies. But that anyone would even consider for an instant that he had had or *could* have had anything to do with a crime of that nature left her breathless. She glanced at the window again, and though the flawed glass made it difficult to make out details, she saw that there definitely were at least five men, loitering in the street in front of the house.

She said, "Surely, Lieutenant," in her most reasonable voice, "if your commander simply wishes Mr. Adams to be available for further questioning, would not a bond serve as well?" She tucked her hands beneath her apron, mostly to keep the officer from seeing them ball into unwomanly fists. "We are simple folk, and not so wealthy that my husband can afford to flee and leave thirty pounds in your hands—I believe thirty pounds is the usual bond for good conduct? Unless you would rather take our firstborn son, but I really wouldn't want to do that to whoever would have to look after him."

Outside, a child shouted something, and a man's voice reproved: "Hush, there, Shimmi, we're not here to make trouble . . ."

And the voice of the guard, "And what are you here for, then, Rebel?"

Coldstone, interrupted in the midst of his reply, frowned. As he walked to the window John stepped closer to Abigail's side, stage-whispered, "You'd price Johnny at thirty pounds?"

She shrugged, never taking her eyes from the officer's

crimson back as he angled his head to look through the thick panes into the street. "We've two other sons."

Coldstone looked back sharply over his shoulder at them, narrow face expressionless. Then he stalked to the table, where his sabertache lay, and from it withdrew a sheet of paper. Abigail helpfully fetched her writing box from where it lay on a corner of the mantelpiece, and set it before him. The officer regarded her in hostile silence, then took the quill she offered him, studied the point critically, adjusted it with his penknife, and wrote:

Mr. John Adams, lawyer, of Queen Street, Boston, is hereby summoned to appear before the Provost Marshal of His Majesty's forces at Castle William on Friday, 25 November 1773 at noon to post bond for his good conduct in the matter of the murder of Mrs. Richard Pentyre of this town. Lt. J. Coldstone, on His Majesty's behalf.

"Do not fail." He dusted it, poured off the sand, and handed the sheet to John as if he were sorry that it was not poisoned. John inclined his head respectfully.

"I will not. Thank you for your forbearance, Lieutenant."

Coldstone opened the door to the hall, snapped, "Muldoon!" in the direction of the kitchen, and the young man appeared, vastly flustered and with crumbs of molasses candy on his jacket. "Get your musket," he reminded him disgustedly. "And come."

John and Abigail walked them to the front door, emerged onto the step to bow another farewell. From the step it could be seen that Queen Street was filled end to end with men: most of them young, though Abigail recognized Billy Dawes the cobbler and the blacksmith Isaac Greenleaf, who had to be in their thirties and masters of their own shops. None were armed, but all were watching the house, and there were a lot of them. More arriving even as the remaining sentry saluted.

Knowing Bostonians, the moment Coldstone turned away, John put his finger to his lips for silence—but when the Lieutenant and his two sentries turned the corner into Cornhill, somebody let out a cheer that was taken up for the length of the street.

Coldstone didn't turn around.

Seven

"We've made an enemy." John closed the door, after thanking the mob, a little stiffly, for its appearance. John was never comfortable with the idea that it was often Sam's mobs, rather than the well-reasoned justice of British Law, that got things done in Boston.

"He was our enemy when he arrived." Abigail went back into the parlor, picked up a beaker of tepid cider. It was well past noon, and she had intended, she recalled, to share breakfast with Rebecca. "Did he say why he was so certain you were the killer? Other than that your name is Adams?"

"In that case, why not call on Sam? Which he clearly didn't, if Sam was able to marshal a mob at short order—"

The parlor door crashed open, and Pattie and the children swarmed through. "Ma, did you see it? Did you see it? Uncle Sam brought them, and Mr. Dawes, and Mr. Revere, and they made that lobsterback captain look nohow!" "Oh, Mrs. Adams, that Irishman said as they were going to take Mr. Adams up for murder—" "Ma, you should have shot him!"

Nabby flung herself silently at John, clutched him around the waist, buried her face in his coat, and burst into tears. Tommy, still very uncertain of his balance, did likewise with Abigail.

"I will say this for Sam," remarked Abigail, as their family tugged them into the kitchen, "he's quick."

"So was the lad who picked my pocket last month in front of Christ's Church, but that doesn't mean I want to see him in charge of the destiny of this colony. I'm quite all right, dear girl." John put a gentle finger under Nabby's chin, raised her eyes to his. "Spartan women didn't shed tears after defeat in battle," he added with a smile. "So why weep for a victory? Keep an eye on your brothers and help Pattie with dinner—Lord, I'm hungry!—while I talk to your mother. What happened?" His voice dropped to a whisper as he followed Abigail to the sideboard, helped her carry to the table the heavy iron Dutch oven and the crock of lard. "Was he telling the truth? Perdita Pentyre! *Did* Mrs. Malvern know her?"

"She must have." Abigail dug in her pocket, brought out the note. "I think she must have been Rebecca's source, for secrets and scandal in the British camp. I suppose there's no doubt that it *was* she, and not another? Her face was . . . much mutilated."

At the other end of the table, Pattie raised a cleaver and whacked off the head of one of the dinner chickens. The other, decapitated, gutted, pale, and naked, lay on a plate before Abigail already. Her empty stomach turned, and she looked queasily away.

"That officer at least was as sure as he could be," rumbled John as he unfolded the slip of paper. "Mrs. Pentyre is indeed missing from her home. According to Lieutenant Coldstone, the stableman there says that Mrs. Pentyre took a light chaise out, fairly late in the evening, and its horse was found wandering loose on the Commons this morning. They're dragging the Mill-Pond for the chaise." He added drily, "I understand that if Richard Pentyre is unable to identify his wife's body, Colonel Leslie knows it well enough to do so."

"It isn't a matter for jest." In a low voice Abigail recounted what she had found in Rebecca Malvern's house that morning, and what she had done about it. "I could have beaten Sam with a broom handle for going through the place as he did," she finished, as she tucked the chicken into its place in the pot. "The more so now, that any trace of evidence that it *wasn't* you has been destroyed. I went to Malvern's after we left Hazlitt's printshop."

"You don't think she'd have taken refuge with him?"

Abigail shook her head. "No. I think she'd have taken refuge with Revere, or with us, or with Orion Hazlitt. But she didn't."

John said, "*Hmmn.*"

"If she had," Abigail went on slowly, drying her hands, "I wouldn't put it past Malvern—I don't *think* I'd put it past Malvern—to take her in, and then lock her up again, as he did before—"

He glanced back at her from the note, which he was studying by the stronger light of the kitchen window. "You truly think he would do something like that?"

Abigail hesitated. "I truly don't know," she said at last. "One hears of it—and not just in novels," she added, seeing the corner of his mouth turn down. "He is—a man who will have his own way, no matter what he has to do to get it. Mostly, I wanted to speak with him before the Watch told him of the crime and Rebecca's disappearance. I knew he'd see no one, afterwards."

"You're probably right about that. And much as I hate to admit it, if Sam and the others hadn't cleared up the scene I suppose Coldstone would have had grounds to arrest me for sedition this morning, instead of being put off with a thirty-pound bond." At that point in Abigail's narrative, he'd snatched off his wig and thrown it at the wall; it lay like a dead animal now on the sideboard near his hand. Without it, his face looked even rounder, his blue eyes more protuberant. His mouse brown hair, short-cropped, was graying, and Abigail had to suppress the urge to kiss the thin spots above his forehead. "You say Sam didn't recognize Mrs. Pentyre? Or know about her?" He turned the note over in his fingers. "Did you take a close look at this?"

She shook her head, set aside the dumplings she was making, and crossed to his side. "When he saw her body, he certainly didn't have any candidates in mind. There can't be that many wealthy women who were friends with Rebecca, who would have been using the code of the Sons." Over his shoulder she studied the paper:

The Linnet in the Oak Tree. Cloetia.

And frowned. She dried her hands again, took from a drawer in the sideboard a much-scribbled sheet on which Nabby—with many blots and scratches—had been practicing the fiddling art of writing with a goose-quill. This she held up to John, her thumb at the topmost line, where Rebecca had written:

All Things Work Together for the Good of Them that Love the Lord.

"Is that the same handwriting?" she asked.

John fished in his pocket for a magnifying lens, laid the two papers side by side.

"The capitals are the same," he said, after a long few minutes. "But look how the small *o*'s and *e*'s want to pinch, while Mrs. Malvern's are naturally round. Not just one or two, but all of them. See there, where the *in* in *Linnet* blots and widens, where he's tried to imitate that little swoop you see in the *in* in *Things*. The same on the downstrokes of the capital *T*'s and *L*'s: that forced change of angle." He offered her the glass.

"I'll tell you what caught my attention," added John, as Abigail verified the wavery changes of line, the odd thicknesses and blots where the writer's hand had struggled to imitate angles unfamiliar to it. "Look at the two pieces of paper. No, Rebecca wouldn't use cold-pressed English notepaper for children's exercises, but would she have had any of it in the house at all? What did she write her broadsides on?"

"Common foolscap, like this. Sam arranges with Isaiah Thomas at the *Spy* to provide her with as much as she needs." She glanced up. "You're saying Mrs. Pentyre was lured there."

"That's what it looks like."

"By someone who knows the code used by the Sons."

"By someone who knew that this code was used between Mrs. Malvern and Mrs. Pentyre."

"But Rebecca did wait up for her," pointed out Abigail. "She was still dressed—at least her day dress and her shoes were gone from the house—and the fire hadn't been banked, nor the candles extinguished. And they *had* been snuffed and mended during the evening. She waited for *someone*. And clearly, she let Mrs. Pentyre in at midnight."

"And the killer as well, apparently," murmured John. He folded the note and pocketed it. "I'll get that," he offered, as Abigail started to lift the heavy Dutch oven, to carry to the hearth. "What time did the rain start here? Ten?" He dumped a couple of shovelfuls of glowing coals onto the iron lid. "If it was coming down as hard as it was in Salem, it would have been easy for someone to follow Mrs. Pentyre's chaise from her house. As to how he would have gotten them to open the door—"

"He was known to one or the other," said Abigail. "He must have been. If he forged the note, he knew the code—"

"And if he forged the note, Mrs. Malvern would not have been still awake," responded John thoughtfully. He set the fire-shovel back in its place. "What time are the Tillets expected back, my Portia?" he asked, using the name they had used in their letters during courtship: she Portia, he Lysander, like heroine and hero of a classical romance. "Do you feel able for a half-mile walk, to see what the Watch have left of Sam's handiwork? Or would you rather rest?" he added, scrutinizing her face more closely. "You look—"

"I look like a woman ready to faint away in your arms,"

replied Abigail briskly. "Yet in either case my conscience would not let me rest, after what I've done to poor Pattie this morning—*and* burdened her with entertaining that young lout of an Irishman . . ."

"Oh, m'am." Pattie dimpled shyly from the table where she was scrubbing potatoes. "Sergeant Muldoon meant nobody harm. Not even Mr. Adams, I daresay. You go," she added. "Mrs. Malvern may even have come back, if what happened there didn't drive her into brain-fever, so that she's forgotten who and where she is."

"If she's forgotten," said John softly, putting on his wig again while Abigail took off her apron and stepped into her pattens in their corner by the door, "'tis a curious thing that none of her neighbors found her wandering and reminded her."

By this hour, Fish Street was a lively confusion of carts and drays coming up from the docks, of pungent smells and the clattering of hammers: shoemakers, coopers, smiths in silver and iron. The North End—technically an island, if you counted the little Mill Creek as a branch of the ocean—was a crowded jumble of rich and poor, of the mansions of merchant families and the tenements offering lodging to those who sailed on their vessels, of tangled alleyways and unexpected courts and yards. Shop signs and laundry, boat builders, hatters, soap makers, and taverns packed shoulder to shoulder like passengers in a too-small coach as they had been for over a century. Among the waterfront taverns and warehouses the smugglers operated, bringing in cognac and linens and tea from France and Holland in flagrant disregard of the British Crown's stringent trade regulations; gangs of thieves, too, pilfering goods from the tall English ships and slipping them out almost at once on the numberless tiny coastal traders that brought in hay and firewood, oysters and butter, from a thousand little towns along the coast. It was among the artisans, stevedores, and laborers of the North End that the Boston mobs arose, ready to hammer down Tory doors or launch themselves into bloody battle with the South End boys during the riotous celebrations of Pope's Day.

Though she would not have wanted to hear that Johnny was playing with the boys from this part of town—or that her brother Will was gambling in any of its many taverns—Abigail liked the North End.

The gate to Tillet's Yard was closed, and—when they tested it—barred from within. Coming around the corner to the shop, the Adamses found not the prentice-boys Abigail had expected behind its counter, but Nehemiah Tillet himself, a stooped and flaccid-jowled man who reminded her of a spider. "Mrs. Tillet thought it best," he said in his whispery voice. His hands fumbled uneasily, straightening an already straight stack of his wife's ready-made shirts. "Every lad in the neighborhood—and men of full years who should have better tasks with which to occupy themselves—wanted to see the place, and broke the lock from the door even, to go in. I spent the best part of the morning turning them away!"

"How shocking for you," sympathized Abigail, who had never liked the man. "To return home to find the place full of soldiers."

"I was very much overset." He fiddled at the edges of the bolts that lay on the crowded counter: linen, cotton, Holland cloth. "Very much so."

"And you've heard nothing from Mrs. Malvern? She's not returned?"

Moist pale eyes regarded them warily under heavy, lashless lids, then glanced aside. "No. No, she hasn't." Again his eyes avoided hers.

And little wonder, reflected Abigail, annoyed. From the first time she'd visited Rebecca here, she'd suspected that Tillet lusted after her friend. This was no great surprise, given Mrs. Tillet's aggressively unpleasant nature—for the past eighteen months, every time she'd come by to visit, Mr. Tillet had found some excuse to knock on Rebecca's door, with advice, or to share some snippet from a newspaper or church business. "He's worse than Charles," Rebecca had said, more than once, exasperated. "He wants to know who my friends are, and whom I visit. I used to think Mrs. T. put him up to it, to see if she could squeeze another five minutes' work out of me, sewing those wretched shirts the customers pay her for. The way he looks at me—" She'd grimaced. "I can't well push him out of the house, since he owns it. And I would rather be here, and put up with the pair of them," she'd added, when Abigail had shown signs of walking across the yard and giving Mr. Tillet a piece of her mind, "than go back to Charles."

Reluctantly, Abigail had agreed. Between Charles Malvern's vindictiveness, and the general Boston attitude that a woman who left her husband must have done so from a preference for profligacy, it had been difficult enough for Rebecca to find a place to live where she might ply any trade other than prostitution. Sewing endless mountains of shirts for Mrs. Tillet and attending three sermons every Sunday at the New Brick Meeting-House were part of what she had to do, to go on living in her little house.

"May we go back there?" John asked now.

"There's naught to be seen," Tillet responded immediately. "The boys coming through after the soldiers, they've tracked all up, and carried away what they could, belike."

"Mrs. Malvern is our friend," persisted Abigail. "If nothing else, we'd like to—"

"There's naught back there." Mrs. Hester Tillet emerged from the back parlor of the shop, a woman of commanding height and substantial girth, with arms like a stonecutter's from a lifetime of carrying bolts of cloth. "Nor will there be. 'Twas the last straw, and I'd had enough of her weeks ago. Disobliging, lazy slut, always finding some reason why she couldn't do a little of the work she contracted to do as part of us giving her the place so cheap. If *I* can turn out a handsome shirt in an hour it's sure anyone can, who puts their mind to it, and nobody needs more than a few hours' sleep at night: I certainly don't. And now she's run off, and left me with twenty orders to fill. I've had enough, and will have no more."

"You can't turn her out for what happened!" protested Abigail, and Mrs. Tillet turned upon her, arms akimbo and jaw protruding like a bulldog getting ready to bite.

"So you're telling me what I can do with my own property now, Mrs. Adams? Well, *I'm* telling *you*, I can't and won't put up with a woman who brings such friends onto my property the minute our backs are turned, to murder one another and bring the whole neighborhood tramping through. We have a position to uphold in our church and in this community, and we won't stand for it." And, seeing her husband looking wretched, she added, "Will we, Mr. Tillet?"

"No. Of course not."

"The woman asked for what was coming to her and was asking for it for some time. I don't wish to seem coldhearted, but I think we all know the difference between the trials that God sends to prove the righteous, and the deserved punishment that befalls those who deliberately put themselves in the way of sinners."

"Do you, Mrs. Tillet?" The stuffy air of the shop made Abigail's head ache, and the woman's grating voice was an iron file on her nerves. "I honor your wisdom, then, because that's something I've never had the presumption to assume that I could determine—nor the callousness to withhold the benefit of the doubt."

She stalked from the shop, expecting John to follow her. He did not, and as the door closed behind her she heard his voice, quick and low, "You must excuse her . . . overwrought . . . closest of friends . . ." She was within an ace of turning back and asking how dared he take their side against her, but was too angry even for that. She strode as far as the corner of Cross Street, then stopped, her temper ebbing and leaving her feeling cold and rather drained.

A few moments later she heard John's step on the cobbles. In a marveling voice, he murmured, "You've *never* withheld the benefit of the doubt?"

"Only from those who don't deserve it," she retorted. Then, blushed. "*Thank you* for covering my retreat. The woman never fails to enrage me, and I won't say my words were uncalled-for because they *were* called-for . . . but I would shake poor Nabby to pieces if she'd said them. I don't know what got into me. I must go back and apologize . . ."

"If you make the attempt I shall put you over my shoulder and carry you bodily home." John took her elbow, guided her firmly in the direction of Queen Street. "I stayed only to keep Mrs. Tillet from following you into the street and pulling your hair out. Send her a note tomorrow, when she'll have cooled down—except that I don't think she ever cools down. As to what got into you," he added grimly, "after this morning's events, I'm astonished you're not in bed with the vapors. I asked if I could come next week and collect Rebecca's things—"

"You can't let her—" Furious, she tried to turn back, and John's hand tightened on her arm.

"I can't very well stop her from doing what she is determined to do. What I *can* do is keep her from selling them at a slopshop. She said she'd have them ready for me."

"After taking out what she considers she's *entitled to* in payment of rent," Abigail grumbled. "Secure in the knowledge that with so many strangers tramping through, the absence of this little thing or that, can be blamed on others and not herself. Who will miss a trifle?"

"If Rebecca returns safe to miss them," replied John, "I

shall be on my knees, giving thanks to God. Now come home and rest."

Abigail wasn't certain she would be able to close her eyes, after what she had seen that morning, and the anxiety about Rebecca's possible whereabouts that gnawed her; nor was she entirely willing to make the experiment. Finding Pattie still (*at three in the afternoon!*) cleaning grates and emptying ashes—with the enthusiastic help of Nabby and Johnny, who were seldom permitted to get themselves that dirty—Abigail would have changed her dress to help her: "If you don't lie down on your bed and be quiet I shall dose you with laudanum and oblige you to be quiet," John threatened. Then, seeing her uncertain face, he added so softly that only she could hear, "I shall stay there with you."

"You don't have to."

"I have briefs to read. What I should have done this morning—and, God help me, what I should be doing tomorrow morning when I'll be out at the British camp."

So Abigail rested, and found herself, as she had feared, back in Rebecca's house, climbing the dark stairs with the stink of blood all around her; hearing Rebecca sobbing in her bedroom, with the door tied shut, and horrible sounds drifting up from the floor below. But when she unraveled the knotted clothes-rope, and got the door open, Rebecca's bed was empty, and instead of that tiny blood-spot on the pillow, the whole of the counterpane was soaked with gore.

Dinner over—dishes washed, pots scoured, scouring-sand swept up from the floor, floor washed, Tommy prevented from falling into the fire—Abigail wrapped up a few pieces of chicken and the extra potatoes she had cooked, added half a loaf of bread and a small crock of butter, and carried this meal to Hanover Street in her marketing basket for Orion Hazlitt. As she'd suspected she would, she found the shop shuttered and the young printer, haggard and distracted, in the keeping room, trying to get his mother to drink another glass of laudanum and water.

"You remember how we used to play in the marshes?" Mrs. Hazlitt murmured sleepily. "You'd pick daisies and mallows, and we'd make long strings of them, you and I . . . We'd both come to evening service wearing crowns of them, my little King." She pushed aside the cup, and framed his face with her hands. "You're still my little King."

"I know, Mother."

"Am I still your Queen?"

"Of course you are."

"And she"—she pointed an unsteady finger at Abigail as she stepped quietly through the rear door—"*she* is the whore of Babylon, the daughter of Eve . . . the worst of Eve's nine daughters. The Meddling Woman, going about the streets, asking what doesn't concern her. *She is loud and stubborn; her feet abide not in her house*—"

"Now, Mother," he said carefully (Abigail was well acquainted with what happened if one contradicted her), "'tis only Mrs. Adams. Surely you know Mrs. Adams? It's quite dark, you just can't see well—" Which was true. Winter dusk set in at four, and it was pitch-black now, though six was only just striking from the tower of the Meeting-House in Brattle Square. A few tallow candles had been lit, but their feeble glow showed Abigail that very little had been accomplished in the way of cleaning. "You shouldn't have," he said, when Abigail uncovered her basket, and she thought he looked ready to weep, with exhaustion and gratitude.

"Nonsense. Even whores of Babylon can see when their neighbors need help. I can help you upstairs with her," she added, glancing toward Mrs. Hazlitt, who had subsided into a stertorous doze. Two of the flat, square black bottles stood on the table, one empty on its side; there was another on the chimney breast. How bad had she been, that he'd needed to dose her so?

"Thank you." He shook his head. "I think I'll let her go as late as I can—a few hours anyway. 'Tis easier—you'll pardon me saying so—taking her out to the privy in this state, than it is managing a chamber pot. She's just . . ." He flinched, the muscles in his jaw suddenly tight. "It has been a bad day."

"No word of Rebecca?"

He shook his head. "I was going to ask you the same. I haven't been out, but Mr. Adams—Sam Adams—must have sent word, if she had . . ." His words fumbled, and he looked aside. *Flinching*, Abigail thought, *from the inevitable conclusion, that the man who has murdered Perdita Pentyre has killed her, too.*

And why not? If she had gotten out of the house, if he had run her down in the alley or the rain-hammered dark of the street, *would* he have carried her body back to the house?

Bracingly, she said, "If he left one body for all the world to find, he would have left two. We've learned who the murdered woman was, though: Perdita Pentyre."

He blinked at her, almost as if he did not recognize the name, then seemed to come to himself a little and said, "*Perdita Pentyre?* Colonel Leslie's—" He bit back the word *mistress*, as if he thought Abigail had never heard the word and didn't know what one was, and cleared his throat.

"I'll tell you of it later." She glanced at the slumbering woman by the fire. "Will that wretched girl of yours be back tomorrow?"

"I hope so. Damnation isn't so bad—"

"What?" Abigail blinked at the non sequitur.

"Damnation. That's her name. Damnation Awaits the Trembling Sinner." A smile flickered across his face. "I'm lucky my mother had me before joining the congregation I grew up in, or I'd be called something like Breakteeth or Doomed unto Hell. As I say, Damnation isn't a bad girl, just . . . lacking." He touched his temple.

"She will perish," observed Mrs. Hazlitt, waking and regarding them with jade green eyes that seemed very brilliant with the narrowing-down of her pupils. "*Four things the earth cannot bear: A servant when he reigneth; a fool when he is filled with meat; an odious woman when she is married; and a handmaid that is heir to her mistress*. Jezebel the Queen was the daughter of Eve, and the Lord smote her, and with her her handmaid that was privy to all her ways. Have you brought us supper?" she asked, with a sudden, dazzling smile. "How very sweet of you, dear, though not at all necessary. It won't take me but a moment to put together a green goose pie and some veal fritters; I'm sure my son has told you how well I cook. The prophet of the Lord says that my cooking would be sinful, if I were not so righteous myself."

And smiling, she fell asleep.

When Abigail returned to her house it was to find Sam in the study, talking quietly with John. "Has there been any word?"

Sam shook his head. "I've put out word to every patriot in the town," he said. "And I've been to see Hancock. He's having all his tea smugglers look in every cellar, every hidey-hole, every warehouse along the wharves—every nook and cranny throughout the town. Revere tells me that white-faced pup from the Provost's office found Pentyre's chaise sunk off Lee's shipyard, and the chaise was all they found. No word of the book, either."

His brow clouded further when John told him of their visit to the Tillets', and Mrs. Tillet's declaration that all Rebecca's things would be put out of the house. "I'll see what I can do, about getting one of our men to rent it," he said. "That way it can be searched properly."

"If you can find someone pious enough to suit Tillet," muttered John.

"Doesn't have to be pious, my boy." Sam grinned, putting on his hat. "Just an enemy of someone—like Charles Malvern—whom Tillet hates."

When Sam was gone, John put an arm around Abigail's shoulders. The kitchen was quiet: the children engaged in playing with wooden soldiers near the hearth, Pattie working at her tatting, a task which to Abigail's baffled disbelief gave her pleasure. The gray tabby cat, Messalina, purred by the fire, dreaming of the slaughter of mice. *Precisely as things had been last night*, thought Abigail: when she'd known her friend was safe, when the doors that looked into households of pain, and sourness, and distrust had all been shut. When she knew that she might sleep and dream of gardening, not blood.

"She'll return." John rocked her softly in the clasp of his arm. "If harm had come to her, they would have found some sign of it by now."

Abigail put her hand over his. "I think you're right," she replied. "Which leads me to wonder—*Why has she neither been found, nor come forth*? And I can think of only two reasons. One is that she received a concussion when she was hit on the head—yet if that were so, would not the people who found her know her? Or at least, have heard by this time that she was being sought?"

"I agree," said John. "Furthermore, if she had been so severely injured, she could not have got far. And the second?"

"Barring the romantical chance that she hid herself in the hold of a ship that is now on its way to China . . . She is hiding because she recognized the man who did it. And he knows she did."

Eight

From Griffin's Wharf it was a voyage of about half an hour to Castle Island. Dozens of small skiffs and sloops made the trip daily over the choppy gray waters of the harbor, bearing provisions for the men and fodder for the horses, firewood to heat the brick corridors of the squat fortress of Castle William and tailors, boot makers, wig makers, and wine merchants to make sure its officers had everything they needed for a comfortable stay. These little craft bore also the friends of the Crown, who were likewise friends of its representatives: the customs officials who relied on the soldiers to enforce His Majesty's duties, the clerks who surrounded the Governor (a large number of them his relatives), the Royal Commissioners who carried out the King's decrees. And, most recently, they carried the consignees to whom the Crown had given the monopoly on the East India Company's tea.

"The Company's on the verge of bankruptcy, from paying for its own troops to take over land in India," said John, as he handed Abigail down into the sloop of a farmer named Logan, who had agreed to carry them to the island. "The King's lowered the customs duty on the tea, so that he can put the smugglers—like Mr. Hancock—out of business . . . it'll barely be three pence a pound. Once it arrives here, there is no way it will not be sold—and then the King and Parliament will have their precedent, that it is legal for the King to tax goods that come to us, without our consent to the tax."

"And who cares about their constitutional right to consent to be taxed," murmured Abigail, "if it means cheap tea?" She gripped the rail as the cold wind caught the *Katrina*'s sails, fixed her eye on the pine and granite tuft of Bird Island, the nearest of the small eyots that dotted the harbor's deep channel. The clammy cold seemed to seep into her joints, and the pitching of the sea turned her stomach.

"Are you all right?" John pulled his own scarf higher and tighter about his throat. "I will be quite safe, you know." As Abigail had feared, she slept little. When John had come to bed after midnight she had been lying with open eyes, fearing what she would see when she closed them.

"I know you can slay any number of British troopers with your bare hands," she replied gravely. "Yet you may need someone to untie the boat, while you battle your way to the wharf."

John slapped his forehead. "I had forgot, we might have to fight our way out." His eyes danced as they met hers. But there was a sober worry in them, that answered the fear in hers, and neither needed to speak of what they both knew. On Castle Island, there was no chance that Sam could summon up a convenient armed mob to outnumber the available British troops. The only thing that might prevent Lieutenant Coldstone from arresting John the moment he set foot on Castle Island would be the fact that if he wished to do so secretly, he would have to detain Abigail as well.

Exhausted as she had been by the time she'd lain down last night, Abigail had remained awake by the light of her single candle, picturing over and over in her mind every room of Rebecca's house, both before and after Sam and the others had gone over it. *What did they forget? What could Coldstone have found that convinced him of John's guilt?* No list, no fragment of paper . . . Had she, Abigail, dropped her handkerchief, for someone to deduce John's presence from? Yet why (her overtired mind had picked endlessly at this detail) would John have been carrying his wife's handkerchief?

If they had found the brown-backed "Household Expenses" book, they would have gone to Sam, or Revere.

The same could be said if their only ground for suspicion was that Richard Pentyre—that wealthy and fashionable friend of the Crown—was one of the consignees to whom a monopoly of the East India Company tea had been granted. John had always held himself aloof from the darker doings of the Sons of Liberty. Even his pamphlets argued in terms of reason and the Constitutional Rights of Englishmen, not Sam's flamboyant demagoguery.

Now, in the gray daylight, with the walls of Castle William bobbing ahead of them, Abigail shivered at the thought, *What did they find in Mrs. Pentyre's room?*

In addition to the four hundred men of the Sixty-Fourth Foot, and the some sixty female "camp followers" supported on regimental half rations, Castle William—the brick fortress on the island to which the British troops had retired after the Massacre three and a half years ago—housed an assortment of servants, sutlers, animals, munitions, and supplies. These in turn engendered the need for offices and service buildings, so that what had originally been a castle indeed on the round-topped green island now had more the appearance of a grubby village, complete with cattle, chickens, children underfoot, and laundry hanging between the rough wooden dwellings of the men. The office of the Provost Marshal was in the fort itself, but as Abigail had feared, she and John were kept waiting for nearly three hours, on a bench in the chilly brick-paved corridor that circled the parade ground. Through a wide archway they watched the men come and go: clerks, grooms, batmen carrying officers' bedding to air. A couple of soldiers edged by them with a crate of wine bottles. Another, brisk and military despite a rather unsoldierly smock, bore a brace of ducks toward the kitchen.

Did Perdita Pentyre have her own rooms here at the fortress? Was that a perquisite of the Colonel's mistress? Abigail wondered who she could decently ask.

Of course, Rebecca will know . . .

And her momentary, reflexive cheer at the answer to her question turned instantly to the haunted pain of dread.

While she'd washed in the icy predawn cold, gone to the stables to milk Semiramis and Cleopatra, she'd strained her ears, listening for footfalls in the yard, for Young Sam or Young Paul: *Mrs. Malvern's at my Pa's, safe . . .*

Nothing. *Orion Hazlitt will be listening, too*, she thought. Waiting as she had waited, in that dark little house as he got his mother up, dressed her for the day, made coffee to go with the bread she'd sent . . . *How well I cook*, forsooth! Mrs. Hazlitt could barely boil an egg. Rebecca had often shaken her head and laughed at Orion's tales of his mother's accounts of her skills as a housewife. *The Lord smote her, and with her her handmaid that was privy to all her ways . . .*

Abigail frowned as that soft voice snagged in her mind. *The handmaid that is heir to her mistress . . .*

She watched the servants come and go. The more smartly dressed looked haughtily down their noses at the mere camp cooks and herdsmen, as was the way, Abigail had seen, of upper servants almost everywhere. What had Perdita Pentyre's handmaid been heir to? To what ways, what secrets, had she been privy?

Her mind turned from the dead woman's hypothetical servant to the known reality of that plump, giggling, sloe-eyed girl who followed Tamar Malvern into the coach in King Street. She would be after Rebecca's time. Abigail recalled, over the five years of their acquaintance, how often her friend had spoken or written of Catherine Moore, her own maid.

She would go to her. If for whatever reason she could not flee to me, or Revere, or Orion—because the killer would know us three as her likeliest refuge—she would seek sanctuary with the woman who was her only friend in that household of anger and lies.

"This is ridiculous," muttered John, face reddening as those who'd arrived after them—town merchants and contractors in victuals, an elegantly clothed Tory judge, and a widow of the town notorious for the gambling-parties held at her house—were admitted to the office almost as soon as they presented their cards to the subaltern who answered their knocks. When that young gentleman finally emerged from the Colonel's office and said, "Mr. Adams?" Abigail rose as well. "I beg your pardon, m'am." The young man stepped, if not into her path, at least enough closer to her to make his point. "The Colonel has said, Mr. Adams by himself."

"Nonsense!" stormed John. "My wife has been kept sitting here, in a cold and drafty hallway, since nine o'clock! I do not propose to leave her alone in the midst of an armed camp, exposed to the comment of every servant and laundress who happens by! You tell your Colonel—"

"I'm quite comfortable, thank you, Mr. Adams." Abigail laid a quick touch on his elbow. "I have brought a book with me."

"I will not have you treated—"

Though she was shivering with the cold, she shook her head again, meeting his eyes. "It is of no consequence. We have been delayed long enough already."

John looked about to say something else, but at that moment Lieutenant Coldstone appeared in the archway from outside, a leather sabertache beneath his arm and his Irish sergeant at his heels. "My apologies for the inconvenience, Mrs. Adams, Mr. Adams. Unfortunately there is no other place to wait. Sergeant Muldoon, would you be so good as to bring Mrs. Adams a cup of tea? Or coffee, if you would prefer, Madame."

"Coffee," said Abigail drily, and the Lieutenant bowed, as if the whole of the colony were not aflame on the subject of tea.

"Coffee, then. Mr. Adams?" He held open the door, and closed it behind them.

Three hours. Abigail opened the book she had brought, then let it rest on her lap. The gauzy quality of the noon overcast brought other clouded days to her, in the little kitchen on Brattle Street: one of those wet mornings when she'd patiently attempted to teach Rebecca how to make Indian pudding that did not end as inedible clots. "He sent her away," Rebecca had said, holding up the note that had just come to the house. "Without a character, Scipio says. Only for having served me." "Does she have family?" Abigail had asked, and Rebecca had said, "A brother. She fled the place; she wanted something other than to be a farm drudge—"

At that point Johnny, who had just turned three, had staggered purposefully toward the fireplace and the discussion had ended, and Abigail never had learned where Catherine's brother lived. From time to time over the ensuing years, Rebecca had spoken of receiving letters from her former servant: a farm somewhere, in the harsh backcountry that still crowded close to the cities of the seaside. Charles Malvern had not scrupled to—

Raised voices came dimly through the office door, faded almost at once. Abigail blinked, frowned. *How long do they need, for John to sign a bond?*

Is there another door out of that office?

She waited for a moment when the corridor was empty—servants were coming and going with greater frequency now, bearing dress uniforms to be brushed, trays of tea things or port bottles—then stepped to the door. Putting her ear close to the crack, she heard Coldstone's chill, measured voice asking something, and John's, loud with his anger, reply, ". . . liver bay, about ten years old, white stocking on the off hind . . ." Balthazar, in fact: John's horse. Had John dispatched his clerk, young Thaxter, to return the post-horse he'd borrowed to get back to Boston on? He must have—she hadn't seen the young man at dinner yesterday afternoon, though he often stayed to eat with the family. She shook her head at herself. *I must have been more tired than I knew . . .*

"Purley himself, for one," John was saying. *They must have asked him, who saw him at Purley's Inn.* "Mrs. Purley, for another. A couple of the Uxford boys, and Elias Norton from Danvers . . ."

"The same Elias Norton, who has been accused of smuggling? I understand, too, that Mr. Purley's sympathies are strongly with the so-called patriots—"

"The sympathies of half the men in New England are with the patriots, man! Will you discount a man's testimony on the grounds of his politics?"

"M'am?"

She turned, sharply, to see young Sergeant Muldoon behind her with a tray of coffee things, and a sort of folding camp table hung over one immense shoulder. Her cheekbones heated with embarrassment at being caught eavesdropping, but she asked, "Is there another door out of that office?" and reached out to take the tray from his hands.

"That there is, m'am," he said, gratefully handing it over and unfolding the camp table. "Into the Colonel's bedroom, it leads, and out into the parade. The cook says, there's precious little cream this time of year, but I got you some, I have, and a bit of cake."

Abigail made herself smile, spread her skirts, and settled on the bench again, there being no way that she could think of to check whether a company of armed men waited in the Colonel's bedroom to drag John away in chains. "Thank you, Sergeant," she said. "Lieutenant Coldstone didn't happen to mention whether anything was found in Mrs. Pentyre's chaise, to hint at whoever might have driven it from the house where Mrs. Pentyre's body was found, to . . . was it Lee's shipyard?"

"That it was, m'am!" The young man regarded her with admiration. "Think of you askin' after that, same as the Lieutenant did, when he looked it over so careful. A chaise is a chaise for my money, and himself that angry that it'd been tipped off the end of the dock there where the water's deep, not to speak of it spucketin' rain like Noah's Flood. Looked it over like somebody'd hid a treasure map under the seats, he did. *And* looked over every inch of the horse they found, like he meant to buy it. He's a caution, he is, m'am, beggin' your pardon, m'am."

"Pardon freely granted." Abigail smiled, and poured herself out some coffee from the small earthenware pot. "And *did* he find aught?"

"Not on the horse nor the chaise, m'am, given they was out in the rain all the night. But just lookin' at the poor lady's shoes, an' at the hems of her petticoats, if you'll excuse me mentionin' such a thing, m'am, and her poor face, he says she wasn't tidied up and laid on the bed by him what killed her, but by others, hours later, for what purpose God only knows." He gave her a bow, and then—not to omit any sign of respect—saluted her as well, before excusing himself and hurrying off.

A caution indeed, Abigail reflected, reopening *Pamela* and taking a nibble of the regimental cook's excellent cake. Wet hems and wet shoes meant she'd arrived in the rain, and the settling of the blood that Dr. Warren had spoken of told its own tale of how long she'd lain on her face before she was put on her back on the bed. *Just because he knows someone tampered with the house doesn't mean he knows who.*

Was that why he suspected John? Because Rebecca would have admitted him to her house without question?

Try as she might to absorb herself into her favorite book—*not*, as Rebecca had described it, "the world's longest shilly-shally," but (Abigail had repeatedly pointed out to her) a serious look at how men and the world regarded a woman's right to choose her own destiny—Abigail found her mind returning again and again to the riddle that lay before her, like a labyrinth plunged in darkness and reeking with the smell of blood.

It was close to two when John emerged at last from Colonel Leslie's office—Abigail checked twice more at the door, as the hour had dragged on, to make sure she could still hear his voice—and he was escorted only by the subaltern who had shown him in. She would have given much to have been able to hear what Lieutenant Coldstone and Colonel Leslie had to say to one another in private, but even had John not worn the watchful look of one who isn't certain he'll actually be allowed to board the departing boat, she couldn't think of an unobtrusive way of listening at the door.

"Damn Sam and his myrmidons," said John softly, as they passed between the red-coated guards at the Castle's gate and picked their way through the straggle of tents, boxes, and sheep pens toward the wharf. "Too many times they've run up against witnesses who'll swear that one or another of the Sons of Liberty was elsewhere than where they know he was, or smugglers who'll slip a man across the harbor at dead of night when the gates are closed."

"That's what they assume you did?"

He nodded. "Left my horse in one of the smuggler barns on Hog Island and crossed in a rowboat, did the deed, then slipped back—"

"But *why*? *Why* do they believe this of *you*, of all people, and why would you have done such a thing? It was an atrocity, John. Do they honestly think you would be capable of performing those acts—"

"They don't know that." John's voice was grim. "Thanks

to Sam, all they saw was her body—slashed, yes, but laid neatly out on a bed, and the blood all mopped away. And we cannot tell them otherwise. You're frozen," he added, chaffing her gloved hand as they descended the muddy path to the little wharf where Linus Logan waited for them in the *Katrina*. "You should not have—"

"They gave me very nice coffee," replied Abigail. "And had I not come, in all this time waiting I'd have gone mad at home, and murdered the children in my rage, and then wouldn't we both have felt silly when you came back safe after all."

No message had come from Sam, or Revere, or Orion Hazlitt in their absence. But after a dinner of yesterday's chicken stewed, when Abigail had milked "the girls" (as she called Semiramis and Cleopatra) and was pouring out milk by lantern light in the icy scullery, Pattie came in with a note. "A boy brought it, m'am. Is it about Mrs. Malvern?" Her elfin face puckered anxiously, as she watched Abigail unfold the scrap of kitchen paper and angle it to the light.

Mrs. Adams—

Forgive me the inconvenience to you entailed in a meeting at six thirty tomorrow evening, in the yard of Mr. Malvern's house, to tell you what I know of Mrs. Moore's whereabouts. These are the only time and place available to me. I will arrange that the gate be open, and that an escort is provided to see you to your home.

I am your ob't etc,
Scipio Carter

Nine

Whatever Charles Malvern might feel—and say—about those would-be imitators of English society who ate their dinners by lamplight, Abigail guessed that with a fashionably minded daughter and son in the house, six thirty was probably the earliest any servant there was going to have a moment's leisure. Which was, she supposed, to the good. Her conscience nagged her painfully about her own work, neglected or, more reprehensibly, shuffled off onto poor Pattie's slim shoulders.

Yet the next morning, instead of setting briskly forth to the market the moment Nabby and Johnny led the cows out of the yard toward what little pasturage the Common offered these days, Abigail brought out her writing desk, and began reading through the twoscore letters that Rebecca had sent to her, in the eighteen months between the family's removal to the Adams farm in Braintree in April of '71, and their return to Boston nineteen months later, in November of '72, scanning for names. In hundreds of desultory conversations, Abigail recalled her speaking occasionally of friends, cousins, her brother's comrades from Baltimore, to any one of whom she would have opened her door on a rainy night. Names Abigail recalled only vaguely, and sought now, in the letters, grimly fighting the temptation to linger on the memories they stirred.

Her anger came back to her, reading of how Charles Malvern had harried her from first one set of chambers and then another; the sadness and pity, at that letter when Rebecca spoke of Orion Hazlitt's growing love for her; grief at the account of little Nathan Malvern's death. And like a mirror in her friend's words, the recollection of her own days on the farm, with John's two brothers and their wives and children, John's indomitable little mother and her easygoing second husband . . . No lying jealousies about stepparents there.

It was well and truly eight o'clock before she set out for the market. Coincidentally, just about the time the Tillet cook Queenie—in Abigail's mind one of the laziest women in New England—generally made her appearance there.

"Wait your turn, you pushy slattern!" the stout little woman shrilled at a young housemaid who was trying to get past her to a golden heap of pears. "The nerve of some people!" she added, loudly, as Abigail came up beside her. "Think they own the market—not that these nasty things have any more juice to them than ninepins, or flavor either. And a penny the slut wants for two of them! Why would anyone want two of the things, or one either—don't you pay her prices, Mrs. Adams, I refuse to stand by and let a good woman be cheated." She dragged Abigail away. "What Mrs. T will say sweetening the fruit, with sugar at three shillings for a loaf, and blaming me that there's nothing fit for the family to eat—"

"How horrible for you," sympathized Abigail warmly, "after the shocking day you had Thursday! I had meant to come yesterday, to see how you did—and I confess I'm astonished you were not felled by it all!—but that vain, *arrogant* officer dared to come and order *John* to go out to the camp, only because he was Mrs. Malvern's lawyer—"

"Oh, my dear, you don't know," gasped Queenie. "You *can't* know how things have been since then! That horrible Lieutenant Coldstone, and those dreadful soldiers, asking me if I'd heard anything in the middle of the night—What would I have heard, sleeping as I do in the west attic and the whole house locked up, and at midnight, too?—and

Mrs. Tillet coming home in the midst of it all, and such a row there was, with all the luggage brought in, I swear my head was pounding fit to split! You know the headaches I get—"

"Oh, *dear*, yes!" agreed Abigail, having been treated to minute descriptions of every single headache whenever she came to call on Rebecca over the course of the past year. If Nehemiah Tillet had a habit of dropping in on his tenant to advise her on how best to arrange the wood in her fireplace, and Mrs. Tillet was constantly in and out of Rebecca's little house to bring shirts for Rebecca to sew and errands for her husband that could not be put off, Queenie was just as intrusive, crossing the yard a dozen times in the course of preparing dinner, with items of gossip, complaints about her health and the ill treatment she was obliged to endure, or simply queries: *Who was that who was just here? Is he a gentleman friend of yours? Don't think I didn't see Mrs. Wallace coming to call on you—is it true she's a spendthrift who has nearly bankrupted her husband . . . ?*

But when Abigail interrupted the catalog of further symptoms to ask, was there anyone Rebecca had spoken of, to whom she might have fled, the cook only bristled, and snapped, "Belike she's run off with her man—after all her talk of how she's pure as driven snow—"

"Her man?" asked Abigail, startled. "Not Mr. Hazlitt—"

"As if her sort stops at one." Queenie sniffed. "The one she let in through her parlor window from the alley."

"Did you see him? Was this at midnight? It could have been—"

The protuberant brown eyes shifted suddenly, and Queenie said, "No, of course not! That is, it wasn't at midnight—What would I have been doing in the alley at midnight? It wasn't Wednesday night at all. I mean to say, I've seen her do so at other times, many other times, and everyone in the neighborhood knows it, too!" she added defensively. "What I mean to say is, this Mrs. Pentyre, if *she* was carrying on with the Colonel of the British Regiment, and had someone else she wanted to meet, a woman like the Malvern is just the one who'd have let her use her house. And I'm sorry to say it," she went on doggedly, as Abigail opened her mouth to protest, "being as I know you were taken in by her cozening ways, but taken in you were, Mrs. Adams."

"No!" Abigail stopped still in the midst of the market crowd. "How dare—That is," she collected herself, seeing Queenie's face redden dangerously, "how could I have been so deceived? Are you sure of this man you saw?"

"Other nights," said the cook. "Dozens of other—"

"Mrs. Queensboro!"

So engrossed had Abigail been in Queenie's rather confused tale, that she had completely neglected to keep an eye out for Hester Tillet. The draper's wife swept up to them now like a Navy Man of War in her dark gown and tall, starched cap, her voice like a bucket of coals falling down a flight of stairs. "I don't come to market to have you stand prattling of our affairs to all the world—your servant, Mrs. Adams." She accompanied her bobbed curtsey with a poisonous glare.

"M'am, I would never—"

"Don't you tell me what you would do and what you wouldn't," snapped Mrs. Tillet. "I won't have it. Come away at once."

Though Queenie was a good decade older than her employer she bowed her head at once and retreated.

"'Twas my fault, m'am," said Abigail quickly, hoping to win herself enough of Queenie's goodwill to elicit further confidences later. "I but asked after Mrs. Malvern—"

"Then shame on you for gossiping with servants," retorted Mrs. Tillet. "The lazy trollop has come to her just and fitting end, and I make no doubt they will find her body, too, in time, at the bottom of the harbor, with her throat cut like her friend's." She closed her hand around

Queenie's arm—a mighty handful of flesh, but the linen-draper's wife had a grip to accommodate nearly anything—and thrust her away ahead of her into the crowd toward the oyster seller's stall.

Though her own market basket was still nearly empty, thanks to her companion's determination not to let her purchase from any farmer to whom she herself had taken a personal dislike, Abigail—with a backwards glance to make sure the towering Tillet bonnet was still moving among the stalls—hastened her steps around the corner of the market hall and out of sight. A small bridge crossed the opening of the town dock, leading to the tangle of lanes that eventually gave onto Ann Street, then Fish Street, along the brisk and crowded waterfront of the North End. It was a walk of only minutes to the alley that led to Tillet's Yard, shadowed still with the wet light of the chilly morning.

The gate was still closed—and still barred, though Tillet and the younger of his two prentice-boys were obliged to help a carter unload several quires of paper, a roll of buckram, and a box of what appeared to be shoes in the street beside the shop's front door, to the great inconvenience of traffic. But Abigail didn't need to enter the yard to refresh her memory. Rebecca's parlor window—shuttered again now—looked out onto the alley, and there was no way that it could be seen from either the main Tillet house, or from the yard.

Had Queenie seen a man entering Rebecca's window, either Wednesday night or on some other occasion? Despite the vindictiveness in her voice, the cook's words had had a ring of truth, before she'd begun to go back on her story and obfuscate . . . What, indeed, *would* she have been doing in the alley, on a night of threatening rain? On a night, moreover, when her master and mistress were away? Selling a pound or two of the Tillet cornmeal, or a loaf of sugar, to put the money in her own pocket?

Abigail couldn't imagine the self-pitying little woman possessed a clandestine lover of her own. Either way, reason enough to come up with any kind of slander to undermine Rebecca's credibility, had Rebecca, for instance, seen her from that parlor window when she opened it to pull the shutters to. Still—

The only window of the L-shaped Tillet house that overlooked the alley was the small gable window of the south attic, a room which Abigail knew had for years been given over to storage, after the overhasty marriage (in her opinion) of the youngest daughter of the house. According to Rebecca, the cramped and stuffy little chamber had been shuttered and out of use for years.

But as she looked up now, she saw—a little to her surprise—that the window's shutters stood open. And just for a moment—though admittedly the angle of her vision was a narrow one, looking up from the straitened confine of the alley—Abigail thought she saw pale movement behind the dingy glass.

Mrs. Tillet's unmistakable voice boomed from the street, shouting to her husband. Abigail moved off further up the alley, to cut through a neighbor's drying yard and garden, and so out onto Cross Street unobserved.

There was no message from anyone, by the time she came belatedly home.

As she swept and cleaned the upstairs rooms, scoured lamps, listened to Nabby and Johnny's lessons, mixed a batch of bread and prepared dinner—with extra provision for tomorrow's cold Sabbath meals—Abigail's mind chased memories.

Rebecca Malvern at eighteen, coming for the first time into the Brattle Street Meeting-House as a bride. She recalled how the dark, self-consciously sober fabric of her dress had been cut and trimmed with a stylish flare that no

Boston woman would ever display. In her own family pew, Abigail had overheard the whispers from the pews on all sides: *Maryland . . . dowry . . . Papist . . . Poor little Tamar Malvern told me only yesterday she said, "I'll teach you to pray to the Virgin and the Pope."* Tamar, mincing with downcast eyes behind her new stepmother, had looked smug; Malvern icy; Rebecca wretched, but head still high.

October of 1768. Abigail herself, she recalled, had been great with the child who had become Susanna—her precious, fragile girl. That was the week the redcoat troops had first come ashore in Boston, setting up their tents on the Commons, and jostling everywhere in the streets. A group of them had passed the meetinghouse after the service, and while Malvern had paused to ask John some question about the vestry—on which they were both serving that year—Rebecca had commented to Abigail, *Are we expecting French invasion, or does the King just think that eight hundred of his armed servants in the town will cause us to sleep better of nights?*

Some in the congregation didn't hesitate to ascribe her objection to the King's troops to a secret Papist's natural sympathy for the Irish, or perhaps the French. But despite the difference in their ages, in Rebecca, Abigail had found a kindred soul. Before long she was inviting the girl to take potluck tea in the kitchen while she herself did the household mending, rather than sit formally in the parlor, and Rebecca had watched in wide-eyed consternation as Abigail performed whatever household tasks needed doing: churning butter or scraping out candlesticks or kneading bread, things that had been done by slaves in the home of Rebecca's father. Later, when Rebecca was living with them—sharing the bed with Nabby and Johnny in the other small upstairs chamber—they'd laughed together about her dismay. "I wish I'd paid closer attention!" Rebecca had moaned during her first lesson with the butter churn. Abigail had replied in her primmest schoolmistress voice: "At least you've seen one before and aren't frightened." Rebecca had flicked droplets of the skimmed milk at her from her fingertips, like a schoolgirl, and they'd both laughed.

How good it had felt to laugh, Abigail remembered, after all those weeks of grieving Susanna's death.

John had promised to return from consulting a client in good time to walk Abigail to the Malvern house, a distance of barely a quarter mile. With the Sabbath on the morrow, and John confined by his bond to the town limits of Boston, Abigail didn't really expect him to conclude his business that quickly, and when the dinner dishes were washed and the pots scoured, the kitchen swept and all the lamps filled and set out ready, she'd gone two doors down Queen Street and made arrangements with young Shim Walton the cooper's apprentice. "I wouldn't *dream* of trespassing on your master's beliefs, Shim, by asking you to do paid work once the Sabbath Eve has begun! But I've had a premonition that I may accidentally drop a halfpenny in the street first thing Monday morning as I go past your master's shop . . ."

A carriage was drawn up before Malvern's front door, as it had been on Thursday afternoon. From across the street, Abigail watched the merchant climb inside, stiff and self-conscious-looking in a satin coat and hair powder. Cloaked shapes that had to be his two surviving children followed him, tall Jeffrey and slender Tamar, trailed by the more robust shape of the giggling maid. Scipio, in his evening livery, bowed them away from the house's single, shallow step, then turned back inside. As he did so, another servant on the ground floor leaned from a window, and closed the shutters against the night.

"I'll be all right now, Shim," said Abigail softly, but the boy insisted on escorting her across the street and down the carriageway to the yard. Scipio must have come straight from the front step to the kitchen's door to meet her, his candle glinting on the brass of his livery buttons.

The fire had already been banked in the kitchen, but the room still pulsed with warmth, exquisite after the night's brutal cold. The glow of the oil-lamp on its chain dimly outlined cauldrons and skimmers, trammels and oil-jars in the shadows, and the brick floor still smelt of the after-dinner wash up. The butler had kept coffee from dinner for her in the pot on the hob, and served her in one of the family cups: blue English porcelain rather than servants' pottery.

"I'm sorry I couldn't come up with the direction of Miss Catherine's brother any sooner than this, m'am," Scipio explained, when Abigail had gestured him to sit. Since it was the house he lived in, she felt strange and awkward inviting him to do so, slave or not, even as she stopped herself from inviting him to share with her the coffee he'd made. *What is the proper behavior between slave and free in this situation?* she asked herself irritably, and concluded that there wasn't any. A truly proper servant wouldn't have admitted a stranger to his master's house in the first place, nor discussed the family's affairs with an outsider. "She wrote to me, and to Ulee in the stables, once or twice over the last year. But we had to look through the letters to find mention of the nearest town to her brother's farm. It's Townsend, but where that might be I don't know. Wenham is another place she speaks of, but she writes as if it's some ways off from her, it sounds like."

"Wenham is some ways off from any spot on the civilized earth," muttered Abigail. "Always supposing Mrs. Malvern could get across the river or through the town gate."

"I understand—" Scipio cleared his throat delicately. "I understand that Miss Rebecca had friends who might have skiffs or whaleboats that could get her across the harbor, even on a falling tide and a rainy night—"

"If she had such," replied Abigail, with equal tact—since no one in Boston, not even the slaves, admitted to knowing anyone either engaged in smuggling or involved with the Sons of Liberty, "and of course I don't for a moment imagine she would know such people—I think they would undertake inquiries amongst themselves, and quickly learn if that had in fact been the case. It does not seem to have been."

"Ah." Scipio nodded. "I didn't think you would be asking after Miss Catherine, if it had. Mr. Adams—"

"—has some fairly low acquaintances. Did Lieutenant Coldstone ask about Mrs. Malvern's possible *friends*?"

The slave shook his head. "Not of me, he didn't. And I think if he had asked Mr. Jeffrey or Miss Tamar, I would have heard. Myself, I don't even know for a fact if she had such friends, though I know that being friends with Mr. Adams, and Mr. Revere, and reading the newspapers and arguing with Mr. Malvern as she did, I shouldn't be surprised to hear of it. As to what Mr. Jeffrey or Miss Tamar might have told him—or their father—I can't answer for that."

Abigail was silent for a time, gazing into the dense shadows of the kitchen. Even under the relatively strong glow of the oil-lamp overhead, the long sideboards, the sturdy bin-table and homely water-jars were barely distinguishable in the gloom. After a time she asked, "Do they hate her so much still?"

The butler sighed. "Not hate, I don't think, so much, Mrs. Adams," he said. "They were her enemies before they even met her. I think Miss Tamar talked herself into hating her—and talked Mr. Jeffrey into it—because it's easier to do evil to someone you hate, than to admit to yourself you're only telling lies and making trouble because you don't want another little brother or sister to come along and cut into your inheritance. That's what it came down to."

"Rebecca—Mrs. Malvern—told me once that Tamar would search her room while she was away, and stole her letters. She said she always suspected it was Tamar who learned, and told Mr. Malvern, about her arranging to pay her brother's gambling debts with part of the household money, and backing her father's bills with Mr. Malvern's name. Mrs. Malvern said she knew she shouldn't have done it, but—"

"People do foolish things for those they love." Scipio poured her a little more coffee. "It's true Miss Tamar doesn't like the idea of having her father's estate cut up into five or six rather than just in two, but it's for Mr. Jeffrey that she started working to turn her father against Miss Rebecca. For Mr. Jeffrey and little Master Nathan—she did her possible, to turn that poor little boy against Miss Rebecca, *for his own good*, as she said. *He'll thank me for it*, she said, 'specially after Miss Rebecca left. But when he was ill there at the end," added the butler softly, "it was Miss Rebecca he would call for."

And it was for Nathan, Abigail knew well, that Rebecca had chosen to remain in Boston, the summer of '72. Hoping against hope that she would have the opportunity to go to the child's bedside.

"Does Miss Tamar still have Miss Rebecca's letters?" asked Abigail. And, when Scipio looked uncertain, she went on, "I'm not fishing for servant-hall gossip, Scipio. Mrs. Pentyre was deliberately lured to Rebecca's house—I know this," she added, seeing the surprise in his face. "Believe me, it is true. She was lured there, and murdered, by someone who knew Rebecca: someone who knew that he could get Rebecca to let him into the house, one way or another. I think she saw him, and I think that's why she fled. It may be someone she knew in Boston—someone I would know, or Mr. Adams, or even you . . . and it may be someone she knew before she married Mr. Malvern."

"Who?" asked Scipio, baffled. "Most of her people—her brother and her father—are dead. The rest of her family cut ties with her, when she gave up her faith."

"That's why I need to see her letters," said Abigail. "Because whoever he is, I suspect that he knows she saw him. And unless we find him—and find *her*—he may reach her first."

Ten

"What I don't understand, m'am, is how Miss Rebecca even knew this Mrs. Pentyre." Scipio kept his voice to a near-whisper as he led Abigail up the servants' backstairs to the upper floor. "She was only a young girl, not even wed to Mr. Pentyre when Miss Rebecca left this house. Unless Mr. Pentyre for some reason thought to learn something from Miss Rebecca, that would damage Mr. Malvern—"

Abigail said, "Good Heavens!" It was something she hadn't even considered. "Would he? I've never met the man—"

"Nor I." They reached a tiny landing and the butler opened the little door there. The hall was near pitch-dark, save for the dim glow of the candles he bore in a pewter branch, and cold as the back corridors of Hell. "Ulee—that's the head groom—has a cousin in Pentyre's stables, though, so every time Mr. Malvern sues Pentyre, or Mr. Pentyre gets the Governor or the Royal Port Commissioner to fine Mr. Malvern or hold up one of his cargoes to search—"

"My goodness. I had no idea. *Every time* . . . Is this a common occurrence? Do they hate one another so?"

"Like a horse hates a snake, m'am—only each of them thinks he's the horse, and the other's the snake. Mr. Malvern's daddy hated Mr. Pentyre's uncle, that was the merchant in the family and he left Mr. Pentyre all his ships and money; they undersell each other's cargoes, they slander each other's goods. You know how Mr. Malvern won't let a matter rest, if he thinks he's been wronged, and Mr. Pentyre, for all he looks like he doesn't have the red blood in him to do up his shoe buckles, is the same. Only, bein' related to the Governor, he'll use that to make trouble for those that make trouble for him."

Halfway down the silent hallway he opened a door. The darkness beyond it was warmer, and breathed of sandalwood and dried rose petals. The candles' light briefly caressed satinwood bedposts, the Venetian glass of an expensive toilet-mirror.

"Back in August, it was Mr. Pentyre who had his agents buy up all Mr. Jeffrey's gaming debts, and call them in, close to a thousand pounds' worth. Then Mr. Malvern put the rumor about that Pentyre was smuggling, and got one of his cargoes seized, and Miss Tamar tried to bribe one of the kitchen staff at Pentyre's to poison Mrs. Pentyre's little dog, in revenge."

"What a charming picture you servants must have of the lives of your masters," Abigail murmured, and a ghost of a smile tugged the slender man's mouth.

"All this is nothing, m'am. Not to what you see if you're a slave in Barbados, where I was born."

Abigail, gathering her skirts aside to draw out the trundle bed from beneath the great bed, looked aside from him, ashamed. Scipio set the candelabra on the little secretaire by the window, and came to help her. The trundle was made up with fresh linen. Either Tamar didn't like to be alone for one minute of the day or night, or her father didn't want her to be. A night rail was laid out ready on the pink silk counterpane of the main bed, the linen as light as silk.

"Does she get love letters?"

"Dozens," affirmed the butler resignedly. "Some she keeps in the desk, but the ones she doesn't want her father to see—or know about—she has delivered to the lady who runs the hat shop at the end of her father's wharf, and sends Miss Oonaugh—that's her maid—down to get them for her. You think they're under the bed?" At Abigail's gestures, the two of them had maneuvered the low bed away from the large one, and Abigail now knelt near the main bed's head.

"'Tis where I hid mine. Not that I set up clandestine flirts," she hastened to add, as the butler grinned. "But when I was young my father considered political pamphlets inappropriate reading for well-bred girls, and I had my older sister's beau smuggle them to me. Dreadfully badly written they were," she went on reminiscently, easing down onto her stomach and reaching as far toward the head of the bed as she could. "And shockingly ill-reasoned, some of them. After a time my conscience grew so bad that I confessed the whole to—Ah!" Her fingers brushed what felt like the corner of a largish box. She flattened herself further, squirmed beneath the tall frame, reaching with both arms and thanking the heavens that Scipio kept the chambermaids strictly up to their work: no nonsense about sweeping only as much of the floor as showed and letting dust kittens breed with abandon in the dark.

She drew it out, sat back on her heels. More quietly, she asked, "Did you ever try to tell their father that Tamar and Jeffrey were telling him lies about Rebecca? About her trying to convert them to Catholicism, or punishing them for not praying to the Virgin?"

Scipio opened his mouth, closed it, then sighed. "You'll think me a coward, m'am. And I daresay I am. But I didn't dare. None of us did. What man would believe his new young wife over his daughter? What man wouldn't believe his daughter, if she—" He hesitated. "If she decided to lie about a slave? And a man-slave?"

Abigail thought about that, and felt her face heat with anger. Hotter, even, than when Rebecca had come to her weeping about the way her stepdaughter had used to twist her every action and word.

"He knew I'd been raised a Catholic," Scipio went on gently. "Miss Rebecca spoke up for me, early in her marriage here, which was a mistake, when Mr. Malvern gets going on one of his rages. He said, we'd conspire, if one of us spoke for the other, after that. Then, too," he went on, "there were those things Miss Rebecca truly did, that were unwise. Things she did for those she loved."

Abigail sighed, and turned the box over in her lap. Twelve inches by twelve, and nearly that deep, with a little hasp and padlock. The sort of thing gentlemen kept case bottles of cognac in, locked away from their servants. When she shook it, both its heft and the dry, whispery rattle inside spoke of folded paper. "I think you're right to tread carefully around Mistress Tamar," she said. "For you, it isn't a case of simply being turned out without a character and having to find a new employer, is it?"

"No, m'am."

How dare the man buy and sell another? How dare any *man put another in the position of being bought and sold like a donkey?*

She took a deep breath, trying to steady herself against the rage that swept her. In a studiedly neutral tone, she asked, "You wouldn't happen to know if any of Rebecca's other letters survived, would you?"

"He burned them all, m'am. And cursed her name as he did it. Since then, Miss Tamar will every now and then come up with, *I didn't tell you this at the time, but she used to do thus-and-such*—threaten her with a red-hot curling iron, I think was one of them. I can always tell when she's done it. I wish she wouldn't. Not just for Miss Rebecca's sake, but for his."

"Well, we have it on the authority of Scripture that the Lord shall avenge the stripes of the righteous, and uphold his children against those who slander them." Abigail sighed. "Though sometimes I wish Scripture were a little more specific about when, exactly, these events will take place. In the meantime, do you know where Miss Tamar keeps the key to this?"

"On a ribbon," said a man's harsh voice from the doorway. "I should imagine it's the blue one, knotted at her waist with her watch."

Abigail slewed around on her heels, aghast. Scipio got hastily to his feet, the dark beyond the single candle's light cloaking, Abigail suspected, the ashen hue of his face.

Charles Malvern said, "You may go, Scipio."

"Sir, I—"

"You may go."

Scipio stayed long enough to help Abigail to her feet. "Mr. Malvern," she said, as the servant's footsteps retreated down the stair, "I beg you not to blame Scipio in this."

"And in what way is a trusted servant not to be blamed, who admits robbers to his master's house while the family is away?" He put his head a little to one side, and the pale eyes that regarded her shrieked rage in a face as calm as stone. "Don't tell me Scipio, too, has been corrupted by this talk of colonial liberties that your husband and his friends vomit forth. Or does he merely seek a share of my daughter's jewelry?" He reached for the bellpull, and Abigail impulsively extended her hand to stop his.

"This isn't jewelry, sir—"

"If it was garden dirt," said Malvern, yanking the bell, "it would still not excuse burglary."

"Mr. Malvern," said Abigail desperately, "I have reason to believe this box contains clandestine correspondence of your daughter's." She felt sick at the thought of Scipio being taken to one of the taverns by the Long Wharf, where dealers bid for slaves to carry south to Virginia. Even if the little merchant went so far as to actually have her locked up in the gaol house by the law-counts for part of the night—with every thief and prostitute in Boston—John would get her out, with no worse effects than perhaps lice in her hair and bugs in her skirts from the bedding.

Scipio was not in the law's hands, but the hands of his master.

Malvern's eyes narrowed: "A girl's love notes." For a moment she thought he was going to snap at her, *My daughter does not receive any such thing . . .*

Of course any father would seek to protect his daughter by knowing who was courting her—particularly a man of wealth like Malvern. Yet it crossed her mind to wonder if he sought to control his daughter's thoughts and movements as totally as he had sought to control Rebecca's.

Footsteps sounded on the back stairs. Dim yellow light mottled the creamy plaster visible through the hall door, making the vines stenciled there seem to stir in soundless wind.

"I pray so, sir," she said, keeping her voice steady with an effort. "Because I fear this box contains evidence of a conspiracy against both yourself, and your wife."

For one instant, familiar with the uncontrollable first rush of his rages, she would not have been surprised had he struck her. Malvern only stood, staring, mouth half open and eyes glittering with fury. Then his lips closed hard, and he stepped to her, and yanked the box from her hands.

A manservant appeared in the doorway, hastily adjusting a badly tied neckcloth. "Sir?"

Malvern was silent for a moment, studying Abigail's face. "Bring me a chisel to my study," he said at last. And he added, as if the words were forced from him at gunpoint, "And bring coffee for myself and Mrs. Adams."

In November of 1770, a few months after starting at Harvard, Jeffrey Malvern had written to Tamar, *Father spoke today of the Papist. It sounded like he begins to have regard for her for making her own way. This does not sound promising. Can you not find him a mistress? There is a woman here named*

Mrs. Bell, who would be willing but has the appearance of great respectability.

John's clerk, young Mr. Thaxter, had told Abigail things about Mrs. Bell of Cambridge, and Abigail thought young Mr. Jeffrey grossly underestimated his father's gullibility, if he supposed the merchant hadn't heard them, too.

March of 1771: *What earthly reason did you give, for not complaining to him at the time, if she indeed threatened you with a hot coal in your face? Surely even for the Whore of Babylon, that is extreme?*

July of 1772—a few weeks after the death of their young brother: . . . *but since he* is *gone, could you not come up with some way that it was the Papist's doing?*

January of 1773, shortly after Rebecca's effort to retrieve her property: *I don't like this talk of divorcement. He's but four-and-fifty, and there's juice in him yet. No sense prying one step-mama away from him only to have him wed another, and then it will be all to do again. The next one may not be so Jesuitical or so obliging about leaving her correspondence where they may be found. What about Clara Wheelock, or one of her fair "nieces"? That carroty one (Jenny?) should keep any man alive busy.*

Abigail looked up from Piers Woodruff's dozenth letter begging and bullying his sister Rebecca to send him money as the clock struck ten. Walking home from their meeting with Malvern last November, with Rebecca silent and shaking at her side, she had wished for worms to consume Malvern from the inside out, as they had consumed Herod Agrippa in the Book of Acts. Now seeing his face, she thought, *I must never wish such ill again, even in my heart.* His was indeed the face of a man whose heart and entrails were being devoured from within.

For the first time in her life, she pitied him. She said, "I'm sorry."

He laid down his son's latest missive—containing only lamentations about debts and hangovers, and a request for Tamar to *get the old man to see reason about my allowance*—and passed a hand over his face. Two hours ago, Malvern had sent his disheveled serving man to Queen Street, with a note to the effect that Mrs. Adams was detained at his house but would return with a suitable escort, and had summoned Scipio from the kitchen to tell him that he need not worry for his position, but should go to bed. "I will see to Miss Malvern, when she comes home," the father had said.

"Has this accomplished all that you had in mind, Mrs. Adams?" the merchant now asked, visibly struggling to control the anger that seemed to be the only emotion he was capable of feeling. He reached for the coffeepot, but lifting it found it empty (as Abigail had, half an hour previously). For a moment he seemed about to hurl it to the floor, but it was an expensive piece, so he set it down again. His pale eyes burned with exhausted resentment as he looked back at her. "Does the knife go deep enough for you, to avenge the hurt I gave your friend?"

"I did not come seeking vengeance." Abigail lifted the yellowing sheets, the looping scribbles of the handwriting of that young wastrel and gambler who had made his sister's life such a misery. "Only information, about who Rebecca might have known, who would have done such a thing to an innocent woman in her house."

"The woman wasn't innocent," grated Malvern. "She was a whore, as her husband is a lying pimp."

"If she was a whore, her deserving would have been an *A* sewed to her garment, in the old way, not to have her throat cut and her body mutilated."

Malvern opened his mouth to shout something about whores and what they deserved, and Abigail steadily met his eyes. After a moment he closed his lips again, settled back into his chair. "You are right, Mrs. Adams," he said, in a voice like the grind of the sea on pebbles after a storm. "If it was reasonable men we spoke of. Yet the woman did her whoring with the commander of the British troops.

And her husband is the Governor's friend and one of the commissioners who's been given the Royal Monopoly to sell East India Company tea. I should think it would be obvious, where to seek for her murderers, and why they would do their deed in—in the house that they chose."

"You think she was killed by the Sons of Liberty, in short," said Abigail, and raised her brows. "Mr. Malvern, if sexual congress with officers of the Sixty-Fourth regiment was considered grounds for murder by the Sons of Liberty, the city of Boston would be littered with female corpses from Copp's Hill to the Neck." She brushed her hand across the letters on the table between them. "I promise you, I have enough friends in the Sons of Liberty to be sure that they were not behind this crime. If I thought they were—or if I knew that Rebecca had run off with them—I would not have risked spending a night in the city gaol trying to find the true culprit. And I certainly would not have risked having an innocent serving man hanged, which I believe is the penalty when a slave robs his master."

He continued to glare at her, like a bull who has pursued a red flag to exhaustion. "And all that you say could be a ploy to convince me of your lies."

"Mr. Malvern," said Abigail, "everyone in town knows that you cannot be convinced of anything."

To her surprise he laughed, a single explosive sputter, then put his face in his hands, so that they hid whatever expression had come over his mouth. He sat that way for some time, staring at his wife's letters, and his son's.

"Rebecca has been missing for three days now," Abigail went on. "For three days the Sons of Liberty have been seeking her—so I am told—about the city, and have found no trace of her. For all I know this man, this killer, whoever he is, seeks her, too. I'd hoped to find something in her correspondence with her family that might help me. She had made few friends here in Boston—"

"She had that printer!" Malvern's hand smote the table with a violence that made Abigail jump. "For all her talk of *my* misdeeds, and *my* mistrust, while *she*—"

"In the years you have been apart," Abigail said slowly, "your wife and I have been as near as sisters. And I will swear an oath on the Testament that she has never regarded herself as anything other than your wife. She has spoken of you in anger—sometimes in very great anger—but never in disrespect . . . Which is more, I'm afraid, than can be said of me."

"It isn't what I've heard."

"From whom did you hear it?"

He was silent again, and in the silence hooves could be heard in the street outside, and the clatter of harness as a carriage came to a halt before the house's outer door. Malvern's eyes moved toward the hall, then returned to Abigail, weary and angry, yet to her the anger seemed to smolder deeper—an inner pain, not a wall against opposition. "You're not telling me all of the truth, Mrs. Adams. You're mired to the neck in the bog of Sam Adams's making—as you mired my wife."

"What I believe—and what she believes—about the rights of the colonies doesn't mean that she isn't in danger now. It doesn't mean that the man who perpetrated a monstrous crime isn't looking for her. Or that I would not move Heaven and Earth, if I could, to find her before he gets to her."

A serving man's shoe-heels clacked in the hall, lamp flame juddering across the papered walls. Abigail's eye slid to Malvern's face, then away as a bright jumble of hushed giggles sounded, a girl's voice crying, "He is not my sweetheart!" and a young man's, "Oh, so you go kiss in alcoves just any officer you happen to meet?" "Faith, how'd ye know that, Master Jeff? Ye weren't out of the card-room but only long enough to piss in Mrs. Fluckner's rose-bed!"

"Good heavens, hand me that sponge, girl! This is what

comes of trying to take rouge off in the carriage—" "Don't be silly, Jeff, the old man's asleep by this time . . ."

And the three of them stood framed, suddenly, in the door of the study—Mistress Tamar in her pink and silver ball dress, her maid a step behind with her arms full of cloaks and her black hair disheveled, handsome Jeffrey with the laughter dying out of his face as they took in the pile of letters on the table, the open box, the grim set of their father's mouth. Tamar took a half step into the room, said, "Papa—?" and cast an uncertain glance at Abigail, then another at the box, and the letters from Jeffrey that lay beside her father's hand.

Then she turned back to her father, tears welling to her eyes, streaming down her face. "Oh, Papa, I can explain! I knew I shouldn't have kept them, but—"

"We'll speak in the morning, child." Malvern held up the letters in Piers Woodruff's Italianate hand. "And before you protest on the subject of whose correspondence is whose business in this house, please be prepared to explain how you came to have possession of letters written to your stepmother by her brother and her father. I trust you enjoyed Mrs. Fluckner's rout-party?" He unpocketed and held out to her a large, clean handkerchief as she began to cry, and his eyes, as he studied her face in the servant's candlelight, held not pity, but a weary disgust and disbelief.

"Please, Papa, please, it was Oonaugh who made me keep them! Oonaugh said she'd—"

"I never!" protested the servant girl, genuinely indignant, and Abigail, watching Jeffrey's face, saw the young man's expression go from surprise to bemusement to sudden, earnest concern.

"Father, I must say that I've long deplored—"

"We'll talk of it in the morning," Malvern repeated, as Tamar showed signs of dissolving into hysterical tears. "Jeffrey, take your sister to her room. Oonaugh, if you'd be so good as to stay?"

"Papa, don't believe her! Please don't believe her! When I found she was *forging* those letters from Jeffrey—"

"I never!" protested the maid, as Abigail closed the study door behind Jeffrey and Tamar.

"Of course you never forged these things, girl," said Malvern harshly. "Don't you think I know you can barely write your own name?" From the litter on the table he picked up a handful of the spicier billets-doux Scipio had told her of, addressed to Tamar by a variety of young gentlemen and containing nothing more incriminating than some of the worst sonnets Abigail had ever read. "And I take it you have no idea how these came into my daughter's possession either?"

"Sorr, I can explain—"

"I'm sure you can," he agreed. "I know my daughter is extremely fond of you, girl, and since I can say with certainty that Miss Tamar is going to be both bored and unhappy over the next several months, I would hesitate to add to her distress by obliging her to train a new servant. Do I make myself clear?"

The girl whispered, "Yes, sorr. But I never forged nuthin', nor told her to keep no letters—"

"It's just a story my daughter made up?"

"Yes, sorr."

"Like other stories she makes up?" His face was mottled crimson with anger, but he kept his voice quiet, more terrifying than a shout.

"Yes, sorr. She—"

"I'm going to ask you to do a favor for me, Oonaugh." He reached into the pocket of his sober gray vest. "Several favors, in fact. I trust you know our conversation is not to be shared with Miss Tamar?"

"Yes, sorr. I mean, no, sorr."

He pitched a coin onto the desk. The maid identified its size and weight in an instant and her black eyes widened. "For a year now I've been paying your wages. I want you to remember, from now on, that you are working for me. You tell my daughter that you forgive her for lying about you—"

Oonaugh's mouth popped open in protest.

"—and whatever she tells me, I expect *you* to come to me with the truth. Is that clear?"

"Yes, sorr."

"Now you may go."

The girl's short little fingers nipped up the coin, and she bobbed a curtsey. As she turned to go, Abigail said, "Just a moment, please. Mr. Malvern?"

He glanced at her, raised one heavy brow, tufted like a bobcat's.

"May I have a word with the girl, please?"

He nodded. "As many as you like. You may cut off her hair and knit stockings out of it—"

Oonaugh clutched at her cap in alarm.

"Mistress Oonaugh," said Abigail. "What is your surname?"

"Connelley, m'am."

"Miss Connelley. Are you acquainted with the maid who worked for Perdita Pentyre?"

"Oh, that was a horror, m'am! I've heard she was—"

"I know what you've heard," said Abigail grimly. "Do you know her?"

"We've spoke at parties. Down the rooms, you know, when the quality are all up flirtin' an' playin' cards an' carryin' on. Thinks the sun shines out her backside, she does, the consayted Frog, but I knows her to speak to."

"Would you be so kind as to carry a note to her for me? I should very much like to speak with her." *The handmaid of Jezebel, that was privy to all her ways . . .*

Malvern brought another coin from his pocket, and held it up for Oonaugh to see. "Please tell Miss—"

"Droux, sorr. Lisette Droux."

"Please tell Miss Droux that both Mrs. Adams and I understand how valuable her time is." There was silence, broken only by the creak of a manservant's feet in the hall, and the scratching of Abigail's quill as she penned a hasty note. "Does she read English?"

"I dunno, sorr." Oonaugh looked puzzled by the question. "I shouldn't think so, if she's French."

"Then perhaps you could ask her, if she would meet Mrs. Adams here at her earliest convenience?"

"That I'll do, sorr. You can depend on me."

"Good." He laid the second coin on the table. "You may go." As the door shut behind Oonaugh, he added quietly, "Shall I call Scipio in and have him make more coffee, Mrs. Adams? You look quite exhausted."

She could hear the half hour striking on Faneuil Hall, and tried to recall which hour had passed. She felt cold, weary to death, and a little ill. Surely it hadn't been only that morning that she'd started reading through Rebecca's letters of the summer before last, before sallying forth to the market to question Queenie.

"Thank you, sir, no. Thank you," she said again, as he came around to her, to hand her up from her chair. "More than I can say." The thick Spanish dollar he'd held up to Miss Connelley would buy, she guessed, any amount of information from Mlle Lisette Droux, and very quickly, if she knew anything of the cupidity of servants—particularly servants who might be facing unemployment in a foreign city.

He rang the bell nevertheless. Scipio appeared, having evidently disregarded his master's orders to take himself off to bed. "Have Ulee harness the chaise, to take Mrs. Adams home. I trust," he added, as the butler turned to obey, "that I have no need to say that I rely on your discretion, about all things concerning the events of this night, Scipio?"

The servant bowed. "You have no need, sir."

"So Mrs. Adams tells me. If I have not said so before," he went on quietly, "and I may not have, for you know as well as I that I do speak hastily when angry—I value very much the discretion that is natural to you, Scipio; as indeed I value all of your good qualities. Thank you for the help that you have extended to Mrs. Adams, on behalf of-of my good wife."

Scipio inclined his head. "Thank you, sir. Mrs. Adams." And he bowed himself from the room.

When he escorted her to the door some ten minutes later, Malvern said, "Let me know what you learn, Mrs. Adams. If you would," he added, like a man recalling a phrase in a foreign tongue. "I'll have the letters from Woodruff to-to my wife"—again he avoided calling her *Mrs. Malvern*—"sent over to you next week; I should like to read them myself again. You probably know as much as I do about—about my wife's family—and in any case it is hard to see, after the lapse of nearly eight years, why someone from her past would choose to do violence against an innocent third party in her house."

"I agree," said Abigail quietly. "Yet the killer has to be someone she knows, and trusted."

"Which doesn't preclude Sam Adams or one of his ilk," retorted Malvern grimly. "There!" he added. "That's the three quarters striking! Ulee had best make a little speed, if you're to be home when the Sabbath begins."

Icy wind clawed them as he handed her down the step and into the chaise. Abigail had protested, while they'd waited for it, that the distance was barely five hundred yards to her own door, but in her heart she was grateful, as the glow of the vehicle's lamps caught on flying spits of rain. "If he's a few minutes late," she replied, "I think we can argue, with our Lord, that it comes under the heading of pulling one's ox from a pit. The Sabbath was made for Man, and not Man for the Sabbath."

"Let me know what you learn," he said. "And how I may help you find—Mrs. Malvern."

Quietly, Abigail said, "I will." But as the chaise rattled

up King Street, Abigail reflected on how little she had learned, since she'd waked in the morning's cold dawn. She had pulled no ox from any pit. And though a small part of her heart rejoiced at what she thought she had heard in Charles Malvern's voice, she was well aware that she was no closer to knowing Rebecca's whereabouts than she had been on Thursday morning, watching the Sons of Liberty mop Perdita Pentyre's blood from Rebecca's kitchen floor.

Eleven

Mrs. Adams

Mistress Lisette Droux will come to the kitchen of my house to meet you at four o'clock this afternoon, having no day but Sunday, to leave her master's house. I hope and trust this meets with your approval?

I remain,
Your obedient humble etc.
Charles Malvern

"I suppose it isn't to be hoped that Malvern could arrange an interview with Richard Pentyre," remarked John, when Abigail handed him the note that had awaited them on the sideboard on their return from morning service.

"On the contrary, I suspect there's a better chance of getting truth out of the maid than out of the master." Abigail squatted to kiss Charley and Tommy, who generally had a hard time of it on Sabbath mornings while the rest of the family was at Meeting. Both John and Abigail subscribed to the belief that profane matters of the workday week included weekday toys and games, something Tommy didn't understand yet and Charley pretended not to. Like many children—Abigail included, at age three—he was deeply puzzled and resentful that God would require him to "sit still and be good" one day out of seven.

"Haven't you told me, John, time and again, that eight murders out of ten turn out to be someone known to their victim?" She rose again to her feet, and spoke softly: oxen, pits, and Sabbath notwithstanding, it wasn't a discussion she wanted small children to overhear. "In spite of the favors and business opportunities that accrued to Mr. Pentyre as a result of his wife's affair with the commander of the British regiment, the fact remains that she was deceiving him, and doing so before the whole of the town."

"And the fact remains that as a firm friend of the Crown, a cousin of our Governor through the Sellars and Oliver families, and a consignee for the East India Company's tea monopoly, Pentyre had no real need of the Army's favors," returned John. "He had, on the other hand, numerous enemies."

"Yet he lives." Abigail hung her cloak on its peg, poured out water to wash her hands: The table for the cold and early Sabbath dinner had been set last night, the food prepared. At three the afternoon service would begin: Young Mr. Thaxter, John's clerk, had agreed to come by with his mother to escort Pattie, Nabby, and Johnny back to the Meeting-House while John remained with the little ones and Abigail embarked on her un-Sabbathlike quest for information. "Why take such pains to lure his *wife* into a trap?"

"Why would Malvern's daughter bribe servants to murder Mrs. Pentyre's dog?" John's face was somber as he picked up Tommy and carried him to the table, where the other children were already taking their places. "There is such a thing as vindictiveness in the world, Portia. I don't suppose, in your conversation with the Malvern servants last night, that you asked after their master's whereabouts on Wednesday night?"

Abigail stared at him, taken aback. "He would not—"

"And I would not," said John. "And yet, someone did."

Lisette Droux was a tiny, dark-haired Frenchwoman in her thirties, with buck teeth and a complexion so pitted by smallpox as to defeat the eye of any but the most willing of suitors. She rose and curtseyed as Scipio showed Abigail into the Malvern kitchen.

"Madame."

"Mistress Droux." A small fire burned on the hearth and warmed the big room, but the neatly stacked dishes, the absence of pans or cooking smells, told her that Charles Malvern held to the Puritan way beneath his own roof. The fire—and the kettle bubbling softly over it—were concessions to Tamar's more fashionable cravings for tea and comforts: Abigail noticed Scipio had provided tea for the maidservant as well. "Did Miss Connelley tell you anything of what I wish to ask you about?"

"No, Madame." At Abigail's gestured invitation, she seated herself on the other side of the table. "Nor would I believe that Irish cocotte if she told me the sun rose in the East. But Scipio tells me you are a friend of the woman in whose house Mrs. Pentyre met her death, the woman who has now disappeared: fled, he says, and perhaps in fear for her life. And since this imbecile from the office of the Provost Marshal seems to think of nothing but that there is a political conspiracy to murder both M'sieu and Madame over this question of tea—"

Abigail said, "What?" and the woman raised her dark, straight brows.

"The imbecile," she explained. "With the pale face and the little nose like a girl's." Her own was a noble organ; had her uneasy shock at this confirmation of Coldstone's inquiries been less, Abigail would have smiled at the description of her adversary's dainty features. "He asked, did anyone follow Madame, did anyone hide themselves about the stables while Gerald was taking out the chaise for her, did she receive letters threatening her life from such a one, or such a one—"

"Which such-ones?" asked Abigail. "Do you recall any names?"

The maidservant considered the matter, with aloof dispassion that seemed to be native to her. It was difficult to tell whether her dark bombazine dress was intended to constitute mourning for her mistress; Abigail was inclined to think not. "*Son of Liberty*," Lisette said at length, pronouncing the words with care. "That was one. *Mohawk* was another he asked after; and *Adam*. And *Novanglus*—that is Latin for . . ."

"*New Englander*," Abigail finished softly. "Yes, I know." *Adam*. Or *Adams*? A mistake would be easy. *Mohawk*, *Son of Liberty*, and *Novanglus* were all names under which John had written pamphlets and articles for the *Gazette* and the *Spy*.

"It is politics." Lisette shrugged. "It is nothing. One does not do murder over politics. You must take tea, Madame, or coffee if you will—"

Scipio brought a small pot over to the table, and a cup. Abigail in fact found coffee's bitterness unpleasant and cursed the Crown for its tax that had pushed the colony into a boycott of her favorite comforter in the late afternoons, but knew she had to accustom herself to drink the stuff. In Malvern's respectable house there was no hope that the tea had been smuggled in by the Dutch, tax-free.

"How long had you been in Madame Pentyre's employment?"

"Three years, Madame. I was taken on at the time of her marriage. These pamphlets, these Sons of Liberty"—she made a very Gallic gesture with one hand—"When first she married M'sieu Pentyre, my lady read them all, these pamphlets. She would stamp her pretty foot and fling up her hands, so! and shake her hair about. She had lovely hair." A trace of sadness came into her voice, like a woman mourning the loss of some particularly fine roses in a childhood home. "And she would call M'sieu a Tory and a dish-licking dog. M'sieu would laugh, and kiss her, and she would be wild with indignation, and storm away out of the house . . . She was very young, Madame. When M'sieu learned that she had fallen in love with Colonel Leslie, and become his mistress, *how* he laughed! 'All it takes is a red coat after all,' he says, and she colors up, and pouts, but we hear no more about the Sons of Liberty."

So much, reflected Abigail, *for The Husband's Revenge.* "And when was this?"

"Almost a year, Madame. They become lovers at the New Year, at a ball at the house of the Governor, in the pantry where the silverware is cleaned. I found some of the cleaning-sand in her petticoat-lace afterwards. But since first she is introduced to him, in the summer at a picnic in honor of the officers of the regiment, she has—what is the word? She has set her hat in his direction."

"Did she love him?" asked Abigail. "Or he her?"

One corner of that wry little mouth turned down: *Eh, bien, what will these Americans think next?* "Oh. Madame. He was quite fond of her—men usually are, if a good-looking woman will consent to go to bed with them. I have heard he is genuinely grieved, and swears that he will hang every Son of Liberty in the colony for the crime. But she—" Lisette shrugged again. "He is the second son of a Scots Earl. Myself, I think my lady was jealous. It was not a month before, that M'sieu took a mistress for himself—"

Abigail tried hard not to look shocked.

"And though he was just as generous to her as he had been before, as I say, she is—she *was*—very young."

Abigail closed her eyes briefly, seeing—as if with the memory of a nightmare—the blood-engorged face, the bitten shoulders and neck. So distorted had the features been by the blood pooling in the tissues it would have been hard to tell the woman's age. But it was very much a young girl's trick, to throw herself at the commander of the occupying troops—a man of power, moderately good-looking, and, as Mademoiselle Droux had pointed out, an Earl's second son. To seduce him with her gay youth, with her beautiful hair: telling herself that her adventure was for her country's sake, like the heroine of a play. Yes. She had been very young.

"How old was she?"

"Seventeen, Madame, when she married M'sieu Pentyre. She was twenty when she died."

Abigail drew in a breath, and let it out, thinking about that very young girl. Had it been her husband taking a mistress, that had determined her on revenge? Yesterday morning, rereading Rebecca's letters, she had found several accounts of trips to Castle Island, in quest of pamphlet-worthy gossip at the camp. Perdita Pentyre would have seen in her first a kindred spirit, then a link with the Sons of Liberty themselves, the organization whose writings she read with such eagerness. *M'sieu would laugh, and kiss her, and she would be wild with indignation, and storm away out of the house . . .*

She could almost hear her daughter Nabby shouting at her one day in fury, *I'll show you—!*

She was from New York, Abigail recalled; without friends or close connections here to distract her from her adventure. And Colonel Leslie, as she had glimpsed him yesterday, was a well-enough-looking man, and younger than one might expect.

As if she discerned the sadness in Abigail's face, Mademoiselle Droux said, "*Eh bien*, Madame, it is not as if the Colonel was her only lover."

Abigail snapped sharply from her reverie. "Was he not?" and at the same moment a flash of disgust went through her. *As if her sort stops at one*, Queenie had sniffed, and standing there in the market yesterday, Abigail had been ready to snatch the cook's cap off, and pull her hair. *The one she let in through her parlor window . . . This Mrs. Pentyre, if she . . . had someone else she wanted to meet . . .*

So it was only a sordid assignation after all.

Oh, Rebecca, no. How could *you?*

Perdita Pentyre may not have had any connection with the Sons of Liberty at all.

Rebecca had only used their code, as the most convenient one to hand, to help another woman as unhappily wed as she herself had been. No wonder Sam had known nothing about her.

Only it wasn't Rebecca, who had written that note.

Abigail turned the matter over in her mind while Mademoiselle Droux went on. "Mrs. Pentyre, she knew it is bad *ton*, to have two lovers at a time; it smacks of excess. She never spoke of him to me. But, *mercredi soir* was not the first time that she would have Gerald put the chaise to for her—and pay him well, to keep his mouth shut." Her lips pinched a little: *disapproval, or merely the ordering of her thoughts?* "I have seen him, this young gentleman, *beau comme Adonais*, watching her so jealously. And when all is said, the Colonel *is* five-and-thirty. To a girl of twenty . . ." She shrugged.

The rain puddle by the window; would opening the shutters account for that amount of water on her skirt? She'd known the Tillets would be away. And yet—Abigail frowned. Rebecca knew that Queenie spied and told tales. With Mr. Tillet loitering in her house whenever he had the chance, and Mrs. Tillet seething with jealousy and annoyance over how many shirts she thought Rebecca should be sewing for her gratis, *would* Rebecca have risked using her house for so small a purpose?

Particularly when there were any number of women on the North End who did *not* have problems with their landladies, equally willing to accommodate would-be multiple adulteresses.

Something did not fit. "Do you have any idea who this young Adonis is?"

Lisette shook her head. "She would have notes from him, I think, from a woman she always met by chance when she went out walking. A little curly-haired woman, dark, with a snub nose—"

"Rebecca," said Abigail.

"I do not know her name, Madame. The notes were always of commonplaces—trees, or birds, or flowers. But for two women who only met in the streets, I thought they corresponded a great deal about trees, or birds, or flowers. I think it was a cipher, *en effet*—"

"She showed you these notes?"

"Madame." Mademoiselle Droux gave her another look of pitying patience. "M'sieu Pentyre paid me two dollars each month, to tell him all the correspondence that came to my lady. It is done in all households, Madame," she added, a note of concern in her voice at Abigail's startled reaction, as if reassuring a simpleton that the booming kettledrums in a military parade were not in fact real thunder. "A man is a fool, who does not pay his wife's maidservant—and a woman a fool, who does not pay them even more. One must build one's nest against the storm, particularly if one is thirty-seven years old, and looks as I do."

I want you to remember from now on that you are working for me, Charles Malvern had said to Oonaugh.

The sinister Mr. B of *Pamela* was not so unreal as Rebecca had thought.

"I know everything that my lady received, and tucked away in the hiding places that she thought were so clever, behind the pictures and beneath the mattress of her bed. Thus I know that no one sent my lady these letters of threat that our maiden-faced Provost kept pressing me to say that she had. And so I told him. Was this woman then she in whose house my lady was killed? This Mrs. Malvern, whose name the Provost kept demanding did I know?"

"That is she," said Abigail slowly. "What did Mr. Pentyre have to say of this other man? A Regimental Colonel is one thing—and useful to a merchant, be he never so wealthy. Was he angry over this good-looking stranger?"

"Now you ask me to speculate on the contents of a man's heart, Madame. He laughed and joked his wife about her lovers, yet if any man crossed him in a business way—even a farmer who cheated him a little on the cost of oats for his horses—he make sure that that man became truly sorry that he had done so. He would have his agents find out, had this man ever broken a law? And *voilà*, the sheriffs would be at that man's door. Or, a rumor would start in the taverns that the man was, what do you call?—was a Tory, and suddenly these Sons of Liberty would break the windows of that man's shop the next time they rioted. Or the man's horses would be hamstrung one night, and blame would fall on these same *Fils du Liberté*. Would such a man truly shrug his shoulders, if his wife lay with another man?" She spread her hands. "That I do not know."

"And where was Mr. Pentyre, on Wednesday night?"

Something—a little glint like a malicious star—twinkled in the lizard black eyes. "He was not at home, Madame. He told the imbecile officer that he was playing cards with the sons of the Governor, but myself, I believe he was at the house of his mistress. She is a lady of the West Indies, named Belle-Isle; she has a little house on Hull Street, near to the *cimitiere*. Would Madame wish me to ask her maid, if indeed M'sieu Pentyre paid such a call that night?"

Quite casually, she extended a hand as she spoke. It was only a momentary gesture, as if accepting a coin. Four generations of Yankee ancestors cried out in Abigail's heart at such venality, particularly since there was nothing to assure her that she would be getting the truth for her money. But she replied, "If you would, Mademoiselle, I thank you. I shall—*er*—make arrangements with Mr. Malvern."

The maid smiled, and nodded appreciation of her tact. "Merci, Madame."

"Was there anyone else? Anyone who might have wished your young lady ill? Either here, or back in New York?"

"All young ladies have their mortal foes, Madame. *Oh, such a one has stolen my hairdresser away from me, I shall claw out her eyes with my fingernails, so! Ah, such another has got herself sat next to that most divine preacher at tea, I will strangle her in her own hair-ribbons!* Does one pay heed to such trivialities?"

"One must, in the circumstances."

"One must, if my lady were found with her eyes scratched out, or strangled in her hair-ribbons," said the older woman somberly. "I saw her body, Madame. I took the clothes off her, and washed her, and dressed her in her prettiest night-dress, that her husband gave her when they were wed, and Madame, I would not admit M'sieu Pentyre into the room until I was done. Even then I kept a cloth over my young lady's face. What was done to her was done by the Devil himself."

Abigail whispered, "Amen," and Mademoiselle Droux crossed herself. "And was she ever afraid of what she could not define? Afraid without reason, of a shadow, or a passerby?"

"*En effet*, Madame, my lady was twenty years old, and the young do not frighten easily. If she had such fears, she did not speak of them to me. I did not make of myself a confidante, as so many maids do, except at the very beginning, when she was lonely and her empty-headed mother and sisters in New York did not write to her, if they *could* write, which I doubt. But I would sooner be a good maid than a good friend. Unless the friendship is extraordinary, it is too easy for confidence to turn into anger, and then one is on the street again, with nowhere to go."

Abigail thought about Catherine Moore, turned out of her job and obliged to return to the farm of her brother, near Townsend (*wherever* that *was*) somewhere in the wooded wilds of Essex County.

In the high kitchen windows the light was fading. This woman would have her duties, back at the great brick Pentyre mansion on Prince's Street. "These notes that Mrs. Pentyre received from the woman in the street. Did she keep them?"

"She locked them away, yes, Madame. Indeed, she took greater care of them, than commonplaces about trees and birds and flowers warranted." She shrugged. "I copied them for M'sieu Pentyre, and the originals, our pretty Provost took away with him. What he shall make of them, I do not know."

"Mademoiselle Droux," she said, "you have been very kind, and your observations extremely helpful."

"When one is forbidden by one's employment to marry," remarked the maid, rising and taking Abigail's proffered hand, "and obliged in it to occupy oneself wholly with the life and concerns of another—and that other, often a person who considers herself the most important object in Creation—one must take amusement in observation, or perish. I hope that I have helped you, Madame. My lady was young and foolish, and a little spoilt as girls are who have never been obliged to work for their livings. But she had no malice in her, which cannot be said of many ladies whom I have served. She did not deserve her fate—Jezebel herself would not deserve such an end. The heathen Greeks had goddesses armed with spears, who hunted down men who did such things to women, and gave them their deserving. I wish you good hunting, Madame."

She made her curtsey again, and signed to Scipio at his little table in the corner, to summon one of the servants to escort her home.

Twelve

"Could you not send a letter?" asked John, following Abigail into the kitchen in the predawn gloom the following morning, where her small portmanteau, cloak, and scarves were heaped, ready to be strapped onto Balthazar's saddle. Young Mr. Thaxter—a stout and good-natured youth related to Abigail through the Quincys—was saddling up in the yard. She felt guilty about not only deserting her husband but taking his horse as well. Still, under the terms of his bond to the Provost Marshal, John wouldn't be going anywhere he couldn't walk to in the next several days. "'Tis a very long way. Thaxter could take it, as easily as escort yourself."

"Indeed, he could," agreed Abigail equably. She walked to the sideboard where John's leather portfolio lay, along with several letters to clients in Roxbury and Cambridge explaining why it would be impossible for him to attend on them until next week or the week after. "Could not Thaxter also take these depositions for you, instead of bearing Mr. Sweet and Mr. Duggan excuses for postponement?"

John slewed around, blue eyes almost bulging. "Thaxter's a boy! He wouldn't know—" He broke off, realizing that Abigail knew perfectly well why a youthful clerk, be he ever so honest, could not be trusted with the task.

"Wouldn't know what questions to ask?"

John sniffed, and picked up her cloak. "Townsend's barely a handful of houses at the end of a farm-track," he said as he laid it around her shoulders. "I doubt they have such a thing as an inn. I don't like to think of you hunting for shelter there, or in the woods between it and Wenham, if it should come on to snow."

"And I don't like to think of the man who killed Perdita Pentyre coming to the same conclusion that I have, that Rebecca might have taken shelter with her maid."

Though it was Abigail's lifelong contention that in America any woman could travel alone through the countryside without fear of robbery or assault—a situation unthinkable in the Home Country—during the final week of November such a solitary excursion was inadvisable for other reasons. The harsh northeast winds and threat of snow that had made John insist that she take the escort of his clerk likewise precluded shortening the trip to the settlement of Townsend by taking one of her uncle Isaac's little coastwise trading vessels as far as Salem. Moreover, Thaxter's mother had kin in western Essex County, and had provided him with clear instructions for getting to Townsend, whence they could inquire for Kemiah Moore's farm.

From Boston north to Salem the road was well-traveled and reasonably well-kept, along the dunes and salt grass above the pounding gray sea. The public stage had already ceased its journeys for the winter, and the coach from Portsmouth wasn't due for another day. An occasional postrider with newspapers or letters overtook their horses, or a city-bound farm-wagon with salt meat and the autumn's cheeses broke the monotony, but for the most part there were only the brown fields inland to look at, swept by wind sharp as broken oyster shells.

Being related to the Quincys, Thaxter had from childhood absorbed huge quantities of miscellaneous information about other merchant families with which his own uncles and cousins had to do, and proved a ready source of information about Richard Pentyre. "Everybody in town thinks he's English," the young man remarked over midmorning bread, cheese, and smuggled tea at the Lion in Lynn. "With those coats he wears, and spending ten pounds on wigs and powder to put on them. But he was born here—in that very house in Prince's Street where he lives now, for all his parents went back to London when he was but a little tot, and sent him and his brother to Cambridge with all the sons of English lords, and only his bachelor uncle stayed on here. But he's a Massachusetts man, back four generations on both sides, and his grandfather was one of the preachers who had a hand in hanging witches hereabouts. Bet the Parliament nobs who think he's so civilized don't know *that* one!"

Abigail chuckled, recalling her glimpses of Richard Pentyre, in his a la mode coats of French brocade, and his immaculately powdered wigs tinted a stylish lavender. *Not for him*, she thought, *the voyages that had made his rival Charles Malvern hard: his was a pleasant, long-nosed face just losing the freshness of a prolonged youth. Vindictive*, Lisette Droux had said, and clever by the sound of it—and by Thaxter's present accounts of the man's manipulations of his relationship with the Governor. Would he have had the wits to decipher the admittedly simple code that Rebecca used to set up meetings with his wife?

More disturbingly, would Lieutenant Coldstone?

And what would those Crown officials, those voters in Parliament, make of this world, she wondered, as they mounted their rested horses, and left the prosperous town of Lynn behind. She was used to thinking of Boston as a great city, with its crooked streets and thronged wharves. Even as a lawyer's wife, she was able to purchase dress goods as fine as any lawyer's wife in London if she had a mind, and paint her rooms in bright fashionable hues like Naples yellow and Dutch pink. The education John had obtained at Harvard was equal to any on offer at Oxford or Cambridge, and in the city's bookstores she could find novels by

Fielding and Richardson, plays by Voltaire and Shakespeare, the poetry of Pope and the philosophical writings of Locke.

Yet outside of Boston, the veneer of England vanished like an early frost. Abigail's girlhood as a minister's daughter had taught her how primitive were the farms that lay only a few hours' walk into the countryside, where vessels were still made from the shells of pumpkins or gourds, and families slept all together in lofts above the single "keeping room" downstairs. Where a child might grow to voting age before he ever saw a clock, or a book other than the Bible. Once they reached Salem, and turned westward, this impression deepened, of traversing time as well as distance, as if they had somewhere crossed the line that separated the eighteenth century from the seventeenth. Away from the sea, and the settled lands along the coast, the woods closed in, standing as they had stood since the creation of the continent: gray and black with winter's coming, fall's tawny gorgeousness only a fading echo of yellow turning to umber underfoot.

Moreover, once one left the main road, all helpful signposts and milestones ceased. Primordial woods closed around them. The innkeeper in Salem provided an assortment of directions along with more tea, more bread, and more cheese—"You take the Danvers road, m'am, but turn off to your right about two miles past Peabody. You can't miss the track, for there's a great oak just a hundred feet down along it, to the left of the way"—but though Abigail jotted what she hoped were the main points on her whale-ivory pocket-tablets, she was disinclined to trust them. "Now, don't pay no mind to the farm-tracks you'll pass, but take the bigger way left, after Great Sellars Pond." "How far?" "Far? Lord, I don't know—how far would you say it is to the Sellars Pond Road, Jemma?" (This to his wife.) "Two miles?" "Never!—all of four . . ."

"Not so far," protested a one-eyed man at another of the tables near the fire. "Old Sellars used to walk it in half an hour by his watch, and he were a fearful rapid walker. The Sellarses used to have all the land hereabouts, on royal grant. One of 'em married into the Olivers—or was it the Governor's kin?—that had their holdings all up into Wenham Township and as far as Topsford . . ." "Be sure you don't take the Topsford Road," the landlord had agreed. "If you get to the Topsford Farm Road, you've gone too far. Old Topsford, he was said to be a warlock, that could raise storms by killing a hare and throwing it in Wenham Pond."

There followed considerable discussion of whether or not the gentleman in question had actually accomplished this feat of meteorology, but no one present seemed to doubt that he could have, had he wished to do so. Neither could anyone be found headed in that direction, to guide the travelers on their way. It was early yet for dinner, and Abigail elected to press on toward Townsend, a decision she regretted some three hours later, with the threat of rain on the wind, and not the slightest idea of whether the muddy, half-frozen cart-track that disappeared into the fading winter twilight before and behind them was indeed the Topsford Road or some other. She and her companion encountered a number of great oak trees, and several small bodies of water that could have been termed *ponds*, *sloughs*, or *pools*, but few signs of habitation. What they had hoped was a farm-road between rock-walled, stubbled fields petered out and disappeared into woods again. "I think that old deadlight back at Salem witched us," grumbled Thaxter.

It was close to dark when they finally stumbled into a village optimistically called Gilead, barely a hamlet clustered around a dilapidated log church, and begged shelter for the night. Hospitality was freely offered by the town's minister, but it had to be paid for, Abigail learned, by attendance at the evening sermon: penance enough to one raised in the dual tradition of old-style predestinarianism and well-written doctrinal argument. The Right Reverend Atonement Bargest was a firm believer in the contention that no one could be Saved who did not tremble before the Altar of the Lord, and Abigail and Thaxter spent three hours on the hard, narrow meetinghouse bench ("The House of Repentance, we call it," confided the Reverend as he escorted them to the front and center seats) while all around them the two hundred or so souls of the congregation trembled, wept, and cried out in terror at apparitions of devils that the preacher pointed to in the candlelit shadows. Thaxter quite frankly dozed off, but Abigail was sorely tried with the effort not to get to her feet in protest as the Reverend pointed and shrieked at the appearance (visible only to himself) of the Nine Daughters of Eve, emerging from Hell to prey on the souls of Righteous Men: the serpent, the nightmare, the witch, the succubus, the harlot, the Priestess of Idols, Jezebel the Queen, the dishonest handmaiden, and most iniquitous of all, the inquisitive woman whose feet are never still.

Women jauntering about the countryside instead of staying home to care for their husbands and children, he implied, would come to no good end. Shivering in her damp cloak, her feet freezing and her thighs cut by the narrowness of the bench on which she sat, Abigail was much inclined to agree with him.

After the sermon was done—it was now pouring rain—the Reverend Bargest arbitrarily assigned a member of his congregation to offer the travelers hospitality, and released them to supper and a bed. As they followed their host to one of the two dozen or so log-built houses within the town's old palisade—like disused barracks, most of them, their upper floors shuttered and dark—Abigail could feel the disapproving gazes of the congregation on her back. "Have you not a husband nor a home?" one of the littler girls of her host's family asked her, as the cold supper of corn pudding and molasses was set on the table—and her elder sister swept her away with a hissed admonition and a glance of sullen dread.

Evidently only the word of "the Hand of the Lord," as they reverently termed their minister, kept Abigail and her escort from being ejected supperless into the road.

Toward the end of the meal the Hand of the Lord made his reappearance with a glowering young man whom he introduced as Brother Mortify. "He shall guide you to Townsend in the morning. It isn't far—five miles or so." He smiled charmingly—he had silky white hair and astonishingly well-preserved teeth for a man in his sixties—and clapped Brother Mortify on the shoulder. "I shall pray for the lessening of the rain, that you may be sped upon your way." For a man who forty minutes previously had been in seizures of terror at the sight of invisible demons appearing out of the back of the House of Repentance, he seemed to have made a remarkable recovery. Abigail's hosts were lavish in their praise for "the Chosen One's" sermon, and the Chosen One nodded grave acknowledgement. *I have only done my duty*, his twinkling dark eyes seemed to say. *Don't I do it well?*

In fact the rain *had* ceased when in predawn darkness the family waked to a frugal breakfast of cold corn pudding and skimmed milk, and Brother Mortify presented himself to put Abigail and Thaxter on their way. "Not many take this way," was his only comment, when they had to dismount and lead their horses over a stream where the bridge had rotted to nothing. "They're Godless, in Townsend—as in other places." He cast a meaningful glower at the travelers.

"And *they're* the only ones saved and blessed, I suppose,"

muttered Thaxter, when their escort finally turned back and the handful of weathered gray buildings that constituted Townsend could be descried through the gray trees. "I wouldn't have believed it, in this day and age." He brushed the last fragments of hay out of his hair and scarf-wool. Despite the raw iciness of the night, he'd slept in the barn. Abigail, who had shared a bed with three of the girls of the family in the boarded-up upper floor of the house, wished propriety had permitted her to do so as well.

"You were born in Boston, weren't you?"

Thaxter nodded. "Born and raised. And Lord, I don't know how people live in the countryside—I mean out here, not in civilized places like Weymouth or Medford. I didn't know places like that still existed."

Abigail sighed. "They exist a good deal closer to Boston than Essex County. They've been feuding in Braintree for years over who got chosen for minister—families who used to be friends not speaking a civil word to one another—and there isn't a county in New England, where a town hasn't split itself off from its parent settlement, because part of the congregation doesn't believe in precisely how the other part conceives salvation. Now with these new preachers coming through, these Evangelists, as they call them—this Awakening they speak of—it's as if all the old arguments over who shall be saved and who damned are all being argued again.

"It wasn't so long ago—I've talked to people who were children at the time—that grown men in Salem, leaders of the community, let themselves be scared like medieval peasants into killing twenty people, on the strength of accusations by a pack of spiteful girls. We think we've come so far toward Enlightenment and Reason, yet even in Boston, rational men who read the newspapers still think a Catholic woman is some kind of devil-worshiper, who would steal her husband's money to give over to the Jesuits."

The young man looked startled. "Well, with Catholics, that's different," he said. "I mean, they *do* have to do as their Pope tells them, whatever it is, don't they?"

Abigail remembered Catherine Moore as a large, calm, good-looking woman in her late thirties whom she had met several times at the Brattle Street Meeting, walking behind Rebecca and Charles Malvern. Rebecca, Abigail recalled, had never asked her maid to carry either her cloak or her Bible, as so many wealthy ladies did. Odd, she thought, in one who had been waited on by slaves every day of her life. In the early days of the friendship Rebecca would always speak of Catherine's unwavering loyalty in the gathering nightmare of spying and distrust that her marriage had become. *Unless the friendship is extraordinary*, Lisette Droux had said, *it is too easy for confidence to turn into anger*. And, *I would rather be a good maid than a good friend.* Catherine Moore, Abigail guessed, in the three years she had served Rebecca Malvern, had managed both.

The woman who came out of the dairy when Abigail and her escort rode into the yard at the Moore farm seemed to her, at first glimpse, to be the elder sister, or an aunt, of the woman she had known in those days. She stooped a little, and her face was weather-beaten; the few strands of hair visible beneath her cap were cinder gray. Only at second look did Abigail recognize her as Rebecca's maid, by her soft little half smile. "Can I help you?" she asked, and the voice—which Abigail had only heard once or twice—was the same.

"Mistress Moore?" She let Thaxter help her from the saddle, her stout boots squishing in half-frozen muck. "I'm Mrs. Adams—"

"Of course!" Mistress Moore's benevolence warmed to delight. "My lady's friend. What brings you here to this"—her mouth quirked, half deprecating, half amused—"this wilderness?" And then, her dark eyes changing as she realized how great a distance her visitor had come on purpose, "My lady is all right, is she not? Tell me all is well." As she said this another woman came out of the dairy behind her, probably just over twenty, Abigail guessed, but looking older, weather-beaten, and tired, with the rounded belly of midterm pregnancy.

"What is it—?"

"News of Rebecca," said Catherine softly, and then glanced back at Abigail. "Isn't it?"

Abigail said, "I'd hoped to find her here."

Thirteen

Though it was only an hour or two past sunup, Catherine's sister-in-law—her brother's third wife—brought them into the big sand-floored keeping room of the log farmhouse, and cut bread and cheese, butter, and cold meat for them. "From all I've heard, those Gilead folk are as stingy with the Godless, as they call us, as they are with their own children. For the good of their souls, they'll tell you," she added with a sniff. "Sit you down, Mrs. Adams, and rest. You look like you've had a cold ride and no mistake."

A crippled boy of perhaps fourteen—wizened and wasted as a little old man—who was working a spinning wheel next to the fire nodded a greeting to them, and added a few billets of wood to the blaze.

Catherine Moore's face contracted in horror when Abigail spoke of what she'd found in Rebecca's house Thursday morning. "Who would do such a thing? And *why*?"

Abigail shook her head. "'Tis what I'm trying to learn. 'Twasn't a madman just wandered in from the street, we do know that," she added. "The other woman—Mrs. Pentyre, a merchant's young wife—was lured there, with a note forged in Rebecca's hand . . . Rebecca didn't know Mrs. Pentyre before Mrs. Pentyre's marriage, did she? Her name would have been Parke in those days, Perdita Parke, of New York."

Mistress Moore shook her head, baffled.

"I know she writes to you—she often speaks of how she treasures your letters. Was there anyone that she spoke of, any friend, any person to whom she might have gone for refuge? Or any name, any circumstance, that by *any* stretch of the imagination might be connected with what happened?"

Catherine sat for a moment, her head tilted to the side, thinking hard though the moment they had seated themselves her hands had taken up sewing on a child's dress from out of her workbasket, automatically, as if no second must—or could—be left idle. "Nothing," she said, and setting aside her work, went to the old-fashioned box-bed built into the wall near the great hearth. From the cupboard beneath it she brought out a lap desk, from which she took a packet of letters. "Mostly she wrote of her pupils, and their progress; of your kindness to her; of her labors at learning to cook and keep house, and that Tillet woman trying to turn her into a sewing-slave for her own profit. Once she wrote of her husband, and even then wouldn't say a word against him."

A look of wearied bitterness flickered in her eyes, swiftly put aside. What had Malvern said of her, Abigail wondered, that had made it impossible for her to find work as a maid in Boston?

Catherine went on, "She said she understood, how he would mistrust her, and blamed herself that he refused to give her any share of her father's money. Myself," she added grimly, "*I* blame that old skinflint, for along with 'holding' the income 'in trust,' he's also lending and investing it at 2 percent, and would have been happy enough if she died, so the property would come to him outright and absolutely. Two thousand acres along the Chesapeake?" She sniffed. "He should have thanked her for keeping it in their family when he was too cheap to lay out for it, not punished her. To say nothing of saving her father from a life of beggary."

She turned her face away, and pressed her hand to her lips, as if what Abigail had told her had only just begun to sink in. Abigail saw how her hand, once the fine deft hand of a quality lady's maid, had grown brown, and rough with calluses, the fingers beginning to deform with arthritis.

"May I take these?"

"Of course. If you can find anything in them to help, you are welcome." Outside the thick, uneven glass of the ill-leaded window a horse and wagon could be discerned, drawing up in the yard. A moment later a boy and a young man strode in, halted uncertainly when they saw Abigail, then went to the cold corner of the big room where all this time the youthful Goodwife Moore had been chopping and mixing the meat and fat of what was clearly a recently slaughtered pig for sausage. The murmur of their voices joined the whirr of the spinning wheel, the drifting smell of sage, as a sort of background scrim, a reminder to Abigail of her own duties and children neglected at home while she wandered to and fro in the world. *Now she is without, now in the streets . . .* Catherine took up her sewing again.

"Did she ever write to you about politics? About her political friends?"

"Not in so many words, no." Catherine's breath went out of her in a sigh. "I knew—Well, you know what a poison that was, between Mr. Malvern and her. Myself . . ." She shrugged. "I'm as loyal as the next woman, I suppose, but it strikes me as only reasonable, that the King nor Parliament neither can understand what goes on here, and what we need. But that's a matter of men of education, men who're trained to it, not for a plain woman—and not meaning disrespect, not for a lady who's trying to get on with her husband, and build a home for him and his children. But she never would see it that way. And as time went on, and Miss Tamar told lies about her to divide her from her husband, it was a refuge to her, though it only made the situation worse."

Sadly, she shook her head, and Abigail pursed her lips and reminded herself that an indignant demand about whether men who made their money out of Crown offices were more to be trusted in government than the plain men and plain women whose pockets were picked by those trained and educated gentlemen, would only lead the discussion far astray. She asked instead, "Did she speak about the Sons of Liberty?"

"I knew she was thick with them." The maidservant sounded grieved. "I feared . . . But surely," she said, looking up from her needle, "surely not one of them would have caused her harm, no matter how heated this politics got. 'Tis only politics, when all's said."

No, Abigail thought. *It isn't politics.* She recalled things Rebecca had told her, things Cousin Sam had said. A man probably wouldn't kill over politics, but he would kill to protect himself, if there were treason in the wind.

A reasonable man, she corrected herself. The man who wielded that knife was no reasonable man.

But would a madman forge a note? Think to dispose of the chaise? Turn the horse free onto the Commons? Why had he not then disposed of the body as well?

Would a madman take Rebecca's "housekeeping" book of codes? Or had Rebecca done that herself when she'd fled, to keep it from falling into the murderer's hands?

Am I looking at madness here? Or treason? Or something else?

At this point Goodman Moore came in, shaking the morning dampness from his hat and glaring suspiciously at his sister and her guest. Both women rose, and Catherine said, "Kem, this is Mrs. Adams, from Boston, a dear friend to my Mrs. Malvern—"

"And is she a Papist, too?"

Exasperated, Abigail said, "Does not *anyone* in Massachusetts believe that a conversion can be sincere? Mrs. Malvern took instruction and satisfied the elders of the Brattle Street congregation, in order to be confirmed. I am honestly curious as to what a woman—or a man, for that matter," she added, thinking as well of Orion Hazlitt, "must do, to convince people that she or he has indeed changed faith."

Catherine's brother regarded both women before him with a kind of chilly contempt, as if confronted with the idiot child of someone he didn't like. "Faith a'nt something you change. If this woman were truly one of the Saints, she would have been born into a family of the Congregation, where her earliest steps would have been put on the path. She wasn't."

"Now, you can't say—" began Abigail indignantly, and Goodman Moore reared his head back slightly, as if shocked that any woman would contradict him with his thought not yet fully revealed in all its glory.

Abigail bit her underlip and reminded herself that this man had sweated to grow the corn and cut the wood that went to make the bread she had just eaten; heaved fodder and mucked out cowsheds, that she might have milk.

"Conversion—" He shook his head heavily, like a bear with a fly in its ear. "Conversion, all you get is those Godless heathens over Gilead way, with all their nonsense about knowing God—as if *that's* going to do a body a single jot of good!—and working toward salvation . . . *Working?* Pah! Salvation must be *given* a man, through no strength of his own . . . *And* laying claim to old Sellars's fields that should rightfully have gone to the Townsend Congregation! Even so did King Ahab conspire to seize the vineyard of Naboth, and seek to do harm unto the Prophet of the Lord who spake against his conspiring—!"

By which Abigail deduced that—as in so much of Massachusetts politics—the disputed fields loomed a good deal larger in her host's mind than the Gilead congregation's doctrinal divagations.

Both Catherine and her brother pressed Abigail to remain and share their early, farm-style dinner, but neither were surprised or offended when she declined. Though it was only midmorning, Abigail well knew that last night's rain would have rendered the roads nearly impassable, and the going would be slow. She had no desire to spend a second night from home, and John, she knew, would worry if she weren't back by the time the town gates were shut and the ferry ceased to run.

Despite their prompt departure, this almost came to pass in any case. The rain had been worse toward the coast, and as she and Thaxter slogged their way toward the main Danvers road the half-frozen morass grew deeper, the horses' hooves sliding in it and the clerk dismounting half a dozen times to scrape the balls of half-frozen clay from the beasts' feet. Icy wind blew into their faces as they reached Salem in time for an early dinner, and though the main road was a little better, it was still closing in on evening when the travelers sighted Winnisimmet's roofs through the trees. "If the ferry's closed down for the night, I'll hang myself," muttered her escort gloomily, as he dismounted once again on the last slope of Chelsea Hill to clear what seemed like monstrous clay boots from his horse's feet. "There isn't an inn on this side of the water that I'd spend a night in." Which wasn't entirely fair, reflected Abigail—but she could sympathize. Across the bay, she could see Boston's tall hills, and the dark spread of houses around their feet. Closer, the British cruiser *Cumberland* moved among the little islands, silent as a dark bird. Allegedly it had been sent to "defend" the town, but everyone knew that like the British regiments on Castle Island, the ship was truly there to put down the kind of insurrection that had shaken the city six years ago, when the King had taken control of colonial officials away from the colonial assemblies and into his own hands, and had eliminated jury trials for anyone even suspected of smuggling: a wide category, in Massachusetts.

No lights twinkled yet in any window, nor in the nearer dwellings of Winnisimmet.

She leaned down to pat the wet, steaming neck of her

horse. "Well, I won't spur these poor fellows to a gallop to make the last ferry," she said. "Always supposing we could. We—"

Flat and soggy in the wet air, a shot cracked out. A horse burst from the woods nearby, running loose with empty saddle and trailing reins; among the trees themselves, a dim confusion of shouts. Abigail turned in her saddle and glimpsed something red in the brown shadows of the woods, a single British soldier bringing up his musket like a club as half a dozen men closed in on him.

Abigail exclaimed, "For shame!" and spurred toward the woods. Thaxter scrambled into his own saddle to follow. Hard as old Balthazar had been ridden all day, the animal responded nobly, and Abigail raised her voice in a shout, "Get away from him, you louts!" before she had any clear idea of what she'd do if those louts didn't. They seemed to be, she could see as she got closer, the rougher types who made up the rank and file of the Sons of Liberty: the poorer class of farmer, out-of-work laborers from the docks of Boston, and two big lads who looked like apprentices playing truant from their work. Such young men followed Cousin Sam and Andy Mackintosh in the violent street battles by which the North End boys and the South End boys celebrated "Pope's Day"—the anniversary of the Catholic Plot to blow up England's Parliament in 1605. At the moment, instead of tearing effigy monks and priests to pieces, they seemed bent on doing the same to the redcoat, who was standing—Abigail saw now—over a fallen comrade in a dark cloak.

She raised her voice again, shouted, "Leave them be!" and the men stopped, more startled than actually obedient. She spurred through them and to the side of the two soldiers, Thaxter galloping up in support, and the men, as she'd expected they probably would, scattered back into the trees. A couple of them shouted "Tory bitch!" and similar sentiments, but none of them was ready to attack a woman—particularly not one who came escorted. Someone threw a rock at them, which missed by yards. Ignoring this completely, Abigail dropped from her horse at the soldiers' side.

"Is he badly hurt?" She pulled away the dark cloak that covered the fallen man's crimson coat, and saw to her surprise that it was Lieutenant Coldstone. Looking up quickly, she met young Sergeant Muldoon's quick glance, before he returned his attention to the darkening woods around them.

"Dunno, m'am—Mrs. Adams. Him and the horse fell together—"

Abigail was already feeling beneath the red coat, and pushed back the stiffly powdered white wig to run her fingers through the young officer's short, fair hair. It was silky as a child's.

"No blood. He may only have been stunned by the fall. Thaxter, help me get this man on my horse. You did well, Sergeant, not to fire at your attackers. The last thing we need right now is another murder trial."

"I did fire, m'am," admitted the Sergeant. "I think the powder's damp."

"Here—" Abigail held up a hand as Thaxter shoved his own horse pistol into his pocket and made to lift the Lieutenant. She took her pin-box from her skirt pocket, selected the longest, and drove the point hard into the unconscious man's leg just below the knee. Coldstone's leg jerked and he turned his head, gasped, "Damn it—!"

"Very good," approved Abigail, as Thaxter helped the fallen man to sit. "He hasn't broken his neck." She replaced the pin in her box. "Are you all right, Lieutenant?"

He was already scanning the woods around them.

"Gang of hooligans, sir," reported Muldoon. "They made off—"

"Can you stand, sir?" Thaxter had risen to his feet and had his pistol at the ready again, though, Abigail reflected, his powder was almost certainly damp as well. She was astonished the attackers had managed to get off a shot. He held down his left arm for the Lieutenant to take hold of, and Coldstone rose, a little shakily, to his feet, and immediately staggered.

"Where's my horse?" he asked. "She came down on my ankle, it feels like—"

"She was well enough to leave the woods at a gallop," Abigail said. "Sergeant—?"

Muldoon shook his head, and waved vaguely in the direction his own mount had gone.

"The innkeeper at the Fish-Tail will advertise a reward," said Abigail. "I think the sooner you two are back in Boston, the better off you'll be. The ferry's stopped running by now—" She glanced worriedly at the gray overcast above the leafless trees.

Thaxter made a noise of disgust as he brought his horse around for Coldstone to mount. "The cook at the Fish-Tail's got to have done for twenty men at least—"

"The ferry will oblige us, in the King's name." Coldstone's face turned wax white when Muldoon boosted him into the saddle, but his expression of arctic calm did not alter. "Thank you, Sergeant." He took the wig that Muldoon picked up for him, but didn't put it on; it was covered with mud and leaves. So was his hat, but he did don that. It fit ill, without the wig. "I trust my sergeant and I will be able to command a bed among the men at the battery, if the weather worsens before we can cross back to the Castle. I am much obliged to you, Mrs. Adams. I guessed you to be formidable, but did not realize you were so fearsome in combat."

Boosted up by her clerk, Abigail settled herself in her saddle. "It does not do to underestimate Americans, Lieutenant. I'm surprised," she added, as they reined back toward the road, and the dim yellow lights of Winnisimmet beginning to speck the darkness, "that they chose to attack you in daylight, so close to the town. You haven't been picking out quarrels with the local worthies, I hope?"

"If by 'picking out quarrels,' you mean, investigating rumors of treason and sedition," replied Coldstone, "I fear that I have, m'am. As you should well know. And, I am not surprised in the least, that such men would lie in wait for an officer of the King."

"He's right, m'am," added Sergeant Muldoon diffidently. "Town's like a nest of hornets, it is."

Coldstone glanced quellingly down at his henchman, but Abigail heard something in the big Irishman's voice that made her ask, "Why is it like a nest of hornets, Sergeant? What's happened? We've been away," she added, turning back to Coldstone.

The officer sniffed. "Have you, indeed? Then you have missed a great deal of excitement. Yesterday the *Dartmouth* put in from England, with the first shipment of the East India Company's tea."

Fourteen

Friends! Brethren! Countrymen! That worst of Plagues, the detested tea shipped for this port by the East India Company, is now arrived in the Harbor; the hour of destruction, or manly opposition to the machinations of Tyranny, stares you in the Face; every Friend to his country, to Himself, and to Posterity, is now called upon to meet at Faneuil Hall, at nine o'clock this day, at which time the bells will ring to make united and successful resistance to this last worst and most destructive measure of Administration. Boston, Nov. 29, 1773.

Movement stirred in every shadow, as Abigail and Lieutenant Coldstone rode down Prince's Street beneath the high darkening shadow of Copp's Hill. Though chilly night now covered the city, every alleyway, every courtyard, every intersection jostled with men as if it were noon on market day, and against the dim lights of every tavern door shadows appeared. Voices muttered from within these establishments, grim voices, not the cheery riot of card players and sailors on their sprees, and the murmur of men's talk grumbled in the night like the fretting of the sea on rocks.

Now and then Abigail glimpsed rough, badly shaven faces, and the coarse textures of hunting shirts and tattered farm coats in the tavern doorways. *They're coming in from the countryside*, she thought, and remembered how Sam and Revere had summoned nearly threescore men to stand in

Queen Street when Coldstone arrived to arrest John. Not rioting, not threatening—just standing there. Standing there and outnumbering the little party of British a dozen to one.

Men shouted at the sight of Sergeant Muldoon's red coat. Someone threw muck from the roadway at them. On every building, it seemed, the rallying-posters for the meeting at Faneuil Hall had been pasted. A dangerous glitter seemed to fill the air, like the smell of lightning before a storm.

John sprang up from the kitchen table when Abigail came in, having detoured a little out of their way to accompany Muldoon and Coldstone to the small stone building that housed the crew of the gun emplacement at the end of Ship Street. When she tied up Balthazar in the yard and crossed to the back door she was almost stumbling with weariness. John caught her in his arms as she crossed the threshold: "What happened? You're frozen!" He was dressed for the meeting already, in his second-best brown suit, the one he wore to plead in the circuit courts, his best wig on his head. Papers covered the big kitchen table. He drew her to the fire, brought up a small table as Johnny darted to drop a swift kiss on her cheek, then dashed through the back door to look after the horse. Nabby left her schoolbook to throw her arms around Abigail's neck—"We were looking for you for hours!"—and Pattie hurried into the icy scullery, to come back with butter, cheese, bread. "We'll have coffee in a trice—"

Abigail cursed the Crown for making it impossible for her to drink tea at this moment.

John chaffed her hands: "Run fetch your mother some warm slippers, Nabby, and her shawl. Was she there?" he asked more quietly, as their daughter dashed away up the tight-shut little box of the stairway. "Did you learn aught?"

"Only that there are as many witch-hunters and religious fanatics in Massachusetts as ever there were in the old days." She put her hand to his cheek as he gently unlaced and drew off her boots and stockings. "Catherine Moore told me nothing of Rebecca's past or family that I did not know already, from Rebecca herself, or from Scipio and Mr. Malvern. Nor can I find anyone who might have had reason to harm Mrs. Pentyre. The only thing I learned was just how impossible it would be for Rebecca to take refuge with Catherine's family, always supposing she could get out of the town at all last Wednesday night. And I suppose Sam has found nothing?"

John shook his head.

"Has he gotten a man into Rebecca's old house?"

"Impossible. The Tillets are refusing to rent to anyone. To tell the truth, once the *Dartmouth* was sighted—and that was but two hours after you left—neither Sam, nor Revere, nor any of us has had many minutes to spare. Griffin's Wharf is surrounded. One customs man tried to force his way through to examine the cargo and was tarred and feathered—"

Abigail flinched, sickened at her recollection of the single time she'd seen that form of mutilation done.

"Not being idiots, the stevedores sent to unload the tea didn't even make the attempt. Sam sent men out to Cambridge, Roxbury, and Dorchester the moment the ship was sighted, and more messengers went out as soon as the time and place for the meeting tonight were set. There's a man on top of Beacon Hill, watching Castle Island, but Colonel Leslie hasn't stirred. I pray God he does not," he added grimly. "The last thing we need is to give the men aboard the *Cumberland* reason to start shelling the town."

"They wouldn't!"

"They won't if they think doing so would cause more damage than rioters. I must go," he added, as Nabby scampered back into the kitchen with Abigail's knitted wool slippers and stoutest shawl. "We're meeting at the Green

Dragon at eight: Sam, Revere, Warren, Church, Hancock, and I. The Faneuil meeting later will be a bear-garden. We need to know in advance what measures to propose. Sam at least knows that we have to move carefully, if we're to keep support in England and not be dismissed as hooligans out for nothing but loot."

Abigail nodded again. She had been aware for years that despite the cries of Democracy, the heads of the Sons of Liberty took care to plan their strategies closely, and leave as little as possible to the whims of the rank and file. Sam kept a finger on the pulse of the poor men, the laborers, the dispossessed and discontented, but he knew well that they could be swayed by the urgings of other men as easily as by his own. John was his balance wheel, his gauge for what would work and what only sounded well.

"By the by, this came for you this morning." He held out a thick little letter, addressed in Scipio's neat hand. The outer sheet enclosed a second missive on much finer paper—though not, she observed, anything like that of the forged note. In nearly illegible French handwriting, it informed her that M. Pentyre had indeed visited the house of Mme. Belle-Isle Wednesday night, leaving shortly after eleven. Clarice, the maid of Mme. Belle-Isle, would not drink rum and so Lisette had been obliged to purchase a bottle of smuggled French cognac for two dollars with which to ply her to obtain this information.

Feeling as if she had stumbled into a more than usually tawdry novel, Abigail brought up a couple of tallow work-candles and wrote out a little invoice for Charles Malvern: *I feel the woman's information is truthful, so far as she has been told the truth. If nothing else, it clears the ground for further inquiry*. She then brought out the packet of letters that Catherine Moore had given her.

Though they—and the remainder of Rebecca's letters to herself, that she'd started to read the previous Saturday—brought back clearly the memories of those times, and stirred anew her anxiety for her friend, they told her nothing new. Rebecca rarely mentioned her family, or the friends she had known in Maryland in her youth. Those were very much of the "Jess will be old enough to start school now," variety—whoever Jess might be.

Abigail blushed once to find her own name, coupled with grateful praise: "She is so patient with my stupidity in the kitchen . . . One day I hope to have her steadiness of heart . . ."

If you think my heart is steady, my dear, it's only because you haven't been around when Charley pissed in the kitchen fireplace. Abigail lowered the page to her lap. In the overcast dark, church bells all over the city had begun to toll, summoning Friends, Brethren, and Countrymen to Faneuil Hall. The strange, slow ringing had a sinister note, profoundly unlike the brisk music of Sunday. Could Rebecca hear them, wherever she was? Sam had had word out for a week now, for all those Friends, Brethren, etc. to be looking for her, and there had been no word of her nor word of her body.

If she were free to leave Boston, why would she not have come to me?

It was nearly midnight when John returned. Abigail, still reading by the fireplace, looked up at the sound of the latch. The men slipped through like fugitives: all the group who met at the Green Dragon regularly over matters of coordinating the patriots in the various Boston wards, and corresponding with like-minded men in far-flung colonies like New York, Philadelphia, Virginia. Her fair-haired, delicate-looking cousin Josiah Quincy, young Dr. Warren, smooth-voiced Dr. Church, and dark Ben Edes, Sam rubbing his hands and smiling with a self-satisfied twinkle in his eye, for all the world like the Reverend Atonement Bargest out in Gilead, soaking up praise for his excellent sermon on the dangers of demons that only he could see.

The resemblance doesn't end there, thought Abigail, smiling a little to herself as the men clustered around her, gripped her hand, all talking a mile a minute and all about their own affairs. She could have been Queen Charlotte or Helen of Troy for all they actually saw her, so preoccupied were they about the announcement to go out tomorrow that all the East India Company consignees for the *Dartmouth*'s tea must report to the Liberty Tree—at the head of the Neck—to resign their appointments, and the plan to have riders go out to farther-flung towns. So many hundred pamphlets from Edes, so many from Hazlitt, so many from Thomas over at the *Spy*—meet again tomorrow to coordinate details—John, you'll get us up a draft of what we're to say to the harbormaster about refusing to unload the ship . . .

Sam smiling at this man, clapping that one on the shoulder, or gripping that one's arm. She could almost see him commanding Brother Lament-Sin to put her and Thaxter up for the night (in that atrocious, *freezing* loft with his daughters), or directing Brother Mortify to guide them on their way again.

And Sam would react, thought Abigail uneasily as she bade them good-night, exactly as the Hand of the Lord would react to the smallest suggestion of unbelief, should she, Abigail, say to him: *I think Perdita Pentyre's killer is a Son of Liberty. I think your organization numbers a madman in its midst.*

John was gone in the morning. Whether under bond for thirty pounds or three hundred, reflected Abigail wryly, it wouldn't keep him from committing sedition against the Crown right here in Boston. Her two days of absence had left a staggering backlog of tasks which Pattie had simply not had the time to accomplish—from cleaning lamps and candlesticks to bringing the household account books up to date—so although her bones ached with weariness and rheumatism, Abigail forced herself to rise when John did, milk the cows, and set about making breakfast while Pattie rinsed and scalded the milk-pails. John kissed her when she brought his cider and oatmeal to the kitchen table: "'Tis good to have you home." And then vanished through the back door, to meet with Sam and the others before the main meeting of Friends, Brethren, etc. at nine.

The bells had tolled all night, and were tolling still. A warning of peril, of invasion, their sound would carry across the bay to Charles Town and Winnisimmet, to Braintree and Lynn; inland to Medford and Concord. Summoning Friends, Brethren, and Countrymen into Boston, to make their stand against the King's assumption that he could arbitrarily clap a tax on whatever goods he thought people couldn't do without—that he could with a scratch of his pen inform the colonists that they must buy their goods only from his friends.

In Scotland, in times of invasion, the men of the clans would burn a cross on the highest hill, that the men of the clan would know to assemble in arms. Even so, thought Abigail, as she dipped water from the boiler on the hearth into the washbowl for the dishes—even so the sound of the bells went out, to that great clan that Cousin Sam had formed with his skill and his charm and his wily understanding of human nature. And in Medford and Dorchester, Cambridge and Lynn, men were turning the management of their farms and shops over to their wives and mothers, and starting out for Boston.

Is *it someone in the Sons of Liberty?* She probed and tested at the thought, as if trying to untangle a necklace without breaking its delicate links. *Is that why he bound Rebecca, shut her up in her room? Or did he do that because he wanted her alive, wanted her to return to him . . .*

Yet she couldn't imagine Charles Malvern taking a knife to a girl of twenty. Exposing her *affaire* with this second

Adonis—if indeed such an *affaire* were not merely Lisette's rather Gallic interpretation of an innocent admiration—certainly. And possibly Malvern's vindictiveness would have extended to spying on Rebecca, by which means he'd have learned of the misdeeds of his rival's flighty bride in the first place. But further than that . . .

Her mind chased itself in a circle, trying to fit what she knew into what she could only surmise.

Richard Pentyre would be hearing the bells, in that handsome house on Prince's Street. They'd passed it last night, riding back from the ferry, its old walls of timber and stone covered over with handsome brick, its old gabled attics remodeled with a fashionable mansard roof. There'd been a handbill plastered to the door already, demanding that Pentyre report himself to the Liberty Tree and resign his appointment, as the tea consignees in Philadelphia and New York had resigned theirs. None of the Massachusetts consignees had yet done so: Probably, reflected Abigail wryly, their father the Governor wouldn't let them. If—

"Mama!" Johnny and Nabby flung themselves panting through the back door, red-faced with the cold. "Soldiers are coming!"

Had Abigail been a swearing woman, she would have sworn. She hadn't yet taken her hands from the washbasin when she heard knocking at the front door, and Pattie's swift step from the parlor where she'd been cleaning the grate—

Abigail strode into the little hallway in time to see the girl open the door and yes, for that first instant the aperture seemed to be filled with the color of the King's Men and blood. She was conscious of Nabby and Johnny at her side, half hiding behind her skirts but at the same time determined not to leave her. The thought flashed through her mind, *Johnny's six! He shouldn't have to be trying to protect his mother from soldiers.* In the kitchen, Tommy started to wail in fright, and from the street outside came the unmistakable *thunk* of a thrown glob of mud and a child chanting, "Lobsterbacks, lobsterbacks . . ."

There's only two of them . . .

Lieutenant Coldstone stepped forward across the threshold, removed his hat, and bowed. "Mrs. Adams? Please forgive this intrusion. May I beg a few minutes of your time? I've come to ask your help."

Fifteen

"In the past eighteen months, two other women have been killed in the same fashion as Mrs. Pentyre." Lieutenant Coldstone stretched his hands to the small blaze in the parlor hearth, newly kindled and struggling, but his coffee-dark gaze remained on Abigail's face.

Abigail stared at him, feeling as if she had been struck. *Two—?* And then, sickened that she had not thought earlier to ask, *Why did I think she was the only one?*

She took a deep breath, yet could think of nothing to say.

"One was a whore, the other a hairdresser—common women—"

"And does a woman's poverty or morals make her more deserving of that *horror?*" She fought the urge to pick up a stick of firewood from the box beside the hearth and smash it over that immaculately powdered wig.

"No, of course not," he replied calmly. "But it does make it curious that the third victim was a wealthy woman, a married woman, and a woman who under normal circumstances could not be easily got at by a stranger who did not have an introduction to her."

Abigail opened her mouth again to snap a response, then thought about his words, and closed it. Her mind darted at once to Charles Malvern's house, and how it was never entirely still: always the distant tread of a servant, the sense of other people at call. When Rebecca had taken up her first set of rooms in that cheap lodging house on the

North End, after six months of living with the Adamses on Brattle Street, she had said, *It feels so queer, to come in from the market, and know I'll be there alone.*

She said, slowly, "And Mrs. Malvern *was* poor, and *she* lived alone . . . as I presume the other two did. And though her landlord had servants and prentice-boys, they were not in the same house with her. *She* fits the pattern, not Mrs. Pentyre."

"Precisely. And, Mrs. Pentyre deliberately took considerable trouble—ordering her husband's man to harness a chaise for her, and driving herself through the rain on a pitch-black night—to put herself into a locality of danger. Why?"

Abigail shook her head. The forged note, in the code of the Sons of Liberty, seemed to her mind to be crying out from the drawer in the sideboard where she had put it, like a kitten in a cupboard. "I can't imagine. Who were the other two?"

"Zulieka Fishwire was found in her own house, on the floor of her parlor, her throat cut and her body mutilated quite as horribly as Mrs. Pentyre's was. It was as difficult to tell the circumstances of Jenny Barry's murder as it was Mrs. Pentyre's because Jenny Barry was a woman of the town. Like the other two, her throat had been cut with what appears, by the wound, to have been a thin, long-bladed knife. I would guess also that like the other two, she was violated as well as slashed, but given her occupation it is less easy to be certain of that."

He spoke matter-of-factly, as if to another man, something Abigail appreciated but found more disconcerting than she had thought she would. John was one of the few men she knew who did not skirt around the subject of the prostitutes who trolled the wharves and serviced the sailors, but he would never have brought the subject up with a woman he had barely met. "Her body was found among the barrels near Scarlett's Wharf. It had obviously been taken there, because there was no blood on the scene, even"—the Lieutenant's cold eye rested disapprovingly upon Abigail—"as there was no blood in the house where Mrs. Pentyre's body was found."

Abigail felt a flush mount to her cheeks. *What hast thou done? The voice of thy brother's blood cries out to me from the ground.*

Not Mrs. Pentyre's blood—the blood of that passionate, not-always-wise girl who sought to get even with her straying husband and help her country at the same time . . . who had wanted to be the heroine of a novel. But the blood of the next woman to die at the killer's hand because she, Abigail, would not describe to this man what she had actually seen.

"I am given also to understand," the Lieutenant went on drily, "that poverty and solitude were not the only things that Mrs. Malvern had in common with the other two. Which makes it interesting to me—"

"If by that you mean that you give credence to that poisonous Queensboro woman's hints that Mrs. Malvern had lovers, it's a lie."

"Is it?" He regarded her without change of expression, but something in his eyes made Abigail realize, with a sudden blast of fury, that Queenie had assumed—because of his legal help, and the fact that for six months Rebecca had lived under his roof—that John was one of them. And that she had told this man so.

"Who did she name? Orion Hazlitt?"

"One of them, yes."

"Orion Hazlitt has been desperately in love with Rebecca Malvern since they met over printing work he was doing. He's an intelligent young man but he was not well educated. Mrs. Malvern, who teaches a dame school, helped him with the spelling and arrangement of manuscripts he was given to print. I suppose it's the fashion to believe calumny rather than innocence, but I have been friends with

Mrs. Malvern for six years, and there was no more between them than his longing for someone in his life other than his execrable mother, and Mrs. Malvern's determination to remain faithful to a husband who treated her like a dog. I take it another of the accused was my husband?"

Coldstone inclined his head.

"As too close a party to the case any testimony of mine would be disbelieved," said Abigail, "so I will not waste your time with trying to prove a negative. And the third, I suppose, was Mr. Tillet—"

"Who owned the house she lived in, which he could have rented for considerably more than she paid him—"

"Had his wife not had in her so convenient a slave for sewing shirts. Mrs. Queensboro is a woman who lives in furtiveness and spite, Lieutenant. I would weigh very carefully any testimony she gives you."

"Including the fact that you were at Mrs. Malvern's door Thursday morning, long before the Watch was called?"

"I had contracted with Mrs. Malvern to do some sewing for me," replied Abigail steadily. "And, as I said to you that morning, I passed by to ask, was there anything I could purchase for her at the market, as I knew it was difficult for her to do so because of teaching."

Coldstone regarded her in silence, his head a little on one side. He still bore a bruise on his forehead, where he'd struck his head when his horse had come down with him Tuesday; its edges were starting to turn yellowy green. Pattie knocked at the parlor door, then entered bearing a tray nobly laden with coffeepot, bread and butter, new cream, and a small dish of hunks of brown Jamaican sugar. The girl laid her burden on the small table that she drew up between them, curtseyed, and withdrew again, and it was some moments before Coldstone spoke.

"Mrs. Adams," he said, "I apologize if I have angered you. I did not mean to do so. I came here seeking your help—"

"To put my husband's neck in a noose?"

"To keep it out of one," said Coldstone. "The Provost Marshal has quite good reason to believe that your husband either did the murder himself, or knows a great deal more about it than any honest man has any business knowing—" He held up his hand as Abigail opened her mouth to snap a protest. "Yet having bettered my acquaintance with you, I cannot believe that you would be party to such a crime, nor that Mr. Adams could succeed in keeping it from you. Much less so, because of its connection with the other two."

"No woman would be."

He was silent a moment. Then, "A few years ago I would have agreed with you, m'am. But one doesn't cross the Atlantic Ocean in the same troopship with British Army camp followers, without coming into contact with the sort of people I had previously assumed existed only in the plays of Euripides. As I was taught in Gray's Inn, I can only speak to what I know 'of my own knowledge.' I do not trust your motives, m'am, nor your loyalties, but I do trust your judgment of the man to whom you are married. I think that you would very likely cover over a murder that Mr. Adams did—but not *this* murder."

"No," said Abigail softly. "I would not." And then, "Bread and butter, Lieutenant?"

"Thank you, m'am. It has been some time," he added after a moment, "since I have tasted either that was not adulterated by Army contractors. Your skills as a housewife do you great honor."

She thought, *Oh, the poor boy*, her heart melting—and mentally slapped her own wrist in disgust. *Knows more than any honest man has any business knowing* indeed!

"What makes your Provost Marshal so sure that it could have been my husband?"

He shook his head. "I'm not at liberty to disclose it, m'am. Physically, he could have committed the crime—"

"He *could not.*" She paused with the coffeepot suspended over a cup, silently wishing she could pour the steaming liquid into her guest's pristine white lap. "He *would* not."

"There is a difference between those two things, Mrs. Adams, as I'm sure, as a lawyer's wife, you are aware. Your husband is in the thick of organizations whose stated goal is to disrupt the smooth working of His Majesty's government here in the colony. He is moreover the associate of men involved in large-scale smuggling operations which aid Britain's enemies. Your husband did indeed spend Wednesday night at the Purley's Tavern outside of Salem, yet a smuggler-craft could have brought him to Boston in an hour—"

"Not in that weather, it couldn't."

"You underrate their skill, m'am. He moreover is good friends with the woman in whose house the body was found: a woman separated from her husband, who has lived under Mr. Adams's protection and whose legal affairs Mr. Adams has looked after, pro bono. Had he wished to harm Mrs. Pentyre, what safer way to do so, than to mimic the methods of a lunatic who has killed two other women and has gone untaken? He chooses a night on which the Tillets are known to be absent. The renter of the house then flees, and you—Mr. Adams being bonded to remain in Boston and being moreover under suspicion—undertake a two-day journey into the backcountry, where an officer of the Crown would take his life in his hands to go—to warn or inform her—"

"Do you honestly think that's what happened?" demanded Abigail, appalled.

Coldstone was silent, studying her face, she realized, as she had studied Charles Malvern's, when she had broken the news to him of Rebecca's disappearance. *She didn't flee*, she wanted to shout at him. *She was imprisoned in her room, her blood was on the pillow of her bed, and on the floor beside the door—*

And Paul Revere and Dr. Warren had neatly mopped it away. She found herself trembling all over.

"No," he said after a time. "No, I don't. All these things—these possibilities—are like objects in a room, like furnishings well arranged. But there is another room, and in that room is the possibility that the same man who killed Mrs. Fishwire and Jenny Barry has started killing again. As all such men invariably will."

"And that matters to you."

"Yes. It does."

Silence again. Abigail handed him the cup of coffee, and looked around for the bell with which Pattie could be summoned to the parlor. Of course it was missing—Charley and Johnny were forever taking it to sound the alarm against imaginary Indian attacks—so she murmured, "Excuse me," went to the door, and called, "Pattie, dearest? Could you bring us some of my marmalade? Do you like marmalade, Lieutenant? And some of your gingerbread, if it's ready—" She returned to her chair beside the fire.

"These other women who were killed. When did it happen? I think I would have heard—"

"Jenny Barry was killed in June of 1772. Zulieka Fishwire in September of the same year."

September of '72. The month Tommy was born. The same month, she remembered, that word had finally reached Rebecca that her father had died the previous May. They had still been at the farm in Braintree then. None of her Smith or Quincy aunts or cousins would have written to her about the murder of a woman with a name like Zulieka Fishwire; certainly not about the death of a prostitute. *Common women*—she heard Coldstone's light, cool voice say the words again. *So worthless are women's deaths held.* "And none since?"

"None that have come to the ears of authority." He stretched his hands to the fire again, his face as inexpressive as stone. "I am certain the owner of the brothel or tavern where the Barry woman met her end hid the circumstances, lest his trade be hurt. There may have been others, between that time and the murder of Mrs. Fishwire."

"Did they know one another? Or have acquaintance in common?"

"That I don't know. They lived in the same part of the town, Mrs. Fishwire on Love Lane, and Mrs. Barry somewhere nearby along the waterfront."

"And Scarlett's Wharf lies not a quarter mile from the Tillet house," murmured Abigail.

"Was Mrs. Malvern acquainted with Mrs. Pentyre? Her maid said, not."

"Her maid didn't know Mrs. Malvern's name," said Abigail. "In fact they knew one another slightly—chance met at Mr. Hazlitt's stationery store, at a guess."

A slight crease flickered into existence between the Lieutenant's pale, perfect eyebrows; he reached into his coat and brought out a folded half sheet, which he held out to her. "Would this be Mrs. Malvern's handwriting?"

Forgive my error beneath the elms on the Common. Your precious Finch. Abigail remembered vaguely that *error* was a meeting, but knew that *the Common* wasn't really the Commons—she forgot what the transposition was. She shook her head. "It does not look familiar." She could always plead nearsightedness if later caught in the lie. "Is this one of the notes that Mademoiselle Droux spoke of her mistress receiving?"

"You've spoken to her, then?"

"Of course. Servants are our shadows, Lieutenant Coldstone. They see ladies without their paint, and gentlemen before they don their wigs in the morning. If one cannot talk to a man about an event, the next best thing is to ask his servants."

"Sometimes the best thing, Mrs. Adams." The cold seraph face suddenly turned human and young with a quick smile. "The man himself is doubtless lying. And did you in fact ride all the way out to Danvers, to speak with Mrs. Malvern's former maid?"

"I did. It wasn't Danvers, but Townsend, a hamlet in that direction—and in fact it wasn't even in the village, but some distance away. A vile journey." She shivered at the recollection of those shuttered-up houses in Gilead, of the twisted little cripple-boy working the spinning wheel with his withered hands, a task he would pursue, Abigail guessed, for life, having nowhere else to go nor any worth to anyone save for that simple chore. "Mistress Moore told me that there was none she could think of, who would have wished Mrs. Malvern harm. But if it is a madman, it would not be—might not be—anyone she knows."

Except of course that it was, she thought, seeing in her mind the dim glow of firelight in the rain as shutters were opened into the alley, the pinched *o* and slightly twisted *in* of the forged note. *The Linnet in the Oak Tree. Cloetia.*

"I take it," she said after a time, "that you have spoken to Mr. Pentyre?"

"I have," said the Lieutenant.

"And did he have an account of his own whereabouts on the night of his wife's death?"

"He did."

"Did you believe it?"

"Madame," said Coldstone, "there is no question of Pentyre's involvement in his wife's death—"

"*Why* is there no question?" asked Abigail. "Because Mr. Pentyre is the Governor's friend?"

One corner of Coldstone's mouth turned down, hard, a prim fold of exasperation.

"Why are you *so* convinced that my husband—and not, I notice, any more obvious member of the Sons of Liberty—had a hand in the killing?"

"Perhaps because the only people who claim to have been with your husband at the time of Mrs. Pentyre's death are known to be speakers of sedition, if no worse, against His Majesty's government?"

"Ah. And only traitors will lie to cover the movements of their friends?"

"You will admit that those who are known to be engaged in smuggling would be less likely to question a 'friend' if he asked them to lie."

"I will admit that they might oblige if asked for an untruth, but I will not admit that they're readier to such a lie than anyone else in Boston, up to and including members of the Governor's family."

It was probably physically impossible for Lieutenant Coldstone's natural stiffness to increase by much, but the slight turn of his head, the flare of his nostrils, informed Abigail that Lisette Droux had at least told her the truth about Pentyre's alibi. She went on, "If I'm wrong, of course, and Mr. Pentyre is genuinely distraught at what happened, I would be the last person to press him with questions about whether he had a hand in it. It is one reason that I do want to see him, if it's possible. Not to ask if he killed his wife, but to see if he knows anything about where my friend may have fled: any fact about the connection between his wife and Mrs. Malvern. Because I very much fear that Mrs. Malvern saw the killer, and that is why she has gone into hiding. We must find her, before the killer finds her first."

There was something about her words that made Coldstone's eyes shift. Something that made him hesitate.

At length he said, "Mr. Pentyre has removed to Castle Island. The families of all the tea consignees, and of every Crown official and clerk in Boston, have been crossing to the island all the morning, asking for the protection of the King's troops against rioting and insult in the wake of agitation by the political organization to which your husband—and apparently Mrs. Malvern, and you yourself—belong. Surely you saw the broadsides," he added drily, "demanding that Mr. Pentyre and the others present themselves at this Liberty Tree and resign their commissions to sell the tea?"

"And yet," returned Abigail quietly, "you—or at least the Provost Marshal—were convinced that Mr. Adams had to do with the murder, while the *Dartmouth* was yet far out at sea and no broadside had yet appeared on any wall."

Coldstone set plate and cup aside—the handle of the cup, Abigail noted, lining up perfectly with the edge of the table. "Mrs. Adams," he said. "You and I are like card players, each guarding the contents of their hand from the other, because there is too much at stake on the table to lay it down. I think—" His frown deepened, as if at the command of that interior blackmailer who was forcing the words from him. "I need your help. I do not think I can find this man without it. And, I think you want to help me, both as a woman, and as a seeker after truth."

"If truth is indeed what you seek, Lieutenant."

Coldstone looked for a moment as if he would have said something else—perhaps, she reflected uncomfortably, turned her statement back upon her. But he only nodded. "I seek the man who would do this to a woman," he said. "I have seen cases like this in London, and such a man will go on killing, until he is stopped. Will you help me find that man, whoever he may be?"

"I will," she said, "if I can. If you will—No." She stopped herself. "I will help you, regardless."

He inclined his head. "Thank you."

"Who was this Mrs. Fishwire? What do you know about her?"

"Only that she was a hairdresser: what they call a woman of the people, meaning she was poor. She was close to fifty, a mulatto from Virginia. The office of the Provost Marshal wasn't concerned in the matter, and only took the report of the city Watch."

"No Mr. Fishwire?"

"None in the report. She was found by a neighbor, a Mr. Ballagh."

Found in the same tight-packed labyrinth of alleys and byways that Rebecca Malvern had perforce made her home. Did that mean anything, or not? Did it mean anything that Richard Pentyre's handsome house lay not half a mile distant, as so many wealthy houses did?

Whose hair had she dressed? Perdita Pentyre's?

"It was over two years ago," Coldstone went on. "Yet surely there will be people in the neighborhood still, who remember the circumstances. If I can track the man from that end of the trail—"

"You?" Abigail's eyebrows shot up. "Lieutenant Coldstone, I may be a suspected traitor, but I am nevertheless a Christian woman. I would not want it on my conscience, that I had sent a British officer into the North End, with or without escort, tea ship or no tea ship."

Stiffly, Coldstone reproved, "I would not go in uniform."

"With that voice and that posture and hair cropped for a military wig, you would not need to. They'll cut you to pieces and feed you to their pigs, Lieutenant. Best let me see to this."

Sixteen

To Abigail, the tight-tangled alleys and narrow, anonymous rights-of-way that made up the North End always smacked more of the village Boston had been a hundred and fifty years ago, than of the thriving colonial city it had become. In fall and spring, the bustle and variety in the crowded streets went to her head like a glass of wine: bookshops, silversmiths', the closeness of the wharves with their tall ships; the smells of sea salt and pine. In the stench and heat of summer, with pigs and chickens and the occasional milk-goat blocking the narrow alleys, she invariably felt a longing for the green quiet and fresh food of Braintree, and today—with winter closing in, and the bells of the city tolling, and an edge of violence in the air—it seemed to her that here in this cramped islet could be found the concentrated solution of the worst of what Boston was.

Boston was a seaport town: sailors, both coastal and deep-water, were to be seen everywhere. The tenements that crowded these narrow streets housed them in their hundreds and—cheek-by-jowl with them—the chandleries, slopshops, and harlots that made up their world.

Boston was a wealthy town: Amid the crumbling squalor of dockside poverty, handsome brick mansions reared, where merchant families had held land for generations while the neighborhood decayed around them. Up until eight years ago, Governor Hutchinson had resided here with his family, in a splendid house up the hill from his wharf. Then in '65—enraged by Britain's arbitrary decision to tax everything printed, from bills of lading to playing cards—rioters had gutted the building, burned the Governor's painstakingly collected library of the colony's oldest documents, and driven his family out into the night. The family lived in Milton now, in the countryside, and the Governor, when in town, had a newer and larger brick mansion on Marlborough Street close to the Commons. The Olivers—relations of the Hutchinsons and the Governor's appointees to the most lucrative colonial posts—had a house on the North End as well, but as Abigail passed it, she noted that its shutters were up, and the knocker taken from its door.

Boston was a town of passions: for religion, for liberty, for riotous street fighting that broke out every fifth of November—Pope's Day—in parades, brawls, battles between North-Enders and South-Enders. As she followed Sam's maid Surry along the cobbled pavement, Abigail could hear voices arguing in taverns, in tenements, in alleyways. In addition to the homes of the rich, the North End held a large concentration of Boston's poor, and though it outraged Abigail's Christian soul, she knew that the refuge of the poor (*if they have not the spiritual mettle to either resign their souls or to better their condition*) was drink, of which plenty was available. The liveliness that elsewhere characterized Boston seemed here to be only a step from violence. On this very cold morning most of the local dwellers were on their way to or from the market in North Square, but gangs and groups of countrymen clustered around the inns and taverns, with rifles on their backs, tomahawks at their belts, and little parcels of clean shirts and spare stockings under their arms.

"Do you remember hearing of the two murders, three summers ago?" she asked her companion, and the slavewoman nodded.

"Was there two? I only heard of the one. Kitta—Mrs. Blaylock's cook"—Mrs. Blaylock was Sam Adams's neighbor—"says Mrs. Fishwire was cut up something horrible. A judgment on her, Kitta says, though to my mind that don't show much of the Christian charity she's always braggin' on that she has." Having been the property of Sam Adams for many years, Surry was easy-tempered and virtually unshockable: a pretty mulatto woman of about Abigail's own age, to whose speech still clung the lazy accent of Virginia.

"Why a judgment? I thought Mrs. Fishwire was a hairdresser."

"Oh, Lord, nuthin' like that." The maidservant shook her head. "For one thing, Zulieka Fishwire was older than Mr. Adams—not that that's ever stopped a woman with a good man," she added with a pixie grin. "But Kitta—and some other folks in this town—thinks that because a woman learned herb-doctorin' from the Indians, and maybe from the country Negroes that come in from Africa, she's got to be learnin' it from the Devil." She sniffed scornfully. "Some of those *white* doctors can't tell the difference between prickly heat and the smallpox . . . Well, Mrs. F. *did* dress hair, and did it well. But folks knew, if they didn't want to be bled or purged or dosed with some of those awful things doctors'll make you swallow, she was the one to come to, to get you well."

The blocks of the North Street Ward had originally been plotted deep enough to permit gardens behind them, but during the course of time this land had been sold, and divided, and built upon for rentals and barns and workshops. In much the same way, old Ezra Tillet had built the narrow little house behind his own, that his son Nehemiah had rented to Rebecca Malvern. The result of this rear-yard building was that much of the North End was a maze of yards and cottages, and alleyways that would admit no more than a wheelbarrow. Down one of these, past the Blue

Bull tavern and behind Love Lane, Surry led Abigail, to a sort of cobbled courtyard surrounded by three or four ramshackle structures of various sizes, aswarm with grubby children barefoot in the cold.

Washing-lines stretched from house to house, and a bonfire burned in the middle of the court under a black cauldron that looked as if it had begun its career on a whaling vessel. Two children who should have been in school were feeding the fire beneath it. A third, slightly older, stirred an acrid burgoo of shirts and chemises simmering within it. The heavy air smelled of woodsmoke, lye, and privies that needed cleaning.

Abigail walked up to the older woman engaged, with yet another child, in hanging shirts of white ruffled linen over the stretched ropes, and asked, "Begging your pardon, m'am, but does Hattie Kern still live hereabouts?" Rachel Revere, who lived two streets away on North Square, had given her this name along with the information that Mrs. Kern took in washing. Sure enough, the woman said, "That'll be me, m'am."

"I'm Mrs. Andrews, from Haverhill." She held out her hand to the warm, laundry-wet grip of those rough fingers. "And this is Lula." Surry curtseyed. "I understand a woman named Fishwire used to live near here; Lula was her niece. We only heard this past summer about the poor woman's death"—in an isolated township like Haverhill, this was not beyond the realm of possibility—"and Lula being her closest relative we had wondered, if any of her things remained?"

"Lord save you," exclaimed Mrs. Kern, and dried her hands on her apron. "I have some of her things—a good few, anyway—and Georgie Ballagh still has that poor cat of hers. Nannie"—this to one of the children feeding the cauldron fire—"run get Mr. Ballagh, there's a good girl . . . Not you, Isaac, you stay with the fire. To think of her having a niece after all!"

"What happened?" asked Abigail, though Rachel Revere had last night given her the armature of the story: that sometime during the night of the twelfth of September, 1772, Zulieka Fishwire had been slashed to death in her house on Love Lane—a house now rented to a tailor named Gridley and his family. ("And a very pleasant gentleman he is, when he's himself," affirmed Mrs. Kern loyally.)

Paul Revere's wife had, like Lieutenant Coldstone, described Mrs. Fishwire as a hairdresser, "But that was just so the church elders wouldn't come pokin' their long noses into her affairs," provided Mrs. Kern. "Between black eyes from the Bull"—she nodded in the direction of the public house—"and round bellies from the girls down at the wharves, if you'll excuse my mentioning what's in front of everyone's noses hereabouts, and children hereabouts comin' down with fever and what-have-you every summer, not to speak of breakin' their arms like my Timmy did climbin' on the back of the butcher's cart like a young idjit . . . Well, Mrs. F. barely had time to fix her *own* hair, poor lady."

"It's why nobody thought a thing of it, that strangers were in and out of her house all the day and of an evening," confirmed Georgie Ballagh, a bent little man who'd lost a leg and a hand fighting the French at Louisburg, over a decade ago. "Mysel', I don't hold with a woman gettin' shut of a child she's carryin', but what's the odds, if the poor mite'll be born to a mother who's workin' the streets for her livin'? Sailors'd come in with their doxies, or by theirselves to be rid of the pox—beggin' your pardon for mentionin' it, m'am—at all hours of the day and night."

He frowned, and ruffled at his thin, colorless hair with the iron hook that had replaced his left hand; Abigail told herself firmly that she must not speculate how many scars he had on his scalp from this habit. "We think a sight more of it now, I'll tell ye. There's not a man or a woman on this yard, that don't prick up their ears when they see a stranger come 'round. But all that's after closin' the barn door when the horse is already gone."

"Did anyone not see who was the last person to visit her house that evening?" Abigail made herself look shocked, and Mrs. Kern, Mr. Ballagh, and three other neighbors poured out a confused tale: it was a lady, at about the time Mrs. Kern was setting out to find where Nannie had got to—no, no, it was a man in a green coat (only Lettie Grace said it was gray) who'd come in a chaise, she thought—No, that chaise belonged to that French feller stopping at the Bull. Mrs. Russell said it was a Negro, but then Mrs. Russell had no use for Negroes on the whole—

As Abigail had coached her, Surry, upon being shown the few effects that Mrs. Kern (and several other neighbors) had taken from the house once the constables of the Watch had been there, asked, "Did no one find among her things a coral necklace? There was a gold bead on it. It was my mother's, that she'd brought from Africa when they came over," which gave Abigail the chance to describe both Rebecca Malvern and Perdita Pentyre, as the possible thieves.

It was a bow drawn at a venture, and if either of those women had visited the tiny shop that Zulieka Fishwire had kept on the ground floor of the little house, nobody had particularly noticed them. Given the proximity of the Bull, and the wide variety of Mrs. Fishwire's clientele, this was scarcely surprising. Mrs. Gridley, whose husband now rented the shop, added that it had costed the landlord six months' rent, that killing had, as no one would rent the place, and she and her man wouldn't have, neither, except the asking price came down so cheap, and then they'd got Father Scully that looked after the Irish in His Majesty's Forces to come over from Castle Island and say prayers, and Mrs. Gridley *still* wouldn't go into that room after dark, not for ready money.

"Slack your fire, lass," said Mr. Gridley easily, from where he sat beside the front window stitching a waistcoat of yellow silk. "There's no such a thing as ghosts." He nodded a genial greeting to Abigail and the rest of the procession that followed her in, agog to display their knowledge of the old crime.

The floor was sanded, after the old country habit, and the ceiling low. The building itself was even more rickety than Rebecca Malvern's dwelling, so that the dashing footsteps of several little Gridleys (there were at least four of them that Abigail could see, and Mrs. Gridley didn't herself look old enough to be out without her own mother) almost vibrated the house. Nails and hooks had been driven into the walls of the small front room: "She had strings back and forth between 'em, with her herbs dryin'," provided Mrs. Kern. When Abigail looked up at the little cluster of hooks in the low ceiling, the washerwoman added, "She'd hang skins up there. Snakeskins, enough to make a Christian's flesh creep. Mornin's, she'd go out to the Commons and catch 'em by the Mill-Pond, or pay the boys hereabouts. Lizards, too. She'd have 'em up there to keep the cats from 'em."

"Had she many?"

"Three," said George Ballagh. "My lad Pirate was one of 'em—" He looked out the open door of the little house, and pointed to a thin, rather delicate-looking black cat sitting on an upper windowsill of a tenement opposite, washing itself with the stump of a missing forepaw. "He a'n't crossed this threshold since that day, an' I can't say as I blame him."

"Because he still smells the blood, do you think?" Abigail knew plenty of people who'd disagree with the enlightened Mr. Gridley and attribute such reaction in an animal to ghosts.

The little ex-soldier's face hardened with hate. "Blood my arse. The man who did it killed the other two, and I found my poor lad hid behind the cupboard with his paw all but sliced off, and cuts on his back where the man'd gone after him as he ran about. There was blood on the step"—he nodded toward the scuffed oak threshold, the shallow brick step outside—"where they three would sit after dark, waitin' for the Fishwire to let 'em in for their dinners, an' the two of 'em gutted like fish here in this room, an' the poor old Fishwire herself in the doorway there, that goes to the back-kitchen. I was one of them as helped clear the dead from Fort William Henry, after the Abenaki had massacred the settlers there." He shook his head. "This was near as bad."

"That Father Scully," put in Mrs. Gridley insistently, "he blessed both this room and the kitchen, and the doorway between 'em. There's nought of evil, that remains here of the deed."

"No," said Abigail softly. "Of course not." While Mrs. Gridley, Mrs. Kern, and others explained to Mr. Gridley every detail of Abigail's story about being the mistress of Mrs. Fishwire's niece, she walked around the little room, set up now as a tailor's shop, with boxes to hold the fabric for various jobs and a little rack of spools of thread of various colors. The resemblance between this place and Rebecca's house lifted the hair on her nape. And yet, she told herself, there was little variation possible in these ramshackle dwellings. It was such a place as any woman obliged to make her own living in the world would take, if she could: a small house on one of Boston's many inner courts, that would be black as pitch once the sun was down, save for the dull gold chinks of closed shutters . . .

"Were the shutters closed?" she asked. "The night of the murder?"

"Oh, aye." Mr. Ballagh nodded, from the doorway where he'd gone to stand talking to Mr. Gridley. "With the species of ruffians that spend their time in the Bull, you want to keep things locked up tight, once the sun goes in. The Fishwire'd keep her door open later nor most, for her trade, an' she was always havin' trouble with 'em."

Another neighbor nodded. "We was all ever havin' trouble with 'em, m'am. One or another—sailors, sometimes, sometimes just the riffraff that unloads the boats—"

"She'd get a gentleman, now an' now, though." The informant—swarthy as an Indian with an Irish brogue that could have been cut like cheese with a wire—explained to Abigail. "From the Bull, y'see. Gentlemen'll come for the cards, an' maybe so-be-it the deacons of their churches won't see 'em takin' a drink—"

"Maybe so-be-it they're deacons theirselves," added a Mrs. Bailey, and got a general laugh.

"Well, sailor or gent, they'd come down here, see the light, an' maybe think it was a whore's house. Or others'd come and pound on her door and curse at her, and call her witch—"

"I throwed a man out, just the week before the killing happened," assented Ballagh. "One of the gentlemen, *he* was, and cursin' like a sailor at her, because he couldn't do his rifle-drill—beggin' your pardon, m'am—with some drab over at the Bull."

"Lord, yes!" Mrs. Kern laughed. "And he wasn't the first or the only—You mind Abednego Sellars, that's deacon at the New South Meeting? He had a ladyfriend lived in rooms at the Mermaid, in Lynn Street; he was here all the time at evening, all cloaked up like he thought nobody here would see his silver shoe buckles, to buy the wherewithal to do his doxy justice. Then when things didn't work out just as he'd planned, he'd be back, midnight sometimes, a-poundin' on the Fishwire's door and screamin' at her that she was a witch who'd put a word on him, to keep him from doin' the deed."

There was general laughter, and Abigail traded a startled glance with Surry. Both of them knew Deacon Sellars, if not well, at least for a number of years. He was a pious and prosperous chandler, a pillar of his church and—Abigail knew—likewise a pillar of the Sons of Liberty, whose pamphlets he was in the habit of taking out of Boston in his deliveries of soap and candles to surrounding towns.

While it was true that Boston was a bustling town that seemed both enormous and crowded to her—particularly when first she had come to live there—she realized that in the five years that she'd lived on and off in Boston, she had come to know, at least by sight, scores of its inhabitants to whom she had never spoken, and by reputation, many more. Those who, like Deacon Sellars, had lived all their lives in the town would know its byways, and where to come if they wanted to deceive their wives or play cards or get drunk out of sight of the elders of their respectable churches.

And heaven knew, you couldn't throw a rock in Boston without hitting someone at least sympathetic to the Sons of Liberty.

On the other hand, she reflected, as she and Surry made their retreat past the Blue Bull and out into Love Lane once more . . . On the other hand, it *was* curious.

And it might behoove her to find out a little more about Abednego Sellars. And she couldn't keep herself from mentally adding, *Carefully* . . .

It was nearly ten in the morning—and poor Pattie was once again saddled with keeping the children at their lessons and beginning preparations for dinner in between her own, heavier tasks—and Abigail turned the corner onto Middle Street with a pang of guilt. A door opened just ahead of her and three men staggered out, dressed for some evening party and laughing with the exhausted silliness of men who've spent the night in the back room of a tavern (and the door was, indeed, of that description). Surry leaped nimbly aside. Abigail, less quick, found herself with one of them in her arms.

She stepped back and released him with an exclamation of disgust.

"Pardon, m'am—pardon, m'am," mumbled the stumbler's friend, catching the stumbler by the elbow. "M'friend's not well, not at all well . . ." The third member of the party hooted with laughter.

"There, Percy, you've gone and offended a respectable matron! Your wife will have words to say to you!" He caught his two friends by the shoulders, and the three of them staggered away down the hill toward Lynn Street, leaving Abigail gazing after them, not certain if she should be troubled or merely bemused.

The young man who'd spoken to her—drunk as a lord and elegant in a coat of blue satin beneath his caped gray greatcoat—looked a great deal like Jeffrey Malvern.

Seventeen

Scarlett's Wharf, where the body of the prostitute Jenny Barry had been found, lay barely four hundred yards from Love Lane. "There won't be anythin' to see now, m'am," warned Surry, as they descended the hill, past taverns and tenements, past public houses where men from the country gathered, quietly talking, and when they fell silent, the tolling of the church bells filled in like the heavy scent of lightning in the air.

"I know."

Had her hair been red? Blonde? Coldstone hadn't said.

Had she been young? So many of the girls who came and went through the doors of the Queen of Argyll tavern near the head of the wharf seemed, to Abigail's eyes, barely children. Others had the bitter faces of crones, though probably no older than her youngest sister Betsy, who was barely twenty-three. Despite her decent upbringing and wary loathing of drunkenness, Abigail felt her heart contract with pity at the sight of them. You could not open yourself to six or eight or ten men a day, she thought, without the assistance of alcohol—of something to keep your mind from what you did and what you'd become. Her thoughts went back to Mrs. Kern and her daughters, hanging gentlemen's shirts on the stretched lines, their hands red with lye. The youngest one—whom Mrs. Kern had sent without a second thought to fetch Mr. Ballagh from the tavern—had looked barely six.

More men loitered on the wharves, waiting their time to

take a shift at guarding the *Dartmouth*'s cargo to prevent it being unloaded. She crossed Ship Street, pattens clanking on the bricks, to the short wooden platform that stretched out over the salt-smelling waters, and behind her caught the words "liberties of Englishmen . . ." ". . . Parliament . . ." ". . . make us slaves, sure as if we was Negroes ourselves!"

From the head of Scarlett's Wharf the *Dartmouth* was hidden by the weathered buildings erected on the quarter mile–plus of the Long Wharf and the clusters of masts beyond; by the shoulder of Fort Hill and the gray stone mass of the Battery. "You think the Governor's gonna call the soldiers, to get that tea ashore, m'am?" asked Surry, when Abigail's eyes turned in that direction. And what did *they* make of it, Abigail wondered: the Scipios and Surrys of the world. Men and women who not only could not vote, but whom the law permitted to be bought and sold, as if they were truly the cattle that Virginians sometimes called them. What did *they* make of all this furor among the whites, over three-pence a pound on tea?

"I shouldn't like to be the commander of the regiment trying to implement the order." She nodded toward a group of newly arrived youths, making their way along the quay under the watchful eye of a bearded older man. "I understand that the *Dartmouth*'s captain has offered to take his cargo back to England, but Governor Hutchinson has ordered the vessel to remain until the tea is unloaded and delivered to its consignees."

"I will purely like," remarked Surry, as they turned south and started to walk along Fish Street toward home, "to see him try." She had, Abigail reflected, been with Sam Adams a long time.

Abigail pulled her cloak tighter about her shoulders as the gray wind cut at her, tucked her chin into the layers of scarves that swaddled her neck. *At any other time, I would be rejoicing.*

At any other time—ten days ago—I would have cried out

against anyone who tried to stop any of the Sons of Liberty from their endeavors, for any reason. Our liberties—our rights as English citizens—take precedence over the misdeeds of any individual.

In her mind she saw the little black cat on the windowsill, washing itself philosophically with the stump of its paw.

. . . deacon at the New Brick Meeting . . . a-poundin' on the Fishwire's door and screamin' at her . . .

Surry strolled beside her, half a pace behind as behooved a slave, but commenting now and then on this or that ship, this or that group of countrymen . . . Comfortable with Abigail, as with a member of the family. And so she was, reflected Abigail, glancing at her: plump and quite pretty in her spotless white head-wrap and calico dress. She had long ago guessed that Cousin Sam used this woman as a concubine, and that Sam's wife, Bess, if not precisely delighted by the arrangement, had accepted it. They were both good-natured women, they were both dearly fond of Sam, and both would rather work together to keep the household comfortable than rend it with recrimination and jealousy. Had she been white, and a free man's wife, Surry would have been precisely what Bess was—as respectable a housewife as she was an "honest" slave.

Thus it was no good asking her if she knew anyone who might have known Jenny Barry. The gulf that divided the respectable from the raffish was deep, and cut across both slave and free. Even a woman as poor and as slatternly as Hattie Kern would feel deeply insulted, had Abigail asked her about the dead prostitute's friends, enemies, clients. *What makes you think I'd know a woman like that?*

A man could cross that gulf, of course. As Jeffrey Malvern obviously did, coming to the North End taverns to play cards and drink—it occurred to Abigail to wonder if he, like Abednego Sellars, had a "ladyfriend" with "rooms" somewhere among these anonymous little rear buildings and yards. No man—anger prickled behind her breastbone at the thought—would suffer ostracism from friends and fellow members of the Congregation, merely for speaking to a publican, a whoremaster, a thief.

Paul Revere could help her there. But Revere was still away, carrying pamphlets and broadsides to every town in the colony, bidding all men who loved their country to come to Boston and stand against tyranny.

As they passed Hitchborn's Wharf, Surry pointed to the whaleboats that were putting out for Castle Island, carrying the families and property of the tea consignees, seeking protection from the Crown against the mob that was growing larger by the day.

Knowing that in all probability she would be immured within her own house for the rest of the day, making dinner and performing the belated tasks of housewifery, after parting from Surry by the town dock Abigail made her way to Hanover Street. She found the shutters up at Orion Hazlitt's shop, but, hearing voices down the narrow passway to the yard, went back and found him endeavoring to explain to his mother why he was going out, yet again.

She was weeping pitifully, her arms around him like a lover. "But why, son? You're always leaving me alone now. You didn't used to. How have I angered you?"

"Mother, I'm not angry. I could never be angry with you. I'll be back this afternoon." He tightened his arm around her, bent his head, to kiss her full on the lips. "I would never abandon my best beloved."

She laid her head on his chest. "But you have," she whispered. "You have left me, over and over. *Please* tell me, how I can win back your love."

"Mother—" he said desperately.

"What if it should rain?" she begged, in a small voice like a child's. "What if the rain should pour down, and the waters rise, and the house begin to float away? *All the high hills, that were under the whole heaven, were covered; fifteen cubits upward did the waters prevail; and the mountains were covered . . . and all that was in the dry land died.*"

"I won't let that happen." Over her starched lace cap his eyes met Abigail's, and there was a haunted flicker in them—*wondering if I saw that kiss?*—as if begging her to understand. He looked as if he had neither eaten nor slept properly in many nights. "I didn't leave you alone the other night, did I? When it started raining, and you were so frightened, I came back."

"You did," she whispered. "You held my hand. *All flesh died, that moved upon the earth, both of fowl, and of cattle, and of beast, and of every creeping thing that creepeth upon the earth . . .*" And she clasped his fingers now, and kissed them with a passion that made Abigail cringe. No wonder the poor man did not feel able to bring a wife into his house. "I could not live without you, now that we are outcasts, exiles, wanderers upon the face of the earth . . ."

"Nor I without you, Mother. Truly, honestly. But I must leave now—"

"Of course, dearest. Just come inside for a moment and see how I've embroidered those new pillowcases for your bed, just the way you liked them—"

"You showed me already, Mother, and they're beautiful." A note of desperation crept into his voice. "And I'll see them again when I return. Damnation—"

A young woman emerged from the house, whom Abigail vaguely recognized as the "girl" indispensible to any household in the town, a lanky, broad-shouldered female with a long, rectangular jaw and dirty hair.

"Son!" pleaded Mrs. Hazlitt, suddenly frantic. "Don't—" She pulled against the grip of the young woman, clutched at her son's hands, then the lapels of his coat, as he tried to step away; she began to struggle and weep. "Why have you stopped loving me, son? Why won't you tell me what

I've done to make you hate me? *There is a generation that curseth their father, and doth not bless their mother! There is a generation whose teeth are as swords, and their jaw teeth as knives . . .*"

The young man turned swiftly, and Abigail walked with him out through the passway to the street. "She'll forget all this by the time I'm home, you know," he said quietly, seeing the trouble on Abigail's face. "I hate it: I hate having to do it. And she—she doesn't understand. She's never understood—" He shook his head, as if trying to shake away sacking wrapped around his eyes and brain. "Have you heard anything? Anything at all?"

Abigail debated for a moment about telling him that at least two other women had been murdered in the same fashion as Perdita Pentyre, then put the thought aside. "I know Rebecca hasn't fled to stay with her maid," she said. "Her husband—"

He had been wavering, caught between his fear for his mother, and the tug of the tolling bells. Now he grew still. "You've seen him?"

"He has been most helpful, Orion."

"If I had—" he began impulsively, then stopped himself, and stood for a moment, looking past her, his face wooden with anger and distress. "He's shown before he'll do anything to possess her, up to and including putting her under lock and key! Do you think you can trust him?" he asked at last.

"I *think* so," she said slowly.

"Do you ever wish—?" He hesitated, then let his breath out in a rush. When she put her hand on his arm, Abigail was disconcerted to feel him trembling. "Let me know," he said, "if you learn anything. If you find anything. I know it's—" He shook his head again, and rubbed his eyes. "Her husband will always be her husband." He sounded like a man reminding himself. "And Mother will always be my mother. I know that. Yet I can be her friend."

Wish what? Abigail watched him stride away down the slope of Wine Lane toward Faneuil Hall. Wish that instead of sitting at home comforting his mother when the rain began Thursday night, he had been still at Rebecca Malvern's, when Perdita Pentyre's killer came knocking at the shutter? Asking in a voice she knew, to let him in?

Wish that he had stood at God's elbow, there at the beginning of Time, and asked that the woman he loved not be given in marriage to a bone-dry merchant with two half-grown children? That he could spend his days with a mother whose grip upon him was an embrace and not a stranglehold?

And in her mind she heard her father's gentle voice: *But we* were *there, my Nab, at the beginning of Time with God. And we saw, and assented to, every single act and event of the lives He drew up for us, seeing in them His wisdom, before we entered into the human condition of blindness day-to-day.*

The sound of the church bells followed her home.

At least one portion of her investigation proved easy, and God had pity on her—or perhaps on poor Pattie, condemned to glean behind her erratic reaping these days. John came home to dinner late, when the meeting was done, with the news that none of the consignees had yet resigned his position, and that the Governor was still refusing to let the *Dartmouth* leave port. "Some of the men are returned, from the villages," he said, ladling the thick stew of chicken out onto the plates held by Johnny to serve parents and siblings. "We're meeting again, at the Green Dragon, at eight tonight. I beg your pardon, Portia, for deserting you again this way . . ."

"Then unless you wish me to behave like Mrs. Hazlitt," she said, "and cling weeping to your coat, may I send to Bess, to pass the evening in her company?"

Bess—born and raised, like Sam, in Boston—brought

her daughter Hannah with her, a lively girl of seventeen, with her father's broad shoulders and sturdy build and her father's quicksilver mind. Both had heard already all about the expedition with Surry into the North End, so there was little explanation necessary. All Abigail had to do was say, at the right point in the exclamations of horror and shock, "The curious thing was, someone spoke of Abednego Sellars as having bought herbs of this Mrs. Fishwire. Surely not Mr. Sellars the chandler? Why, he is a deacon!"

"Nab," said Bess, wisely shaking her head, "you're the smartest woman I know, and married to the most long-headed man of my acquaintance, yet it's plain you come out of a country parsonage. A whited sepulchre," she said, with an expression that added, *There are plenty of those around*.

Abigail leaned forward in the deep gold light of the work-candles, with an expression of rapt fascination, and had the whole of Abednego Sellars's business and personal life deposited neatly in her lap.

Abednego Sellars did indeed have a ladyfriend in the North End, though probably not the same ladyfriend he'd had eighteen months ago at the time he'd made an exhibition of himself for the amusement of the inhabitants of the Love Lane Yard. "He's a man full of juice," sighed Bess. "When Penny Rucker married him back in '52, my Ma said he'd make her weep, and it's sure he has. Even then he liked his dram, for all he'll get up at meetings of the Session and roar against drunkenness before the face of the Congregation. Goes up to the sailors' taverns in the North End, where he thinks nobody knows him, as if Sophy Blaylock's cousin doesn't run the Queen of Argyll *and* gossip worse than any woman in the town. These days—" She shook her head again, and made a little noise, as if urging on a recalcitrant horse.

Pattie got up to put more hot water in the teapot. Bess had brought a quarter of a brick of good Dutch East India

Company oolong, respectably smuggled and ambrosial after many months of coffee and sassafras.

"He's always seemed so respectable," lamented Abigail encouragingly.

"There's a good many men in this town who *seem* respectable," chimed in Hannah. Like her mother, she didn't seem particularly put out by this fact. Abigail wondered if she guessed about her father and Surry.

The picture emerged of a man of lusty appetites, of quick temper, of sharp acumen where money and business were concerned; a man disinclined to keep rules where they interfered with what he considered his rights as a man, whether those rules were laid down by the Crown or the Congregation. He had many cronies, and made friends easily; was on good terms with one of his daughters, but the other two tended to be bitter over his way of life. His one son had gone to sea, and had been taken from his uncle's ship off Barbados, and pressed into the British Navy. Steps had been taken to get him out, but he had died before he could return home.

Abigail asked, "When was this?" no longer wondering at the man's dedication to the cause of rights for the colonists.

"Three years ago?" Bess paused in her sewing—baskets of sheets, shirts, the children's clothing lay on the big kitchen table between them, the eternal work of a household. Abigail didn't wonder at it, that Mrs. Tillet had pressed poor Rebecca into servitude to keep up with extra stitching for money. "Sixty-nine, maybe? I remember he vowed then that he'd mend his way of life—that was the same year there was trouble with the elders of the Congregation. But it takes great strength, to alter the way a man lives. The hunger for the old ways grew on him, I guess."

"If he'd left Boston, he might have stood a better chance of mending his ways," remarked Hannah, bringing two of the work-candles close, so that she could thread up a needle by their light. "Here, if a man wants to make a change, he has to almost abandon all his friends. If he was out in Essex County, it would take a deal of trouble to find gambling houses and bad women."

"He would only have ended up seducing his neighbors' wives." Bess turned a shirt right-side out, to inspect a darn. "But you may be right. He went back, in any case. I suppose only knowing that it was just a few minutes' walk, to the Mermaid or the Queen of Argyll, was too much for him. Especially if he didn't really think there was anything wrong with what he was doing in the first place."

"Is he a relation of Richard Pentyre's, then?" asked Abigail, after the four women had sewed for a time in quiet.

"Oh, Lord, yes! There was bad blood between them, you see, over the land that Pentyre's mother inherited: Well, to my mind the bad blood was inherited, too, because it was Abednego's father that got passed over in the will, not Abednego himself. But it was Pentyre he went to when his son was pressed into the Navy, see—as family, you know. I don't know a great deal about the British Navy," she added, setting her sewing down for a moment, to sip her tea. "Nor do I know, how long it takes even for a man who's a friend of the Crown, to get them to turn loose of a common sailor, even if they can find the man, on all their ships all over the seas. So, I don't know the right of it. Abednego claims Pentyre was lazy, and put the matter off, as not important to him, for nearly a year, before they even located what ship poor Davy was on. And by then it was too late."

Eighteen

Rain started late that night, raw and cold. Abigail, since childhood a subject to rheumatism, felt the change of weather in her sleep, and turned restlessly, seeking John's steady warmth, like a heated brick. Seeking, in her dreams, his unquenchable flame of spirit.

But all her dreams were drawn toward darkness. In her sleep she heard Mrs. Hazlitt's wailing: *All flesh died, that moved upon the earth . . . fifteen cubits upward did the waters prevail; and the mountains were covered.* Though even in her dream her reason told her that the vision was simply a confused old woman's hallucination, she went to the window and looked out, and saw all of Queen Street drowned in rising waters. Water climbed the brick walls of the opposite houses, rain-pocked in the blackness yet visible with the all-seeing knowledge of dreams. Church bells tolled their wordless warning of danger, and she saw in her dreaming Nabby and Johnny in the next room, clinging together in fright as the water poured silently in over the windowsill. The *Dartmouth* floated by, laden with its burden of tea, its crewmen waving their cargo manifests and asking to be allowed to vote.

Rebecca is out there somewhere. A prisoner in one of those attics, with the water rising. She will drown, before we find her. Abigail leaned from the window, feeling the slick wet coldness of the windowsill, the sting of the wind on her face. "Where are you?" she screamed, but her throat would produce no sound. The gale whipped her hair around her face, a vast sable cloud. From the window the whole of the world seemed to be a waste of water, a thousand dark roofs and blind black windows. Rebecca could be trapped behind any one. The bells tolled like thunder, and lightning from the coming storm flickered over the face of the deep.

"Don't give up!" Still no sound. She gasped, trying to force the air from her throat. "We're coming!" And woke upon a gasp, as John touched her shoulder.

"Nab," he whispered, and she clung to him in the darkness that seemed so black after the luminous cat-sight of dreaming. "Beloved—"

At the sound of the church bells she shivered violently. "Who is ringing the bells?" He drew back a little in surprise at the mundane question, and she heard the muffled snort of his chuckle.

"Sam's got men at it, turn and turn about," he said. "All along the waterfront, too, ready in case the *Cumberland* tries to put in or Leslie brings his men over. Is that what you were dreaming of, dear friend? The bells? Do they trouble you?"

She shook her head. "Just a dream. They'll trouble the British a good deal more." It was good to be able to seek refuge in his arms.

There was no great difficulty in ascertaining whether Abednego Sellars had passed the previous Thursday evening where others could see him, particularly not with Boston in a ferment and half the merchants in the town absent from their shops. Abigail abstracted a book of sermons from the top shelf of John's library, wrapped it in rough paper and string, and waited until John left for Old South Church, where the meeting was that day. Though not one of the inner circle of the Sons of Liberty, he was always gone during these gray, louring mornings, at the hour when the countrymen who crowded the streets seemed to vanish as if by magic. Walking from Queen Street down to Milk Street, where Sellars had his chandlery shop, Abigail passed Old South, and saw the backs of men clustered in its doorway, and heard the muffled outcry of voices within. *Sam?* she wondered. *He could always get a crowd going . . .*

Again the thought crossed her mind of the Reverend Bargest out in Gilead, rousing his congregation to just such an outcry: *Behold them! Aggh, there she is! Do you not see her? The serpent, with its glaring eyes—Lo, can you not see where the Nightmare comes? There!* There! And everyone in the little congregation wailed, *We see her, we see . . .*

You must see! You must*! Behold the witch! She comes NOW through the wall, glowing with the corpse-light of Hell—!*

Only it was Sam's voice she heard in her mind, *Can you not see the King? He comes through the wall, glowing with the fires of Hell, holding a bayonet to the throats of your children—*!

The case is not the same, Abigail told herself, vexed that the comparison had even crossed her mind. *In any case Sam doesn't control the lives of the families of the men who look to him for leadership.* Even if he did get carried away with his rhetoric and start taking liberties with provable facts.

As she'd known would be the case, only Abednego Sellars's youngest prentice-boy was in the chandlery shop on Milk Street. Bess had informed her—after a few discreet questions—that Penelope Sellars's sister had recently given birth, so there was little fear of encountering the New South deacon's wife in the shop, something Abigail felt guiltily unwilling to do. She had been raised to abhor gossip, and made a careful point, in her discussions with her sisters and Bess of the affairs of various friends and acquaintances, not to spread evil rumors unless they could be definitively substantiated, and *then* to put the best face on the matters if possible . . .

But, she told herself, *the case is not the same here, either*.

Even so, she was glad Penelope Sellars wasn't in the building.

"It might have been Mr. Sellars," said the apprentice, to Abigail's story of a visitor last Wednesday night, just before the rain started, who had been gone before she could be called in from the cowhouse and had left this package, and Pattie had said she thought it might be Mr. Sellars. "In truth he spent that night from home. He was called out to Cambridge, just after dinner, and didn't return in time, and the gates were closed on him . . ." He glanced around the empty shop, with its neat packages of candles and rope, soap and nails, as if for listening ears. His voice sank to a whisper. "Mrs. Sellars, she wasn't any too pleased, either. The squawk she set up!"

Abigail said, a little primly, "Well, if Mr. Sellars was in Cambridge Wednesday night, he could not be the man who left this book upon my husband's doorstep, could he? I think it would be a favor to them both, if you mentioned nothing of this."

"No, m'am." He looked like he might have said something else—mentioned the deacon's latest "ladyfriend" on the North End?—but only repeated after a moment, "No, m'am."

Drat men. Abigail's pattens clinked sharply on Milk Street's cobblestone paving. *If they have an aversion to a woman, why wed her? If they want to tup harlots, let them marry the hussies to begin with*—then *they'd see there's more to happiness than four bare legs in a bed.*

Orion Hazlitt's face returned to her, harsh with sudden anger at the thought of Charles Malvern. *Do you ever wish*—?

Yet Rebecca Woodruff had pledged herself to Charles Malvern for her family's sake, long before her path had ever crossed the young stationer's. *What God hath joined, let no man put asunder.*

Rebecca had said that to her, on her first evening in the new house on Queen Street, when she and John had come back to Boston from Braintree a year ago. Rebecca had helped her, Bess, Hannah, and Pattie scrub every surface with hot water and vinegar, move pots and kettles into the kitchen, make up the beds. After dinner was done for all friends and family, Rebecca had remained, to help clean up, and to tell at greater depth the small events that had made up her life during Abigail's year and a half of absence from the town. Orion's name had come up early in the conversation: "He is a good man," Rebecca had said, perhaps too quickly, when Abigail had mentioned the number of times his name had arisen in her letters. "Cannot a woman take pleasure in a man's conversation without all the world winking and smirking, if he but walk her home from church?"

Abigail had replied carefully, "If she is living apart from her husband, it behooves her to take care how she shows her pleasure. Either to others, or to him."

Rebecca had reddened a little in the pallor of the winter twilight, but it was anger that sparkled in her dark eyes, not shame. She had bent over her sewing again. "Those who walk with their gaze in the gutters will see mud wherever they look," she replied after a time. "He tells me his mother is the same. She thinks that any woman who speaks to her son is 'on the catch' to take him away from *her*. She's never forgiven him for coming to Boston in the first place, he says, *As if he were running away from me!* Which of course is exactly what he was doing. She thinks the young ladies of the Brattle Street congregation are heretics, let alone me, whether I were married or not. And I *am* married," Rebecca went on. "Abigail, I do not forget that. *What God hath joined, let no man put asunder* . . . not even the man who has cast me out."

It had been on Abigail's lips to ask, *What if things were different?*

But they were not different, nor would they be. So she had held her peace.

"Mrs. Adams?"

Startled, Abigail turned, as she came into the open space between the Old State House and the Old Meeting House—the very place where, three and a half years ago, British troopers had opened fire on a mob of unarmed civilians—to see a man approaching from the doorway of the State House, wrapped in a thick gray cloak. His hat shadowed the pristine gleam of hair powder, but even before he came close enough for her to see his face her heart leaped to her throat.

"Heavens, man, are you insane?" She strode over to him, and he removed his hat and bowed: It was Lieutenant Coldstone, sure enough, and in uniform beneath that very military-looking cloak. He wasn't even accompanied by the faithful Sergeant Muldoon.

"On the contrary," said the young officer, "you could scarcely call upon me, m'am. And we are not half a mile from the soldiers at the Battery."

"With all of—oh, what is it? Twenty troops? Do you think they'd even turn out, if they heard a mob going after a Tory who wasn't smart enough to keep off the streets at a time like this? What on earth are you doing here?"

"My duty," he responded stiffly, as Abigail caught him by the arm and almost dragged him down King Street toward the relative safety of the Battery. "We were sent to escort the Fluckner family across to Castle Island"—Thomas Fluckner was a crony of Governor Hutchinson's—"and I thought to improve the occasion by asking if you had had time to pursue inquiries on the North End. I left a note with your girl, that I would return at three. The town seems quiet enough."

"That's because they're all at Old South Church, listening to my husband's cousin tell them the Crown has no right to tax British citizens without the consent of their elected representatives in Parliament, *or* set up a monopoly on any item for the benefit of his personal friends."

Coldstone's lips parted on the words *Three pence a pound*— and closed again. She thought he might have followed this up with an argument beginning, *Nevertheless, it is the law* . . . but that look, too, passed from his eyes. He only said, "You are quite right, Mrs. Adams. It was foolish of me."

For a moment King Street was quiet indeed, save for the eternal tolling of the bells. Then he continued, "Last night I reviewed the notes I made at the time of the Fishwire murder, and those of my predecessor. The regiment had only just taken up post at Castle William. The previous Provost Marshal seemed to have the attitude that a woman who has been reduced to selling her body deserves whatever befalls her, and merely noted the savagery of the postmortem slashing. I was angry, both that he would make no more of it than he did, and because it was plain to me that his neglect in pursuing the first murder had left the culprit at large to commit a second. For that reason, though it was deemed a civil matter only, when the constable reported it to the Provost Marshal—in his usual weekly report, and thus some days after the event—I asked permission to visit the Fishwire house."

"And did you have dung thrown at you by the local children?" inquired Abigail. When he did not reply, she glanced sidelong up at the young man's face, and added, more kindly, "There are few enough in Boston who would take such trouble, for a woman who made her living fixing hair and selling herbs."

"Few in London either." Coldstone didn't return her glance. His dark, clear eyes roved to the muddy flats that lay on their left as they emerged from Kilby Street, the rough, open ground on both sides of the Battery March below the slope of Fort Hill, as if seeking signs of danger.

"Are you from London, Lieutenant Coldstone?"

That brought his eyes back to her, and put that little crease back in the corner of his mouth. "Not originally. My parents lived in Kent. They didn't start bringing me to London with them until I was seven or eight. I've always preferred the country. Even as a child, I think I sensed that London was a place where a poor woman could be slashed to death, or a poor child trampled by a rich man's horse, and no one would really care. This seems to hold true in Boston as well."

"I think it holds true in many places." Abigail made a wry smile. "As Londoners consider themselves the pattern-cards for the conduct of all the world, I suppose this is as it should be. What did you make of the house when you saw it? Or the victim?"

"Little enough." Below them, among the scattered buildings around Oliver's Wharf, two redcoats stood on guard while three British sailors, in their striped jerseys and tarred pigtails, helped the crew of a small sloop unload barrels of provisions. For the men of the Battery, Abigail assumed: the soldiers whose little palisaded barrack stood at the foot of Fort Hill to their left. Just ahead of them on the other side of the Battery March lay the walled park of the guns themselves, thirty-five cannon set to defend the Harbor against the French who had never come.

There were, Abigail observed, more soldiers on guard there than was usual, but not so great a number as to provoke fears of a landing or an invasion. Her estimation of Colonel Leslie's good sense rose. Beyond the line formed by Milk Street and School Street, the southern portion of the Boston peninsula was but thinly inhabited, open fields, cow pastures, vegetable gardens, builders' yards, and rope-walks prevailing along the unpaved lanes. In general the soldiers stationed at the Battery kept themselves strictly to themselves, did their drinking on-post, and did not venture into the town even in times of quiet.

Beside her, Coldstone continued, "The constable had already given the landlord leave to clear the place up. Fools—" His brow darkened. "Any sign the killer might have left behind was gone, and of course none of the neighbors had a word to say to me. It was clearly the work of a madman, yet there is something—" He shook his head. "At the risk of sounding like the very men I derided a moment ago, I will say that my observation has been that a harlot—and Mrs. Barry was well known about the wharves, apparently—puts herself in danger by the very nature of her work. It is not at all uncommon, for one to be slashed, or even killed."

"I suppose in London," said Abigail softly, "one would see a good deal more of that sort of thing, than here."

"As you say, Mrs. Adams. But why this man, whoever he was, would have attacked a *hairdresser*, and a woman of some fifty years to boot—"

"I know not whether this lightens or darkens the issue," said Abigail. "But dressing hair was not all that Mrs. Fishwire did. She was an herbalist, a healer, and an abortionist. Some called her a witch. It was not unusual for her to have visitors at odd hours, well after dark."

"Was it not?" Coldstone halted, where a broad flight of wooden steps led down past John Rowe's warehouses to Rowe's Wharf. On the wharf itself, two redcoats stood guard over a mountain of trunks, crates, and hatboxes, which servants were loading into a launch. In the roadway before Abigail and her escort, a coach had come to a halt, from which a black manservant was handing a massive, red-faced gentleman in a crimson greatcoat. Thomas Fluckner, Abigail identified him. One of the richest merchants in Boston and the proprietor of a million acres of Crown lands in Maine.

"Excuse me, m'am." Coldstone bowed, and strode to meet Fluckner, who shook a handful of papers at him and harangued him at some length in his sharp, yapping voice.

Abigail caught the words *transport . . . rights as citizens . . . adequate guard . . . Milk Street* (which was where Abigail knew the Fluckner mansion stood) . . . *always supported His Majesty . . .*

"Yes, sir. Yes, sir. You would need to speak to Colonel Leslie, sir . . ."

Fluckner went back to his carriage and cursed the footmen. Coldstone returned to Abigail's side. "Forgive me, m'am."

"For doing your duty? Nonsense."

"Even so." He bowed again, as if in a drawing room. "And were Mrs. Fishwire's neighbors any more forthcoming to you than they were to me, about who they may have seen on the night of her murder?"

The name of Abednego Sellars flashed through her mind, only to be thrust aside at once. It was ridiculous, and besides, if he were arrested for murder—particularly one he did not commit—once in the Castle Island gaol, the danger of what he might say about the Sons of Liberty wasn't even to be thought of. "The court is black as a tomb, once dark falls," she said, in what she hoped was a completely natural tone. "The honest folk that live there—and they *are* honest folk, who make up the greater part of the North End—close their doors when things begin to get lively at the tavern at the head of the alley. It surprises me none would have come to a woman's outcry, but I should imagine there's a great deal of ruckus most nights . . ."

"And if a man keeps a knife hid up his sleeve or under his coat," said Coldstone quietly, "all he has to do is wait for a woman to turn her back on him, to seize her. Many times there is no outcry."

Abigail looked away. It seemed to her that she could smell the blood in Rebecca's kitchen again. At the head of the wharf a straggly haired youth loitered, a thief, probably, totting up the value of the trunks. A footman helped first Mrs. Fluckner—stout and pretty and fussing angrily at everyone in sight—from the carriage, then Miss Fluckner, heiress of the house, a tall, strapping, black-haired girl of fifteen in a dress of mustard-colored silk.

"He killed her cats," Abigail said after a moment. "Two of them. Slashed them to pieces, as he did her." But when she looked back at the Lieutenant's face, there was no more expression there than he would wear if he were playing cards.

"It seems, then," he said, "that Mrs. Barry and Mrs. Fishwire were more similar to one another than we had known—that there were those who would consider the latter as reprehensible, in her way, as a woman of the town would have been. And the gap widens between them and Mrs. Pentyre."

"One could say that," returned Abigail levelly, "if one did not regard Mrs. Pentyre as a whore herself." His back stiffened. *Does he truly believe that when a fine lady takes lovers it is different in the eyes of God from the act of some poor woman who is only doing it to buy herself bread?* "As some—whom I shall not name—regard Mrs. Malvern."

He thought about that for some time before saying, "You are quite right, m'am."

"And no politics in sight."

Something changed in his eyes, and she knew as if she read it on a piece of paper, that in his mind was whatever it was that made him—and Colonel Leslie—so certain John had a hand in the killing. Whatever it was that he would not tell her.

As she would not—could not—speak Abednego Sellars's name to him.

A pretty black maid, slender as a dark lily, got down from the coachman's box to collect the odds and ends left in the coach: a book, a scarf, vinaigrette, an overfed lapdog who whined and licked her hands. As if she heard Coldstone's speculations the maid turned quickly, trying to get a look at the loitering watcher. But the young idler slipped away out of sight. *Too many soldiers about?* Abigail wondered. Or had he simply been told to report to some master-thief, that the family had indeed departed for Castle Island, and the house could be robbed at leisure?

"You said to me the other day that killers such as this one—of whom I presume you have heard more in London—invariably continue with their killings," she said. "Why would he have waited fourteen months, between the second murder and the third? You're certain there have been none between?"

"After Mrs. Fishwire's murder," said Coldstone quietly, "I have been watching."

"Fourteen months is the length of a sea voyage, and a stay in some other land."

"I had thought that. I will send to the city magistrates of New York and Philadelphia, to ask if there have been similar crimes."

Abigail hesitated, then said carefully, "There is a man—a friend"—not a completely accurate statement, but it was the best she could manage on the spur of the moment—"who got into a quarrel with Mrs. Fishwire, more than once, I understand. He is . . . a connection of the family of Mr. Pentyre's mother, who were involved in a dispute over property. I cannot give you his name—"

Coldstone made an impatient gesture.

"—because he has been so unwise as to speak out against the King's Governor in the past . . . not an uncommon topic of conversation, in this colony. Because of the situation of his poor wife"—Would he care for this argument? She didn't think so—"I fear lest he be harassed, merely on suspicion of this crime. Have you had the opportunity to ask Mr. Pentyre if he is willing to speak with me, so that I may ask him of this?"

"Of this?" He raised one eyebrow. "Or to further your personal theory that he might be the murderer himself?"

"Lieutenant!" Mr. Fluckner strode back up the wooden steps to street level again, swinging his silver-headed cane. "Lieutenant, I have twice indicated to you that we are ready to depart! Need I remind you—"

"Forgive me." Lieutenant Coldstone turned quickly toward the red-faced merchant. "I came ashore to accomplish two duties, and am guilty of neglecting the one in pursuit of the other."

Fluckner glanced at Abigail, his thick lips wry, as if gauging both her politics and her morals from the cost of her plain green wool cloak, the muslin cap visible beneath her hood. He said, "M'am," but didn't sound enthusiastic about it, and touched the brim of his hat.

"Mr. Fluckner, Mrs. Adams," Coldstone introduced them, as the daughter came up, followed by the mother's querulous voice.

"They're not going to come rushing out of the town to shoot us on sight, you know, Papa," the girl protested, as she reached her father's side. "All they're asking for is their rights as citizens." She stared with fiery fifteen-year-old defiance at Coldstone, and Fluckner said sharply, "Hush, girl. The only rights they're interested in is the right to take property from those who've worked for it. Begging your pardon, Mrs. Adams," he added, turning back to Abigail. "We'll miss the tide if we linger." By the smoldering suspicion in his eyes—presumably at the name of Adams—he was clearly considering the possibility that she was delaying their departure until the protest meeting was finished and a concerted attack could be arranged.

"I fear Mr. Fluckner is quite correct." Coldstone turned back to her. "If you can cross tomorrow at this time," he said, "I can arrange an introduction. Would that satisfy you?"

"Thank you. I am very sensible of your assistance."

"Enough to share with me the results of the interview?"

She smiled. "Even that."

He bowed over her hand. "Until tomorrow then, m'am. Curtis—" He signaled one of the soldiers on the wharf. "Please escort Mrs. Adams back to Queen Street—"

"Good heavens, do you want the poor man killed?" Abigail stepped back. "This is Massachusetts, Lieutenant, not London. Women are quite safe to go about by themselves."

"Not all of them," returned Coldstone quietly. "But have it as you will, Mrs. Adams."

He followed the merchant and his daughter down the steps to the wharf, where the last of the baggage had been loaded onto the launch. Mrs. Fluckner had gone aboard, too, and stood, cradling her lapdog, unwilling—for whatever reason—to set foot once more in the place that had become so suddenly dangerous for her and hers. Abigail stood for a time on the roadway, looking down at the gray green water lapping around the piers and the vessel's black-wet sides, the bloody splashes of the soldiers' uniforms, the brilliant hues of Miss Fluckner's skirt where the wind took her cloak aside. Last of all the black maid was handed into the boat, and for a moment stopped and turned back.

And what does she *think of it, who has not Scipio's position in the household, nor Surry's unshakeable trust in Sam's ability to keep his family safe? Does she wonder what will become of her, should the family suffer financial reverses in the course of this unrest over the tea?* In such circumstances, Abigail was well aware, frequently the first luxuries to be sold off were the chattel servants.

And yet for the briefest moment, Abigail had the feeling that the young woman was not looking at Boston, but at *her*.

Mr. Fluckner's voice snapped, an angry and audible

shout, "Philomela, get down here! Your mistress is calling!"

The slave turned away, and disappeared among the confusion of men as they made sail. Abigail tightened her scarves about her throat, and made her way back along the Battery March toward the town.

Nineteen

"You are crossing to Castle Island?" John set the basin of hot water on the corner of the table, brows diving down over his blunt nose the way they did in court when opposing counsel tried to slip some fact by him in a millrace of rhetoric. Abigail gathered up the last of the forks.

"Lieutenant Coldstone has offered to arrange an interview between myself and Richard Pentyre. I could ask you to escort me, but since I had rather our children did not grow up as proscribed orphans in the wake of your hanging, I think it would be better for all if Thaxter came with me instead."

"And what will you ask Mr. Pentyre when you see him?" inquired John sarcastically. "If he murdered his wife?"

"Something of the kind." Instead of coming back directly from the Battery that morning, Abigail had taken a long detour to the North End again, and had stood for some time on Prince's Street, studying the bland brick frontage of Pentyre's handsome house. Of the original dwelling, only the lintel over the door remained unchanged: ANTONINUS SELLARS—1697. The stylish slate roof with its numerous tiny dormers towered above the older gables of its neighbors, but of the half-dozen chimneys, only one—probably that of the kitchen—vented a drift of smoke.

Abigail wondered if Lisette Droux still remained in residence, or whether she had gone on, to feather her nest elsewhere. *Now you ask me to speculate on the contents of a man's heart . . .*

A short walk took her thence to Hull Street, and a few inquiries among the neighbors had identified the residence of Mrs. Belle-Isle, likewise closed. Unlike the immense Pentyre house, the modest two-story dwelling—set back, like Rebecca's and Mrs. Fishwire's, behind a larger building, but infinitely more snug and stylish—bore the appearance of complete desertion. A young woman crossing the yard from the bigger house to what appeared to be a small hen-coop affirmed that indeed Mrs. Belle-Isle had taken her servant girl with her when she'd left.

"It may be a complete coincidence, that he left his mistress's house not long before his straying spouse was due to arrive at the home of his enemy's wife," Abigail went on as she laid the dinner dishes beside the basin, dipped up a little soft-soap onto her rag. "As it may be mere happenstance, that he arranged with his friends—and fellow tea consignees—the Hutchinson boys, to swear that he was playing cards with them until three thirty in the morning, which is when he returned to his house. If that be the case—and his quite natural grief for a wife he was betraying is genuine—I would not scrape salt into his wounds by accusing him of doing such a deed himself.

"And indeed," she added thoughtfully, and set out the washed cups on a towel on the opposite side of the basin, "there's no reason that Richard Pentyre has to have done the killing himself. He's a wealthy man. He could have hired someone . . . As I suppose you could have found another Son of Liberty to do the murder while you were at Purley's Tavern—"

"Always supposing I—or Richard Pentyre—didn't mind paying blackmail for the rest of our lives," snapped John.

"There is that," Abigail agreed. "But answer me this, John. If a woman has been betraying her husband quite profitably with the Colonel of a regiment—who can provide the husband with contracts and protection for his property if he happens to be about to take a whacking great consignment of tea from the East India Company—and that woman then becomes entangled with a young Adonis to whom Colonel Obliging may take exception, whose whereabouts would it be more reasonable to inquire after when she's found dead? The twice-betrayed husband who may be about to lose both contracts and protection due to his wife's romantic self-will, or a total stranger who has done nothing worse than object to the import of tea?"

"A hit, Portia." John's hand closed over her wet and soapy one. "A palpable hit. Yet I remind you that your Lieutenant Coldstone is not a stupid man, and what you have told me, he already knows. And yet whatever else he knows—or thinks he knows—causes him to believe that I, and not the deceived husband, wielded the knife."

"I wonder if there's a way to ask the Lieutenant to be in the room with me when I speak to Pentyre?" said Abigail. "I'm sure there is. For I'm very curious what Pentyre's reaction will be when I mention that someone of my acquaintance saw him—or someone very like him—walking down Hull Street at eleven thirty Wednesday night, only a half mile from where his wife was found dead. I don't expect he'll cry out or anything, but as Hamlet says, *If he but blench . . .*"

"Not a bad idea," agreed John. "And I've done the same myself in courtrooms. Yet I urge you to remember, Portia, what happens to Hamlet at the end of Act Five."

Once the dishes were washed up John wrapped himself in cloak and scarves and vanished into the slow drizzle of the rain. Colonel Leslie had proclaimed a curfew on the town but no one was keeping it: John calculated that some four thousand countrymen had come into Boston so far. As she stitched at the mountain of household mending—and tried to keep her attention on her children's reading—Abigail reflected that the tea crisis and subsequent presence of the mob in Boston may have been the only reason John hadn't been arrested for the Pentyre murder already, if Coldstone were that certain of whatever it was that he refused to tell her.

"*And Jacob vowed a vow, saying, If God will be with me, and will keep me in this way that I go, and will give me bread to eat, and ra . . . ra-i*"—"Raiment," whispered Nabby at his side—"*and raiment to put on, so that I come again to my father's house in peace; then shall the Lord be my God: and this stone, which I have set for a pillar, shall be God's house, and of all that thou shalt give me I will surely give the tenth unto thee.*"

But it cut both ways, she reflected, her mind straying, yet again, from her son's childish drone. Now more than ever, Colonel Leslie and the Provost Marshal would be seeking a reason to arrest John—and any other Sons of Liberty they could prove were in collusion with him—for a shocking murder, rather than for standing up for the rights of colonial Englishmen.

"That's very good, Johnny." Abigail set aside the shirt she was working on, helped the boy close the heavy book.

"Ma, would God really have forgiven Jacob for cheating his brother, just because Jacob promised him back a tenth of what God gave him?" Johnny sounded worried. "Didn't God love Esau and Jacob the same?"

"Later on, Jacob cheated his uncle Laban, too," added Nabby.

Abigail was still disposing of this piece of divine favoritism—not to say bribery—when she heard footsteps in the yard. The door opened to reveal John, with Sam at his side. Her eyes went to the clock—shocked—Yes, it really was half past eight—and she got quickly to her feet. John's lips were cold as marble, his mantle flecked with the last of the rain. "Now, it's past time you children should be in bed," she said, as Johnny and Nabby threw themselves on their father and their uncle Sam. "You may ask your father about Jacob tomorrow," she added, since the six-year-old showed signs of opening the subject with a more satisfactory authority: understandable, given that, like the much-put-upon Esau, he was the firstborn son. "Now—hot bricks!"

These Pattie had ready by the hearth, each wrapped in layers of towels. Abigail collected a candle from the sideboard, lit it at the work-candles on the table, woke the sleepy Charley from the settle where he'd been curled up, and gathered Tommy from his crib. She kept her voice cheerful, though Sam looked grim and John looked troubled: It was one of her foremost rules of the household, that though politics might be argued and the iniquities of the King freely aired, the darker matters of the Sons of Liberty must be kept separate from these four little souls whom God had elected to launch on their childhoods during this confusing era.

Only when she came down to the kitchen again did she ask, "Sam, what brings you here tonight?"

Sam glanced at John, who looked aside, being a firm believer in letting people fight their own battles. Sam, Abigail had noticed over the years, had a habit of getting between Bess and anyone who wanted to have words with her. She didn't know whether this was because he considered Bess his property, or because he liked to control the flow of information, and edit it if necessary for the good of all concerned. Taking John's silence as tacit permission, Sam turned back to Abigail and said, "You do, I'm afraid."

John sat down on the settle where Charley had been sleeping, and picked up the nearest book, which Abigail had been reading earlier in the day. Had the rest of the house not been freezing he would have left the room. Sam clearly waited for either John or Abigail to make some remark, and when neither did, went on grimly, "John tells me you're going to Castle Island tomorrow, under the auspices of the British Provost Marshal."

"Corrupting his servants was proving rather costly, I'm afraid, so I thought I should save money by making my inquiries direct."

"What have you told that Lieutenant?"

"Nothing," said Abigail.

"You're sure of that, are you?"

She folded her arms. "Obviously, not having been party to any of my conversations with him, you're not."

Sam's face seemed to darken in the flickering light. "You're not to go."

"Ah," said Abigail in an enlightened voice. "You know where Rebecca is, then. I must say, that relieves my mind—"

"Don't you be pert with me, Nab—"

"And don't you be bossy with me," she returned. "I'm trying to save a woman who is almost certainly in appalling peril—"

"And I'm trying to save the liberties of our country. Something I think you're in danger of forgetting."

"Not at all," responded Abigail. "And the reason we seek to retain our liberties, is so that the life of a single individual—even if she *is* a *mere woman*—does not get snuffed out or thrust aside because it isn't expedient for those in charge to take the time to save her."

Sam opened his mouth, glanced sidelong at John—his nose still in *Pamela* and giving no sign of having heard a word—and seemed to settle a little, like oatmeal taken off the boil. Very quietly, he said, "I have had every patriot in this town searching for her, for seven days now. Cellars, attics, warehouses . . . smuggler hidey-holes and the hulls of ruined ships. You forget that we're not only hunting for Mrs. Malvern: We're searching for the book that contains our codes and ciphers, and the lists of our contacts in other colonies where we are perhaps not strong enough to protect those the British would seek to arrest."

"I don't forget."

"If you haven't forgotten, then you're a fool," Sam gritted. "You don't think that every time you open your mouth around that lobsterback pretty boy of yours he isn't noting down every word and fitting them together like pieces of a mosaic? He only waits until he has a picture complete, to charge me or Hancock or John over there with that murder, or with complicity in covering it up. Do you want the Tories putting it around that John or myself will be hanged not for fighting for our liberties, not for standing up against a monstrous attempt to make the whole of these colonies the personal fiefdom of a fat German princeling, but for murdering a woman of our own organization who disagreed with us?"

Abigail looked aside.

"Now Bess tells me you've been asking questions about Abednego Sellars, of all people—"

"Who held a grudge against Richard Pentyre."

"Then why didn't he murder Pentyre?"

"Why would he have—might he have—murdered a woman in precisely this same hideous fashion fourteen months ago in the North End, a woman he claimed was a witch—"

"Now you are insane." Sam's hand struck flat-palmed on the top of the sideboard next to her, a crack that made her flinch but did not cause John to stir a hair. "You're accusing everyone, casting about at random, muddying the waters, and putting us all in peril. I forbid you to go."

"And I defy you to stay me," retorted Abigail.

"And I forbid you to make any inquiry, or put about the slightest suggestion, that any Son of Liberty might have had the slightest involvement in, or knowledge of, Mrs. Pentyre's death! Good God, woman, that's all we'd need, at a time like this!"

"A time like this," said Abigail, her voice suddenly deadly quiet, "is the time—eight days—that a woman who is my friend, a woman who helped me through a time of grievous pain, is . . . somewhere. Somewhere that your smugglers and patriots and South End boys have not been able to discover, *if* they have been searching as hard as you say they have and not attending your meetings and carrying pamphlets to every village and town in riding distance to protest against the landing of a cargo of tea. You can't have it both ways, Sam. Either Rebecca is in hiding with the ciphers in her possession, and afraid to contact the Sons of Liberty for reasons I will leave *you* to conjecture . . . or she is dead at the bottom of the bay and the ciphers are in the killer's possession, and have been so for a week. Either a woman's life is more important to you than ninety thousand dollars' worth of tea, or it isn't."

"I forbid you to go!" thundered Sam, and turned back to the fire. "John, I order you to bridle this wife of yours and keep her from interfering, either with our own men or with that damned cold-faced Provost! I will not have our endeavor jeopardized, and I warn you, John, kin or not, I'll take whatever steps I need!"

And snatching up his hat and cloak from the sideboard, he strode to the door, and vanished into the night.

Twenty

"Pa! Mrs. Adams is here."

"I know fifteen Mrs. Adamses." Paul Revere grinned, emerging in his shirtsleeves from the back room of his shop, an apron around his waist. "Yet somehow, I knew it would be you, m'am." He winked at his son behind the counter, stepped aside to let Abigail past him, into the wide-windowed little workshop with its shelves and tools and blocks of wax.

"Because Sam has ordered you not to speak to me?"

"Of course. I have tea here—" The kettle was hissing and muttering to itself on the edge of a small forge near the back door. No need to ask whether so much as a farthing's tax had been paid on it. "What do you need to know?"

It was midmorning, and wind blew icy across the harbor, rattling gently at the windows that formed a band of grayish light, halfway round the workroom. Abigail prayed it would grow less by three, when—with luck—Lieutenant Coldstone would meet her at Rowe's Wharf. Even now it wasn't bad enough to keep boats from passing over to the Island, but her stomach did anticipatory flip-flops at the thought of being on the water in such weather. "Were you acquainted with a woman named Jenny Barry?"

He started to make a good-natured grimace, a comment on the dead woman's way of life: then she saw in quick succession recollection, angry horror, and sudden speculation fleet across his dark eyes at the name. "She was killed—" he began, and Abigail finished for him, "—eighteen months ago, give or take. Her body was slashed—"

"—like Mrs. Pentyre's, after she was dead. Yes. I knew there was something . . . Another woman was killed that same summer, Zulie Fishwire—" His dark brows knit sharply down over his nose.

"I went to her house the day before yesterday," said Abigail. "Spoke with her neighbors, which apparently the local constables barely troubled themselves to do at the time. Did you see either of their bodies?"

"I don't live in that ward." Revere shook his head. "I heard of them, of course. Everyone in the neighborhood did. There was a scare, but it seemed to come to nothing after all but tavern-shouting and vows to protect wives and daughters." He made a little space on the table that occupied most of that room to set a teacup before her, then sank into his barrel-chair. On the table between them Abigail saw pamphlets, engraving plates and tools, sketches of the *Dartmouth* at anchor on Griffin's Wharf. On a shelf above them a half-finished set of dentures grinned, discolored ivory in silver wire. Abigail felt a pang of gratitude that even the bearing of five children had left her with her teeth intact.

"You think it was the same man?"

"I don't know," said Abigail. She told him of her words with Coldstone, of the help Malvern had given her, and the accounts of Zulieka Fishwire's neighbors. "Sometimes it looks to me like the act of a lunatic, and at others, like a cold-blooded crime masquing as one."

"Why the delay?" he asked. "Zulie Fishwire was killed—what? A year ago last September? If it is the same man, why did he stop? And why did he start again?"

"I thought he might have left Boston and come back. If

he were a sailor on a deepwater vessel, for instance, or a whaler. Lieutenant Coldstone is writing to the authorities in Philadelphia and New York. John says he thinks the note we found in Mrs. Pentyre's pocket, arranging the meeting, is a forgery, but whether that means the killer is in the Sons, or Mrs. Pentyre had simply given him the code for another reason, or whether he just had access to her correspondence, I don't know."

Quickly, she sketched out to him all that Lisette Droux had told her about the young gentleman, *beau comme Adonais*, and what the inhabitants of Love Lane had had to say about Abednego Sellars. "I suppose it would lie beyond the bounds of coincidence for him to be Mrs. Pentyre's mysterious lover—"

"Not unless Mademoiselle Droux is singularly desperate or singularly blind," put in Revere. "Abed is a well-looking man—and God only knows what women see in any man—but *beau comme Adonais*? Never." He shook his head. "And yet—he's never been the same, since word came to him of Davy's death. In the time between their getting word that he'd been pressed into the Navy, and word of his death—over a year, that was—he was . . . I feared he'd go out of his senses. I think it was that, put a wedge between himself and Penelope. He'd take out his rage on her, then go try to drink himself unconscious, and all the while keeping up his position in the church, and running his business." He fell silent, and a muscle in his temple stood out, with the clench of his jaw.

In time he said, "He was one of the constables of the Cornhill Ward, during the summer of '72. He would have heard the details of the other murders. And," he added with a sigh, "he was in town the night of the twenty-fourth, for all his prentice-boy said he was in Cambridge. I know, because I saw him, drinking at the Green Dragon."

"At what time?"

"About seven. Long after the gates had been closed."

Revere poured her out tea. "It does seem like two criminals, doesn't it? One mad—and maybe dead by this time—and the other . . . pretending to be him, for his own ends."

"And Lieutenant Coldstone is certain—for what reason I don't know—that that second criminal is John." She folded her hands around the teacup, grateful for its warmth. "Not you, not Sam, not any of the actual leaders of the Sons of Liberty . . . specifically John. And in all of this, Rebecca has still made no appearance, nor has her body been found. I think—" She turned her face aside, and found herself suddenly having to work to keep her voice level. "I think it would actually be rather difficult to conceal a body in a town this crowded, for this length of time."

"Easier in winter than in summer," said Revere gently, and Abigail nodded.

"There is that. Now tell me—" She took a deep breath, and brought her gaze back to his. "Now tell me about Jenny Barry."

"Jenny Barry." Revere handed her a two-penny pottery sugar bowl—he who made the most exquisite silver ones in the colony—and sat for a time, collecting his thoughts.

"Myself, I think it was only a matter of time, before she met the end she did," he said at last. "She was one of your bawdy whores, who reveled in being a disgrace. A big well-made Irish girl, with hair like a bunch of carrots. If she had money she'd spend it, on gimcrack ornaments and rum. I doubt she drew a sober breath since before she was a woman, and she could not have been twenty-five when she died. Everyone on the North End knew her, if not to speak to then by sight: There wasn't a man who crossed the Mill Creek by day or night she did not approach. There's a story—" He grinned suddenly at the recollection. "'Tis said one day Governor Hutchinson's coach was stopped by some pigs in the lane, and she climbed in and sat on his knee, and offered him a drink from her bottle. She followed me once the whole length of Ship Street, shouting to the world how I was afraid of a real woman, as she called herself . . ."

"And were you?" asked Abigail, amused.

"Petrified. Still," he said more quietly, "her death was an obscenity. I don't know why I didn't think of her, the moment I saw Mrs. Pentyre."

"Possibly because hers was a death that falls more often to poor whores, than to rich ones?"

"Possibly." He sounded sad.

"Lieutenant Coldstone says she was killed somewhere else, and brought to the wharf—"

"Lord, yes. In the summer the whole world's out on the waterfront 'til all hours." Revere's fingers, long and deft, toyed with the carved-horn spoon. "Jem Greenough—he was constable of the ward that summer—said he thought it must have been done at the Queen of Argyll, across the way, which was where she generally took her men-friends. The landlord there is a cold-blooded rascal, and keeps open 'til dawn in the teeth of church and Army and all. He has rooms on his yard that nobody sees who goes in and out; all the girls use them. If he found her in one of them, as we found poor Mrs. Pentyre, he'd have done as we did."

Abigail sniffed. "At least Sam didn't put Mrs. Pentyre's body out in the road. Or was that only because Mrs. Pentyre wasn't found until daylight?"

"Where Sam is concerned, and the liberties of Englishmen," returned the silversmith quietly, "I would put nothing past him."

"You said Abednego Sellars was constable over in the Ninth Ward, in '72 when Mrs. Barry was killed," said Abigail after a time of thought. "Davy Sellars was taken in '68 or '67, so Sellars would have been frequenting the taverns in the North End pretty heavily by then—"

"Well, he always did," said Revere. "And he knew Jenny Barry, if that's the direction I think this is heading. I saw them together on three or four occasions, at the Queen or the Shores of Paradise. Did it mean anything?" Revere shrugged. "For that matter, she'd had a kiss or two off Sam, at a Pope's Night parade . . . and there was more in one of Mrs. Barry's kisses than there is to some marriages I've seen. Certainly to Abednego's. But whether that means he'd murder the woman, and two others, and lure one of them to the house of one of our own pamphlet-writers instead of out to someplace like the Commons or the far side of Barton Point . . ."

He looked up at the tinkle of the shop-bell, and the boy's voice called from the shop, "Pa? It's Mr. Adams."

Abigail said, "Drat!" and Revere handed her to her feet, gave her her marketing basket, and led her to the small door to the yard.

"The gate there past the shed will take you out to Wood Lane, by the Cockerel Church." He pointed. "Just one request, in trade for the information I've given you, Mrs. Adams. Talk to me—or to John—before you take any steps."

She tilted her head warily. "So you can forbid me, for the good of your endeavor?"

"So we can make sure someone goes with you," he said quietly. "Good luck." He stood in the rear door of his shop until she was through the little gate.

Abigail turned them over in her mind, as she walked back toward Queen Street. Jenny Barry, Zulieka Fishwire, Perdita Pentyre. Coldstone had spoken several times of the differences between them: *In what way*, she asked herself, *are they alike?*

Are we in fact seeking two criminals here, or one?

Just because Perdita Pentyre received a note luring her to the place of her death, it does not mean that the other two did not.

One killed in a tavern, another in her house, a third in the house of a friend. She saw again the single column of smoke rising above the mansarded slates of Richard Pentyre's mansion; heard the constant soft stirrings and creakings that had murmured at the edges of her interviews with Scipio, with Charles Malvern, with Lisette Droux in the Malvern kitchen.

Maids, butler, grooms at Pentyre's house had been the guarantee of Perdita Pentyre's protection. Those servants who knew everything, who slept beneath the same roof albeit in their maze of little attic chambers up beneath the rafters. Had it been chance only, that the murder had taken place on the night the Tillets were away?

A group of men passed her, newly in from the country, rifles on their shoulders and powder horns at their belts. They stepped respectfully out into the center of the street, to let her keep the higher and less mucky ground close to the wall. In their way, they were precisely like the Pentyre servants. Their mere presence was a guarantee of protection. *It is when we are alone that we are vulnerable.*

She wondered if she were insane, for agreeing—nay, demanding—to go across the harbor to Castle William that afternoon. Of course, she told herself, Colonel Leslie was highly unlikely to clap her into a cell and send word to John to present himself alone and unarmed somewhere at midnight or he'd never see her alive again . . .

Considered in that light, her peril (if there was one) sounded as far-fetched as the situation in *Pamela*, which always caused Rebecca to roll her eyes at the ceiling. John, too—last night, as they'd gotten into bed, John had said, "That farrago is *honestly* your favorite novel?" Rather defensively, Abigail had replied, "And why would it not be?"

"You honestly think that a rich and powerful gentleman would—or would be able to—hold a young woman prisoner in the attic of a country house, with the connivance of not one but two entire staffs of servants, *and* of every other person in the countryside—"

"You've obviously never seen a family putting pressure

on a girl to marry a man of property and power whom she doesn't like," she'd retorted, and the quibble had passed to other matters. Perhaps it was that discussion which had touched her thoughts, perhaps her dream of rain and darkness.

But as she walked along the street with the morning sky pale pewter beyond the line of the gables above her, she thought, *An attic.* Sam's patriots had been poking into cellars, snooping around smuggler-caches, investigating warehouses for nine days, finding nothing . . . All those places where the smugglers hid their packets of tea and casks of cognac and other goods that the English Crown forbade English colonists to buy from any but English merchants. And those places all had this in common: that they could be entered by a stranger from the street.

With the complicity of the household, Rebecca could be hiding—or be hidden in—any house in town.

Or her body could be buried in any cellar.

The thought halted Abigail in her tracks, in the middle of the street; a coldness fell on her like the shadow of a storm. *She's being held.*

And the next instant: *That's ridiculous . . .*

Isn't it?

But her heart was beating fast, and she felt as she'd felt when, as a child, she'd grasped the logic that linked mathematical principles, or had understood for the first time why God *must* know who would be saved and who damned: that sense of seeing gears mesh, of facts falling into place. Before the eye of her mind flashed the open shutters of the Tillet attic, closed for the year that she'd been visiting Rebecca on Fish Street. With the Pentyre household in an uproar over its mistress's murder, would Lisette Droux even be aware, during that first day or two, of someone being kept in one of those myriad little chambers marked by the stylish mansion's dormer windows? Would she have thought to mention it? Particularly if some other explanation had been given that required her silence. *We must make our nest against a storm—*

Ludicrous. The immediate, overpowering sense of reasonableness faded as swiftly as it had come. John was quite right: *You honestly think* . . .

No. She didn't. Not honestly.

But the case Mr. Richardson had made—for a young girl who was powerless, with no family connections and no one to inquire after her, being held captive—returned again and again to her mind as she hurried her steps toward home.

She reached Queen Street in time to do her own share of the housekeeping—sweeping, cleaning the lamps and candlesticks, making up the aired beds with Nabby's assistance—before plucking and dressing the ducks she'd bought and putting into the oven the bread she'd set early that morning to rise. She should have done laundry Monday and Tuesday, while she was out gallivanting through the countryside, she reflected. *It must certainly be done this week.* And . . . and . . . and . . .

Charley and Tommy clung to her skirts one moment, then caromed off back to their blocks and gourds.

In between all that she ate a quick nuncheon of bread, butter, and cheese, knowing she'd get nothing until supper. When everyone else was eating dinner she, God preserve her, would be on her way across to Castle Island—and probably too seasick to even think of food.

The thought brought another one. Before she left to meet Lieutenant Coldstone, she wrapped up a small crock of butter, a wedge of her mother-in-law's justly famous cheese, half of one of her new-baked loaves and some of the pears she'd bought, put them in one of her baskets, and left the house slightly early, to give herself time to carry this offering to Hanover Street. The Hazlitt bookshop was closed.

When she went round to the back, she could see through the shed windows a great stack of paper beside the printing press, a much smaller pile of finished pamphlets, and a dozen hung up to dry. From the half-open door of the keeping room came the sound of voices, Mrs. Hazlitt's very fast, running over Orion's interjections—

"—Don't interrupt me, darling, you never listen to me now, you used to care what I had to say. Now you don't even care that I love you. That I have given up everything, everything in my life for love of you—"

"Of course I love you, but—"

"Then listen to me! Please, sit down and listen to me for once—"

"Mother, I always listen—"

"You don't! You're always thinking about just dosing me with that horrible laudanum—don't go looking around the room for it while I'm speaking, please, please, my darling—"

Orion caught Abigail's eye as she stood in the doorway. He'd clearly been interrupted in the midst of a print run, his sleeves rolled to his biceps, his shirt, apron, flesh all smudged and sticky with ink. He moved his head, with a slight, desperate jerk, toward the open door of the staircase (*And with the cost of wood it's no wonder he can afford no better help than Miss Damnation, with the heat wasted . . .*). Remembering what he'd told her about laudanum, Abigail set her basket on the sideboard and moved swiftly to the narrow door.

If the house itself, shop and all, covered more ground than a couple of good-sized tablecloths she would have been surprised. The second floor boasted one moderate bedchamber and a sort of windowless cupboard where paper, ink for the press, and the slender stock for the store were kept. When Abigail had first encountered Orion Hazlitt, upon moving to Boston, he'd had an apprentice who'd slept downstairs in the shop, and an elderly and crotchety housekeeper who'd slept in this cupboard. This good woman had left the household in high dudgeon when Lucretia Hazlitt had arrived, bag and baggage, and had informed her son that she would now live with him and keep his house. The bedchamber that had been Orion's was, when Abigail ducked into it in quest of the laudanum bottle, crowded with trunks of his mother's dresses, and the housekeeper's sleeping-cupboard crammed with printing supplies. Rebecca had written to her that Orion kept that room locked at night and frequently during the day, for his mother had a tendency to go in and dump the contents of the household chamber pots there, if she felt she was being ignored or put off with excuses.

The laudanum bottle stood on the corner of the mantel—a fresh one, by its fullness—and Abigail noted that a cozy fire burned to warm the room despite the fact that Mrs. Hazlitt spent most of her day in the keeping room. The bed had been neither made nor aired nor, by the smell of the room, had the chamber pot been emptied. *Poor Orion!* There was a trundle bed half pulled out beneath the big one, presumably for Damnation. At a guess, Orion would be sleeping on a pallet in the keeping room . . .

At the head of the stair, laudanum bottle in hand, Abigail paused, her eye caught by the ladder that led up to the attic. On impulse she went back to it, and climbed to the trapdoor—

The tiny space below the steep-slanted roof was crammed with more trunks, all the things Mrs. Hazlitt had bought in the nearly two years she'd lived with her son: dresses, sets of chinaware, clocks, birdcages, an ostrich egg packed in straw. One couldn't have imprisoned a lapdog up there, let alone a full-grown kidnapped maidservant.

You have indeed read Pamela *too many times.*

Abigail descended to the keeping room once more.

Mrs. Hazlitt was in tears by the time Abigail emerged from the staircase (and thriftily closed the door after herself), Orion holding her in his arms and covering her face with kisses. But in his own countenance was only exhaustion and revulsion, and the haggard desperation of a man who sees no light at the end of his road. He beckoned Abigail up, and it took the two of them to get his mother to swallow the medicine: She spit the first mouthful at him, cried when he forced her to swallow the second by holding her nose and keeping a hand on her mouth.

"When she gets excited like this, I'm always afraid Damnation will give her too much of the stuff," he said, when they'd finally guided the stumbling, disheveled woman to her chair by the keeping room fire. "I *must* finish the pamphlets, and I *must* get to the meeting this afternoon. Please don't think—" he began, with a glance back toward his mother. He brushed a lock of hair from his forehead, making the mess worse. "She wasn't always like this, you know."

"I know." Though in fact, Rebecca had written to her last year that according to her son, Mrs. Hazlitt had always been a horror.

"Bless you—" He lifted the napkin from the basket, his tired face lighting up. "You are indeed an angel, Mrs. Adams. Now I must fly—" His face altered, suddenly twisted with dread, fatigue, grief. "You have heard nothing, I suppose?"

Looking up at him, she wondered when he had last slept. She shook her head. Now was not the time, she knew, to lay upon him her own inconclusive findings and nightmare surmises. He was a man who bore trouble enough.

"It will be over soon." Abigail placed her hands over his, on the basket's plaited handle. "I'll make a little extra for dinner tonight, and send Pattie over with it. John tells me the *Dartmouth* must unload her tea by Saturday—a week from today—else it will all be confiscated to pay the harbor tolls. Whatever happens, it will only be a week."

He caught her wrist as she was turning away, looking up at her with ravaged eyes. "And then what?" he asked softly. "Rebecca—Mrs. Malvern—"

Saved or endangered, dead or alive, *femme seule* or spouse abused . . . Rebecca would always be some other man's wife.

Abigail said quietly, "God knows. But God *does* know—and will inform us, in due time."

Twenty-one

Visiting Castle Island on the previous Friday, Abigail had received the impression of crowding and bustle, in the brick corridors of the little fortress, and in the village of tents, huts, cow-byres, sheep pens, and laundry-lines that had grown up around its walls. When the two sailors from the *Cumberland* landed her there today—in company with the family of an English customs clerk named Burrell, two gentlemen related to the Olivers, and towering mountains of luggage—Abigail saw her earlier error. It seemed to her that at least as many tents and huts again had been newly erected, not only for the servants of the refugee Tories but for all the lesser officers and their clerks and servants who had been displaced from the fort, so that the likes of the Hutchinsons, Olivers, and Fluckners could have its sturdier roof over their heads. Smoke from cook-fires wreathed the walls and stung Abigail's eyes as she and Thaxter picked their way up from the dock. Every step was impeded by camp servants putting up shelters, sheep penned in the thoroughfare, bales of provisions, and prostitutes. The whole place smelled like a privy.

Lieutenant Coldstone met her a few yards from Castle William's gate.

"Mrs. Adams." He bowed over her hand. "I beg your pardon. I had meant to come to fetch you—"

"Good heavens, Lieutenant, with this many soldiers shifting their arrangements about I'm astonished you have a few minutes to meet me here. Did you have civilians quartered upon you?"

The chilly reserve broke into a grin at this reversal of the usual civilian complaint of the military being quartered in private homes, swiftly repressed: His eyes still smiled. "I have lived under canvas before, m'am; and that, recently enough that it is no catastrophe. The civilians forced to take refuge here, from fear of the mobs in Boston, have been neither trained to it, nor are they for the most part physically suited to such hardships. Not only the men by whom your husband and his friends feel wronged, but their wives, who have surely wronged no one, and children as well."

"And, as the Lord says to Jonah, *also much cattle*," remarked Abigail, stepping out of the way of a girl in a dirty skirt, driving half a dozen pigs through the gate. "Lieutenant Coldstone, you recall Mr. Thaxter, my husband's clerk? I assume Mr. Pentyre has consented to see me?" She took Thaxter's arm again and followed Coldstone after the pigs up to the gate, the muck of the path sucking and clinging to her pattens.

"With certain stipulations, yes."

"Stipulations?" Abigail raised her brows, and got an enigmatic glance over Coldstone's epauletted shoulder in reply.

"He has asked that I be present at the interview—at a sufficient distance that conversation in a low voice should be private enough if you choose," he added, anticipating Abigail's protest, though in fact what she felt was relief that she would not be obliged either to broach or explain the matter of his presence herself. "And he has requested that you be searched."

Abigail stopped short under the low brick tunnel of the gate. *"Searched?"*

"With all due decency." Coldstone's voice, like his features, seemed wrought of polished marble, ungiving and absolutely smooth. "I have asked the wives of five of the sergeants major here: respectable women, and honest. You may choose which of them you will, to perform the office. He would not meet you, else."

Abigail opened her mouth, outraged, then closed it again. *Why would he ask that?* Her eyes searched the face of the man before her. "He sounds like a man in fear for his life."

"Were he not," replied Coldstone civilly, "he would not be living in a single clerk's room on this island. Nor would any of the other lawyers, Crown officers, merchants, and their families currently eating Army rations. Your husband is, I might remind you, known as one of the leaders of the Boston mob—"

"He is *not*!"

"Forgive me for contradicting a lady, m'am, but he is indeed *known* as such, whatever his true position might be. And if he will take such a position, his wife must needs suffer for it, even as Mrs. Oliver and Mrs. Fluckner and the Apthorp ladies do—and, I might add, suffer to a considerably lesser degree. Will you agree to submit to the conditions?"

Abigail smiled. "I would not miss it for worlds."

The wives of the sergeants major were red-faced, thick-armed, good-natured-looking women of the kind one would meet in the marketplace any day, not the slatternly trulls described in pamphlets from one end of New England to the other (*I have been listening to too many of Sam's diatribes*). Abigail selected the one who looked most talkative, and remarked, as they retired behind a screen (there being no spare rooms in the fortress at all besides this single office), "I had no idea I was considered so formidable. Does Mr. Pentyre truly expect me to assault him?"

"That I don't know, mum. He's sure no so fussy about

others that see him—and his poor wife *did* come to a terrible end."

"Were you acquainted with her, Mrs.—?"

"Gill. Maria Gill. And only to give a good day to; as sweet and condescending a lady as you could ask, which is somethin' you don't often find in Americans, begging your pardon, mum. Not like that nasty—" She stopped herself. Abigail could not but wonder if the next words out of her mouth would have been, *that nasty Mrs. Belle-Isle*. "She'd often stop and talk with us, or with the women who did laundry or sewing here—not the girls that do for the men, you understand, but the town women who do fine work for the gentlemen. She had what my mum used to call 'the common touch': permittin' no liberties, of course, but not bein' so high in the instep as some I could name, that treats honest women as if they were the dirt in the streets."

"She was here fairly often, was she?" Abigail stepped out of her skirt and stood back while Mrs. Gill pinched and shook her petticoats ("With your permission, mum—"), turned her bodice inside out, and conscientiously removed and held up every item in her pockets and set them on the chair in their screened sanctum ("Are you sure you're warm enough, mum?").

"Well"—Mrs. Gill half hid a little conspiratorial smile—"all those town ladies, they were back and forth to dine, of course. And the officers would invite them sailing, or to reviews, or to hear the regimental band. So yes, Mrs. Pentyre was often here."

"With her husband?"

"Not always." The stout woman cast a quick glance at Abigail's face, as if asking herself how discreet she should be, then whispered, "She and the Colonel was good friends, if you take my meaning . . . *good* friends." She winked. "But Mr. Pentyre, as often as not he'd come dine with them, or ask the Colonel over to that big house he has in Boston, and why should he play dog-in-the-manger? T'wasn't as if he was sittin' home alone weepin' into his beer, nights."

"Really?" Abigail leaned forward, discreetly agog.

Pleased, Mrs. Gill said, "That's the truth, mum. A West Indian lady, a Mrs. Belle-Isle, that he set up in a house not two streets from his own, and has had brought over here—*and* got her a room for herself, when respectable people are doin' without or livin' in tents behind the cow pens—for fear that if riotin' breaks out in the town over this Donnybrook over the tea—and what on earth would Americans balk at? You can't get it at home for such a price!—there's some that would give her her deservin' for the way she lives."

"You don't say?"

"I *do* say." Mrs. Gill handed her back her bodice with a self-righteous nod. "The jewelry he's given that woman—and her not half as pretty as poor Mrs. P!—and the airs she's taken on herself . . . and casting eyes on Major Gray and Major Garrick, and even the Colonel himself, poor man."

"Was the Colonel very grieved?"

"He was shocked, of course." Mrs. Gill started to lace her up again, neat and swift as a chambermaid. "You can't not be, you know, even if you barely know someone, who's killed sudden and terrible like that. Why, our Captain when we was stationed in Halifax, he robbed the men somethin' cruel, holdin' back their pay and sellin' their rations to pocket the money himself, an' havin' my Fred flogged when he complained of it to the Colonel . . . yet when the Hurons killed him, I swear to you I cried, and not the only one in the regiment neither. And Mrs. P was a sweet young lady. The Colonel liked her by him. He had her ride with him in town like she was a queen. She'd stand at his side when he reviewed the soldiers, all pink and pretty—not like these Boston ladies who go about with faces like boot-scrapers as if a bit of rouge has got to be the Mark of the Devil, beggin' your pardon, m'am, and to each 'er own I says. Even Mr. P would joke, that she'd become queen over the regiment. But still, you know, mum, Colonel Leslie is a soldier; and these things come and go. 'Tisn't as if she thought he'd marry her, or either thought it would last. She flung herself at him, when all's said—and he didn't duck."

"Well." Primly, Abigail shook out her petticoat. "She sounds like a bit of a flirt to me, God rest her. If the Congregation didn't frown upon gossip, I'd wonder if Mrs. Pentyre gave the Colonel cause to be jealous as well."

"As to that, I'm sure I never saw sign of it." Mrs. Gill sighed. "Even when the other young officers would be gallant—as they are, you know, being so far from home, how can you blame them?—she'd let them know it was the Colonel who had her heart, at least for the time being. And as for the Congregation," she added with a grin, "if good men haven't anything better to frown at in this sorry world, m'am, I say, Let 'em frown, eh? Gives their face a bit of exercise, not meaning no disrespect."

Abigail permitted herself a smile. "And none taken, I'm sure."

Like nearly everyone else in Boston, Abigail had seen Richard Pentyre from a distance. Like nearly everyone, she had for years thought him an Englishman, and the caricature of one, at that: slight, girlish, excessively tailored and intensely peruked. He bowed to Abigail with great politeness, and took a seat on the opposite side of the heavy table like a man who providentially finds the chairs so arranged, rather than one who has insisted on their placement to keep the greatest distance from his caller. He said, "Mrs. Adams," in his wisp of a voice, but did not offer to touch her hand.

"Mr. Pentyre." Lisette Droux's voice came back to her: *He laughed and joked his wife about her lovers, yet if any man crossed him in a business way, he make sure that that man became truly sorry that he had done so.* "Thank you for seeing me."

"The honor is mine." His eyes were dark, intelligent, and wary: because he knew more than he was saying concerning his wife's death? Or because he expected that at any moment she would whip a pistol out from beneath her skirts? "Lieutenant Coldstone said that you thought I could be of assistance in some way?"

"I know not if anyone can be," said Abigail, hoping her voice and expression combined to express wearied resignation. "But I know not where else to turn. I am a friend to Mrs. Malvern—the woman in whose house—"

He raised a hand to stay further words, and turned his face aside. "Yes," he said quickly, though his expression registered nothing. "I know who Mrs. Malvern was."

"Pray forgive me for bringing up a subject that I know must grievously distress you." *Was?* A thoughtless trick of speech? Or—Knowledge of something that others didn't have? "Yet I—and, I might add, Mr. Malvern—are grasping at straws, in the matter of Mrs. Malvern's disappearance."

Annoyance flickered across his face at the mention of Malvern's name. "Pray believe me, m'am," he said, "though I sympathize with you in your concern for your friend, I had no idea that my wife had formed so distasteful a connection. While I'm sure Mrs. Malvern was a paragon of virtue and beauty, her husband's habit of using members of his family—in particular his son and daughter—to obtain information about his trade rivals would have caused me to forbid the acquaintance, had I known of it."

He was watching her again, with an intentness that she found hard to attribute merely to grief for a wife who had betrayed him. Trying to read her, she thought, as she—her eyes downcast in a counterfeit of confusion—was trying to read him.

"They had no acquaintance in common that you know of?"

"In the past, I'm sure they did. Given Mrs. Malvern's current circumstances, I can hardly imagine any woman with whom my wife was associated, who would acknowledge the connection."

The revival of the implication that Rebecca had deserted Charles Malvern out of a craving for low company brought a flush of anger to Abigail's face, and though she lowered her head in submissive assent, she took a good deal of pleasure in saying meekly, "Of course, sir. And would you know what to make of the story that I have heard, that you were seen in Hull Street, at half past eleven on the Wednesday night, on foot and walking toward the waterfront?"

Pentyre couldn't stop himself. He threw a fast glance over his shoulder, to see if Coldstone had heard.

If he but blench . . .

"That is a lie," he said—not loudly enough for the words to carry to the Lieutenant.

"Is it?" said Abigail in a normal tone. "I understood that—"

"I am a man with many enemies, Madame, and as such I cannot hope to keep track of the calumnies that may be circulated about me by the disgruntled. Fortunately, it is well attested—by the sons of Governor Hutchinson—that I was at cards with them, in their father's mansion on Marlborough Street, quite at the other end of the town." As he spoke his eyes shifted, and for a moment, behind the wary anger in them, she thought she saw fear.

Why fear?

"I'm sorry that I could not be of more assistance." He was on his feet. At the other side of the office, looking the tiniest bit surprised, Coldstone rose from his chair.

Hamlet, or Viola, or the wily Odysseus, would have had

precisely the right question to call the merchant back, to pique his vanity or his curiosity or his fear of what she might know and thus elicit further revelations . . .

And all she, Abigail Adams, could do was incline her head, and say, "I thank you for your trouble, sir—and for the information you have given me."

Would a murderer have turned back, asked in not-quite-concealed concern, *And what information was that, pray, my dear Mrs. Adams?*

Richard Pentyre got out of the room as promptly as he was able—she had the impression he only barely kept himself from backing from her presence.

"Please wait here, Mrs. Adams." Coldstone favored her with a slight bow, and followed him out.

Abigail folded her hands, her heart beating hard. She had touched him on the raw, beyond a doubt; frightened him. It crossed her mind to wonder what he was going to say to Coldstone, who might very well have seen or heard something. Or would it suffice merely to play his trump card: *I am the Governor's friend. The law does not apply to me.*

In certain matters it didn't. The fact that the Governor's friends, like the King's, could get away with financial peculation and chicanery with the customs was one of the things that most maddened Sam, and John, and others. In a question of murder, however, he was likely to find matters less amenable to influence.

Or was he? The thought was a disconcerting one. In *Pamela*, as John had derisively pointed out, the lustful and demanding Mr. B held his power precisely as Governor Hutchinson held it: because every man's livelihood depended upon his whim. No one considered a servant girl's honor more important than keeping a roof over one's own head or food on one's family table.

The door opened. Abigail got to her feet, lips parting to ask Coldstone what Pentyre had said—

Only it wasn't Lieutenant Coldstone in the doorway, but a tall, buxom, black-haired young girl in an overly colorful parakeet green dress.

In fact—Abigail belatedly identified the newcomer—it was the Royal Commissioner's daughter, Miss Lucy Fluckner.

"Mrs. Adams?" The girl's husky hesitancy, Abigail guessed at once, was not her usual habit. "We need to speak to you. I-I think it's on a matter of life and death."

Twenty-two

The Fluckners had two rooms in what was clearly the officers' quarters of Castle William: Abigail wondered who had been displaced to make way for them. The suite had obviously been intended to house an officer and his servant, for a door connected its rooms, and in addition each had a door and a window looking out onto the parade ground. A light burned in the window of the smaller chamber, an uneasy reminder that, though daylight remained in the sky, evening was coming on fast. The wind, which, as she had prayed it would, had slackened for her crossing, was now getting up again, and whistled shrilly around the fortress walls. It would be a bitter night for those lodged under canvas. As she crossed the parade in Miss Fluckner's wake, Abigail checked her watch, reflecting that she had best hold fast to what she had instructed Thaxter to tell Lieutenant Coldstone: that she would return in one hour.

The Lieutenant's probable reaction, when he returned to the office and found John's clerk there instead of herself, she put from her mind. Instead she mentally marshaled the arguments she'd have to present to this decisive-looking young lady—or her irascible father—about where she, Abigail, was supposed to spend the night—

And tried to salve her conscience about playing sleuth-hound on the Sabbath yet again.

A matter of life and death?

"No one will believe Philomela when she says she's

in danger," said Miss Fluckner—who was, Abigail was pleased to see, one of the few women of her acquaintance who walked as briskly as she did herself. "They say—Papa says—she just doesn't want to be sold, because I indulge her and she's afraid that another master wouldn't." Though Colonel Leslie had clearly given orders that the open parade in the center of the fort was to remain open, all around its edges pens had been set up for sheep, cows, pigs. As they approached the doors Abigail was obliged to gather up her skirts lest they be caught on the corners of makeshift chicken-coops. "Papa says she's sly, playing on what he calls my 'romantical fancies.' Papa says all Negroes are liars."

"I expect a good number of slaves do learn to lie, if 'tis the only way they'll escape a beating," remarked Abigail rather drily. "And since their masters would sooner blame them than themselves for things that go wrong, one can scarcely take issue with this evidence of intelligence on their part. I am pleased that you're treating your servant's danger seriously, but what prompted you to come to me? Don't tell me my reputation for detecting wrongdoing has spread beyond this affair of Mrs. Pentyre?"

"But it *is* about Mrs. Pentyre's murder." Miss Fluckner stopped before the door, regarded her with wide eyes of a jewel-like blue. "Mr. Malvern's Scipio told Philomela that you were looking for the man who did it—that you'd gone to talk to Mrs. Fishwire's neighbors, because she was killed the same way—"

"Wait a moment," said Abigail, with a sense of shock. "Are you telling me that your servant Philomela—the young woman I saw with you on Rowe's Wharf yesterday, I presume—"

Miss Fluckner nodded, black curls bouncing.

"—believes herself to be in danger from the same man who killed those other women? How does she know this? Has she seen him?"

"She thinks so. She doesn't know, Mrs. Adams, but she's mortally afraid." Miss Fluckner opened the door.

Philomela got to her feet. Abigail's impression of yesterday was confirmed. Slender and graceful, even in the neat chintz frock and mobcap of a maidservant, she was probably the most beautiful woman Abigail had ever seen. She sank into a curtsey as Miss Fluckner said, "Mrs. Adams, this is Philomela."

"Thank you, m'am, for coming." The young woman's voice was as lovely as her face, and her golden brown eyes were not those of a girl who indulges in "romantical fancies." "And thank you for believing me, and Miss Fluckner. For a swear to you as I'm born, I'm telling the truth, so far as I know it."

"And what is the truth?" At Miss Fluckner's gesture Abigail took a seat in one of the room's two cane-bottomed chairs; Miss Fluckner herself sat on the bed. Rods had been rigged from the ceiling, and calico curtains, in an approximation of a half-tester—cryingly necessary, thought Abigail, given the chill of the room and the doll-like petiteness of the fireplace. "That the man who murdered Jenny Barry, Zulieka Fishwire, and Perdita Pentyre seeks also to kill you? What makes you think this? Please speak freely," she added, seeing the automatic look of reserve—so common to even the best-treated of slaves—that flickered across the back of Philomela's eyes. Abigail glanced at Miss Fluckner for confirmation, then said, "Nothing that you say will be repeated, or will be held against you."

A ridiculous assertion, she railed at herself the instant the words were out of her mouth. Even the most trusting bondswoman wasn't about to state some of her real opinions in the presence of members of a race who could get her whipped if they didn't like what they heard. But it seemed to reassure Philomela.

"I don't know about Mrs. Pentyre, m'am," said the servant after a moment. "And I don't know why this is happening to me. I swear, I have never spoken to this man in my life. Even as I say it, it sounds—" She shook her head, peeped apologetically at her young mistress. "It sounds like something out of the novels Miss Lucy is always reading."

And Miss Lucy—to Abigail's relief and doubtless Philomela's as well—only grinned in good-natured acknowledgment.

Philomela took a deep breath, let it out. "This is what happened. It doesn't sound like much."

And it didn't. *And yet*—thought Abigail, the hair prickling on her nape. *And yet . . .*

Philomela's master in Virginia had sold her to Thomas Fluckner in April of 1772, because Mrs. Fluckner's maid had had a child, and could no longer (Mrs. Fluckner said) devote herself to the interests of her mistress as she properly should. When Philomela had been in the household about six weeks, someone started sending her poems.

"They'd be slipped in under the kitchen door at night, or poked through the cracks in the shutters. Mr. Barnaby—Mr. Fluckner's butler—would bring them to me, and joke me about having an admirer, and that's all I thought they were."

"You do read, then?"

"Oh, yes, m'am. Back home, my mistress liked to be read to. And one of my mistress's sons would write me poems—one of his friends, too. That's all I thought these were: young gentlemen's foolishness." She looked aside slightly, and down, her bronze lips tightening in a way that told Abigail that these offerings were probably not the only *young gentlemen's foolishness* that Philomela had had to put up with in her old mistress's home. She wondered how much those first poems had had to do with the decision to sell Philomela . . . far away from Virginia.

"I did show Miss Lucy," Philomela added quickly. "And I asked her, Should I show Mrs. Fluckner? I didn't want to do wrong, yet I did fear Miss Lucy's mother might blame me, for having an admirer, though I didn't know who this man was."

Lucy Fluckner put in, "Mama would have said, Philomela was encouraging him, and would have asked Papa to sell her. I thought as long as I knew, it was all right."

Abigail pinched her lips on the words, *And what possible business could it have been of yours* or *your mother's?* If Pattie had acquired an "admirer" in Boston, she herself would certainly want to know if the man was a thief who only wanted access to the household. She settled for, "Of course. You both acted very properly. Did you keep the poems?"

"At first I did," said Philomela. "Though they weren't very good, I didn't think. The first two were just about how beautiful he thought I was—" Her voice stammered a little over the words. "Then he started writing how I came to him in his dreams at night, and the things I said . . . and things we did." The room was too dim, and her complexion too dark, to show her blush. "Not the way some gentlemen write, that they dreamed of me lying in their arms and how beautiful I was in the moonlight and all how it would be a good idea if I'd make their dream come true. You know that kind of poem—"

She caught herself a little guiltily, but Abigail smiled, and said, "I have received such, yes. And very tiresome I found them."

A dimple flicked into place beside the girl's perfect mouth: vanished in a flexure of uneasy disgust. "This man wrote as if I'd truly come to him, while he was asleep and dreaming. As if that was truly *me* who'd said I loved him, who'd given herself to him, and not . . . not just a phantom out of his own head. And as if *I*—the real me—was held accountable for what his dream-me had said and done. But since I didn't know even who he was I couldn't tell him, *Grow up. It's just your dream.* I thought then he might have been a young boy, you know how they get, when they've never had a woman . . ."

She caught herself again and glanced at Abigail's face, as if worried she'd gone too far, but again Abigail nodded. "I know." She remembered her brother William at fifteen, in poetical ecstasies over one of the local Weymouth belles. Like Romeo on the subject of Rosalind—a state that had ended abruptly when William's good-for-nothing friends had taken him to one of the Boston brothels.

"And he'd write how he watched me, going about my business in the town. Not like Mr. Petrarch writing about his Laura, *I saw you crossing the bridge today and my heart stood still* . . . Specific things. *The way Mrs. Fluckner handed you that basket of apples at the market . . . How, you look so beautiful in that yellow dress with the blue flowers.* He was watching me, Mrs. Adams. I can't tell you how that made me feel. And then he wrote that in his room the night before, I'd turned away from his mirror so that he guessed that I was a demon; that I was feeding on his love, and his love would damn him. But, he said, he loved me anyway, though I was the devil's minion and his soul was in peril because—"

She stammered a little, and turned her eyes aside. Then she finished, "Because he enjoyed it when I raped him."

Abigail said softly, "Oh." And felt it to be true, in that instant, that whoever he was, he had indeed killed the others. And the awareness turned her sick with fear.

"After that I watched for him," Philomela said softly. "I burned that poem, and all the others. You know how it is, when you're scared? Everything seems . . . distorted. You almost can't tell what's real and what you only imagine. Every man on the street could have been him. There was a man I'm pretty certain *was* him—handsome, dark-haired—he'd sometimes be on Milk Street when we'd come out and get into the carriage, and he didn't seem to have much business there. But of course I only glimpsed him. And I was afraid to turn and look harder, in case it *was* him and that made him think I was in love with him, or whatever it was he thought. About a week after that Mr. Fluckner got an offer to buy me, from a Mr. Merryweather, who's a dealer in slaves and bloodstock horses and such things. Acting for someone else, our butler said. And I knew it had to be him."

"When was this? What month?"

"June," said Philomela. "The middle of June, 1772. About two days after I heard there'd been an offer for me, I heard about there'd been a murder near the docks, a woman—Mrs. Barry—killed and slashed up; I didn't think anything of it. I mean, I was shocked, of course, but I didn't think it was the same man. Then not long after that I got a long poem, an awful poem, talking about how sometimes a man has to strike down the thing he loves, to save his soul. Two of the verses talked about killing a red-haired demon with a woman's face."

"Do you still have the poem?"

"Not with me," said Philomela. "I hid it. I didn't want to look at it, didn't want to think about it."

"He also talked about killing her," said Lucy Fluckner somberly. "In the same poem, about killing her as they made love. But it was all so flowery, if you didn't know what was going on, you wouldn't know what was going on . . . if you know what I mean. Not just in the poem, I mean, but the whole situation. And this Mr. Merryweather who was trying to buy Philomela from Papa, they couldn't come to an agreement about price. Papa's incredibly stingy. He paid four hundred dollars for Philomela, and he wasn't going to take a penny less. Mr. Merryweather—and I guess his client—was very persistent for about two months. Then he stopped sending notes." Lucy shrugged.

"Two months."

September, 1772. Apple-picking time, when Tommy was born.

"I think his last note came just before Mrs. Fishwire was killed," said Lucy after a moment. "Philomela and I were just terrified, because I'd already talked to Papa about not selling her and he gave me his lecture about how she wanted to stay with us only because I spoiled her, and all Negroes lie, etc. etc. And Mama gave me *her* lecture about how that wasn't any of my business anyway, and young ladies shouldn't concern themselves with men's business etc. etc." She reached across the short distance that separated them, and gripped her servant's hand.

"And after that," said Philomela quietly, "nothing. This man I'd thought was him . . . I didn't see him anymore. But for a year and a half now, every time I go outside, it's terrible. That poem is still under a floorboard in my room, but it's like a burning coal, that I smell the smoke of, every waking moment."

"It's like the Sword of Damocles in the story," agreed Lucy. "For months—over a year—we've been waiting for the thread to break, and the blade to drop. But at the same time, you know how easy it is, to think, *Were we really making that up? Did that* truly *happen?* Or was it like the games you play when you're little, about being a princess in danger, and all the time you know that nobody *really* gets carried off and held captive in a big house far from anywhere, and has their captor fall madly in love with them. And then Philomela told me about Mrs. Pentyre."

"From whom did you hear that?"

"The woman who comes to help with the laundry, the next day. I was scared, and when I went to the market Saturday I asked about. And Mrs. Adams, it truly sounded like the same man who'd killed the others. Then a few days later Scipio told me you were asking about it, because of Mrs. Malvern disappearing, and that you'd talked to Mrs. Pentyre's French maid, and were really looking, the way the constables and the magistrates never did . . . Scipio's a sort of friend of mine," she added. "He lived for years in the same part of Virginia I come from—though he was long gone from there before I was ever born. But he knew a lot of the people I grew up with. I didn't know you by sight, but on the wharf yesterday, Miss Lucy heard the officer introduce you to her father, and knew you would be coming here today."

"And you thought you would tell me what you know of the matter? Can you remember—"

"It isn't just that," Lucy broke in.

After a slight pause—because no well-bred servant would follow into even someone else's interruption of a white lady—Philomela said, "The day before yesterday, I saw him again. Watching me the way he used to, on the way to the market."

Twenty-three

"Are you sure?"

"I'm sure." There was not a shadow of doubt in her voice. "But the problem is, m'am, I can't *be* sure. When he would watch me, the summer before last, he wore summer things: a blue coat with a good trim cut to it, and stockings and shoes, not boots. Thursday he was muffled up in a greatcoat, and boots, and a scarf, for 'twas bitter cold. But it was the man. I saw his face, and the way he stood and moved. It was the man."

Abigail was silent for a time. Throughout this recital she'd held her watch cradled in her palm, and the time stood very near four thirty. Light was nearly gone from the sky. Yet if she could not cross back to Boston, then neither could Thaxter, or anyone. With matters as they stood, would John have the good sense to wait until morning? Would he show up, alone and unarmed, in the boat of one of Sam's smuggler friends, like the hero of a gothic romance to attempt a rescue? Under ordinary circumstances, of course—

She looked back at the two young women, Lucy in her gaudy silk, Philomela who wore her extraordinary beauty like a nimbus of light. *What other victims has this man sought? Is this man still seeking?*

She took a deep breath. "What color greatcoat?"

"Gray. A sort of stone gray."

The same color as John's. And Orion Hazlitt's. And Charles Malvern's. And Paul Revere's and Nehemiah Tillet's and Mr. Ballagh on Love Lane and several score more of Abigail's male acquaintance both in and out of Boston. "Caped?"

Philomela closed her eyes, calling the scene back. "Yes. I think so, yes."

Voices sounded suddenly loud in the other room, two women bewailing the inconveniences of the island and the savage barbarity of the traitors whose insanity had taken over Boston. One of them expressed a strident hope that Sam would be hanged. Recalling Sam's outright command to John to keep her from this expedition today—and his probable reaction if John came to him with the news that Abigail had not returned—she felt inclined to agree. "And the scarf?"

Philomela's forehead puckered, trying to call back a moment that she would rather forget. "Red? Dull red, I think. What we'd dye wool at home, with madder-root."

Abigail owned three of that color, including the one she had on at the moment. "I must go," she said, rising. A man's voice cut through those of the ladies next door, gruff and rumbling. "Else I won't be able to get home at all. Is there anyone left at your father's house, Miss Fluckner?" And when she nodded, "You say this poem is under the floorboard in your room?"

"Yes, m'am. 'Tis on the second floor, between Miss Lucy's room and her mother's. There's a loose board beside the head of the bed, near the wall. Mrs. Adams, thank you—"

"Don't thank me yet. Miss Fluckner, can you send me a note, as soon as may be, authorizing me to whoever is in charge at your father's house? We live in Queen Street, anyone there will know where. I must—"

A knock on the connecting door: "Lucy, dearest? Are you ready?"

"Drat it—tea with Commander Leslie—" Lucy bounded off the bed, turned her back on Philomela. "Get me unlaced . . ."

"Lucy?" bellowed Mr. Fluckner's voice.

"I'll be dressed in a moment, Papa."

Abigail curtseyed and left through the outer door. Behind her, framed in the lamplight, she saw Philomela rapidly divesting the girl of her brilliant day-gown in a cloud of green and yellow silk.

John Thaxter was pacing the bricks fretfully outside the commander's office, looking in all directions. When he saw Abigail across the parade he strode toward her, followed by the sturdy, towering figure of Sergeant Muldoon. Rather despairingly, Abigail added Thaxter to the list of men she knew who owned caped gray greatcoats. "M'am, I've been to the wharf, the men say—"

"We're going," promised Abigail, and obediently turned her steps toward the castle gate. Distantly, the tolling of Boston's church bells carried over the three miles of tumbled gray harbor, dreary and ominous in the failing light. "Is Lieutenant Coldstone—?"

"He's with Colonel Leslie, m'am." Muldoon saluted her respectfully as he spoke. "In a rare taking he is, and the Provost Marshal, too, and trying to get shut of a mountain of business before the Colonel's to take tea with the Royal Commissioners and the wives of all these rich nobs from Boston, beggin' your pardon, m'am." He nodded toward a small group of men crossing the parade, the torchlight borne by the soldier who preceded them glittering on the bullion that decked the Colonel's dress uniform, gleaming on the marble smoothness of powdered hair. Beside the Colonel, resplendent in a caped greatcoat of some dark hue that could have been liver brown or indigo in the darkness, walked Richard Pentyre, gesturing with his quizzing glass and speaking with what appeared to be a ferocious intensity.

No sign of Coldstone. *Drat it.*

"I hope your talk with Mr. Pentyre went as you hoped it would, m'am?"

Abigail shook her head. "It wasn't a wasted trip, but Mr. Pentyre was hardly forthcoming."

"Well, you can scarce blame him, can you?" remarked Thaxter, as the freezing draft dragged at Abigail's cloak and they entered the lamplit tunnel of the gate. "Between the lawsuit over the Sellars land that's to be decided next month, and being served notice by the Sons of Liberty to—"

"What lawsuit?"

"Up in Essex County, m'am. If all this isn't solved, the thing looks to be dragging on into another session. It's been up in the courts, or some other nuisance suit that he's brought in aid of it, every time Mr. Adams and I have had a case on the docket there."

"Not—" She glanced at Muldoon, stopped herself from saying, *Abednego Sellars*, and to turn the subject said instead, "Not likely to be settled soon, if trouble comes of this tea business. I know he had notice to report to the Liberty Tree and resign his position, but I'd scarcely consider that grounds for having his visitors searched before they're permitted to see him."

"Damn it!" They emerged from the gate, into the mucky chaos of the camp around the walls. With a hasty, "Excuse me, m'am!" Thaxter dashed ahead, to intercept two sailors in striped jerseys and tarred pigtails, making their way up the torchlit path. Presumably, guessed Abigail, with deep forboding, the men who were to take her back to Boston. Their obvious reluctance to have anything further to do with the project was understandable: Darkness was closing in, and beyond the range of each smoky little campfire among the close-crowded jumble of tents and wash-lines, virtually nothing could be seen but a sense of movement in the shadows, and the occasional flash of an animal eye. Around Thaxter and the sailors, more civilians were coming up the path from the wharf: not rich merchants, but ordinary citizens of the town. Angry and harried-looking, they bore makeshift bundles and glanced right and left at the chaos with the expression of people who have been cheated of their rights. A small child was crying.

We have all been cheated of our rights, thought Abigail, pitying them yet knowing there was no good answer to their distress. *We* will *all be cheated of our rights, unless we take a stand against the Crown while yet we have a little freedom to do so.*

Beside her, Muldoon said, "T'cha! Searchin'—that's goin' a bit far, beggin' your pardon, m'am, note or no note."

"Note?" Abigail turned her head sharply, her mind still running on poems stuffed through shutters, hidden under floorboards. "What note?"

"The note Mr. Pentyre had, m'am. About how the Sons of Liberty were going to kill him and his wife both."

She stared at him, aghast, and Thaxter came striding back up the path, coat flapping. "They say they'll do it, Mrs. Adams, but you must come *now*."

"Where did they get it? Who sent it?" She took Thaxter's arm, her pattens slipping in the mud as they descended another two yards of path, turned a corner around a makeshift tavern, found themselves suddenly at the dock itself.

Muldoon shook his head. "That I don't know, m'am, I'm sorry."

"Does Coldstone have it in his possession?"

"Mrs. Adams, you *must* come—"

"I don't know, m'am. I'll ask him—"

"Mrs. Adams—!"

She allowed herself to be helped into the boat, what was called in New England a whaleboat: like a large rowboat with a sail. Scarcely what one wanted to be on the water in, on an overcast winter evening with wind howling down the bay straight from the North Pole . . .

"Who signed the note?" she asked, standing up precariously as the boat moved from the dock. "Whose name was on it?"

Muldoon looked puzzled, fishing in his memory. "Something Latin," he said. "No-vangelus?"

Novanglus. New Englander.

John's pseudonym.

And John, of course, was away at a meeting when Thaxter finally walked her up from Rowe's Wharf to Queen Street again. "Mrs. Adams, you must be froze!" Pattie almost dragged her and Thaxter indoors. The warmth of the kitchen—redolent of soap and wet bricks, for Pattie had Johnny and Charley in the tub before the fire and Nabby was drying her long blonde hair—wrapped her like a shadowy amber blanket. Woozy as she was with residual seasickness from the crossing, Abigail was suddenly, crashingly conscious that she had consumed nothing since the bread-and-butter nuncheon just after two.

On that thought came another, of the promise she'd made poor Orion. It was nearly full-dark—the sailors had grumbled about having to spend the night with the little Battery garrison, instead of rowing back to the safety of Castle Island—and Abigail was almost certain that for the pious Hazlitt household, the Sabbath had well and truly begun. Still, she reflected, she could but try.

And she knew she'd better try now, because if she so much as sat down and took off her pattens, she knew she wouldn't want to stand up again.

"Hercules—" She put her hand on Thaxter's arm. "Could I trouble you for one more Labor before you turn in for the night?"

Abigail suspected that this particular Labor would be in vain, and so it proved. The little house on Hanover Street was closed up tight, the feeblest glimmer of candlelight leaking through the cracks in the rear shutters visible only by the comparative blackness of the yard when she and Thaxter groped their way to the back door. No one answered her knock, though she thought she heard the droning voice within pause in its reading of Scripture.

When it resumed, she sighed. "No sense adding to the poor man's trouble by leaving bait out for rats." She settled the basket more firmly on her arm. "But, I couldn't sleep tonight, without having tried."

Wind screamed along Hanover Street as they made their way back, cutting through Abigail's cloak and jacket as if she wore gauze and lace. This corner of Boston, along the footslopes of Beacon Hill, was but thinly built-upon yet, and the neighborhood along Hanover Street lacked the crowded liveliness of the North End. With all shutters closed, and the moon hidden in cloud-wrack, the darkness was abyssal, swallowing the wan flicker of Thaxter's lantern and causing Abigail to wonder what people did, who were abroad in such darkness who didn't know the way. *Even thieves*, she reflected, *would have a hard time—*

She stopped, and turned to look back.

"What is it, m'am?"

What had it been? She stood for a moment, wondering if she should say anything . . . "I thought I saw a light behind us," she said.

"There's naught now." Thaxter raised his lantern—not that the single candle inside could have put out enough light to show up a regiment of dragoons at ten feet. The two of them might have been sewn up in a sack, for all either could see.

With the wind, the whole of the night seemed to be in motion: creakings from shop-signs, the constant whispered rattle of shutters in the darkness.

"Could have been a cat," the young man opined.

It could have.

"Or there's no reason that we're the only ones abroad tonight."

None.

It was only a few hundred feet, to the narrow passway that led back into the Adams yard and the warmth of the kitchen door. Abigail looked back over her shoulder half a dozen times, but never saw a thing in the darkness.

When John came home and heard what Sergeant Muldoon had said about the threat made in the name of Novanglus, his face took on that congealed, heavy look of rage that Abigail knew so well—then he shook his head, and let it go. "I must say I'm a little insulted, that the British believe I'd be such a booby as to announce murderous intentions under the name that pretty much everyone in New England knows is mine." He pulled off his wig, folded it carefully, and laid it on the corner of the table, then vigorously scratched his scalp. A small pot of cider—and two larger ones of hot water—steamed gently over the fire, and Abigail went to fetch cold chicken and a couple of slices of corn-pudding for him from the crocks where tomorrow's cold Sabbath dinner waited, cooked and ready.

Of her account of Richard Pentyre's reaction to being asked about his movements on the night of the twenty-third, he said, "In truth it's no more than I expected. Even if he didn't murder his wife, he might have been up to a dozen things he'd rather the Provost Marshal didn't know about. The fact that he's a friend of the Crown and a consignee for the East India Company's tea doesn't mean he isn't elbow-deep in smuggling cognac, silk, and paint-pigment from the French."

"Is that something Sam could find out about?"

"I suppose." John poured molasses over the corn-pudding. "If you feel like explaining to him that you're still investigating this murder."

"I do," said Abigail grimly. "While on the island I spoke to Lucy Fluckner—"

"What, Tom Fluckner's heiress?"

"And a true-blue Whig, it sounds like," said Abigail. "She told me that at the time Mrs. Fishwire and Mrs. Barry were murdered, a third woman—the Fluckners' maidservant Philomela—was having horrible poems sent to her, and was being followed, by a man whom she suspects was the killer."

"Suspects—?"

"Because of something in one of the poems, about killing a red-haired woman. A few days ago—less than a week after Mrs. Pentyre's murder, in other words—he started following her again."

John whispered, "Damn. Is she sure? Not that it's the killer, but that it's the same man who followed her the summer before last?"

"She's sure." Quickly she outlined all that the girls had told her. "There was no time to seek out Lieutenant Coldstone after I learned this, or I would have been stranded on the island for the night, and Heaven only knows what Sam would have had to say. I'll write him tomorrow. Coldstone, I mean, not Sam. At least she shall be safe there at the fort . . ."

"If the man isn't a Tory himself, and there among them," murmured John, and carried his plate to the sideboard. "Or masquerading as one. With the island that crowded, and people coming and going on business to the town, it would be easy. It does sound as if he's been away, doesn't it?"

Together they brought the tin tub from the corner where she and Pattie had stood it earlier, brought up the screen to protect it from drafts, and poured the hot water in. "There's nothing to tell us that he lives in Boston and not New York or Halifax, for that matter," said John, as he took off his coat. "In fact, nothing in any of this indicates that the man who killed Perdita Pentyre has anything to do with the man who killed the others and now, apparently, has resumed his pursuit of another woman who, like your precious Pamela, has neither friends nor family strong enough to look out for her."

"Pamela." Abigail, who had gone to fetch the candles from the table, came back around the screen. "John, tell me if this sounds mad, but—it occurred to me today—is there any chance that the reason Rebecca has not come forward—has not even gotten a message to me or Sam or Orion—is that she's . . . she's being *held prisoner* somewhere?"

He paused in the act of removing his neckcloth, regarded her in the softly flickering light with a kind of gentleness, as if she had an injury that would reawaken in agony if touched. "I think it far likelier that she is dead," he said.

"I do—I would—because of course in any house in Boston where she could be locked in an attic, she could also be buried in the cellar. Except this man, whoever he is . . . he doesn't hide the bodies of his victims."

John took the candles from her hand, set them on the chimney breast. "The man who killed Mrs. Barry and Mrs. Fishwire doesn't hide the bodies," he said. "The man who killed Mrs. Pentyre—if he is *not* the same man—only left in the open the body that he *wanted* the Watch to find. Why go to pains to imitate a crime, if not to have someone blamed for it? The point of this crime," he went on, "now does not seem to be to kill Mrs. Pentyre, but to kill *me.* I admit I will be most curious to see the handwriting on that poem sent to Fluckner's girl. Now might I persuade you," he added, "to wash my back for me, before it becomes the Sabbath?"

Twenty-four

A note from Lucy Fluckner awaited John and Abigail on the sideboard when they returned from services the following morning. Either the Fluckner household wasn't one in which the Sabbath was regarded with Puritan strictness, or its heiress had found some outright heathen among the hangers-on about Castle William to carry her message across the bay. When Abigail broke the seal, she found requests from both Miss Lucy Fluckner and Philomela Strong, that Mr. Barnaby permit the bearer to enter the house and the chamber of Philomela, to take possession of the document they would find hidden under the floorboard near the head of the bed.

Please say nothing of this to Papa, Lucy's paragraph added. *It is from the man who wrote those awful poems to Philomela the summer before last. We have reason to think that he has done something dreadful, and Mr. Adams is looking into the matter on Philomela's behalf.*

"And if I discovered my butler was keeping intrigues like this from me, at the behest of my sixteen-year-old daughter and a servant girl," remarked John, pocketing the paper, "I'd sack him. We'll be fortunate if he lets us into the house."

"You're known throughout the town as a respectable man," Abigail replied soothingly.

"I'm known throughout the Tory community as a fomenter of sedition," grumbled John. "Were I a Royal Commissioner, in hiding from the mob, *I* wouldn't let me in the house . . . particularly if my daughter has expressed, as you say she does, leanings toward evil Whiggish doctrines like our right as Englishmen. I wonder who's been sneaking the girl pamphlets?"

"The other servants, belike." Abigail put on her apron and went to the pantry, as Johnny and Nabby hurried to set the table. She shook her head in mock disapproval. "It all comes of teaching girls to read—" Both children glanced around at her, and John added gravely, "And of not beating boys soundly enough."

Solemn Johnny flashed him a rare grin.

After a cold Sabbath dinner they returned to Meeting with Pattie, leaving Nabby and Johnny home to watch the younger boys. As Abigail had suspected would be the case, the sermon, which ostensibly concerned King David, had a great deal more to do with tea and taxation than with the affairs of ancient Judea. Yet through it all her mind roved again and again to attic windows, shuttered or unshuttered, to forged notes and skillfully crafted lies. Though she had long trained her mind to shut out the profane in contemplation of the divine (which was more than Pastor Simmonds seemed inclined to do just now), she found her thoughts drawn again and again to the image of the lovely fifteen-year-old servant girl in *Pamela*, kept prisoner in the midst of a respectable community . . .

Ridiculous, she reflected uneasily. *John is right.* She had always justified her fondness for the novel with the argument that it was a paradigm of how every woman was treated, if not physically then emotionally and socially. Never before had she seriously considered whether it would be possible for someone to actually do. *I fear to be turned off without a character*, one servant quails in the novel; *He*—meaning the lustful and powerful Mr. B—*has it in his power to give or withhold a living from me*, another excuses himself.

And in truth, on several occasions Charles Malvern had actually imprisoned Rebecca for periods of days or weeks, when he suspected that she would use her liberty to get in touch with her family (as in fact she had). He was, Abigail reflected, probably holding his daughter under a similar form of house arrest at this very moment, and neither she nor any man in Boston would think twice about his right to do so.

But 'tis a long way from that, to holding a woman captive when you have no legal right to do so—isn't it?

Resolutely, she tried to force her thoughts to a more sacred direction, though the pastoral tirade on the subject of the rights of God's chosen to cast off the bonds of unjust rulers hardly qualified as that. The meetinghouse was packed to the walls, as it had been for the morning service, and as they had for the morning service, John and Abigail shared their pew with half a dozen complete strangers, young farmers from Chelsea and Brookline and one from as far away as Worcester, brought into the town by the tolling of the bells and the word that was circulating the countryside: *Your Country is in Danger. The King's demands must be challenged if we are not to be enslaved.* These young men listened to the sermon with deep appreciation, shook hands afterwards with John, and said they'd heard him speak at Old South Thursday: "We're ready for anything, sir."

Reflecting on the number of things that could go wrong in the eleven days between now and the deadline for the tea's unloading, Abigail thought, *We had better be.*

The Fluckners lived in Milk Street, a new and extremely handsome house, suitable to a man who was not only Royal Commissioner of Massachusetts but proprietor of a million acres in the Maine district to the northeast. Beyond a doubt it was crammed to the rafters with expensive furniture, fine silk clothing, costly silver and china, and similar lootable goods. "Sam claims there will be no looting," murmured John, surveying the tightly shuttered brick façade. "The Sons of Liberty learned their lesson when Governor Hutchinson's house was gutted; there are standing orders that anyone who loots the houses or goods of the Tories will be punished. If we lower ourselves to the acts of criminals, we will lose our support among men of good character, both here and in England, and justify the Crown in treating us as such."

"Which includes murder as well as theft."

"Precisely." His mouth tightened. "I dearly wish there were a way you could ask to see this 'Novanglus' note of Coldstone's without displaying in turn the one that was on Mrs. Pentyre's body. 'Twouldn't take a clever man long to guess the code, if he knew already that she met her end on a Wednesday night at close to midnight. Nor do we know how close they are to unraveling whatever other papers Mrs. Pentyre may have left—including, you say, all Rebecca's previous notes." He shook his head, forestalling her unspoken question. "It can't be risked." He led the way across the street.

But the knocker had been taken from the Fluckners' door. When they walked around the side of the house to the carriageway, they found the gate into the back quarters shut and locked. John glared at the shuttered windows, and returning to the front, pounded on the door with his fist.

"The droppings I saw through the gate of the carriageway were fresh," provided Abigail. "And there's smoke in the kitchen chimney."

"Fluckner's probably given orders to open to no one they don't recognize." John gave the portal an impatient and un-Sabbathlike kick. "And it's too much to hope, that he'd permit his daughter to come back to town to get his servants to open up the house—even to someone who *wasn't* under suspicion of treason and murder. Always supposing," he added, as he came down the single brick step, "that telling Fluckner of the poem in the first place wouldn't cause him to sell the poor girl out of hand, to spare himself trouble."

"For something she couldn't help?" Abigail stopped in her tracks, half inclined to go back and have another try at the door. "For receiving poems that she didn't want, from a man who is clearly insane? Knock again, John, they might—"

"And pigs might fly." He put his hand at her back, started to lead her down the street. "I've argued in the Commonwealth courts for thirteen years, my girl, and if I had a shilling for every man who would sell a slave rather than deal with more than an hour's 'nonsense,' as men like to call it, from people that slave might attract to the household . . . Well, I'd have bought you a house as big as that one, and a new lace cap to wear in it."

They turned the corner onto Cornhill. It was barely four, yet lamplight shone in many windows, where children in their Sabbath best sat politely in parlor chairs while mothers read the Scripture to them, or told them Bible stories as Abigail's father had told them to her. The taverns and ordinaries were of course closed, yet in every one they passed, Abigail saw lights behind the shutters, where the men lodged there gathered, muttering with talk.

It is a dangerous game they're playing, Sam and Mr. Hancock and Dr. Warren and the others, she thought. All those meetings, at Old South and Faneuil Hall, were not just to keep spirits roused and angry—and to keep that potential mob of farmers and countrymen in town—until the date passed on which the tea must be confiscated.

The Sons of Liberty had to keep that anger just below the boiling point. To keep it from erupting into uncontrolled violence, from giving the Governor an excuse to call in extra troops, an excuse to say, *These men are criminals, not defenders of Englishmen's rights as they claim.*

Her hand sought John's. "Should I try if I can get Lieutenant Coldstone to help us open Fluckner's door?"

"If you think we can guarantee he won't make that poem disappear, since it proves I'm *not* the killer."

"In other words, we need a witness to its discovery."

"We need a witness who won't be intimidated by a British threat," said John. "That is, always supposing the poem has any bearing on the Pentyre matter at all. It may not."

"Do you doubt that it does?" asked Abigail, surprised.

"Not the slightest."

Abigail looked for Queenie the next day at the market, turning in her mind possibilities that seemed, when viewed from one angle, to be the fantasies of a schoolgirl dream. Yet her mind kept returning to the lakes of blood on Rebecca's kitchen floor, to the stains of mud and dampness on the green and white counterpane, the glint of scissor-blades in the shadows of the hall, and she knew that the lunacy which she suspected possessed Hester Tillet was as nothing compared with the madness whose existence could not be denied.

Even a man who would deliberately mimic such crimes, for whatever goal of politics or vengeance, is no more sane than the devil who originally perpetrated them.

As if that brief glimpse of madness had opened some terrible inner door, she seemed now to be conscious of lunacy everywhere. *What had Lucy Fluckner said? You know how easy it is to think, 'Were we really making that up . . . ?'*

She didn't know.

All she knew was that she wanted, by hook or by crook, to get into the Tillet house and have a look at the south attic.

Queenie was nowhere to be found at the market. Abigail spotted Mrs. Tillet's tall, starched cap almost at once among the stalls, and kept well clear of her. The cook could be ill—according to Rebecca, Queenie was a determined malingerer. Yet, Mrs. Tillet was an even more determined taskmistress, and ferociously disinclined to let any member of her household abdicate their duty.

Curious.

I'm going to feel very silly indeed, Abigail reflected as she moved swiftly, lightly away from the market square—her basket still empty—in the direction of Fish Street, *if I find that there is some perfectly simple explanation to the yard being kept locked up, the rear house going unrented, and the Tillets' obvious desire to keep people away.*

The gate into Tillet's Yard was still locked when Abigail reached the alley. Stepping back until her shoulders touched the opposite wall, she craned her neck to look up, and saw the south attic's shutters had been opened again. The inner sides, folded back against the rain-wetted dark of the gable, were dry, the glass beneath them unbeaded with any trace of last night's showers.

Surely it isn't possible. Mrs. Tillet isn't that *mad.*

She pulled her hood up to conceal her face, and moved inconspicuously to the end of the alley, in time to see a porter with a laden handcart engaged in an argument with Nehemiah Tillet outside the door of his shop. The handcart blocked traffic, but Tillet was gesturing impatiently to have it unloaded into the shop, as before, instead of into the yard.

Of course, she reflected as she retraced her steps down the alley, to circle around through somebody's garden and pigyard into Broad Alley and thence to Fish Street on the other side of the Tillet shop . . . *Of course a violent murder in his rental house could have changed his mind about leaving the gate open. But surely not in broad daylight?*

It didn't seem to have affected the landlords of Zulieka Fishwire's house—or that residence's ultimate rentability.

As she approached the shop from the other direction, Tillet, his apprentice, and the porter were struggling with a large box. Abigail slipped casually into the shop, and passed through it to its rear door and into the yard. Though she was tempted to investigate Rebecca's house—closed-up and forlorn near the locked alley gate—she made her way instead to the kitchen, where Queenie was as usual sitting at her ease at the kitchen table drinking a cup of tea.

"Mrs. Adams!" She sprang to her feet and looked immediately—her face contracted with guilt—at the tray that rested on the other end of the table. Wicker—like everything else in the kitchen rather battered and grimed and clearly picked up secondhand from someplace else—and bearing a pottery pitcher of water, and a pottery plate on which lay one slice of bread, rimed with the barest film of butter. Beside it sat an enormous basket, stacked with cut and folded packets of muslin and calico: the component parts of shirts.

"My dear, I've been sick with worry over you!" cried Abigail. "I was afraid you were ill, knowing how sensitive your system is to horrors and strain!"

"If only you knew the whole!" groaned Queenie, and passed her wrist over her sweatless brow, with the air of an enslaved Child of Israel stealing momentary respite from the task of building the Great Pyramid single-handedly. "I know not where 'twill end! And Mrs. Tillet is like a woman possessed!"

"How is this?" Abigail dropped, unasked, into the other rush-bottomed chair and puckered her brow in earnest readiness to listen to whatever Queenie had to say—noting, as she did so, that the teacup Queenie was drinking out of was one that she, Abigail, had given Rebecca. Though Nehemiah Tillet had on Monday dropped a small box containing "Mrs. Malvern's things," a glance at the sideboard told her that the Tillets had in fact appropriated plates, glasses, and silverware—anything expensive or of good quality—for their own.

"I have warned her," cried Queenie, shaking her head and pouring Abigail some tea. "She will not listen! Not to me nor to anyone! No good will come of it—"

"Of what, for Heaven's sake?" She took care to make herself sound profoundly concerned and not ready to grab Queenie by the shoulders and shake the information out of her.

"And the whole thing is simply shredding my nerves, Mrs. Adams! From the moment Mr. Revere shouted to me to come—"

So that's how they did it—

"There has not been a moment, when I have been free of migraine, or palpitations of the heart, or the sweats . . . Feel my forehead, if you don't believe me, Mrs. Adams! Last night I could not get a wink of sleep, not one single wink, and what it's done to my digestion I daren't think! My husband was the same way, all nerves, poor soul . . . Of course I was stronger then—"

"You have always inspired me with your strength, Mrs. Queensboro," affirmed Abigail desperately, knowing Mrs. Tillet was not a woman to linger in the marketplace.

"No more." Queenie shook her head, and raised a sigh so piteous and profound that—as Shakespeare had said—it seemed to shatter all her considerable bulk. "No more. Not since his death, taken as he was in the flower of his prime . . . I have never been the same, you know . . ."

"What is it that she's done?" asked Abigail, throwing caution to the winds. "Surely she isn't making *you*, on top of all else that you have to do to run this household, sew those wretched shirts that she charges the customers seven shillings for?"

And she cast a meaningful eye toward the basket.

"Alas, if it were only that!" Queenie pressed a hand to her eyes. "Even with my migraines, that I get from doing close work—and even the smallest effort at it will set me off for days—"

Heavy footfalls shook the parlor floorboards. Had she not known the yard gate was locked, Abigail would have made a smiling excuse and taken her leave at that point, but she knew she was cornered. She turned toward the parlor door with an expression of pleasure. "Why, Mrs. Tillet—"

"Mrs. Adams." The linendraper's wife filled the doorway like the Minotaur emerging from its cave. "To what do we owe this visit?"

"I'm terribly sorry to intrude, m'am, but I was in the neighborhood and Mr. Adams had asked me, about a volume of Tacitus he had lent to Mrs. Malvern some weeks ago. It was not among the things you so kindly sent; I had wondered if by chance it had been mistakenly set aside?"

"If you're saying we might have stolen it, the answer is no," snapped the big woman, broad face flushed with anger. She slapped down her market basket on the sideboard. "And what my cook would know about the matter one way or the other I cannot for the life of me think."

"Mrs. Tillet," said Abigail, getting up, aggrieved and puzzled. "I'm most dreadfully sorry if I've given you reason to think—"

"Well, I'm sorry, too, m'am," returned Mrs. Tillet coldly. She was resolutely not looking at either the tray with the bread and water, nor the basket of sewing. "I'm sorry that *you* have nothing better to do with your time—and with growing children in your home!—then to go about the town talking to people's servants and keeping them from their honest work. Now, good day to you."

Her face stinging with rising blood as if the other woman had slapped her, Abigail was halfway back to the market square when she remembered the detail that had caught her eye as she'd come out of the shop's back door, crossed to the kitchen—a difference in detail that had snagged her attention without transmitting, at the time, any meaning.

On dozens of mornings over the past year she'd crossed from Rebecca's door to the kitchen door, to ask one thing or another of Queenie, and had noted the small furnishings of the yard repeatedly: hayfork for the cowshed, woodpile in its shelter, line of chamber pots outside the kitchen door, emptied but waiting to be scoured. (More laziness of Queenie's—Rebecca had always scoured hers with ashes, soap, and boiling water even before breakfast, one of the first things Abigail had taught her when it had become clear that Rebecca was determined to live on her own. Abigail's mother always said—a saying which Abigail had passed along—*Worst goes first*.) Rebecca's chamber pot had been a hand-me-down, like everything else in her house: yellowware with a white and blue stripe around its middle.

This morning it had been sitting in the line of the Tillet household china on the step.

Abigail slowed her steps, calling the picture back to mind. Of course, given Mrs. Tillet's penny-pinching ways, it was natural that she'd appropriate her vanished tenant's thunder mug as well as her plates and forks . . . But *why*? None of the Tillet china had been missing. Half closing her eyes, Abigail was sure of it, because the four Tillet vessels didn't match one another, either. The Tillets' blue-and-white chinaware, and three rather plain pottery vessels in different colors for Queenie, the prentice-boys who slept in the shop, and whatever orphan Mrs. Tillet was half starving and working to death that year.

So who was using the other chamber pot?

Twenty-five

"Mr. Butler." Abigail paused in the door of the cooper's shop. Mrs. Tillet's words still smarted in her mind, accompanied by other remarks made by other friends, about people who went around gossiping with servants. A little hesitantly, she said, "Might I beg a few words with Shim?"

The cooper grinned at her. "Nar, I think Shim's too set on cuttin' staves to spare a second to rest," and the boy—already hopping gratefully down from the workbench where he had been performing this tedious and finicking task—grinned back and threw his master a salute. Mr. Cooper opened the door to the shop's tiny rear parlor for them and went back to fitting hoops to a half-assembled barrel.

At least everyone *doesn't think it's a sin to want to talk to someone other than the head of the family.*

"Shim," said Abigail softly, setting down her market basket, "do you know any of the prentice-boys along Fish Street on the North End?"

"Yes, m'am." Small and wiry for his eleven years, Shimrath Walton had a quick mind and a friendly nature, even—up until recently—with the redcoats. Jed Paley—apprenticed to a house-carpenter a little farther up the street, and nearly seventeen—was acknowledged leader of the boys on Queen Street, but Shim combined a tendency to rove everywhere in town with an almost compulsive desire to talk to anybody about anything. He went on,

"Zib Fife and Rooster Tamble, we're going to all go to the meeting after dinner at Old South, about the British injustices and the King trying to make us all slaves. Mr. Butler says we can," he added quickly, with a glance through the door into the shop.

"Excellent," approved Abigail. "Do you happen to know the prentices of Tillet the linendraper?"

"Where the murder took place, m'am?" Something altered in the boy's expression: more than just the eagerness of one who has had a sensation. Almost wariness. A look of putting things together, that he has heard or overheard.

So it isn't my imagination.

"Yes," said Abigail quietly. "Listen to me, Shim, this is important—and it's doubly important that neither Mr. Tillet, nor his prentices, know that you're asking questions. But I need an agent—a spy."

Shim nodded, his soul aglow in his eyes.

"I don't think it has anything to do with the murder," she said. "Not directly, anyway. But I think there's something funny going on in that house, and I need to know what it is. Can you find out for me?"

"Yes, m'am."

"Can you find out without anyone else knowing that you're asking? That's important."

"Yes, m'am." The boy nodded again. "If they get word of someone asking, they'll move what they're doing away from there, won't they? Like if they're meeting with Tory agents, or sending out signals to the British . . . And then you won't know where to start looking again. Is that it?"

"Something like that," said Abigail. "But it isn't Tory agents or signals to the British. And you mustn't say that, or anything else, to anyone. If I'm wrong, you know how terribly gossip can hurt someone, even if the gossip isn't true."

The boy's face changed again, anger this time, and hurt. "I know that, m'am," he said quietly. "Ma had a hired girl, and she was *not* doing anything wrong, but the mother of one of the young men on our street took against her, and started stories—it was terrible, m'am. The old witch! And everyone in the church believed her, just 'cause she was the pastor's wife! It got so bad, our girl had to go away."

"Well, I don't know if what I *think* is going on is really true or not. That's why I need someone trustworthy to find out for me. So you must speak of this only to me. Furthermore, I don't know who's behind all this, so I don't know who's likely to tell on you—and me—if anyone suspects they're being asked about."

"Would they kill us?" He could not have been more thrilled had she told him he was in line for the crown of Great Britain.

"They would get *you* turned out of your apprenticeship without a character," said Abigail severely, and picked up her market basket again, with its brimming load of turnips and fish. "In which case your father would kill you—and me as well." She hesitated, not wanting to add to the drama of the occasion but unable to put from her mind the smell of the blood in Rebecca Malvern's kitchen, or the sight of a small black cat cleaning itself with the stump of a cut-off paw. "The fact is, Shim—the person who's behind this . . . I don't know what he's likely to do, to protect himself. So I want you to be *very* careful. Don't take *any* chances. All right?"

"All right, m'am." Had it been evening, he would have glowed in the dark.

"Cross your heart?"

"Cross my heart." The boy did. "I'm true-blue, and will never stain."

"I would not have asked you"— Abigail smiled, handing

him a halfpenny she had saved from her grocery money—"if I thought you were anything else."

Scouring pots, changing Tommy's clout, cleaning lamps and chamber pots, sweeping and making the beds that were Abigail's portion of the housework—all that was one thing. Abigail's conscience, if not precisely clear on the subject of pursuing her search for Rebecca while Pattie was left home doing all the work, could at least be salved by the reflection that because the girl's parents had too many children and not enough money, Abigail was in fact providing Pattie with an alternative to labor still harder and more degrading.

But there were no two ways around laundry.

It should have been done last week, when Abigail was wandering around the countryside with young Thaxter and listening to hysterical sermons delivered by the Hand of the Lord. With winter weather threatening, there was no way to tell when it would become impossible to wash the vast and accumulating quantities of shirts, chemises, dish clouts, and rough-rinsed baby dresses. As she and Pattie drew quantities of water from the well, tended the fire under the cauldrons in the yard, and filled tubs with water and lye, Abigail thought despairingly, *Forgive me, Rebecca . . .*

We are women, and bound as women are bound, to the labor of caring for those they love.

Curiously, the suspicion that had formed in her heart gave her a strange hope. *If she's being held captive in the Tillets' attic (madness! surely madness!) she at least is safe as long as Mrs. Tillet's supply of shirts holds out . . .*

Tommy tried to eat one of Johnny's toy soldiers and nearly choked. Charley and Johnny decided they were Indians and ambushed Nabby with clubs of firewood. Messalina threw up a hairball into the drawer of clean shirts.

More wood. More lye. More shirts.

John put in the briefest possible appearance for a dinner of roast pork and apples, then vanished to meet Sam and the others. After cleaning the dishes, scouring the pans, sweeping and washing the kitchen floor, and checking the fires under the cauldrons in the yard, Abigail changed her cap and assembled a dinner for Orion and his mother. "*You*," she ordered Pattie, "sit down and crochet or something until I get back. I *refuse* to have you turn a hand at the laundry until I'm here to help you."

"Yes, m'am. No, m'am."

A servant is worthy of his hire—Heaven only knew what riches were Pattie's true worth, if anyone had that kind of treasure to pay her with.

The printshop on Hanover Street was closed. The girl Damnation was in the keeping room, stolidly cleaning lamps that obviously hadn't been cleaned in days and should have been scoured that morning: *She'll have the house aflame if the soot in them catches fire*, Abigail reflected.

Mr. Hazlitt wasn't in. Hadn't been in since early morning. Did Damnation know where Mr. Hazlitt might have gone? No, m'am.

"Mrs. Hazlitt, she's near to crazy weeping over it. She says, she knows he's run off and left her, the way he did before."

And small blame to him. "Oh, I'm sure he'll be back before nightfall."

"Yes, m'am." The girl dipped her cleaning rag into a little basin of sand that had been reused so frequently that the sand was nearly the color of the soot it was intended to eradicate, and continued to rub doggedly at the nearly coal black surface of the brass. "He'd have told me, if he'd gone back off to Gilead."

"Gilead?" Having set her basket on the corner of the table, Abigail paused on her way to the door.

"Yes, m'am. The Hand of the Lord, he's wrote to Mr. Hazlitt two and three times to come. He grows main angry, when I bring him letters from Mr. Hazlitt saying as how he can't." She went to the sideboard, produced from among the litter of papers there half a dozen ragged sheets, clearly endpapers torn from the backs of books, decorated with the same virulent scrawl Abigail recognized at once from the sermons Rebecca was preparing for print. Words leaped out at her—*further excuses . . . turn thy face for the work of the Lord . . . scorn his Chosen One and set up idols before thee . . .*

Heaven forbid, reflected Abigail sourly, *that even the fate of English justice and English liberties should come before the sacred cogitations of the Hand of the Lord.*

A hundred things Orion had said to her about the conditions under which he'd grown up now returned, with the recollection of those shut-up, weathered buildings, of the hysterical atmosphere in the "House of Repentance" where sinners trembled and shrieked before the Chosen One's version of the Lord. Rather smugly, Damnation added, "I was a bride of the Chosen One," and Abigail didn't even feel surprise. Only a kind of outraged disgust.

"Are you indeed?" she asked in what she hoped was a polite voice.

"Oh, not no more, m'am. The Lord became displeased with me, and told Reverend Bargest to put me aside, because my spirit used to walk abroad in the night and pinch the babies in their cradles, and let the mice into the kitchens. I tried not to let it," she added worriedly. "Nights I'd lie awake, trying to hold my bad spirit in." She clenched her sooty fists illustratively, pressed them together against her breast. "But it always did get away, the Reverend said, and walked about the world doing evil. He saw it, he said, and others did, too. So he had to put me aside."

When she outgrew childish prettiness? Abigail studied

her face. She could not have been as much as nineteen now. *Had I known*, she thought, *I would have slept in the woods rather than take the man's hospitality.* "And did he turn you out of your home, as well as put you aside?"

"Oh, no, m'am." Damnation seemed shocked at the suggestion. "The Hand of the Lord would never turn out one of his children! It was for us that God gave us the land we live on, so that none of us can ever be turned away. The last time Mr. Hazlitt came to Gilead, the Reverend Bargest commanded me to come here to take care of Mrs. Hazlitt, in return for Mr. Hazlitt printing his sermons for him. But this Realm of Iniquities is not my home."

"My child—" The stairway door opened. Lucretia Hazlitt stepped out. Perfectly dressed, hair coiffed beneath a lace cap, she moved steadily, except for her head, which had a slight waver to it, as if the world before her eyes was in constant motion and needed to be tracked. When she came close—to take Damnation's arm—Abigail saw by the last fading light of evening that despite the gloom, the pupils of her eyes were narrowed to pinpricks with opium. "My child, I'm going out," she announced. "I shall be back in a few minutes—"

"I'm afraid you can't, m'am," said Damnation. "Mr. Hazlitt told me I wasn't to let you, and—"

Lucretia Hazlitt's face convulsed suddenly, swiftly, with an expression of agony, and her green eyes turned wide and desperate. "You must let me go," she said. "My son is dead. He met with an accident, a terrible misfortune. I saw him."

"Mrs. Hazlitt," said Damnation gently, "you know that wasn't really him."

"It was!" she insisted. "He came to me, blue and glowing. He sat beside my bed and took my hand, and I saw then that a great beam of wood had been driven into his chest! I saw the blood, my child! I saw the bruises on his face, where it had been crushed in—"

"M'am, that isn't true." The girl took her mistress's hand in one hand, and gripped her arm with the other. "You know it isn't." She turned to Abigail, added in a whisper, "That didn't really happen, m'am. It's just the opium, that makes her see things. It wasn't a *real* spirit."

"Of course it wasn't," said Abigail, startled at the girl's assumption that it could have been and that Abigail would probably believe it.

"You must let me go find him!" pleaded Mrs. Hazlitt, as Damnation steered her firmly toward her chair. "You must let me speak to him, beg his forgiveness before it is too late—"

"Of course, m'am, but first you sit down—"

Without being told, Abigail checked the mantelpiece and the sideboard for the opium bottle, then darted upstairs to the bedroom. As before, the bottle stood on the mantelpiece there; as before, a brisk fire burned in the grate, warming the room; and as before, though it was close to nightfall, nobody had cleaned the room or tidied the bed that day, nor even pushed the trundle bed away out of sight. Lying across the foot of the trundle bed, discarded at waking presumably, was a man's nightshirt. Yesterday's stockings, that lay on the floor by the trundle's foot, were a pair of yellow ones that Abigail recognized as Orion's.

She returned downstairs, and helped Damnation dose the struggling, weeping woman beside the fire, despite wailed threats that the Lord would smite them both and cast them down with Jezebel from the window to be eaten by dogs, and pleas that she had seen her son begging for her to come to him.

Walking home in the early falling darkness, Abigail tried to put aside the lingering distaste of that frowsy, smelly room. The nightshirt and stockings called up other images, of Mrs. Hazlitt dragging her son's lips down to hers: *my treasure*, she had called him, *my King* . . .

No wonder the poor man threw himself into his work

for the Sons of Liberty with such passion. Anything to be doing something other than what his life was with her . . . anything to have even the illusion of real life.

The Lord seeth not as man seeth: for man looketh on the outward appearance, but the Lord looketh on the heart.

Abigail found herself wondering very much what the Lord saw when He looked on Nehemiah Tillet's heart.

Twenty-six

Midmorning—the first break she had in transferring garment after waterlogged garment from the lye-tubs in which they'd soaked all night to the cauldrons of boiling rinse-water—Abigail changed her dress, smoothed her hair, and walked with John—who had himself spent the morning with Thaxter trying to catch up on legal papers neglected in favor of leading meetings and writing pamphlets—to Milk Street again. She had hoped that yesterday would have brought a letter from Miss Fluckner to Mr. Barnaby, but though the whiff of smoke still floated from what Abigail guessed to be the kitchen chimney, no window was unshuttered, and no footman opened to John's repeated pounding at the door.

"I'll write to Coldstone," said Abigail, as they walked back home. "Sam can change his precious codes—or explain to Philomela, on Judgment Day, after she is murdered by this monster, why he thought their preservation as they stand was more important than her life."

She thought John might have said something about how short the time was until the seventeenth—the day by which the *Dartmouth*'s cargo must be confiscated to pay the harbor dues—but he remained silent.

Shortly after she, Pattie, Nabby, and Johnny commenced the horrendous task of lifting out each dripping, steaming shirt, sheet, chemise, or baby-clout from the slowly cooling rinse-water to wring and hang to dry, Thaxter appeared in the kitchen door with the information that Mr. Malvern was here to see her.

As it had been during Lieutenant Coldstone's call last Wednesday, the parlor was arctically cold, but as on last Wednesday, Pattie—by some miracle of efficiency—had already that morning swept the grate and laid a fire. Flames crackled cheerily as Abigail entered to receive a bow from her guest. She had been used to thinking of the tough, grim-faced little merchant as old before his time, yet seeing him now she was struck by how facile her earlier judgment had been. A week and a half ago, he had been merely weatherworn and wrinkled. Now he was old. His shoulders bowed, and the lines of his face had not merely deepened but slackened under the burden of dread.

Abigail cried, "Sir!" in consternation, and instead of curtseying, clasped his hands. "You ought not to have come."

"You think I fear the rabble that have flooded into this town?" He sniffed, and took the seat that Coldstone had, only after Abigail herself sat down. "The lascars in Singapore would eat the lot of them for breakfast, and I managed to deal with *them* smartly enough. If His Majesty—" He caught himself, took a deep breath, as if forcing down the crimson anger rising to his face. "I'm quite well, Mrs. Adams," he added, in a quieter voice. *He will never be capable of gentleness*, she thought. But she had the impression of looking at a granite slab that had been broken, to let the first shoots of green peep through. "And feeling a bit of a pokenose, for I know had you learned anything—anything at all—you would have writ me, as you said."

"And so I would," said Abigail. "In the past week I have run up one blind alley and down another, chasing specters—"

Like poor Mrs. Hazlitt, conversing with the glowing blue ghost of her son, conjured by her frenzied need not to let him from her sight? She pushed the thought from her mind, though it made her stammer a little.

"I take it communication with Mrs. Moore yielded nothing?"

Abigail shook her head.

"Might—Forgive a man who's lived hard, for his suspicions—You do not think Mrs. Malvern might have instructed her to write that she was not there, when in fact she was?"

He brought the words out carefully, not like a story thought-out beforehand but like phrases in a foreign language, recently learned: an effort to break a long-held pattern of rough and hasty speech that touched Abigail strangely. Whether this new learning would hold the first time he lost his temper was another matter—she knew how desperately hard it was, to break a habit even as trivial as biting one's cuticles—but he was clearly trying. She wondered who he'd asked for pointers. Scipio?

"I think not, sir," she replied. "I made the journey out to Townsend myself—"

"Good God, woman! In this weather?" His old self slammed out of the shadows of self-imposed restraint. "It's at the ends of the bloody earth!"

"So I learned." She hid a smile. "Yet I had to be sure."

"Of all the damfool harebrained—" He caught himself in hand, and added, "Thank you. I would not for the world have asked it of you. No, no," he added, as she reached for the handbell—in its proper place, for a marvel, not that Pattie or anyone else was in the kitchen to answer it—"I can see I've taken you in the midst of your work, and will not keep you from it. I just—"

He was silent a moment, big hands clenched, staring into the fire. Then his hard gray eyes flicked up to Abigail's again and he said, "If you—when you . . . Please let her know that I stand ready to protect her, with all that I have, from anything, no questions asked. I am her husband," he added. "It is my duty—and my desire."

"I'll tell her. I pray I will have the opportunity."

He took a deep breath. "Tell her that I was wrong, to treat her as I did." He pulled out the words like arrowheads from flesh.

A few weeks ago Abigail would have sniffed, *Well, there's a first!* Now she said, "You were deceived, sir. That's all."

"I was deceived," he said, anger hardening his face at that recollection. Then he sighed. "But I was also wrong." He stood, and Abigail rose, too. He grasped her hand again, a brief, businesslike grip. "I'll not trouble Mr. Adams," he added, as Abigail handed him his hat and gloves. "I reckon he's got *his* work cut out for him. You may tell him from me that I hope it fails. Good day, m'am. Thank you—for standing a friend to Mrs. Malvern."

She said, "We all need friends."

More shirts. More sheets. The gray overcast of the sky thinned, engendering hopes that the garments would all actually dry this afternoon and tomorrow. The yard took on the aspect of a labyrinth of clothes-rope and poles, of linen flapping slowly, like sails in the doldrums, in such dreary puffs of wind as sneaked down the passways between the houses. As always, a path was left to the cowhouse, down which in due time Johnny would herd Semiramis and Cleopatra after an unprofitable day on the Commons. Abigail had just gone into the house to put together a scratch washday dinner of pork and cabbage—early, because John would be meeting with the chiefs of the Eighth Ward again—when the kitchen door darkened behind her and she heard Orion Hazlitt's knock.

"I can't stay." He set his hat on the sideboard with a

hand so uncertain that it almost fell. "I only wanted to thank you for helping Damnation with Mother yesterday. She told me—Damnation did—"

"Is your mother feeling better?"

His jaw tightened so hard that she thought it must break itself, of its own strength.

"I'm sorry—"

"No, it's nothing . . . There's nothing, really, that can be done. I've tried to act for the best," he went on, in a voice taut with frustration and pain. "But I can't be two people! Sometimes I feel—" He shook his head violently. "And Mr. Adams—Mr. Sam Adams—is on me hammer and tongs about these pamphlets, and this broadside Mr. Revere is engraving. I know the case is urgent. Mother doesn't understand—"

He stopped himself, took a breath, and with a gallant recovery of a normal tone of voice, and the actions of a man unsavaged by expectations beyond human accomplishment, flourished the market basket he'd brought. "Thank you for bringing food." He set the basket on the sideboard beside his hat. "Did we dwell in Paradise and were Mother—were Mother as calm and saintly as yourself—Damnation would still be the worst cook in the civilized world. You have once again saved our lives. You have—"

Again he fumbled for words. "You have heard nothing?" In the gray windowlight she saw that he was unshaven, and his green eyes had a restless movement to them, like a man haunted by things that only he could see.

Abigail shook her head. It did not seem to be the time, to speak of Charles Malvern, of her own questions and doubts. *Time enough*, she thought, *when we know Rebecca will be alive to choose.* Only a monster would slam the door of hope on this overburdened young man and leave him in darkness with his nightmare. "You did not tell me you grew up in Gilead."

He blinked, startled. "I didn't know you'd ever heard of the place."

"I was there—"

His eyes widened with alarm. *As well they might . . .*

"Was your mother also the Chosen One's bride?"

He sighed, and looked away. "Can you doubt it?"

"And that was why you fled?"

"Who can tell why one does what one does?" He made a helpless gesture. "I had to get out—had to get away. From her, from him . . . She said she would kill herself, if I ever left her. I knew she wouldn't—" A wry grin twisted his mouth. "She loves herself far too well. But it was like cutting off my own arm, to leave her, even knowing her the way I do. And in the end I had to sneak away like a thief. I knew Bargest would look after her. It was almost a year, before one of his people here in town saw me, and wrote to him—to them—where I was."

"His people?"

He sighed again. "Like Damnation. Like me. People who lived on Gilead, whom he can still command." And seeing her raised brows, he asked more gently, "How do you think I could look after Mother, without his ordering Damnation to live here and help me? Say what you will about him, for better or for worse, he never leaves one of his people to make their way in the world unaided and alone."

Not even Lucretia Hazlitt, reflected Abigail sadly. Even though her craziness had probably gone beyond what even the Gilead Congregation would put up with. She recalled those boarded-up houses, those shuttered upper stories. The place must have been much bigger, when little Orion and his mother—how old had he been then?—had come there, Lucretia afire with the words of the Chosen One, her "little King" dragged along by the hand. How many others, like Orion, had fled the community there? How many could the Hand of the Lord still call upon for service, here in Boston or in the communities along the bay?

Was it by his command that Orion had opened his house to his mother, despite what he knew it would cost him? Or had it been simply because she was his mother—because of that entangling love?

"I'm sorry," she whispered, and he shook his head again, and made a gesture of pushing some unseen thing away.

"'Tis all right. There's naught to be done, and I'm used to her now. I can't—" He rubbed his hand over his face, breathed in deep, and made a smile. "I keep thinking there was something else I could have done, but I don't see what it is. Please don't think ill of her."

"No, of course not."

"Tell Mr. Sam Adams that I'll have his pamphlets done for him, right enough." He bowed to her again, lifted his hat. "Now I must get back to her. She doesn't do well alone."

Abigail settled the pork and cabbage in the Dutch oven, ringed with potatoes, and buried the whole under shovelfuls of coals. The Reverend Bargest's father had been a minister, too, she recalled one of her unwilling hosts saying at some point during her night's stay—clearly one of those who'd believed in the spectral evidence of the devil's presence in Salem—and she remembered wondering at the time what would become of those young girls she'd shared that cold attic bed with: illiterate as dogs and knowing nothing but labor on the farm, the emotional ecstasies of the House of Repentance, and the Prophet's authority.

What was it Bess had said, in another context, a few days ago? *It is almost impossible to change one's way of life . . .*

She and Nabby were clearing up after dinner when Shim Walton appeared at the back door.

"Mrs. Adams," he said worriedly as she stepped out into the bedsheet maze in the yard with him, "I remembered what you said, about not telling a soul, and I haven't. But since I talked to Tim Flowers this morning—he's the brother to Hap, that's Mr. Tillet's junior apprentice—I've been thinking about it, and thinking about it, and if you don't tell someone I'm going to have to tell Mr. Butler. Because Tim says, that Hap says, that Mr. Tillet is keeping a lady locked up in his attic."

Twenty-seven

Nehemiah Tillet's brother-in-law was the magistrate of the Third Ward, and Abigail knew instinctively that he would speak to Tillet before paying a visit to the house.

Thus, Abigail wrote a note to Lieutenant Coldstone, and after a word with Mrs. Butler—Shim's master being already gone to the ward meeting with John—she dispatched Shim to find a boat over to Castle Island. The boy was back in a few minutes, not much to Abigail's surprise, considering how quickly dark was falling. With the onset of night, and the brisk wind now setting off the bay, no more boats were putting forth that day.

"But, m'am, they're saying all along the wharf—and I could hear the men shouting about it in the taverns, too—that the other two East India Company ships have been sighted, the *Beaver* and the *Endeavor*. They'll be at Griffin's Wharf, they're saying, with the flow of the tide."

"I would not have believed it." John held out his hands to the kitchen fire, rubbing them as if he'd never get his fingers warm again. Most of the household was abed. For an hour Abigail had waited up by the kitchen fire, listening to the monotonous tolling of the church bells that penetrated even the thick walls of the brick house. "Shall I write *Pamela*'s author a letter of apology?" He raised an eyebrow, which Abigail answered with a wry half smile as she brought up the bowl of bean soup that had been waiting for him on the hob.

"According to Shim—by way of poor little Hap—the south attic, whose window looks onto the alley, was unoccupied and used for storage until Thursday the twenty-fifth. The house was in an uproar that day, of course, with Coldstone and his henchmen questioning Mrs. Tillet, who returned with the luggage at about ten. Hap says, he thinks Mr. Tillet came in later, but he isn't sure because everything was at sixes and sevens, but at about eleven Mr. Tillet suddenly came downstairs and asked what the commotion was."

"Came *downstairs?*"

"As you say," murmured Abigail. "Hap had just come into the front hall and saw his master come down the stairs and walk straight into the parlor, still in his travel clothes, cloak, and hat. He said, 'See here, what's going on?' and said that he'd just then returned."

"Whereas in fact he'd returned and gone upstairs—for how long, we don't know."

"The following day—the day that you and I spent most of kicking our heels outside Colonel Leslie's door at Castle William—Hap was in the south wing of the house, where Mr. Tillet has his study, and heard what he thought were footfalls in the attic above. He'd just left both Tillet and Queenie downstairs, and of course being only a little boy—he's nine, and young for his age I think—he immediately thought it was a ghost. He tiptoed up the attic stairs and found the door locked, which it wasn't usually up until that time. But from that day the entire attic floor has been kept locked, with only Queenie keeping the key."

"At least your blameless imbecile Pamela was permitted to go about Mr. B's house." Despite his jocular tone, in the firelight John's eyes were grave. He set the empty soup bowl on the hearth beside him, stared for a time into the low-burning flame. "Madness of a different sort," he murmured after a time. "And one more difficult to prove, than the kind that carves people up with knives."

"As you say." Abigail thrust the poker beneath the logs, sending up a shower of sparks. She would have returned to the settle where she had been, but John put an arm around her waist, drew her to his knee. "Someone—probably this second lover of Mrs. Pentyre's, but just possibly Richard Pentyre himself—forced the alley window of Rebecca's house just after the rain began—possibly while Rebecca herself was at the front door asking Queenie just what she was doing lingering by the yard gate. The intruder knew the code and knew that Mrs. Pentyre would be at the house at midnight. When Rebecca came back into the house he struck her over the head, bound her, put her in her bedroom—the best evidence we have, I think, that he had heard about the two murders in '72, but was not the killer."

"Were the shutters barred or unbarred?"

"Unbarred, I think they must have been at that point. If Rebecca had sewing to do, or correcting proofs of the Hand of the Lord's wretched sermons, she would still have been awake when the rain began. He tied the bedroom door shut, then waited downstairs for Mrs. Pentyre to arrive. Rebecca came to her senses, managed to get the scissors from her sewing basket, cut her bonds if she was tied, and got the door open sufficiently to allow her to saw through the rope that held it shut. The murder must have been taking place in the kitchen when Rebecca slipped downstairs. She fled to the Tillet house, quite possibly only semiconscious from her head wound. Queenie let her in, and Rebecca may very well have muttered something about 'Don't tell anyone,' because she remembered that she hadn't concealed her book of contacts. Queenie got her up to the south attic where she lost consciousness."

"And this wretch of a cook wouldn't have spoken even

to you, whom she knows to be Rebecca's closest friend, when she saw you at Rebecca's door next morning?"

"At all events she *didn't*," said Abigail. "If Rebecca were groggy she may very well have begged Queenie to tell no one, and Queenie took her at her word. Then, too, Queenie may have made up her mind to have a look through the place herself before telling anyone anything."

"Was there any evidence she'd done so before you, Sam, and Sam's jolly henchmen returned to completely obfuscate any sign of who the killer might have been?"

"I saw none, but then, I was so shaken by what I'd seen that I may well have missed something. Then, too, the family was due back that day. If I know Queenie, the Tillet house hadn't been properly cleaned since they'd left for Medford, and it was market day into the bargain. She could well have gone to the market while we four were at the house, and returned just in time to have Sam and the others 'call on Rebecca' so that they all went in and 'discovered' the corpse in the bed where Sam had left it."

"And still didn't tell Sam or the Watch."

"That all depends on what Rebecca said to her," said Abigail. "And what she thought she could make out of the matter. The fact remains that when the Tillets returned to find the Watch and the Provost Marshal's men going over Rebecca's house and questioning the servants, Queenie *did* confide in her mistress, who sent Mr. Tillet upstairs at once to investigate. She herself—Mrs. Tillet, I mean—strode in and claimed to Coldstone that she had just arrived with the luggage, and Mr. Tillet would be along shortly."

"And Mr. Tillet—or more likely Mrs. Tillet—decided that as long as Rebecca Malvern had disappeared without a trace, now might be an excellent time to acquire a permanent sewing woman who had no family and very few friends to inquire as to her whereabouts?"

Something in his voice made Abigail ask flatly, "You think it's absurd, don't you?"

"Actually," said John, "I don't." He shifted her weight on his lap, dug in his pocket for pipe and tobacco. "Your father's parish at Weymouth is in a long-settled and peaceable town—"

"*Hmph*. You weren't there for the last uproar by those who don't approve of his views on Arminianism."

"Well, at least your neighbors are a fairly civilized crew. I've been trying cases for years in the backwoods circuit courts, in Essex and Worcester and on up into Maine. And you do find men—mostly in isolated settlements, isolated farms—who consider themselves perfectly justified in all kinds of outrageous behavior, that somehow always redounds to their material benefit: keeping sons and daughters as virtual indentured servants; robbing and killing Indians and kidnapping their children to raise in kennels like dogs . . . sometimes taking multiple wives, like your friend the Hand of the Lord, because God told them they might."

He leaned around Abigail to reach the tongs, brought up a coal from the fire to light his pipe. The sweet-cured scent of the tobacco mingled with the smell of the bread slowly baking in the oven. "God knows, with sufficient justification on their side, even men of accredited sanity, in Virginia, will have girls of twelve and fourteen whipped for stealing food from the kitchens, or locked up for weeks in conditions one wouldn't make a dog endure, only because those girls happen to be Negroes, and not one of their neighbors thinks twice of it. Rebecca Malvern had left her husband—branding herself a Daughter of Eve in no uncertain terms. She 'owed' Mrs. Tillet sewing work, she had been 'slack' and 'not doing her share,' in an effort that Mrs. Tillet obviously sees as necessary to the material welfare of her family. And, as you say, with the murder she would be presumed dead: She would be officially accounted for. Therefore, no one was likely to search the Tillet house. Is the boy sure?"

"*I* am sure." She told him of the attic window, unshuttered now after years closed, and of the dim shape she had seen behind it; of the basket of sewing, the jug of water, the bread on the plate, the extra chamber pot beside the door. "Hap says that he's seen his mistress carrying bread, water, and sewing up to the attic two or three times in the past week, and once he sneaked up the attic stair, and thought he heard a woman weeping."

"Hmn." John knocked the ember from his pipe. "Well, we shall both look nohow if we go bursting in there with full military escort only to find the room being readied to rent—not to mention what Sam will say."

"You tell Sam," retorted Abigail, "to come and talk to me."

John took the precaution of being absent from home the following morning.

When Abigail went to the front door at the sound of a military knock—it was barely nine; Shim Walton must have flown down to the harbor and taken one of the first boats across—the first person she saw past Lieutenant Coldstone's square crimson shoulder was Paul Revere, lounging in the opposite doorway wrapped in his sorry old gray greatcoat (*with a red scarf, drat him!*). The second person she saw—and third, fourth, fifth, and on through at least twenty—were various neighbors, patriots, idlers, smugglers, and countrymen who'd come to town on account of the tea, also loitering here and there along Queen Street.

How wise of John, she reflected, to make sure the Sons of Liberty had been alerted to the Lieutenant's visit so that they could form a cordon sanitaire around him and his men.

She waved to Revere, nodded to Sergeant Muldoon and his red-coated companion posted outside her door, and led the way to the parlor: "Lieutenant Coldstone, would your men care to go around to the kitchen for some hot cider on this dreadful cold morning? I'm sure they'd be more comfortable. The local children do make such pests of themselves."

"Thank you, m'am." As usual, the young officer gave the impression of having swallowed his own ramrod. "I'm sure the children do their best to obey their parents' wishes."

"To be sure they do." She smiled dazzlingly, and went back out to send Muldoon and the other man—the same short and disgruntled private who had accompanied him here on the last occasion—around to the back, then reentered the parlor and sat beside the crackling fire. "Thank you so much for coming."

"Are you certain of your accusation, m'am?"

"How certain do I need to be, Lieutenant?" she asked quietly. "Was the figure I saw in the window pounding the glass to get out? No. Have I seen baskets of sewing, and a little bread and water, waiting to be taken up—baskets similar to what one of the prentice-boys in the house has seen being taken up to the attic? Yes."

"So you're going on the accusation of a prentice-boy against a mistress he hates?" Coldstone didn't speak the words scornfully, or with any kind of irony. He sounded rather like John had last night, or when John was testing out a client's arguments with how they might sound to a jury. "You realize you're risking a lawsuit."

"'Tis a risk I'm willing to take. A woman disappeared on Wednesday night, and Thursday morning we have the sudden mysterious appearance of a locked attic, an extra chamber pot, food and sewing being taken up, and no one not of the household permitted anywhere near the house. The civilian magistrate of the ward is a close relative of the kidnapper, and the victim, a woman who through no fault of her own is considered beneath the notice of most of its respectable citizens. I've asked you to help me because you are able to move swiftly and independently, and to take the perpetrators of this—this mad scheme—by surprise, before they can cover their tracks. And I've asked you because I judge you to be a humane man."

"Fair enough." Coldstone inclined his head, and picked up his hat.

And if Rebecca has Sam's precious "Household Expenses" book on or about her person, thought Abigail, *Sam will eat me alive.*

When the party reached Fish Street—still surrounded by a loose ring of Revere's North End boys, to keep off unscheduled demonstrations of disapproval against Royal power and red uniforms—Lieutenant Coldstone signed the grim-faced little private to watch the yard gate, while he, Muldoon, and Abigail entered the shop. Nehemiah Tillet came around the counter smiling. "What can I do—?" before it dawned on him how extraordinary the presence of any British officer must be in Boston at this particular time.

The next moment he saw Abigail behind the Lieutenant, and his face blenched a little in the gray light of the shop.

"An allegation has been laid against you that you are unlawfully keeping a woman—who is herself wanted for questioning in the murder that took place here on the night of the twenty-fourth—prisoner under lock and key in this house." Coldstone laid a paper on the counter. "Here is a warrant from the Provost Marshal, to search your house and ascertain the truth."

"It isn't true!" gasped Tillet. "She's my daughter—my niece, I mean—she isn't right in the head! We keep her locked up for her own protection—"

"Shut up, Tillet!" His wife appeared in the doorway, face even less attractive than usual due to its mottled flush of rage. She stabbed a furious finger at Abigail. "That slattern would say anything to disgrace us, before our church and before our friends! Bringing soldiers here, in broad daylight, to turn all our neighbors against us! She has always been jealous of this household, and worked as a go-between to ruin the marriage of an honest woman! Her accusation is ridiculous!"

"The question is not about her relations with your family," responded Coldstone evenly, "nor whether her accusation is ridiculous, but whether it is true." The two prentice-boys, Queenie, and the scullery maid had assembled in the doorway behind her, and Abigail saw the glance that went among the three youngsters. Queenie was staring at her, her big hands working and unmantled hatred in her eyes.

"Hap," snapped Mrs. Tillet to the younger boy, "you go now, at once, to Mr. Goss the magistrate over at Wentworth's Wharf and bring him here." She turned furiously back to Coldstone. "My sister-in-law's husband is the magistrate of this ward, sir! We'll see if your warrant stands up to his authority!"

"By all means send for him, m'am." Coldstone stepped aside from the doorway. "Yet this warrant has the King's authority, and save for your messenger boy, none of the household shall stir from my presence until I have seen that attic."

Nevertheless, Mrs. Tillet refused to budge until the magistrate—a man of Mr. Tillet's age, bluff and red-faced from his profession as a ship's carpenter—appeared, grumbling and snorting at being called from his work and glaring at his red-faced sister-in-law. In the interim, Mr. Tillet repeatedly began his long train of explanations: "—my niece, sir, and subject to violent fits; 'tis only out of the goodness of my wife's heart that we took her in at all—" which invariably ended in his wife telling him to hold his tongue. For her part, Mrs. Tillet spent the half hour or so that the wait occupied in railing against Abigail's morals, personal habits, marriage, family, housekeeping, and sanity, despite Lieutenant Coldstone's reiterated warnings that her words were being taken note of, and would lay her open to action for slander.

"Let her sue me!" shouted Mrs. Tillet, pounding her chest with one massive fist. "I'll repeat every word I've said to the whole of the General Court, and then they will all know her for the slut and unbeliever she is!"

Abigail listened in stony silence, only praying that Sam wouldn't get word of all this and show up to further complicate matters.

And that, once in Coldstone's hands, Rebecca would not reveal that the killer was, in fact, Abednego Sellars or some other member of the Sons.

Sam didn't come. With the magistrate's appearance, the whole of the party filed upstairs, to find that the door of the attic stair was indeed locked. This ultimately debouched into the wide, freezingly cold space at the top of the house—not even Queenie's chamber at the west end, above that of her master and mistress, gleaned any warmth, for obviously no fires were kept up on the second floor at all.

The door of the small room called the south attic was also locked. The bolts on the outside of its door looked new. Beside the door stood a water pitcher, a plate innocent even of crumbs, a basket filled with newly sewed shirts, and beside them, a short, braided-leather whip, of the kind hunters used for beating dogs away from a kill.

"The woman's got to earn her keep," stated Mrs. Tillet fiercely. "She'd eat us out of house and home if left to herself, a glutton and a wittol. 'Tis only Christian charity that we took her in, and she refuses to turn a hand to help us or support herself. She should be put out into the road—"

"Why then do you lock the door on her instead?" Coldstone took the key, and opened the door. "Strange charity, m'am."

The woman seated on the bed had already staggered to her feet—probably at the sound of footsteps and strange voices—and dropped the chemise she was sewing, flung herself on her knees in front of Coldstone, and threw her arms around his legs. "Please, sir, please, tell her it wasn't my fault I didn't get them done!" she babbled. Her long blonde hair, pale as flax, hid her face, and the marks the dog-whip had left stood out purple on her cold-reddened arms. "I couldn't help! 'Tis I couldn't hold a needle right with the cold, and I did try! Please tell her!"

The room was like an icehouse. Coldstone reached down and grasped the woman's arm—she wore only a chemise, with the bed's single blanket wrapped over it—and brought her to her feet. Tears poured down from her eyes, and snot from her nose, and her fingers left little traces of blood on the officer's white gloves as she clutched at his hands.

"Make her let me go, sir! I promise I'll do whatever she asks, but tell her to let me out!"

Coldstone turned to Abigail. "Is this Mrs. Malvern?" With a gentle hand he brushed back the greasy strings of graying blonde hair from a face square, broad, and slightly animal-looking, with its level bar of dark brow and its sloping forehead.

Abigail had already come forward with her handkerchief, gently wiping at the tears, stroking the woman's shoulder in a way that she hoped was reassuring. "I've never seen her before in my life."

Twenty-eight

It was well past dinnertime by the time it was agreed that Gomer Faulk—that was the woman's name—would be taken to Abigail's house for the next few days, until it could be decided what to do with her. Hester Tillet had a great deal to say, at the top of her lungs, about her "niece's" inborn inability to tell the truth on any subject whatsoever, and bawled that Abigail would hear from her lawyers for taking from her household one of its members, though as Gomer was a good thirty-five years of age and, according to the disgusted Magistrate Goss, no relation whatsoever to the Tillets, it was hard to discover on what grounds Hester thought she had jurisdiction over her.

"Faulk? Nobody named Faulk in the family. There was a Faulk out in Medford—a drunk good-for-nothing who abandoned his family, as I recall it—but they were no connection of ours, thank God . . ."

Gomer herself clung alternately to Abigail and Lieutenant Coldstone, shivering and wiping her nose with her fingers. "Just don't let her lock me up again. There's rats at night, sir, m'am, big 'uns, and they talks to me. I'll sew for you all you want m'am, sir, just don't let her whip me again." She was clearly, as Orion Hazlitt had said of his servant girl Damnation, "lacking." She couldn't recall the names of her parents other than Ma and Pa, but said that she'd lived with one family and another in the farms around Medford, the most recent being that of Nehemiah Tillet's sister and brother-in-law. "They hit me now and now, but they didn't lock me up. Let me sleep in the cow-shed. I like cows, m'am. I takes good care of 'em . . .

"She and that man"—she pointed to Tillet—"come to my uncle Reb's wedding, and Uncle Reb and Miss Eliza, they said they had to go away, and I couldn't come with 'em—"

"Someone had to look after the girl," protested Tillet. "My wife was unsatisfied with the woman then helping her with sewing for the shop—"

Like the crippled boy turning the spinning wheel at Moore's Farm out in Essex County, reflected Abigail sadly. Handed off, to provide labor to whoever would support him. At least Kemiah Moore and his wife appeared to be willing to feed that boy the same rations they gave their own family, and let him sit among the kitchen's distractions. But maybe, her darker soul whispered, that was only because he was incapable of wandering away.

"An unfortunate story," said Coldstone, as they walked back along Fish Street in the gathering dusk. "But not a new one."

"A letter to Medford will yield more information on the subject," said Abigail. Her head ached—she prayed Pattie had made some kind of dinner for John and the children, and had thought to save some for her—and she felt infinitely tired. Though she knew Mrs. Tillet's spew of invective had been simply that—the vomiting forth of a poisoned mind—she felt as if she were physically smeared with filth every time the young Lieutenant turned his eyes upon her. "I do beg your pardon, Lieutenant."

"For using the King's authority as it should be used?" he asked. "As a tool to protect those incapable of protecting themselves?" He glanced back at Gomer, walking between Sergeant Muldoon and Trooper Yarrow, seemingly oblivious that her ankles were exposed by the hem of Queenie's borrowed dress. "What will you do with her? She's obviously incapable of looking after herself."

"I'll write to my father," said Abigail. "He's the pastor

at Weymouth, across the bay to the south. He'll know a good family who can take her in and will treat her decently. She seems willing enough to work."

"Oh, I'll work, m'am," provided Gomer, hurrying her steps to close the distance between them. "Just please don't lock me up with the rats. I got so hungry up there in the attic, and cold. I'll even sew for you, but I'm no good at it."

Abigail thought about the single slice of thinly buttered bread, the jug of water. Even the harsh laws of Leviticus enjoined the Hebrews to look after their beasts, and to treat the lowest of their households with common humanity. Which obviously—since the frugal Tillets had smuggled her into their attic while the rest of the household was in turmoil on the day of the murder—they had had no intention of doing, even from the first. Free labor, and the cheapest possible food . . .

At least the slave Philomela, thought Abigail, was worth four hundred dollars to somebody.

She stopped, and laid a hand on Lieutenant Coldstone's arm. "Lieutenant," she said, "might I impose upon you for one more favor? And this one," she added, "*will* advance us on our way, to finding the murderer of Mrs. Pentyre."

She had the notes from both Philomela and Lucy Fluckner still in her pocket, but the Fluckner butler Mr. Barnaby barely glanced at them. "A shocking thing it was, m'am," he said. "Well, there's always young men who'll try to get up an *affaire* with a maidservant, especially one as beautiful as Miss Philomela, and some of them do send poems. Terrible lot of tosh, most of them." He glanced back at Coldstone, who followed them up the stair—a broad and handsome flight, open in the fashion of wealthy English houses where presumably there was more money to be spent on heating. "But this, sir—m'am—there was something about these, after the first two or three, that made my blood run cold. I didn't know Miss Philomela had kept that last one. Terrible frightened she was over it—and no wonder! The first few weeks after she got it, I thought she was like to faint, going outside the house."

He opened the door to the maid's room, which was a narrow chamber on the main bedroom floor, between the overdecorated demipalaces allotted to Mrs. Fluckner and her daughter. Philomela's room was very like the girl herself, Abigail thought. No frills, no fuss, though she probably could have gleaned any number of gaudy castoffs from either of her mistresses. On a little table beside the bed lay a book of Sir Philip Sidney's poems.

The more sinister poem in question was, as Philomela had said, under the loose floorboard beside the head of the bed.

Abigail saw immediately that it was written on the same expensive English paper as had been the note that summoned Perdita Pentyre to her death. Her heart beating hard, she unfolded it, carried it to the window where the last of the daylight still lingered over Boston's peaked roofs. She remembered what the girls had said of its contents, and braced herself for horrors.

But the words of those first lines were blanked from her mind by the handwriting itself.

No. Oh, no.

She felt sick, almost dizzy with the rush of surmise and horror, pieces of some monstrous mosaic falling into place . . .

And worse than that, the vertiginous shock of how close she'd stood to the man.

Dear God in Heaven—!

"Mrs. Adams?" Coldstone was watching her face narrowly. Quickly she turned to the second page, aware that her fingers were shaking. "Do you know the hand?"

"No. It's—" She shook her head, stammered—groped for some other reason to account for her distress. "It's just that it's a little like my father's, at first glance—that rounding of the letters . . . It shocked me for an instant, that's all." *Had I babbled, 'Good Heavens, it looks exactly like the Emperor of China's,' it would not be so obvious a lie . . .*

"Mrs. Adams." The officer took the sheets from her hand, and his dark eyes traveled swiftly over the lines. Then he returned his gaze to her, and she looked aside, fighting to keep her thoughts from her face and aware she must be white-lipped and distracted as one who has seen a ghost. *"What is it?"*

"Naught." She could barely get the word out.

"Naught," he repeated, and it was the first time she saw emotion—rage—blaze in his eyes, cold as the northern lights. "Even with what you know. *Naught.*"

Abigail looked away. "My secrets are not mine to tell."

"Nor are mine," said Coldstone quietly. "Yet I have spoken with those who have been magistrates in London for many years, and on one fact they all agree: that these men do not stop their crimes. How many more women are you willing to have die, Mrs. Adams, before you conclude that protection of the innocent is more important to you than shielding politically suspect friends? May I take these?"

"Let me keep two pages." Her voice sounded stifled in her own ears. "In case one of my politically suspect friends recognizes it."

Without a word he pocketed the other three sheets, and preceded her down the handsome stairs. Mr. Barnaby glanced at them inquiringly, but neither spoke. At the outer door Coldstone looked up and down the darkening length of Milk Street. At least two dozen of Revere's North End boys loitered still, hands in pockets, studiously paying not the slightest attention to the two soldiers stationed beside the Fluckner door. "Go on to the wharf," said Abigail. "You won't be molested, and there's enough light left, for you to return to Castle Island. I will circulate these"—she touched her pocket—"and see if the hand is familiar—"

"And if it belongs to one of the Sons of Liberty, will that be the last I hear of it?"

He was so angry she could almost see it, coming off him like frozen smoke. In a voice held steady with an effort, Abigail said, "We aren't savages, Lieutenant. Even as we are not traitors."

He faced her in the thin twilight. "*You* are not a savage, Mrs. Adams," he replied. "Yet you are devoted to a cause—which you feel to be right—which is being led by men who feel themselves justified in breaking the King's law. Whether that law is just or unjust is immaterial in the face of the fact that you—and they—believe your cause to be above law. Even as those killers of witches in Salem a generation ago believed theirs to be. Such an attitude, m'am, makes you as dangerous as they."

He bowed, and left her on the steps. The circle of patriots followed him and his men, like sharks around a ship's boat, out of sight in the gloom. When they had gone, young Dr. Warren emerged from the shadows of a nearby alley, raffish-looking in a mechanic's corduroy jacket and rough boots. "May I escort you home, Mrs. Adams?"

Later, Abigail recalled that she'd talked with him of something, but didn't know what, and she was hard-put not to simply answer his remarks at random. Her mind seemed to return, again and again, to two things:

These men do not stop their crimes.

And the poem about the slaughter of a red-haired whore, written in Orion Hazlitt's hand.

"Will you come with me to Sam's?" John picked up his boots, which he'd already pulled off by the fire by the time Abigail handed him the two sheets of fevered verse. "It's gone beyond choice, now. You didn't do anything foolish like try to see Hazlitt, did you?"

"I walked down Hanover Street." Abigail took off her

apron, closed the sewing box that she'd been working on when John had returned home. Upstairs, the children and Pattie slumbered in their beds. "The shop was shuttered, and there was no light in the upstairs windows. I had not the courage to do more."

"You had more sense, you mean." John fetched their coats and cloaks from the pegs beside the door—his own still cold to the touch—while Abigail climbed to the little room Pattie shared with the younger boys and now with Gomer Faulk. She gently woke Pattie, and bid her watch until they returned. Only then, wreathed in scarves and cloaks and hoods and hats, with a lantern bobbing ineffectually from John's hand, did they step out into the windy night.

"Is Coldstone right?" asked Abigail softly after a time. "Have we become like the hanging judges years ago? Like medieval Inquisitors, who would kill a man to save his soul? Abrogating to ourselves the right to do so, because we *felt* it was right?"

"The only ones who do that," replied John after thought, "are those who see the world as they did, with only a single answer, not only to *that* problem, but to *all* problems. And the single-minded certainly do not number Sam among their ranks, you know. Nor will he condone murder, just because a man has served the liberties of his country."

"No," said Abigail. "No, I know that. Orion—no wonder he didn't harm Rebecca! And no wonder she went into hiding—"

"*If* it was Hazlitt who killed Mrs. Pentyre." John held aloft the lantern as they entered the square before the State House and the Customs house, where the Massacre had taken place. Every shutter in town was barred, and at this hour, most of the windows behind them were dark. The night watchman's cries drifted to them from another street, barely to be heard beneath the steady tolling of the bells.

The wind made the feeble light sway even in John's hand, and the waning moon, breaking through the clouds, showed Abigail movement stirring in the alleyways. A chip of light flared, where someone closed a slide over a lantern. " 'Tis all right," he said softly, when she caught at his sleeve. "Sam's boys, most like."

"And was it Sam's *boys*," she asked, vexed, "who've followed *me*, when I've been abroad at night?"

"Damn his impertinence," growled John. "But likely, yes. I'll have a word to say to him." They walked on in silence.

"When you say," said Abigail after a moment, "*if* it was Orion who killed Perdita Pentyre—You still think there were two criminals, and two crimes?"

"I don't doubt he committed the others, and that it's he who has been following that poor slave-girl and sending her poems. But killing Mrs. Pentyre—" He shook his head. "To say nothing of throwing the blame off onto me. There are men whose loyalty I've doubted, Abigail, men I think Sam needs to be more careful in his dealings with . . . but not Hazlitt. For God's sake, why commit the crime in the house of the woman he loves? And why steal her list of contacts?"

"What else would he have done with it?" countered Abigail. "Left it for the Watch? Handed it back to Sam?"

"But in Rebecca's house—"

"Where else," asked Abigail softly, "could he be sure of getting Mrs. Pentyre alone? These other women whom he—he fixed upon, to whom he was drawn in some unholy fashion—these women he convinced himself were the Daughters of Eve. They were, as Lieutenant Coldstone said, *common women*. Women whom any man could come to and find unprotected . . . or in poor Philomela's case, a woman whose access he could purchase, though thankfully it was beyond his price. Perdita Pentyre wasn't. Yet to him she was Jezebel the Queen."

"Jezebel—?"

"Remember Bargest's sermons that I told you of? About the Nine Daughters of Eve, that lie in wait to destroy a man's soul? *The serpent, the witch*—we know Mrs. Fishwire had any number of serpents in her shop, besides her poor cats—*the harlot. The succubus*—the demon female who torments a righteous man's dreams. Or would he consider Philomela a nightmare? Poor Mrs. Pentyre, riding at the Colonel's side to review the troops, with her face painted and her head tir'd like Jezebel—"

They walked on, Abigail's pattens clinking on the cobbles of Kilby Street and her heavy skirts flapping against her legs. Fort Hill loomed before them, pricked with spots of yellow where the few soldiers left on the mainland manned the guns. At the wharves below, ships stirred and creaked, restless wooden animals in the dark.

"Saying it is Orion," said John quietly. "And saying that he wouldn't have killed Rebecca . . . How can you be sure that she's in hiding?"

"I looked in his attic."

The lantern-light flashed as John turned his head. "You thought then—?"

"No. It was nowhere in my mind. But I'd just realized she might be being held prisoner *somewhere*, when I went into his house and he sent me upstairs for laudanum for his mother. I had to look up into the nearest attic, to see how possible it would be. I think at that moment I would have run down the street looking into the attics of every house in turn. It's only a tiny space up there, you know. One can't stand up in it, even right under the ridgepole, and there's no other space in the house, where a woman could be kept."

Across the open ground, and down the hill to their left, they could see the glow of torches around Griffin's Wharf, where men still sat up, muskets in hand, around the *Dartmouth*, and now the *Eleanor*, as they had mounted guard now for ten days. Out in the harbor the *Beaver* lay at anchor, where the harbormaster had commanded she remain until the members of the crew had either died of the smallpox that had broken out among them, or were recovered enough to be in no danger of spreading the disease. No word yet, of the Governor sending for troops, from either Britain or Halifax, but surely it was only a matter of time . . .

"Oh, good," Abigail said, as they emerged from the narrow throat of Gridley Lane to see, a few houses down the street, the weak glow of candles behind the shutters in the downstairs room which Abigail knew to be Sam's study. "At least we won't be waking him."

"You're tender of Sam's rest, all of a sudden. I'd have thought you'd delight in shooting him out of bed in order to say, *I told you so . . .*"

"But what a horrid thing to do to Bess. Besides, after all that's happened today I'm not sure I could support the sight of Sam in his nightshirt."

Predictably, Sam was not only awake and dressed, but drinking cider with Dr. Warren and Paul Revere, the latter preparing to take over charge of the guard on Griffin's Wharf at midnight. With them were two or three others of Sam's South End cabal that guided the Sons of Liberty, including—a bit disconcertingly—Abednego Sellars. These lesser captains retired to the kitchen while John and Abigail laid before Sam the poem: "'Tis Hazlitt's hand, right enough," said Abigail, and John nodded agreement. Revere lighted half a dozen more candles and brought them close.

"They're right." He read the verse before him, and his dark brow plunged down over his nose in shocked disgust; his dark eyes flicked up to meet Abigail's. "Good God."

"Not really," she murmured in response.

"Do you have the note he sent to Mrs. Pentyre? The one supposed to be from Mrs. Malvern?"

Abigail produced it, and the silversmith held them close together, then produced a glass from his pocket to study them in detail. "The light isn't good enough," he said at length. "And the hand is well disguised. *Would* he have jeopardized one of our own?"

"Would one of Jesus' disciples have jeopardized *Him*?" retorted Sam, putting on his greatcoat.

"He could be simply too mad to care," put in Warren.

"We have seen nothing to tell us," insisted John, "that Orion Hazlitt is in any way involved in the murder of Mrs. Pentyre, or the disappearance of Mrs. Malvern—or of your precious codebook," he added. "All we can be *fairly* sure of, is that he was the author of the two crimes, and the man who has pursued Fluckner's girl. The rest I presume we can ask him about in due time."

"Will you take Mrs. Adams home, John?" Sam wrapped a scarf around his throat—another madder-red one, Abigail noted automatically: *Really, Boston has entirely too many things in it that too many people have . . .* "Or will you come?"

"We'll go home," said John. "If you'd send someone to let us know the—outcome—of your visit, I think we should both rather hear it tonight, than wait until I see you tomorrow at the meeting. And to add to that, after the meeting this evening, a man told me there's a rumor afoot, that a ship is coming across from Lynn within a few days, to take the tea off the *Beaver* before she even comes into harbor."

"'Tis what Paul and the doctor came just now to tell me," responded Sam grimly. "'Twill have to be looked into, and at once, tomorrow—"

"It can't be with the Governor's approval—"

"I wouldn't put it past him to hire the Devil himself to get the tea landed. Can you meet with us at nine?"

John nodded. As the other men left, he led Abigail once more out into the night. The wind had scattered the clouds; the night's cold was worse. In most houses, the thin chinks of lamp- and candlelight had failed. The streets lay stark, under the watery blue of the moon.

"And do you think," asked Abigail softly, "that Sam, and Dr. Warren, and the others, will wait long enough to ask Mr. Hazlitt whether he in fact knows anything of Mrs. Pentyre's murder? They won't dare to turn him over to the authorities, you know."

"I think you're right about that."

"Then is this not in fact putting our own cause above the law?"

"Were we in England," pointed out John, "and did Orion Hazlitt happen to be a friend of the King's, or a member of the nobility, I doubt he would even be prosecuted. Come," he added, and put his arm around her shoulders. "One way or another, we shall hear something before morning, and then we will know what we must do."

But as the chimes of midnight mingled with the tolling of the alarm bells, Paul Revere—looking uncharacteristically haggard and shaken in the feeble shudder of the candlelight—brought the news that Orion Hazlitt had fled from his home.

"The place was shut tight as a drum when we got there; Sam broke a window in the printing shed, to get us in," he said. "He wasn't about to wait, you understand, for Hazlitt to pick up some rumor in the morning and disappear with Mrs. Malvern's cipher-book and list of names, always supposing he had them. Hazlitt wasn't there. Neither was the book. Sam searched the place."

Of course Sam searched.

"What *was* there," went on Revere steadily, "was Mrs. Hazlitt. Dead, like the others." He was silent a moment, his eyebrows standing out very dark in the dim glow of her lamp, as if his face was still chalky from what he had seen. "*Just* like the others."

Abigail put a hand over her mouth, trying to push from her mind the sight of a fresh bite in the wax yellow flesh of

Mrs. Pentyre's shoulder. *The serpent, the harlot, the witch, the nightmare . . .*

What nightmares had tormented Orion Hazlitt's sleep, on the trundle at his mother's bedside while she murmured in opiated slumber?

What nightmare had he sought to flee, in the sanity of friendship with a woman he couldn't have?

"The Sons are out looking for him," Revere continued after a few moments. "Sam has asked me to tell you, that this isn't to go any farther. We'll look after our own."

"I will at least send a letter to Miss Fluckner," responded Abigail, "alerting her slave-girl—whom—" Her throat closed on Orion Hazlitt's name, as her mind flung up at her a hundred conversations, a hundred memories, of that handsome and quiet young man. "Who was surely marked for the next victim. I will swear Miss Fluckner to secrecy—she is a fierce partisan to our cause—and Sam surely cannot object to that. And if he does," she added mildly, "assure him that I will spend the next six months weeping with chagrin at his displeasure."

Despite his look of having quietly thrown up his supper not long before, Revere managed a wry grin. "Depend upon me to do so, m'am."

Twenty-nine

My dear Miss Fluckner,

Thank you for the help you have given us, beyond what I can express.

The man who wrote the poems to Philomela is a printer named Orion Hazlitt. He is being sought by authorities now, for yet another crime. My suspicion is that he will flee the district, yet the possibility remains that he may attempt to cross over to the Island. Please be alert, and both you and Mistress Philomela take care about going anywhere alone. Yet I beg you, for reasons which you must take on trust, do not speak of this, or show this letter, to anyone, unless you should return to the mainland, or see him on the Island.

I will advise you, when I hear that he has been apprehended. I do not feel that it will be long.

Your friend,
A. Adams

This note John carried down to the waterfront, to send across to Castle Island, when he left the house in the morning to meet Sam. "Don't wait dinner for me," he said as he kissed her. "Nor supper either. The Lord only knows how long it will take, to trace this rumor and find out who exactly is planning to take off the *Beaver*'s cargo—if indeed anyone is at all."

"I shall leave a bowl of food for you on the doorstep,"

Abigail promised, neatly tying the tapes on Tommy's clout. "Right next to Messalina's."

He put a hand on her shoulder and leaned to kiss her nape. "Portia, your price is above rubies."

Gomer Faulk, coming in behind Pattie with her arms full of ice-cold linens from the yard, said, "Good-bye, Mr. Adams," as he passed. Making a place for the big woman in the household would be awkward, reflected Abigail, for the little time she'd be there—*I MUST write a letter to Papa today as well, and get Thaxter to take it*—but at least she was good-hearted, eager to do what lay within her simple understanding, and loved children.

"Well, she's living proof that the Lord does provide," remarked Pattie, with a twinkle in her eye. "Here she's come just on the day when we need help with the ironing."

AND a letter to the pastor at Medford, to find out who the woman really is related to . . .

Abigail shivered, as she and Pattie returned to the yard for another load of shirts and sheets, at the thought of how easy it was for a woman with no family connections to drop out of sight without a trace. Her mind roved, not to Pamela in the novel, but to Jenny Barry, to the children of Mrs. Kern the laundrywoman in Love Lane Yard—little six-year-old Nannie who'd been sent down to the tavern to fetch Mr. Ballagh, as casually as if she'd been a grown girl able to defend herself—to Philomela, after whom no one would inquire once money was handed over. Even to the maddening, clinging, outrageous Lucretia Hazlitt, whom everyone avoided if they could . . .

That, she supposed, in spite of its absurdity, was why she came back to *Pamela* again and again. Because at its heart, it was true. No one really cared about a girl who was poor, more than they cared about themselves.

Movement in the passway to the street caught her eye. Turning—her thought going at once to Sam and his "boys"—she saw Sergeant Muldoon. He saluted, and she quickly draped the garments over her big wicker clothes-hamper and hurried across to him: "Good Heavens, man, are you mad? I'm astonished you weren't set upon, on your way here."

"Well, there was a bit of a botheration." He craned his head around to look over his own shoulder at splotches of fresh horse dung smeared on his back. "But 'twas just bad words, when all's said, and none tried to stay me. 'Tis early yet. Though I'll be hopin'," he added a little shyly, "that you'll be so kind as to find a minute, to walk me back to the wharves. I've this for you, from Himself."

He held out a sealed note.

My very dear Mrs. Adams:

When we parted yesterday evening I expressed myself harshly, being very angry. Yet on reflection I see that we are equally accessories after the fact.

If we do not trust one another, at least insofar as this case is concerned, the next victim's blood will be upon both of our hands. Sooner or later, one of us must surrender the high ground of safety with proof of good intent.

Therefore, as I am detained today upon the island, I enclose the reason that Colonel Leslie is so sure that it was your husband who was responsible for the murder of Mrs. Pentyre. I trust, first, that you will show this to no one—not to your husband, nor to anyone whom you may know or suspect to be associated with the Sons of Liberty—and that you will return it to me.

I hope that this gesture will prompt a reciprocal sharing of at least some of the information which I know that you have been keeping from me, concerning the circumstances of Mrs. Pentyre's murder. I promise you, that I will keep silent concerning what you tell me, save where it touches that which would immediately endanger the lives of the soldiers under Colonel Leslie's charge. I know you to be a woman of profound integrity, and loyalty to your husband and to his cause; even as I have my loyalty to my King and to my Regiment.

Your obedient servant,
Lieutenant Jeremy Coldstone
King's 64th Regiment

She unfolded the enclosed note.

Pentyre—

The hand of Liberty lies heavy upon you, and shall crush your wife and yourself for your Sins against your Country and those who Love her.

Novanglus

For the second time in just over half a day, Abigail was smitten dizzy with the vertiginous sensation of being bombarded with too much light. As if she had opened a door long closed, and before her a vista of doors slammed open in such swift sequence that the sight of what lay beyond one was immediately overwhelmed by what lay beyond the next. Her breath stopped—she had the sensation it was minutes before she was able to draw it again, and she fought to keep her hands from shaking.

Rebecca.

DEAR GOD!!!

She folded up both notes. She was almost surprised, to see her yard with its mazes of clothes-ropes exactly as it had been five minutes before. "Can you read, Sergeant Muldoon?" she inquired in her sweetest voice.

"Oh, not me, m'am. I can put me name good and proper, but more'n that our priest never did manage to teach me."

"Hmm," said Abigail. "Well, Lieutenant Coldstone writes here that you are to disregard all former orders to you, and accompany me. You and I are going on a little journey."

Dearest Friend,

I pray this letter will reach you quickly. Shim Walton is good at finding people in the North End. I have sent another like it to Sam, and a third—suitably excised—to Lt. Coldstone.

The man who wrote a threat of death, under your name, to Mr. and Mrs. Pentyre was the Hand of the Lord Atonement Bargest, for the simple reason (I will confirm this with Abednego Sellars or his wife before I leave for Gilead this morning) that the Gilead congregation has been in a lawsuit with Pentyre over the former Sellars lands in Essex County, lands upon which much of Gilead stands. The suit as I recall is coming up for final judgment at the next Session. To kill Pentyre alone would be insufficient, as Mrs. Pentyre would inherit the lands—and the lawsuit—in the event of her husband's death. The next heir—Pentyre's brother—lives, with the remainder of the family, in England.

Therefore, you must undertake at once to protect Richard Pentyre, and to find Orion Hazlitt before he reaches him. He will, I assume, have gone to Castle William.

I am not sure, but I suspect that Hazlitt may have killed someone—probably a young woman—at Gilead years ago, and that Bargest knows it. Certainly he has a hold of some kind over the man, beyond mere superstition. I don't believe Hazlitt even knows that Bargest wrote the threat, directing suspicion toward the Sons of Liberty (and away from Gilead).

My fear is, that Rebecca, having escaped imprisonment in her room, saw Orion, and was apprehended by him before she could get out of the house. If he did not immediately kill her—and I do not believe he did or would—the only place he could have sent her was to Gilead itself, keeping her and his mother both dosed with laudanum while he dispatched Damnation to the settlement with instructions to Bargest to send (or come) to fetch her from one of the smuggler-barns across the bay from Boston, to which Hazlitt could take her one night. I think she must have been in the bedroom overhead, unconscious, even as I talked to Orion and his mother on Thursday, and that she was in one of the deserted dwellings in Gilead when Thaxter and I passed through there the following Monday night.

For this reason I have commandeered Sergeant Muldoon—who is under the impression that he is obeying his commanding officer's orders—and am on my way to Gilead even now. I beg of you, send reinforcements after us at once, for should Bargest discover that he has been implicated in this crime, I do not put it past him to incite violence against us, to protect his own position.

Likewise I have warned Thaxter, Gomer, and Pattie to keep the children close to home, and to let no one see them until you have given them word.

I trust that you (and suitable assistance) will catch us up on the road.

Your own,
Portia

They spent the night in Salem. The modern seaport town had had little to do with the witchcraft trials that had spread over Essex County like a poison-rash not quite eighty years before. "They weren't in this town at all, then?" Sergeant Muldoon sounded disappointed.

Rain rattled the darkening casements of Purley's Tavern, as Mrs. Purley—who always reminded Abigail of a dried apple-doll—set before them a dish of stew and a fresh-baked loaf of bread. Wind shrieked around the eaves. Abigail gratefully drank the landlady's excellent cider, feeling that she would never get warm again.

"There may have been one or two here, once the accusations were started," she said. "When people found they could accuse their personal enemies of sending out their spirits to do evil, when the accused themselves were demonstrably elsewhere, a great many found they knew people who *must* be witches . . . But the accusations themselves began in Salem *Village*, about eight miles west of here. They changed the name of that settlement to Danvers."

"I can see why they'd do." The young man shook his head, and mopped busily at the gravy. The men at the other table—clerks and supercargoes, they looked like, from one of the many ships at anchor—burst into talk and laughter over some witticism, their voices loud in the ordinary-room that had no other customers. After a time he asked, "'Tis what this Hand of the Lord told this Hazlitt, then, isn't it? That Mrs. Pentyre was a witch, and had sent her spirit to do some wicked thing?"

"I think he must have. Or something very like it." Abigail glanced at the window as the wind shook it again, praying at every moment that each sound was John—with a suitable troop of Sons of Liberty at his back—coming to her assistance. "Mrs. Pentyre and her husband, who evilly contested God's will that had given the land to the Gilead Congregation. How could such ill-intentioned people not be in league with the Devil?"

Muldoon said, "T'cha!" and reached for another hunk of bread with an enthusiasm that gave Abigail a very bad impression of His Majesty's generosity to his servants. "Sounds like me Aunt Bridget," he added. "She's got it well in her head, that the Divil's got naught to do but spend his days urgin' folks on to make her life harder for her. Says she can see him, in the shape of a black bird, or a black cat, or sometimes a spider, whisperin' in the ear of

Grinder Givern—that's our landlord's rent-agent—or Mrs. O'Toole the tavern keeper's wife, just before they go ask her to pay up her bills or whate'er it is that she's diviled about that day. She's still got friends that believe her, mostly 'cause she tells them she sees the Divil urgin' on folks to make *their* lives miserable, too, but mostly in Ballyseigh—that's home—they just say, 'Well, there's Bridget Muldoon on a tear again.' She's never told any to go do no murder."

He shrugged back his cloak in the warmth of the hearth, and one or two of the men who shared the ordinary-room with them glanced warily at his red coat. He had accepted Abigail's assurance that Coldstone's note to her was in fact orders to him to accompany her and obey her commands, and didn't seem in the least troubled by the fact that the whole northeast section of Massachusetts had for two weeks been flooded with pamphlets describing the British troops as murderers intent upon enslaving the population in the name of the King. *No imagination?* she wondered. Or simply a stolid sense of duty as unshakeable as Coldstone's own. Perhaps the fact that he was alone—and clearly acting the role of bodyguard to a civilian woman—lessened the chances of random assault, but Abigail was very aware of being watched, and undoubtedly discussed in whispers in the shadows of the ill-lit inn.

"Bein' that the Hand of the Lord did tell him," he went on after a worried silence, "sure and he didn't tell him to . . . to cut her up the way he did, and all the rest of it. He wouldn't have told him *that*."

"I'm sure he did not." Abigail put her hands around her mug of cider, slowly feeling the warmth returning to them. "Being unable to see beyond his own vanity, to the point of madness, himself, I'm sure it never crossed his mind that a man who is mad cannot control the shape his madness takes, nor when it will seize on him."

She was silent a moment, remembering a man named James Otis—a great thinker, a great organizer, a pillar of the Sons of Liberty, who had slowly gone mad as a bedbug. His sister—to whom Abigail still wrote—had spoken to her of his torments, knowing that he could no longer be trusted, of her wretchedness at watching that brilliant mind eclipsed, and knowing that there was nothing anyone could do to save him.

When Orion is sane, she wondered, *does he know that he's mad?*

Or does he only suspect it in his dreams?

When Muldoon excused himself to her and rose, and crossed to the other table to make the acquaintance of the men with whom he'd share one of the beds in the big chamber upstairs that night, Abigail sat for a time in thought. She should, she knew, put in a half hour with quill and paper, composing orders purportedly from Lieutenant Coldstone to Sergeant Muldoon instructing him to go where she told him and do what she said, in case it later occurred to him to ask someone else to verify the document she'd shown him.

Instead, when Mrs. Purley came in with another pitcher of steaming cider, Abigail beckoned her. "My dear, I hope that soldier with you doesn't mean your Mr. Adams is still in trouble with His Majesty?" said the innkeeper's wife softly. "What a *fuss* they made, over that horse he left here lame—and by the by, Mr. Thaxter left his pipe here on accident when he came to fetch the beast, and we've got it saved for him in the pantry—"

"Thank you." Abigail smiled, and clasped the woman's hand. She'd become well acquainted with Mrs. Purley in the years that her own sister Mary and her husband had lived in Salem. "Remind me of it tomorrow . . . And no, all is well, Sergeant Muldoon is inquiring after another matter . . . Would *you* know," she asked artlessly, "the name of that girl who was slashed to death so horribly, about ten years ago out toward Townsend?"

1763—or thereabouts—was, she knew, the year that Orion Hazlitt had come to Boston.

Jemma Purley's round face clouded, and Abigail knew before she spoke, that she was right.

But Mrs. Purley asked, "Which one?" and Abigail stared at her, aghast.

"There was more than one?"

"Oh, dear, yes." Mrs. Purley set down her pitcher, dried her hands in her apron as she looked down at Abigail with sorrow and anger in her eyes. "The one from Gilead, we only heard rumor of: Those Gilead folks has always kept their doings to themselves. Purley says, nobody would ever have heard of it at all, except for it being Rose of Sharon Topsford that found the body, and the poor thing has never been quite right after that, seeing what had been done to the girl. But Frankincense Banister—" She shook her head. "It doesn't do to speak ill of the dead, and whatever the poor girl's failings—and it *was* only foolishness, and having her head turned, so pretty as she was—the way she would flirt, and with boys she didn't know well, we were all afraid she'd find herself in trouble one day, though of course no one expected . . . Is that who you meant?"

"Yes," said Abigail tonelessly. "I-I knew it was some name of the kind. From a farm, wasn't she? Near Wenham?"

"A few miles south of Wenham Pond, yes."

Within a few miles of Gilead.

"And did anyone try bearding that wretch Bargest in his den about it?"

At the mention of the Hand of the Lord, Mrs. Purley's mouth tightened up. "Well, as I recall it, every single one of his flock was accounted for, the day the poor girl disappeared. But there's more than one hereabouts, who'll be pleased when that court case is resolved, and those Boston folks that own that land put the sheriffs onto them and turn them out. Their title's no good to about three quarters of their fields," she added, in reply to Abigail's inquiring look—though in fact Abigail had ascertained nearly as much from Penelope Sellars before leaving Boston. "The case has been dragging on for years, with some Boston merchant whose mother was old Antoninus Sellars's granddaughter—*and* who's put the sheriffs onto old Bargest's 'Chosen Brides.' A disgrace, the lot of them." She shook her head.

No other women were traveling abroad that dismal night, so Abigail had the smaller upstairs chamber and its cold—but dry, aired, and bug-free—bed to herself. There was even a small fire in its fireplace. She wrote out the orders from Coldstone to Muldoon, then blew out her candle and lay awake, listening for horses in the court beneath the drumming of the rain.

Though rain, and wind, and the rattling of the window sash were all the sounds that broke the deep stillness, she dreamed of church bells.

Thirty

In darkness she woke—with the instincts of one who has milked cows for most of her thirty years—and in darkness dressed. Downstairs she heard the small sounds of the inn servants making fires, tidying the ordinary, taking bread from the oven.

The wind was less; the rain had ceased. Abigail's bones ached with the damp.

You will not *be sick*, she told herself firmly. Descending to the ordinary, she congratulated herself that she'd written a note to John and his reinforcements last night, while she still had candles and the room was still warm enough that she could hold a pen.

Male voices drifted up the stairway, and for one moment her heart gave a leap. But of course it was only Muldoon and the other male guests, consuming bread and cheese and joking one another about who snored and whose names got amorously murmured in sleep.

"—Oh, and Fleurette—who the bloody 'ell is Fleurette . . ."

"My dearest wife—"

"Aargh, 'er and Nan . . . *and* Margot . . ."

"I have many wives, *mes amis*; behold, I am a Mohammedan . . ."

All stood as Abigail came down the stairs, and Mrs. Purley brought her corn pudding—as befit her more elevated station—and coffee. *The horses are ready like you asked, Mrs. Adams*—and *a nice bit of bread and cheese for you both, and oats for the beasts—Why, thank you, m'am—Will there be anything else, Mrs. Adams?—Yes, we'll hand it to him as soon as he arrives . . .*

Under a racing cover of cloud, the world was just light enough, at eight, to make out the details of the Danvers road as it turned inland, toward what had once been Salem Village.

"D'you know the place, then, m'am?" asked Muldoon, as Abigail drew rein. From her last visit to Gilead she remembered the old house that lay a little distance down the overgrown track to their right: remembered it because, in the near-darkness in which she and Thaxter had been riding, she hadn't been able to see the end of the woods some hundred yards ahead, and had hoped to find shelter.

Now in midafternoon, with the woods filled with a sickly rinsed-out light, she could glimpse the ruined walls, the holed and sagging ceiling, in clearer detail. As she had on that first visit, she dismounted, and led Balthazar to the broken door. What had been simply a pitch-black cavern on that night showed up now as a primitive keeping room, the puncheon floor—under its carpet of dead leaves—an assurance that they wouldn't fall through broken boards into an unsuspected cellar.

She led the horses inside, slipped the bits from their mouths, loosened the saddle cinches, and from the saddlebag poured two little heaps of oats on the floor. Muldoon, who'd lingered in the doorway looking down the road at the fields glimpsed beyond the thinning of the trees, came in to help her: "Is that there Gilead, then, Mrs. A?"

"Beyond the fields, yes. My impression was that the place was larger ten or fifteen years ago. Several houses looked completely deserted, and many of the inhabited ones had their upper stories shuttered up, even in the daytime when we rode out. But it was the end of daylight when we reached here, my husband's clerk and I, and we were taken immediately to their House of Repentance for evening services. It was well and truly dark by the time the Hand of the Lord had had his say."

"Then we'd best have a careful look round." The sergeant took his musket in its wrappings of oilcloth from the back of his saddle, and after it, the pistol that John kept in his office desk under lock and key. "How close are the woods to the buildings?"

With half-closed eyes Abigail summoned back the wet twilight, the impression of trees crowding in on those decaying gray buildings. "A hundred feet?" It was hard to put aside her horrified anger at herself, that she and Thaxter had undoubtedly spent the night only a few dozen feet from where Rebecca—almost certainly—was being kept. "They'll have gardens, between the houses and the woods, but those will be cleared off now."

"Aye, but their fences'll still be up." The young man led the way from the house, looked down the road toward open ground, blue eyes narrowed. In Boston, Patrick Muldoon's air of countrified good nature had made him seem naïve, primitive, and rather harmless despite his imposing size and crimson uniform. Faced with the prospect of an escape through woods in overcast darkness—she knew precisely how far her lantern would cast light and she knew it would be next to useless—Abigail felt suddenly grateful that she was with an Irish farmhand used to the ways of bogs and fields, rather than the cleverest of Boston law clerks. "Moon's on the wane, too, and them clouds don't look like breakin'. We'll barely be able to see, goin' in. Comin' out, we've got to strike a fence and know which way to follow it, if we're to make it back here with both feet. Thank Christ the road's good and rutted."

"And that it's December and cold as a well digger's elbow," murmured Abigail. "They'll all be indoors."

As if to mock her words, the crack of a gunshot sounded somewhere in the brown and silver woods, a hunter seeking to make the most of what game there was before the last of the squirrels retired for their winter naps. "Almost all," she temporized primly, and Muldoon grinned.

"Better watch out for them behind us, then, if they take it into their heads we're the divil's henchmen. All over the barrack, they say colonials grow up with guns in their hands, an' don't have to be taught to shoot 'em, like we do that the landlords have up for poachin' if we so much as throw a rock. Lead on, m'am."

For nearly a mile they skirted the edge of the open fields that lay to the eastern side of the village. The rain had been much less here, inland from the sea, but the going was slow, wet leaves and broken branches treacherous underfoot. The thicker undergrowth along the edge of the woods screened them from sight of the village itself, but within the woods the ground was clearer, the world bathed in a cold shadowless light. Now and then Abigail and her escort would work their way through the knots of hazel and bindweed, to the ditch that demarcated the fields. Beyond the ditch, low stone walls kept wild pigs, deer, and—probably more effectively—saplings and creepers at bay.

"Looks a right mess to get a plow through," whispered Muldoon, gazing across the brown field with its pocked, uneven ground. "What do they grow hereabouts?"

"Maize—Indian corn—mostly, and beans and pumpkins between the rows. The Indians used to not plow at all, just make hills for each plant, and bury a dead fish in each hill, to put heart into the plant. We grow corn on our farm—south of Boston, in Braintree—as well as wheat and rye, but 'tis a hard crop on the soil. If you're to grow corn you need three times the land you're going to plant, plus meadows for hay."

"And it all belongs to somebody else anyway, you say?"

"A great deal of it. It isn't that unusual, for boundaries to get mixed up, especially if the land goes through the hands of a speculator. When Bargest originally sought out land for his congregation he bought what was cheapest without looking into title too closely." Abednego Sellars himself had been absent when Abigail had called at the chandlery on her way out of Boston—evidently a good many of the Sons of Liberty were out investigating the rumor that the *Beaver* was going to be surreptitiously unloaded at sea. But Penelope Sellars had provided a wealth of detail about her detested in-laws' legal troubles, with considerable spiteful satisfaction, including the information that indeed, the case was scheduled to be settled at the next General Court. Legal details aside, Abigail couldn't imagine anyone thinking that the decision would go against a good friend of the Crown who dined regularly with the Governor.

'*And I will give unto thee the land wherein thou art a stranger, for an everlasting possession*,' the little woman had told her; *That's what their Hand of the Lord wrote on his court deposition, when they asked him for proof of where he'd got title to have his folks farming those acres. And, 'This is the land which I sware unto Abraham, unto Isaac, and unto Jacob, saying, I will give it unto thy seed . . .' just as if HE were Abraham, Isaac, and Jacob all rolled into one. AND he had his congregation run off the bailiffs, that Pentyre had sent out—just as if the man wasn't in a position to have this Hand of the Lord taken up for debt and bigamy, too . . .*

What had Thaxter said of Richard Pentyre? *God help you if you cross him . . .*

And God help you, thought Abigail uneasily, *if you cross the Hand of the Lord.*

And Perdita Pentyre, who would have inherited the lands were her husband to die, had been merely a detail to be cleared from the path of the righteous.

The woods grew thinner around them, sumac and sapling pine replacing the immemorial heaviness of hickory and oak. The ground became more even underfoot, and the broken remains of a wall slanted away before them. Following the woods' edge, Abigail saw the houses of the village much closer, and the remains of what had been a palisade in the days when Indian attack was a real possibility. Above the gray overcast, the sun had passed noon.

"Well, that place looks a fair mansion, anyway—"

"The Reverend Bargest's, at a guess," Abigail murmured. It was the handsomest and best-kept in the village. Troublingly, men and women stood about in front of it with an air of people waiting for news. Now and then someone would emerge from one of the other houses, cross to the waiting knots. Even at this distance, Abigail could see the tension of question and reply.

"Would he be ill, then?"

"What, he?" Despite her uneasiness, Abigail couldn't keep the sarcasm from her voice. "Surely he can cure himself of anything with a touch? Perhaps his most recent Bride has gone into labor." But the sight filled her with dismay. She had counted on three solid hours of the Chosen One's evening sermon, to allow her to get in, release Rebecca, and make good an escape before total darkness set in. The possibility that the Reverend would be ill and unable to preach had never crossed her mind.

"Well, let's get in a smitch closer, and sit and watch a spell. 'Mostly you don't need to ask questions,' me mother always says, 'if you'll just hold your peace and keep your eyes open.'"

"She sounds like a wise woman, your mother."

"Ach." He shook his head. "When I'd tell her so, she'd roll up her eyes at the rafters an' say, 'I'm scarcely that, boy-o; I married your Da', didn't I?' Yet she always did give me the best advice." He fell silent, as they moved closer yet to the buildings. There were perhaps forty houses, not counting cowsheds and outbuildings, straggling along a single rutted lane which perished in the yard of the last dwelling in the town. Another lane crossed it, joining the Reverend's house (as Abigail surmised it) with the House of Repentance. Nearly half of these dwellings clustered within the ruined quadrangle of the old palisade, and three appeared to have been part of its curtain wall.

As she watched the inhabitants of the village moved about their circumscribed winter chores—cutting kindling or hauling in sledges of wood from the surrounding wilderness; feeding chickens in their coops or tending boiling pots where by the stink of it soap was being rendered. Most, Abigail knew, would be laboring at indoor winter tasks: spinning, weaving, carding, sharpening tools, and mending harness. *Orion grew up here.*

She could almost see him, toddling adoringly at his mother's heels down that muddy street. Beautiful, like her, with her raven hair and green eyes. And she'd thought nothing of dragging him along with her to live under the domination of her monomaniacal lover. And he, who had only his love to use, to draw her back to him, had been trapped in the sticky webs of neediness and domination.

I've tried to act for the best, but I can't be two people!

Would things have been different, if he had been brought up in anything approaching normal circumstances?

Or with madness, did it make a difference?

Yet while her mind ran on all this, Abigail's gaze moved over the squalid little settlement, picked out details. Who went into which doors, who came out, how long they remained. Which houses had the look of habitation—cows, chickens, dogs, gardens harvested recently, smoke in the chimneys, outhouses that smelled of use—and which did not. She and Muldoon shifted their position several times in the course of the afternoon, watching patiently as hunters, not even knowing quite what they looked for.

"You say he kept her stupefied with laudanum before he took her across the bay—"

"He had plenty in his house. I don't see how else he would have kept her quiet."

"Oh, aye. Our landlord's mother had the habit of it, and God knows she didn't know Easter from Christmas for months on end. But you had to watch her. Lord Semphill, he'd keep her locked in her room, but you couldn't leave a candle with her, and they had to bar the windows, for she'd sometimes try to break 'em. Would they still have her under it now, d'ye think, ten days later?"

"I have reason to think she was struck over the head," Abigail murmured back. She shifted her cloak, where it had become entangled with the small horn lantern at her belt, and its little satchel of candles. "I don't know how badly. Nor can I guess what the Reverend Bargest told whatever family is in charge of caring for her. They must be well and truly under his sway, for if she's capable of speech, what she tells them will be disquieting to say the least. And they'll see—they *must* see—how harmless she is . . . In the end, he knows he's going to have to kill her."

"Oh, aye," said the young man again, as if it needed no saying. "Just as soon as he knows Mr. Pentyre's been took care of, belike. They won't have done for the poor lady already, d'ye think?"

Abigail shook her head, not shifting her gaze from the village down the hill. She'd already thought of that. "If he *did* bring her here, it would be because she saw him. She knew him. Whatever Bargest told him about why Perdita Pentyre must die, Orion had clearly made up his mind not to harm Rebecca. The Hand of the Lord must have had a nasty shock," she added grimly, "when his chosen weapon came back to him with a witness, saying, *You keep her safe, or I won't kill Pentyre.*"

"It's mad. Your boy must have known the old man couldn't let her live."

"He knew for two years that she was another man's wife," said Abigail. "Yet he hoped that things would somehow turn out right in the end. But—" She broke off, and said, "Damnation!"

"What?" Muldoon grinned. "An' don't think it ain't a treat, to find a good Puritan lady will swear now and then—"

"No," whispered Abigail indignantly. "That woman there, coming out of that house . . . It's Damnation Awaits the Trembling Sinner. The servant to the Hazlitts."

"Damnation indeed." He raised an eyebrow curiously at Abigail, as the tall young woman made her way along the muddy street. Abigail nodded assent, and cautiously they moved through the brown tangles of dead fern and leafless hackberry, where the edge of the woods paralleled the way. Beyond the broken stumps of the palisade, and the last cowsheds and woodpiles of the village proper, lay half a dozen houses, farther and farther apart; one of these, two stories tall, had the look of an old defensive blockhouse. Its upper floor projected over its lower, and its walls were stoutly constructed of squared logs. The sheds around it stood empty, and what had been its garden was a knotted thicket of dead weeds, ringed by straggly fence-posts whose rails had long since been taken away for other purposes.

Before this house Damnation halted, and stood staring up at its upper windows. Across the road and with a field between them, Abigail couldn't see the woman's face. But she did see her walk back and forth before the house, and partway around both sides, looking.

Muldoon touched Abigail's arm, pointed. By the door,

Abigail saw, were three little piles of cut wood, as if someone had been assigned to bring an armload to the place, and had simply dumped their burden and gone away.

Abigail said, "That's it."

Thirty-one

A woman came out of the house nearest the one that had attracted Damnation's attention—which lay nearly fifty feet away—aproned and wrapped in a heavy shawl. Though the servant woman's brown dress was the plainest serge obtainable in town, still it looked modish and new against the villager's crude homespun. The village woman caught Damnation's arm, explained something to her, with gestures and shakings of her head. As she led Damnation away, back toward the main village crossroad, the servant looked back over her shoulder at the empty house.

"A closer inspection, Sergeant?"

To avoid crossing the road under the eyes of possible watchers in the two nearest houses, Abigail and her escort had to work their way for nearly thirty minutes along the edge of the woods, past the last house in the village (which was occupied, Abigail noted—What half-believing heart had settled thus far from his neighbors?) and so back to the rear of that closed-up former blockhouse. Even so, nearly a hundred feet of open ground lay between the woods and the rear of the house. Its original defensive purpose was clearest on that side, for there were no windows at all on the ground floor, and only rifle-slits above, facing the fields.

It was so wholly and indisputably a prison that Abigail shivered, and wondered, *Is his Word so paramount to them, that they'll follow him even in that? Incarcerating someone only because he says they should?*

Fifteen centuries of religious histories in her father's

books, and John's, snickered up their sleeves at her: *You think that's odd?* The Salem witches shook their heads at her naïveté.

She's a born liar and a conniver, the wicked Mrs. Jewkes in *Pamela* had said to the other servants, *don't believe a word that she says*. Or had the Hand of the Lord chosen Mrs. Tillet's justification? *I know more about this than you do . . .*

Dark as it had been when she and Thaxter had come out of the evening service, she doubted she'd even been able to see this house.

Yet still, unreasonably, she felt, *I should have known . . .*

The more closely she observed the house, the more certain she was.

Only once in the course of the short, fading afternoon did anyone go near the place. The same woman who had drawn Damnation away returned some hours later, a basket on her arm. Going in, she reemerged almost at once—without the basket—and fetched in a few sticks of the firewood. A few moments later, Abigail saw the white puffs of new smoke rise from the chimney. *Good Heavens, it must be like an icehouse in there—!*

She came out again to bring in a pail of water, and to empty a chamber pot, which she rinsed briefly with another splash of water drawn from the well, but didn't wash. This she carried back inside, then reemerged, picked up her empty basket, and hastened away down the darkening street toward the groups gathered outside the house of the Chosen of the Lord.

By that time, the wintry daylight was almost gone. At times Abigail barely noticed that she was shivering, so violent was her rage, shock, horror; at other times she felt a kind of bone-deep exhaustion coming over her and thought, *I'm going to get sick if I'm not careful*. But there was nothing to be done about that. She and Muldoon worked their way along the edge of the woods, observing every house in the town, but they all appeared to be normal—

"Or as normal as this place can be, under the command of a hypocritical madman!" whispered Abigail, when they returned to their post among a thicket of young hazel, opposite the old blockhouse.

"Who may be dying," breathed back Muldoon. Men came in from the woods—some with wood, others carrying braces of dead squirrels or groundhogs—and the anxious groups keeping watch around that handsome house coalesced into a crowd. Though at that distance it was difficult to be sure, Abigail thought the watchers kept turning, looking in the direction of the blockhouse. Several pointed.

"You don't think she had the smallpox, and has give it to him?"

"If she had, the Tillets would have it as well," Abigail whispered back. "As would Mr. Hazlitt, and I myself."

"Did she bite him, d'you think, and it's mortifyin'?"

"Serve him right if it were." But her chuckle swiftly died. "They would kill her."

"T'cha!"

"If she were responsible for his death, or his illness? For robbing them of his counsel? Of course they would." As she spoke the words a cold suspicion took her heart, as to what was actually going on in the village.

John—Where was John? Or—though she could not imagine that John wouldn't come to aid her himself, and be damned to the Provost Marshal's thirty-pound bond—where were those he would, he *must*, send? She had listened all day for them, consumed with dread lest they ride straight into Gilead and let themselves be talked into leaving, having given the game away . . .

"Don't worry after 'em, Mrs. Adams," whispered Muldoon. "We can get the poor lady out of there right enough. All we need's a bit of time to get ourselves ready."

As the gray light thickened, they worked their way back to one of the broken fence-lines that crossed the light second growth of what had been fields, the sergeant marking the way by cutting saplings half through with his knife, and bending them down so that they formed a sort of chain as far as the fence. "Even if the moon's covered, keep a hand on these," he breathed. "It'll lead ye's to the fence. The fence'll lead us to the ditch and wall round the great fields, and we can follow those to the road. 'Twill be slow going, but once at the road we can keep one foot in a rut, and thirty of my strides'll take us to that shanty where the horses are tied."

"I have a lantern—" It had been dragging at her belt all the afternoon.

"Agh, m'am, it won't shine a foot before us, but'll show us up for a mile. And, I never did go out poachin' with a winker but that I managed to drop it and the candle fell out of it."

"How'll we find our way from the house to the first sapling?"

"We'll do like that old Greek feller." Muldoon tapped the side of his nose with an expression of wisdom. "The one that treated that poor girl so scaly: I misremember his name. But we'll have to step pretty lively, I'm thinkin'. Night's fallin' fast."

It was, in fact, about the hour that Abigail and Thaxter had entered the village before, when she and Muldoon came opposite its main crossroad again. Lights had been kindled in the House of Repentance, but—as Abigail had feared—few were going inside. Instead they lingered around its doors in the twilight, or gathered, thicker and thicker, before the big and handsome house, whose windows also began to glow. She recognized Damnation among them, by her height and by the relatively stronger color of her dress. She was one of the ones gesturing, talking, passionately it seemed, and pointing back toward the blockhouse.

"Mr. Hazlitt must have sent her away Wednesday evening, just before the town gates were shut," Abigail whispered, now shivering in earnest as she stood beside the sergeant's comforting bulk. "I can't see how she could have come into town much before this morning, even with a few hours' start on us. I don't know where she would obtain a horse. What's going on now?"

The house door opened. Six men emerged, carrying a sort of bier between them, as if for a dead man. But the Reverend Atonement Bargest, the Hand of the Lord, was far from dead. On the bier he writhed, arms threshing, head rolling, and even across the distance Abigail could hear him moan and cry out, though his words were lost to her.

"What the divil—?"

"The divil indeed," murmured Abigail. "He's being tormented by witches—invisible, of course—even as those girls were in Salem Village, all those years ago." She glanced up at Muldoon. "Or your Aunt Bridget. Something tells me we're here just in time."

Men, women, a few children and adolescents came hurrying from the houses to join the little procession that crowded around the bier and followed it to the church. A few bore lanterns. Most carried pine-knot torches, the light yellow and wild on their faces, like an uneasy whirlpool of flame. Muldoon signed to Abigail, and the two made their way farther up the edge of the woods, finally breaking cover at a small house that stood a little distance from the old palisade, one of the few in the village which they had observed included no dog. Muldoon led the way across the fallow garden, circled on the side away from the street, and yanked the latchstring to let them in. The downstairs keeping room was a chasm of almost total dark, save for the glow of the banked fire, at which Abigail lighted her lantern's candle. She'd already guessed what Muldoon sought.

"Good for her, she's spun a fair bundle of it." He dug through the willow basket beside the spinning wheel, pulled out hanks of thick yarn, for stockings or scarves rather than the finer thread that would feed the great loom that crouched in the far corner. *So the old Greek he had in mind was Theseus, following the thread-clue to the labyrinth's heart . . .* as she had followed first one clue, and then another, to lead her here. "Is there a shed for laundry?"

Abigail shook her head. "She'll have her clothes-rope strung upstairs in the attic, this time of year. Will we need rope?" She glanced toward the window, her heart beginning to pound with the sense of panic, of time running out, that had driven her from Boston the moment she had seen Bargest's handwriting on the threat to Pentyre. *Orion killed his mother because he knew he would not be returning to care for her . . . because he was going to make his attack on Pentyre last night.* She shuddered at the thought: *Had he meant only to cut her throat? Was it that blood that triggered his madness, as it triggered his outrages on Perdita Pentyre's body?*

Was that the message he'd sent here with Damnation? To tell the Hand of the Lord that his Will would be done?

Then Bargest would know that his tool—his human weapon—would either not be returning here at all—that he would be killed—or that he would *return, and demand Rebecca's release.* Either way, Rebecca would be no longer of use.

The attic was crammed with supplies—sacks of corn, barrels of apples, smoke-black hams hanging from the rafters to keep them away from mice—but no clothesline. By the attenuated glimmer of the single gable window, and the weak flicker of Abigail's candle, they eventually located a stout coil of it downstairs in the porch, after what felt like half an hour of hunting. By that time the ground outside was a mere blur of iron gray, the sky barely to be distinguished above the coal-black line of the trees. "Can you find the thicket?" Abigail slipped the lantern-slide shut on her candle, and Muldoon nodded. "Then go now, and rig a line to the blockhouse," she whispered. "I don't know what I'll find there, or how long it'll take."

"Stand at the corner of the house toward the wood,

then," whispered the sergeant, "with the lantern-slide open toward me, or I'll never find the place comin' back."

Abigail obeyed. As she stood waiting, she could hear the drift of sound from the House of Repentance, a single voice, crying out in terror, shrieking in horror at the spirit of the witch that assailed him. Now and then, like the gust of wind in the trees, the congregation gasped or screamed in response.

Like the Sons of Liberty, she reflected, when Sam would shout at them, *Do you want to see your homes overrun, your goods plundered, your children at the point of British bayonets . . . ?*

No—! Like the hammer of the sea . . . or the slow tolling of Boston's bells . . .

For a time she could make out the black shape of the sergeant, his heavy military cloak belling out behind him, moving over the paler ground. Then she blinked, and could see him no more. She herself could scarcely find the blockhouse, though she oriented herself carefully toward the dark bulk of it against the final limmerance of sky. She followed its wall around, opened the lantern-slide, pointed it out toward the wood.

Herself a Daughter of Eve—the ninth and worst, she recalled: the woman who goes about the town poking her long nose into things that weren't her affair—Abigail would have given much, to tiptoe down the empty village street and put her head through the door of the House of Repentance. She recalled how an uncle of hers described the girls at the Salem trials, screaming in agony and pointing at the old woman whom the jury had just voted as innocent: It was she, she, who was doing this to them! Did they not see her glowing spirit, squatting on their chests, strangling and pinching and grinning? The jury had reversed their verdict, and old Mrs. Nurse had been hanged.

Sergeant Muldoon's footfalls crunched in the dark, but Abigail saw nothing of him until he appeared suddenly, a yard from her, in the lantern's feeble light. The sky was black overcast, thin wind running like scared rats over the fallow fields. The sergeant tied the end of his yarn-clue to a sliver of kindling, which he rammed between the logs at the corner of the house. "Let's not lose that," he said.

Abigail shut the lantern-slide. The dark was absolute. They followed the log wall of the blockhouse back around to their right, and Abigail almost broke her shin on the pile of firewood by the door. Opening the slide, they could just see the latchstring.

The remains of a fire glowed in the hearth of what had been a keeping room downstairs, long as two ordinary rooms and smelling of dirt and mold. Searching for the stairway, Abigail had the dim impression of a big table, a litter of broken baskets entangled with the knots and slag-ends of wool. Broken shuttles, and a whittled wood "wheel-finger," told her that at some point this room had contained spinning wheels and probably a couple of looms, where the women of the village had pursued the wholesale task of cloth-making. Neither looms nor wheels remained. Along the back wall lay the stairs, a sort of heavy ladder that it would have taken all of Abigail's strength to raise to its place alone. The room was as cold as a tomb.

The ladder, put in its place, hooked onto pegs in the wall just beneath a bolted trapdoor in the ceiling. This opened into darkness only warmer by the most minute degree, a darkness that smelled of dirty blankets, mice, decades of mold, and of chamber pots long uncleaned.

Abigail said, "Rebecca?"

There was no reply.

The dark lantern showed only edges, spots, and then only when Abigail had cautiously advanced to be nearly on top of what she saw. The room was a large one, lined—Abigail saw as she moved toward the wall—with two tiers of roughly constructed bunks. Some of these retained mattresses of ticking stuffed with what had once been straw.

On others, only heaps of mousy-smelling husks remained. Wild skittering at the other end of the long room, and the lantern-beam glittered on a half-hundred little mousy eyes. Abigail walked toward the place, the light held out before her, knowing what she'd find close to that many mice.

And she did. A bowl of porridge and a hunk of bread, comprehensively chewed by the vermin. A red pottery pitcher of water. The rinsed-out chamber pot, and the trailing end of a very dirty striped blanket.

She held the lantern higher and closer.

Rebecca. *Asleep.*

Thirty-two

Abigail saw her breast rise and fall beneath the blankets. Someone had thrown a couple of those thin straw mattresses over her, for extra warmth. Rebecca was so emaciated as to be almost unrecognizable, her black hair cut off short and a dark, bruised area just back of her right temple, a half-healed cut in its center. A black bottle—and two dead mice—lay beside the bed. Another bottle stood next to it, exactly the same as she had seen in Orion Hazlitt's house.

Abigail knelt beside the bed. "Rebecca, wake up." She shook her, gently but urgently. *"Wake up!"*

She hefted the upright bottle. Nearly full. Concussion would have made laudanum almost redundant, though she suspected Orion had poured at least some down Rebecca's throat the first night he'd carried her to his house, to keep her silent as the dead while he sent Damnation back to Gilead with the message: *I have done as you asked but you must keep this woman safe, or I will do no more.* She remembered herself downstairs, with Sam and Revere and Dr. Warren, like an utter fool talking with Orion while his mother, stupefied into near-unawareness, argued with customers and sat in the keeping room.

"Rebecca!" She dipped her hand into the pitcher—checking first that there was no mouse within it—and first flicked, then splashed water on her friend's face. Muldoon prowled from window to window—there were three on the street side of the upper room, and one at one of the gable ends—trying to open a casement, to relieve the stuffiness of the atmosphere. It could scarcely get any colder: No wonder, in Rebecca's state, it was nearly impossible to wake her. "You have to wake up!" All four of the windows were shuttered, and the shutters padlocked. Muldoon set aside his musket and the rope he still carried, and worked his knife beneath the iron hasp. "Rebecca!"

"Abigail?" Rebecca turned her face from the cold of the almost-frozen water. "Stop it."

"You have to wake up."

The brown eyes opened, blinked up at her, sleepy and incurious. Abigail held the candle close and saw the pupils wide, not narrow with opiates. Rebecca flinched from the light, then gasped, "Abigail!" and clutched suddenly at Abigail's wrist. "Oh, God!"

"We have to get out of here. Now, this minute. Can you sit up?"

"I did—Yesterday—first time." Rebecca groped for her shoulder, dragged herself up. "Mary Mother of *God*, it's cold—"

Abigail pulled her own small clasp knife from her pocket, dragged the blanket from beneath the ragged mattresses and cut a slit in it, so that it went over Rebecca's head like a crude garment. All they had left her was her chemise. It was filthy, but nowhere was it marked with blood.

"Cut one of those ticks." Muldoon turned his head from the window, and tossed Abigail the coil of clothes-rope, followed by his cloak. "Wrap up her feet."

"Who's he?" Rebecca's eyes were wide at the unmistakable cut and color—visible when his arm came near to the light—of a British infantry coat.

"Mrs. Malvern, may I present Sergeant Patrick Muldoon of the King's Sixty-Fourth Regiment of Foot? Sergeant

Muldoon, Mrs. Malvern—the sergeant has been good enough to escort me here, and I hope at some point John and others will—"

"Damn!" Muldoon pulled the shutters to instants after he got them open. "Here they come!"

"Who?" gasped Rebecca shakily, as Abigail left her to dart to the window. "Abigail, where *am* I? I saw—Oh, God! Orion—"

"I know all about it." Abigail peered grimly through the crack in the shutters. Her training held good and she said, "*Oh*!" instead of some of the more choice expressions Muldoon was using, but rage swept her, almost drowning out fear at the sight of the thirty or so men striding down the unpaved lane toward the blockhouse, burning billets of firewood aloft in their hands. The women—perhaps two thirds of the Congregation—swarmed among them, crying and shouting and pointing. The man in the lead wasn't Bargest, but rather the dark-browed Brother Mortify, who had guided her and Thaxter out of the village lands.

She flung herself back to Rebecca, pulled her to her feet, and threw Muldoon's cloak around her. "They'll see us use the door—"

He was already working, ripping and levering at the hasp that locked the shutters of the single window in the gable wall. It faced at an angle, away from the street. Through the shutters on the street-side windows the torchlight showed up fiercely yellow, and Abigail heard the crash of the door opening downstairs. But instead of footsteps on the floor below, there was only the light, sharp crack of torches flung in, followed at once by billows of acrid smoke. Someone shouted, "Stand ready! She may fly!"

"I've my gun—"

"There she is! There she is!" screamed a woman—Rebecca was still leaning on Abigail's shoulder, nowhere near any of the windows. "I see her! Look, she's flying!"

Rebecca muttered, "I wish I might!" She took a step,

staggered, and someone outside fired a gun. "Don't tell me they think I'm a witch!"

"Yes."

Someone else yelled, "There she is!" and more guns boomed. At the same moment Muldoon flung open the gable window. Smoke was now pouring up the stair, and through the open trapdoor Abigail could see the red flare of firelight.

Wretch! Lying, hypocrite wretch! He planned this from the moment Orion told him he must keep Rebecca safe! This building is isolated—one of the few in the village that could burn without danger to its neighbors!

"Give her here." Muldoon jerked the knot tight on the doubled rope, wrapped around the nearest bunk-frame, crossed himself, scooped Rebecca up, and put her over one shoulder like a sack of meal. "Hang on, m'am, if ever you did. Mrs. Adams, wrap the rope around your arm like this, play it out, put your feet on the wall and lean back—"

Abigail said, "Oh, dear God . . ."

"Throw me down me musket to me first. And don't drop that winker!"

Dear God—She fought panic at the thought of descending as Muldoon descended, playing out the rope around his arm. The distance wasn't fearful—she'd fallen from higher trees as a girl. But in the blackness, with the red wildness of firelight reflected from the front of the house and flame beginning to crawl up the dry wood of the ladder—for a moment she could think nothing but, *I'll be killed. I'll be killed*—

Her mind flashed, blindingly, to the night a number of years ago, when one of the wild mobs of the North End, stirred up by Sam's furious pamphlets against the Stamp Act, had mobbed, broken into, and gutted the Governor's house—the last time Sam had let a mob get away from his control. Governor Hutchinson and his daughter had escaped out a back window, she had heard later, and fled through the winding alleyways of the North End to take refuge with friends. *What horror—!*

Trembling, she dropped the musket down out the window, tied the lantern to her waist, the heat of the metal palpable even through several petticoats and a quilted skirt, wrapped the rope around her arm as she'd been shown and hoped fervently she was doing correctly—

"There they go!" screamed someone, and as Abigail swung herself out the window—and the rope constricted like an agonizing garrote around her arm—two or three men came around the corner of the house. "She's getting away!"

Muldoon has time for one shot. The thought passed, very coolly, through Abigail's mind and, bracing her feet on the house-wall, she began to lower herself as rapidly as she could. Someone fired a shot, then another, followed by a great deal of shouting and cursing and Muldoon's voice bellowing, very unlike his usual good-natured self, "And the next one goes between the eyes of the first man steps forward!"

He has John's pistol.

Then she was on the ground. She ran to the sergeant's side, scooped up the musket that he'd dropped to the ground to draw the pistol: "Go!" he said, and she went. The yarn-clue was there, and she fled along it, the musket weighing pounds in her hand, the spreading firelight showing her up. At the thicket she waited, gasping, hearing shots behind her in the dark and seeing the black figures of men and woman silhouetted on the red glare of the fire.

Men and women both. The words ran in a circle in her head. *Men and women both . . .*

The way she herself, and Rebecca—and poor Mrs. Pentyre—had arrayed themselves at the sides of the men, in their fight for the colony's rights?

She shoved the thought from her as she'd have struck a

mouse away that tried to climb her skirts: *We're following the principles of justice! The rights that Englishmen have fought for—*

But she knew perfectly well that many members of the Sons of Liberty were in the organization simply because they were following Sam Adams.

It isn't the same. She knew it in the marrow of her bones.

His recent outburst against her notwithstanding, would Sam hesitate to order killed a man he saw as a threat to the Sons?

It isn't the same.

But at that moment, kneeling, gasping, in the wet ground by the hazel thicket, it seemed frighteningly close.

"Mrs. Adams?" "Abigail?"

Whispered voices, hoarse with exertion and fear. "Here." She shot the slide back for one instant, then closed it again.

"Bide," said Muldoon.

Rebecca caught at her arm, her shoulder, her weight frighteningly slight. How few days ago had she wakened and been able to eat and drink? At the same moment the pistol was put into her hand, the musket taken, and she heard the oily snick of the lock, the faint noise of a cartridge being ripped. A moment later, the clink of the rod rammed home: once, twice, thrice. Every man in the militia whined like a schoolboy about drill—*How many times we got to show them we know how to load our bloody guns?*

It wasn't until she heard Muldoon loading his rifle in seconds, by touch, in the dark, with the torchlight coming toward them, that she understood why British foot soldiers had to drill for hours. So that you load your rifle—cartridge, ball, powder, patch, ram—with no more hesitation than you bring your spoon to your mouth; the way she, or her mother, could knit in the dark.

The blockhouse was ablaze. The light covers that had blocked the rifle-slits inside had burned away; flame jetted out like the emanations of demon eyes. A single great column of fire roared from the broken roof. Rebecca's hand clutched tighter on Abigail's arm. Deeply as she had been asleep, thought Abigail, she would not have waked until the fire had climbed into the room. Her hand closed hard around her friend's.

Across the dark meadow, torches were beginning to spread out.

Muldoon said, "We ain't out of the woods yet, ladies."

The night was freezing, the darkness absolute. Though she'd put on her gloves, Abigail's fingers were numb with the cold and it was nearly impossible sometimes to distinguish the branches and saplings Muldoon had cut and bent during the day; she stumbled repeatedly on the uneven ground, the bent roots and old stones of the woodland edge. Thorns tore and grabbed at her skirt, her hair, her face. Through the thickets to her left she glimpsed the fire of the burning blockhouse, and sometimes the moving yellow flare of a torch. But no light penetrated the thin woods through which she and her companions moved. Had Muldoon not spoken softly to her she would have despaired a dozen times: She wanted to cry, *Don't leave me!* like a child. But every time she reached the end of one sapling, and couldn't find the next, she managed to keep her voice adult and level and soft—"Sergeant?" "Here, m'am. This way." *He must think I'm a complete idiot—*

They reached the fences. Knots of torchlight flitted from tree to tree in the blackness, but nothing close. Abigail leaned on the first fence-post, trembling, and very near her, heard that light Irish voice ask, "You still with us, Mrs. M?"

"I regret—I am," whispered Rebecca. "Hoped—I was dreaming—all those other dreams. What *is* this? Who *are* those people? Orion—Orion killed Perdita—" Her voice cracked a little, and Muldoon said, "Have a bit of this. Mrs. A?"

"I was rather hoping it was a dream as well." Abigail dug in her skirt pockets for the remains of the bread and cheese they'd been given by Mrs. Purley. They'd eaten most of it, watching in the woods that afternoon. "I know what Orion did, dearest. We've been looking for you for two weeks." She divided the cheese—pitifully tiny morsels, when pulled into three—and handed the others chunks of the bread. In return she received Muldoon's canteen, and a smaller flask which proved to be half full of British Army rum. "You've been in Gilead—"

"That horrid place where Orion grew up?" Her voice was weak, but she sounded very much herself. "Then—it wasn't a dream—"

"What wasn't?"

"The Hand of the Lord. Bargest. He was standing by my bed. Not that I ever saw him in my life, but he looked exactly like"—her voice stuck a little on his name—"as Orion described him to me."

"He spoke to you of him, then?"

"Heavens, yes. I've been helping him edit those nasty sermons of his for a year and a half now. Poisonous, dirty-minded, and *so* vain." She leaned against the fence-rails: Abigail felt them shift in their sockets, smelled the moldy stink of the blanket she wore. "I asked him, why did he put up with that man's interference. Constant finicking—nothing ever right. Everything we'd settle on, Orion would ride back there for approval and there was always something wrong. I knew he was getting nothing for it. He said, *I owe the Reverend more than I can ever say.*"

"What he owed him," said Abigail softly, "is that the Reverend knew that Orion had killed a girl here. Two girls."

She heard the hiss of Rebecca's breath, and felt slight

movement through the fence-rail. Wondered if her friend had so far forgotten her conversion, as to cross herself.

Rebecca whispered, "He is mad."

"Bargest, or Orion?"

They moved off again, following the line of fence-rails. "I think—both. Orion—it wasn't a nightmare, was it?" Rebecca stumbled, and Abigail, immediately behind her, caught her.

"No. I think Bargest told him that Mrs. Pentyre was one of the Nine Daughters of Eve—"

"God, not that horrible thing! He polished that sermon like a jewel—Orion said he must have given it once or twice a year, the whole time Orion was growing up here. Simply vile! All Woman's fault, that Man sinned—" She stumbled again, with a soft sob of pain.

"Here, m'am, this won't do." Muldoon's voice sounded very close, and by the swish of clothing and the fence-rail brambles, Abigail guessed he'd picked Rebecca up again. "Up you come. You good for another piece, then, Mrs. A?"

Abigail sighed. "Lead on."

It was harder to speak softly enough for safety, and still be heard. She whispered, "Gilead's about ten miles from Townsend, but we must stick close to the Salem road. John and others will be coming. I know they'll be coming."

"Well, if we start wanderin' about in the woods we've had it for sure," remarked Muldoon matter-of-factly.

The fence became a stone wall, and they followed the wall in the blackness. The harsh wind carried the smell of open fields and smoke. Behind them, Gilead was a cluster of coals around the dimming ruby of the blockhouse. The trees on their right muttered like live things disturbed in their sleep. Abigail said, "They can't let us escape."

And Muldoon said, "Aye. That they can't."

"Pentyre owns most of the land under the Gilead fields," she explained softly, as the young sergeant helped her over the wall. "Bargest was swindled when he bought the place, it sounds like. The case has been in the courts for years—"

"I know. Half those sermons were about how the Chosen of the Lord is being persecuted for his beliefs—"

"For his belief that he can do whatever he likes, maybe—including bigamy and fornication, which Pentyre had him up for as well. Perdita was her husband's heir, of course. The next heir would never come back to this country to straighten things out. Bargest sent Pentyre a letter, threatening him *and Perdita* with murder by the Sons of Liberty. Signed with one of John's names, which he must have got off a pamphlet."

"Fly old duck," muttered Muldoon. "You got to admit, 'tis clever."

"If he's so clever," murmured Rebecca, "will he have his men waiting for us at the road?"

Abigail felt as if she were eight years old again, and that her brother had struck her in the wind with a chunk of firewood. Sick, and cold, and suddenly too tired to move another foot. "They'll have found the horses—"

"That shanty's a bit off the track," said the sergeant, as they moved on. "Watch it here, m'am—" A hand groped for her elbow in the dark, supported her where the ground turned to a morass whose surface ice crunched sharply underfoot. "As I said, we can't leave the road. And if we don't get 'em, sure they'll catch us by daylight come mornin'. I been watchin' for torches coming this way from the village, and seen none, but that doesn't mean they're not usin' a dark-lantern. We'll just have to take a sharp listen, 'fore we go in for the beasts."

They trudged in silence. Though Abigail fought to keep her concentration sharp, cold, hunger, daylong fatigue, and bone-deep exhaustion dragged at her thoughts, which kept returning to a gnawing anxiety about where John and the others might be. She found herself a dozen times obsessively calculating how many hours had passed since she'd sent off her notes—*good heavens, did any of those notes actually arrive*? Had ill befallen Shim, or Jed Paley, or the others in carrying them? Had Orion accomplished Pentyre's murder after all? Had John and the others all been arrested?

For that matter, had their arrest (if it had taken place) triggered rioting? Was there fighting in Boston? Her mind fretted at the memory of cries and gunfire barely a street away in winter twilight, of running to King Street in the icy night four years ago, to see the bodies lying in the churned-up snow, of the stink of gunfire hanging in the raw air.

Abigail, stop it! she told herself firmly. *They've just got lost.*

A more prosaic and likely reason, and one which just as surely condemned her and her companions to wandering in darkness until the witch-hunters found them. But at least it didn't involve British cannon opening fire on Boston.

"Bide here." She heard the rustle of Muldoon's cloak, and the blanket as he lowered Rebecca to the ground. He took the musket from Abigail's hand. "The beasts should be hereabouts, t'other side of the road. If I call, *Mrs. Adams*, you cross the road, follow my voice. If I call, *Mrs. Malvern*, you know they're there and they've got me."

"You're very good at this," Abigail whispered admiringly.

"Saints, m'am, I spent the whole of me boyhood poachin' Lord Semphill's rabbits. Me an' the other lads, we had it worked to fare-thee-well, how to keep from gettin' a thrashin'." With barely a rustle he moved off through the trees. Rebecca's hand closed over hers, cold as ice, and Abigail groped around them in the darkness until she found what felt like the remains of a deadfall tree. To this she guided her friend, and sat beside her, unbuckling her belt to bring the shuttered lantern between them. She hadn't dared crack the slide so much as a half inch for light, for most of their flight, but the hot metal was a comfort to fingers nearly frozen.

Above the wind in the trees it was nearly impossible to distinguish smaller sounds.

Then a gun fired like the breaking of Doom, and Muldoon yelled, "Mrs. Malvern, run for it!"

And at half a dozen points around them, dark-lanterns shone out suddenly among the trees.

Thirty-three

Knowing exactly how far the light of her own lantern illuminated the darkness around her—which was not at all—Abigail immediately shoved Rebecca backwards off the log where they sat, snapped open the slide of her lantern, and got to her feet, holding the lantern before her to illuminate her own face and plunge everything around her into still blacker night. At the same time she faced into the woods and shouted, "Rebecca, don't come any closer!" Rather to her astonishment, five of the dozen or so men coming toward them out of the woods immediately whirled and raced off in that direction, lanterns aloft, shouting, "I see her! I see the witch! Hark how her eyes glow!"

Rebecca, under Muldoon's dark army cloak, had the good sense to lie perfectly still as Abigail strode away from her to intercept her captors.

"I suppose the Chosen of the Lord is waiting courageously back in the safety of the village?" Abigail demanded briskly. "While you blunder about in the woods to face an armed man? Get your hand off me, sir," she added, as one of the men moved to seize her arm. "Now that my friend has fled to safety I have no reason to flee from you. You can't murder every outsider who passes through your village, you know."

"'Tis no crime, to exterminate a witch." The very tall, very young farmer who faced her seemed to be the leader of this portion of the mob. He had narrow-set eyes, thin mousy hair, and a mouth like an ill-natured dog's.

"Not according to the Book of Leviticus," agreed Abigail. "How awkward that the Bible doesn't give similar instructions for identifying them."

"By their deeds shall ye know them," replied Dog-Mouth darkly. "All these days, that the hag's been lyin' in the Devil's sleep, *we've* known. We seen our Reverend growin' sicker an' sicker; seen the fires that have broke out, here and there about the town in dead of night; and the very beasts in their stalls struck by plague, since she's been here."

Abigail wondered whether the Hand of the Lord had used an accomplice to set the fires and mix nightshade with the fodder, but knew better than to do so aloud.

"Reverend, he wouldn't hear word against the witch," said another man, as they ringed Abigail and made their way toward the broken-down shanty. "Not at first, so great is his heart with love." Torchlight flared in the cracks of the walls, the broken-out holes of what had been windows. "Yet those vexations began, the first night of her bein' in the blockhouse, and him cryin' out in his sleep for terror. *We* knew. All the village could see him weakenin' day by day—when he'd writhe in pain, or clutch at his heart when he stood up before the Congregation at evenin' services. When he'd cry out at the shape of the devil, flyin' like a glowing bird, he said, about his head. *We* knew who that glowin' bird was!"

Abigail raised her eyebrows. The Hand of the Lord was a more astute mountebank than she'd thought. "And is this the first time your Reverend has been set upon by demons?" she inquired. "Or have others he's disagreed with all turned out to be witches, too?"

The young man brought his hand back to strike her. Abigail—whose younger brother had the same hot temper and ready hand in his cups—stepped back fast, turned face and body so that the blow flashed past her. "Is that all you know how to do?" she snapped, as he started to raise his hand again. "What good servants of the Lord your Reverend has taught you to be, to be sure." She wheeled swiftly, and led the way toward the glowing doorway before he could gather himself for a response. Anything, she thought, to get them away from where Rebecca lay.

Unshaven, untidy, but giving no other evidence of spectral vexation, the Reverend Bargest stood in the restless red glare of the torches, his arms folded and his eyes like pits of shadow beneath silver brows. One of the half-dozen village men grouped behind him had a lantern, and from it the torches had been kindled, that were now thrust into cracks of the broken walls all around the little room. Farther back still in the shadows, the eyes of the horses glowed gold, and the beasts stamped and shifted at the scent of Muldoon's blood.

Abigail ran forward to where the sergeant lay by the wall, and Dog-Mouth and Brother Mortify caught her arms, pulled her back. She could see Muldoon still breathing, though his eyes were closed and there was blood in his red hair. "Behold another of them," proclaimed Bargest, and Abigail whirled to face him, righteous anger drowning her consternation and fear.

"Don't be an ass," she snapped. "Is *everyone* who goes against you a witch?"

"It takes but one witch to corrupt a multitude, as leaven works through a loaf, so that they do her bidding, and through her, her Master's. Where is she?"

"Halfway to Wenham by this time, I should imagine," retorted Abigail.

"Hear it lie," he said, as if she were not really there. "The hag could scarce walk."

"What?" said Abigail. "A woman who can fly? A woman who can reduce you, Reverend—Chosen though you may be—to writhing in agony on your bed? Until it's time to do something that you really want to do, like rise up and convince people that she's the cause of all their problems."

"Satan is the cause of all of their problems," replied Bargest quietly. "And Satan wears many guises. And the most deadly of his guises is that of the Anti-Christ, the False Shepherd who leads men astray with arguments that sound like reason. So don't chop logic with me, Mrs. Adams. These my children are the tried and true remnant of the People, Gideon's faithful Three Hundred, who remain true to the Lord's testing when all the rest have fallen away. They know the Voice of the Lord, and they will not fall away, though you show them all the Kingdoms of the Earth."

He turned to the men. "Satan her master has forsaken the witch," he told them. "Yet as long as her body remains, Satan can return to her, and she will not cease to vex us, until I am dead, or she is destroyed. And when I am dead—when I am no longer able to stand between her and you with the shield of pure faith—then she will come for the rest of you. Believe this." His deep, quiet voice filled the room with its power, and such was the force of his personality that Abigail thought, *Now I can understand, how Prophets stood up to Kings . . .*

"Believe it?" retorted Abigail. "The way that poor mad murderer Orion Hazlitt believed it, when you told him an innocent woman was Jezebel, only because she owned land that you want? It is *you* who played King Ahab, sir, not the other way about."

"The whore was not innocent," said Bargest quietly. "None is innocent, who raises her hand against the children of the Lord. Even as the witch Malvern"—here he raised his voice—"has lifted the Devil's red and dripping hand to smite me down!"

"Rebecca Malvern has been barely conscious for weeks! Since when—?"

"The Devil dwells in the flesh of a witch!" thundered Bargest, and flung up his hands as if calling down the power of God from the heavens. "*He* never sleeps! Nor will he ever, until the Righteous lie dead in their blood! Find the woman and kill her." His blazing eyes, the sweep of his arm, took in all his followers, and ended with one long, bony finger pointing at Abigail. "This one as well. She is the Daughter of Eve, apt to the hand of the Devil . . ."

Those were the final words of the Chosen One. A gunshot crashed from one of the holes in the crazy roof. Bargest flung up his arms as he staggered back, a red hole appearing in the white of his open shirt-front, eyes bulging with shock and an expression of astonishment that was nearly comical.

Brother Mortify grabbed Abigail's arm as the men in the little cabin convulsed into panic movement. Abigail, furious, turned in his grip, shoved her face close to his, flung up her free arm, and screamed as loud as she could.

Taken completely by surprise, Mortify dropped her arm in shock. At the same instant Muldoon sat up, blood oozing from a wound in his shoulder, pistol in hand, barrel leveled on Dog-Mouth, who was one of the few who had a weapon ready. Abigail dived for the sergeant's side as men began to stampede for the door. Her eyes went to the biggest of the holes in the ceiling in time to see another pistol thrust through it, nearly invisible in the shadows. The second shot cleared the room.

Bargest rolled over, gagging on blood. His hands fumbled about, trying to rise, to crawl after them. Then he fell, sobbing and groaning like a child. Abigail dragged Muldoon clear of the horses, which were rearing and stamping in fright. She thought she would have gone next to the Reverend, but there was a slither and thump outside the wall, and the next moment, Orion Hazlitt appeared in the broken doorway of the house.

At the sight of him Abigail's nostrils seemed filled with the smell of blood. All she could see was the dishonored horror of the young woman's body on Rebecca's kitchen floor. Muldoon drew her close to him, pistol ready in his hand, unaware, Abigail realized, who this unshaven, exhausted stranger was.

No more than do I. No more than anyone in Boston ever has.

Hazlitt stopped before her. "Is she safe?" His green eyes—his mother's eyes—were sane. Sane, and very tired.

"She's in the woods. We'll—"

"May I?" Orion bent down, took the pistol from Muldoon's hand—it was John's, Abigail noted—turned around, and shot Bargest between the eyes. "Don't fear," he said, handing the weapon back to the startled Muldoon. "I won't"—he stopped, took a deep breath—"I didn't kill Pentyre," he said. "I couldn't get near him. I—there were—Sons of Liberty—on Castle Island. Everywhere I looked, among the crowd. Someone must have—They were watching for me—"

Softly, Abigail said, "They know."

He closed his eyes. The breath went out of him in a sigh. "Rebecca, too?"

"Yes."

"Everything?" His eyes opened, went to Muldoon, who was busily reloading the gun.

"Everything about *you*." Her mind screamed, *How could you not have known?* and along with Perdita Pentyre's slashed-up body she seemed to see the black cat Pirate, cleaning himself with the stump of his cut-off paw. To read again the horrible verses about slitting the throat of a red-haired devil so that she would not tempt him again, as he was tempted by the dark-skinned succubus who haunted his dreams.

How could I have sat at Rebecca's table with this man? Shoulder to shoulder with him, not just one night but dozens? How could I have talked politics with him, commiserated with him about servant-girls, made dinners for him—for him and for the mother he murdered not forty-eight hours ago? How could I not have seen and smelled and felt all that horror inside him?

She knew she should feel something—*fear? Rage? Disgust? Hatred?* But all she felt was strange, separated from herself, as if she were coming down with fever. For a moment she thought that she stood on the threshold of Hell, speaking to someone just within its doors.

Orion Hazlitt drew breath again, and let it out. "Would that anyone," he whispered, "knew everything about me." He turned away.

A part of her wanted only for him to leave. Muldoon, with the blood soaking into his jacket and his eyebrows standing out ghastly in the torchlight against his waxy pallor, could not have saved her from an attack. Yet she knew Hazlitt would not raise his hand against her. She asked, "Where will you go now?"

He looked back. "I should say, to Hell," he said softly. "Except that I am there. I was raised there. I suppose I'll go where God sends me, who made me as I am."

Had he not turned back to speak to her, she thought he might have gotten clear away. The night was pitch-dark, and even with a small lead, he could have been swallowed up by the native woods of his childhood, and so gone on to the West beyond the mountains. But when he looked away from her, and started again for the door, it was to find Lieutenant Coldstone standing in the aperture, his coat as red in the torchlight as the Reverend Bargest's pooling blood and not a hair of his marble white wig out of place. He had a pistol in his hand and two very large soldiers of the Sixty-Fourth at his back. "Orion Hazlitt?"

Abigail caught the officer's eye, and nodded, knowing that with him, she handed all his knowledge of the Sons of Liberty over into the hands of the Crown.

"I arrest you for murder, in the King's name."

"Don't worry," said Hazlitt, when they stood together while two of Coldstone's men dug a shallow grave. "I am what I am—but I'm not a traitor to Liberty. I'll tell them nothing."

Seated on a tree stump, wrapped in her own cloak and Coldstone's, too, and shivering as if her bones would shatter, Abigail looked quickly up at him.

"God made me what I am," he repeated softly. "But I chose to fight for our rights." He looked across the torchlit clearing, to where Coldstone knelt, talking to Rebecca. "Please tell her that."

"Would you wish me to ask her," said Abigail, "if she will speak to you?"

Men carried Bargest's body out of the broken little house. There was no time, nor a horse to spare, to bear him back even as far as Salem with them, and there was no knowing whether the Gileadites would themselves return to bury him before the vermin of the woods came to feed. Coldstone had brought six men in all—enough to provide protection but by no stretch of any Patriot imagination a threat of armed force—and two of them stood on either side of Hazlitt, watching the darkness all around them with frightened eyes.

After England's tame fields, Abigail thought, the woods of America must seem primeval beyond description, and what they'd seen recently—both in Boston and here in the hinterland—could not have been reassuring.

Across the clearing by torchlight, Coldstone pressed Rebecca's hand, and helped her rise. Exhausted as her friend was, Abigail guessed that she would be capable of coming up with a convincing explanation of why Perdita Pentyre would have come to her house at midnight, without the slightest reference to the Sons of Liberty or insulting pamphlets about the British on Castle Island.

Orion said, "Thank you, Mrs. Adams, but no. I don't want to upset her, and I know she would never understand. Only Mother—" He stopped himself, and turned his face away. His hands were bound behind him but Abigail guessed that the blood on his shirt-cuffs was his mother's. "Only Mother truly understood that I don't want to be what I am," he finished quietly. "I wish she hadn't seen me. Not because she'd tell, but because . . . Her good opinion . . ."

His voice broke off in a whispered laugh, and he shook his head at himself, for even thinking of such a thing. "God made me like this. The Reverend Bargest said, after I—after the first—the first *time*," he stammered, "that God never does things without a reason, and therefore, it was God's will, that I am what I am. That I am seized with— That there are times when it is as if my soul goes into another world, where nothing looks the same, and God's commands are different. In that world, I hear those commands shouting at me out of my heart. I did fight it," he added, as another trooper brought up horses for them both. "The second time, when I woke up in the woods, and came back to the village and everyone talking about the Banister girl's death, and I knew it wasn't a dream . . ."

He shook his head. "Bargest told me, to pray God to show me a different path. A different way to combat Satan. It was the saving of me, for five years. There were bad days, bad times, in Boston, but nothing I could not put aside, with the help of God.

"Knowing Rebecca helped. Knowing she . . . she cared for me, without wanting to eat my soul. I thought then, that maybe I could choose another road." One corner of his mouth turned down, with a breath that could have been a sigh, or another, whispered, laugh at his own absurdity. "Then Mother came."

His mother had left Gilead, and appeared on the printshop doorstep, in May of 1772, Abigail recalled. She remembered it because Rebecca's letter spoke of seeing John, when he'd gone to the session court at Cambridge in that month.

"And Perdita? Did you . . . Did you go into this other world you speak of?"

"Not—No. Yes." In the torchlight by the house, Coldstone helped Rebecca to mount behind a trooper, stood speaking to her for a few moments more. She did not look in Orion's direction.

"It was the blood," said Orion at last. "I thought I could kill her without . . . I thought I could do what the Lord commanded me to, and no more. But then I saw the blood. Smelled its smell. The Hand—Bargest," he made himself use the man's name. "Bargest came to Boston at the beginning of November. With more sermons for the book I was printing, but also to attend on the court. Afterwards he came to the shop, took me aside. He told me that he had proof that Pentyre and his wife were in league with the Devil, that they were the Devil's chosen instruments to break up our Congregation and drive us from our lands. I had fought—for over a year I had fought—to put these thoughts, this terrible sense, from me, that inevitably I would go back to what I had done . . ."

"And he told you," said Abigail softly, "that God had forged you to be His Weapon?"

Orion nodded, his face ghastly in the flickering yellow light. Soldiers came, knocking grave-dirt from their hands and boots, to help him onto a horse. Abigail wondered if the men of the Gilead Congregation would come at daybreak, to dig the Chosen of the Lord up again and bury him in Gilead itself. The energy that had kept her going through flight and confrontation, scouting the town boundaries and climbing down ropes from the burning blockhouse, was long gone. When someone brought up Balthazar to her, she could only gaze aghast at the saddle; one of the men had to help her mount. She reined him over beside the sturdy middle-aged trooper behind whose saddle Rebecca clung: "Will she be all right?" She was mildly astonished that Rebecca hadn't fainted long ago.

The trooper saluted her. "I'll look after 'er, mum, don't you worry." He showed her where, under his cloak, he held Rebecca's wrists tight together against his chest with one big hand. "She starts to shift or slack, I'll feel it 'fore she feels it 'erself, won't I, Mrs. M?"

Her head pressed to his back, Rebecca barely had the strength to nod.

Abigail recalled one of Sam's choice broadsides, about every redcoat being the scum of the London backstreets, whose sole wish was to bayonet every honest American woman he saw.

The little troop started away down the road, one man walking ahead with a torch to light the road. Tarry flakes of fire dripped down from it, to hiss out on the wet earth; the horses moved among rising threads of steam. The world smelled of smoke.

John and his party finally met them, halfway back to the Salem–Danvers road.

Or, rather, Coldstone's party was intercepted by a gang of unknown men dressed up and painted to look like Indians, who stopped them at gunpoint and searched the saddlebags on Orion's horse, something Lieutenant Coldstone had neglected to do. As one of the Indians—who under all his paint looked suspiciously like Paul Revere—brought out of the bag a brown-backed quarto-sized notebook labeled "Household Expenses," another—short, chubby, sitting his horse with the uncomfortable stiffness of a man who has his dignity to consider—reined up beside Abigail. Blue, slightly protuberant eyes met hers worriedly from a black-painted face.

Abigail inquired coolly, "Did you get lost?"

The Indian nodded, and said, rather unwillingly, "Ugh."

"*Ugh* indeed."

He looked as if he were struggling against strict orders not to say a word in English, and Abigail, relenting, said more quietly, "I'm quite all right," which was not strictly the truth. She could feel fever coming on her, from chill, exertion, and clothing damp from the wet of the woods. She realized she was very lucky to be alive at all. Rebecca, slumped behind the King's bloody-back savage, was shivering, too. The Indian reached out a hand to her, but Abigail, mindful of the soldiers watching them, kept her grip on the reins.

In a quiet voice she asked, "I take it you didn't get my message until the town gates were shut for the night. Was the storm too bad to get a boat across the bay?"

"Ugh." He looked, first at Rebecca, his eyes filled with pity, then at Orion.

"The Reverend Bargest is dead," said Abigail. "Hazlitt shot him—goodness knows what his followers are going to do." She coughed, fighting to still it, then gave the Indian a smile. "It is very good to see you, dearest friend."

He smiled back, and saluted her with his tomahawk. "Ugh."

The Indian who looked like Paul Revere slipped the account book into his own saddlebag, and signed to his men. Two of them took the reins of Orion's horse. Orion turned in the saddle, and sought Rebecca's eyes, but did not speak. With him among them, the whole tribe disappeared into the night.

Thirty-four

Presumably this same tribe of Indians, five nights later, boarded the three tea ships at Griffin's Wharf—the *Beaver* having docked, cargo intact, the day before—and dumped some $90,000 worth of East India Company tea into Boston Harbor while six thousand armed countrymen stood around the docks. There was no attempt on Colonel Leslie's part to interfere.

Abigail herself only heard the men go by in the street, from the bed where she lay in the weak aftermath of fever. Though her window was closed and shuttered by that time, still the tramp of their feet came to her, quiet and well-disciplined, though some of them sang. *Not a mob*, she thought. *An army.*

"And not so much as a belaying-pin on any of those three ships was stolen or damaged," Rebecca Malvern reported the next morning, when she came after breakfast with fresh-baked scones and a hot ginger tisane. "The Indians even swept the decks clean afterwards."

"How very tidy of them." Abigail—dressed for the first time since being put to bed with a feverish cold—tugged her several shawls closer about her shoulders, and sipped the tisane. "Sam does nice work."

"It makes me wish I could write a poem about it." Rebecca smiled, and drew over to herself the papers that Thaxter had left on the big kitchen table for them: notes copied from the Essex County court records, which showed just how much of the Gilead congregation's lands actually belonged to the Sellars family, and through them, to Richard Pentyre.

Abigail looked across at her, and raised an inquiring brow. After being sick herself for two days, nursed by Gomer Faulk in the tiny chamber from which Tommy and Charley had been temporarily evicted, Rebecca had been on her feet again and helping Gomer and Pattie nurse Abigail—thus Abigail had witnessed the meeting between her friend and Charles Malvern.

It had been awkward—no self-respecting novelist would have produced the fumbling dialog between the elderly merchant and his estranged and rescued wife—but, Abigail thought, not painful. The afternoon following—which was Wednesday—Malvern had called again, and Wednesday evening, Scipio had arrived with a light gig, to take Rebecca home.

Rebecca continued, "Perhaps I will write a poem, at that. I'll keep it in my desk drawer, until—until we know how any of this will turn out." She smoothed the folds of the dark wool dress she wore, a dress that bore the signs of neat refitting and was laced as close as it would draw around her wasted body. Framed in the neat dark wig she wore, her strong-boned, triangular face had a waifish look.

Still, she'd been enough herself to smile and laugh when Johnny and Nabby had greeted her back with embraces, and demanded help with their sums, at which they were working at the other end of the table: "Will you be teaching us again?" Nabby had wanted to know. "I've told Gomer she can come to your school, too." And Rebecca had replied, "I would love to have you again—and you, too, Mistress Faulk—but it may not answer, now that I'm to be Mr. Malvern's wife again."

Now Abigail asked, "And what does Mr. Malvern say to last night's events?"

"Everything that he always did." Rebecca's smile turned a little wry. "I knew his promise not to speak of politics wouldn't hold—I think he'd go off in an apoplexy if he tried to keep it. But at least so far he does remember, that we have 'agreed to disagree.' Having Tamar gone helps," she added. "She went on a great deal about prisons and convents, when her father broke it to her she was being sent to her aunt's. But I think the prospect of living in New York cheered her, before she even got on the boat. I still keep to my own room, and Mr. Malvern to his." She turned on her wrist the little bracelet of pearls, that Abigail did not remember among her things before. "And we will see, how it all answers, in time."

Silence lay between them, and Abigail drank her tisane. Pattie and the children went out into the scullery—Pattie had promised to make a syllabub for after dinner—and the kitchen was quiet. Oddly so, it seemed, without the church bells that had rung over Boston for two weeks. Indeed, the silence seemed a little ominous.

"I must say I'm a little surprised, that the Indians unloaded all three ships," remarked Abigail after a moment. "What came of the rumor that someone was going to unload the *Beaver* secretly—?"

Rebecca laughed, and flung up one hand in exasperation: "Do you know who was behind that? *Richard Pentyre.* Sam told me only yesterday: 'tis what Pentyre was trying to arrange on the Wednesday night, that his wife—" Her voice faltered, and she put her hand quickly to her lips.

To call her thoughts back, Abigail said, "He guessed there'd be trouble, and sneaked off after seeing his mistress, to hire smugglers to circumvent it?"

Rebecca nodded, and made herself smile. Abigail saw the tears flood to her eyes.

"And of course he guessed there'd be trouble because that wretch Bargest had sent him a note, threatening his life."

Rebecca drew breath, to steady herself, and let it out again. " 'Tis lucky he had the note, or he'd have been a suspect himself."

"Don't think I didn't suspect him." Abigail refilled her cup. The silence returned.

At length Rebecca said, "I dreamed about it last night. Again. In daytime I barely remember it, but at night—"

" 'Twill pass."

"I know." Rebecca pressed her hands to her eyes for a moment, and sighed again. "I don't even know if the things I see in my dreams really happened or not. I remember—I think I remember—waking up lying on my bed with my hands tied, in the dark, but I have no idea how I got there. Orion had come earlier, of course, with some more of the Hand of the Lord's wretched sermons, but I know he left. And I remember going out a little later, and seeing Queenie standing in the alley gate, talking to one of the men who buys kitchen leftovers—grease and suet and such, only of course Mrs. T. forbade her to sell them. The way she started when I spoke to her, I suspect she was selling other things, like the odd spoon, or a few ounces of Mr. T's cognac."

Abigail sniffed. "I wondered if 'twas something like that. The way she lied and prevaricated about having been in the alley, or having talked to you—"

"Miserable woman. I suppose," she added, "that living under the same roof with Mrs. Tillet would make anyone miserable, let alone a thief and a liar. I remember talking to her, and going back into the house as the rain was starting, but nothing after that."

"We think—John and I," Abigail said slowly, "that Orion must have unlatched the window in the parlor when he was there earlier, and slipped back in that way while you were out talking to Queenie by the gate. Yours was the only house, you see, that he knew he could get Mrs. Pentyre to come to alone."

It was the blood, Orion had said. *I thought I could kill her without . . . But then I saw the blood. Smelled its smell . . .*

Had Bargest told him, *You're a Weapon in the Hand of the Lord, but for God's sake don't go crazy and cut the woman to pieces like you did those others . . . ?*

A Weapon in the Hand of the Lord.

Was Sam? Was she herself, as Lisette Droux had hoped?

"I dreamed—I don't know even if this really happened," whispered Rebecca. "I dreamed I saw him through the kitchen door, standing above her body . . . Blood all over his hands—"

"Don't—"

She shook her head, pressing on as if driven to purge the scene from her thought. "Blood all over his hands, and he looked down at them, at her, as if he knew not for a moment how it had got there. Then he looked up, and in my dream I swear I saw the light of Heaven, falling from far-off on his face, and he cried, *Why have you done this to me? Why did you create me this way?* Abigail, why *would* God create a man that way? Will he be punished—is he now in Hell—for being as God made him?"

Abigail murmured, "Only God knows what was in his heart."

"That's no answer." Her brown eyes blazed with anger, with helplessness—with a passion, Abigail thought, that would never let her rest.

"No more than 'tis to say, *The man was born a monster, for reasons no one knows*. But 'tis the only answer God gave Job, when he spoke to him out of the whirlwind. And poor Orion was not the worst monster in the case."

She looked up as John walked into the kitchen, passed through it catching up his hat and greatcoat, and on out into the yard. "I see Lieutenant Coldstone has come to call," she remarked.

An instant later, Thaxter appeared in the hall doorway. "Mrs. Adams? Lieutenant Coldstone is here."

"Is there a fire in the parlor?" She tidied up the legal notes, the morning papers with their account of the drowning of the East India Company's precious tea. "Well, I suppose 'twill warm up soon—Pattie, would you bring us some coffee? Lieutenant," she greeted him, as she and Rebecca entered the small—and icily cold—chamber where the officer was trying to warm his hands before the newly kindled hearth. "I'm sorry Mr. Adams is away—"

"You astonish me, Madame," said Coldstone drily. "Your servant, Mrs. Malvern. I hope you are recovered? And yourself, Mrs. Adams—"

"Have you come to question me instead, about the events of last night? I assure you I've only just finished reading the *Gazette*'s account of them—"

Somberly, the young man replied, "My business is justice, m'am, and the law. What took place last night was an act of insurrection, nothing less. I came only to see how you go on. And I must say," he added, with a bow that took in both women, "I am extremely pleased to see you looking well. You especially, Mrs. Malvern. And I came to inform you," he went on quietly, "that the body of Orion Hazlitt was found yesterday evening, in a wood not far from Salem. He had been dead about a week, shot through the head."

"God have mercy on him." Rebecca put her hand again, briefly, to her lips. "He had to be stopped—and I think that only death could have stopped him—but he did save my life. And yours, Abigail. It should count for something."

"Were the world just," replied Abigail softly, "it might. Thank you, Lieutenant. How is Sergeant Muldoon?"

For the first time an expression of human warmth cracked the young man's face, and he smiled. "Recovering—and cursing at the regimental sawbones for keeping him in quarters. The ball broke his collarbone, but did little other damage beyond the loss of blood—and the lad's tough as boot leather. I cannot say I was particularly pleased to get word from you that you'd kidnapped him as you did, but following Hazlitt that night, when he fled Castle Island, I was glad that it was Muldoon you were with."

"So that's how you turned up so pat," remarked Abigail. "I wondered how you knew where Gilead was. Even some tribes of Indians," she added wryly, "got lost looking for the place."

Coldstone's face stiffened. "In fact, it was Miss Fluckner who alerted me to the fact that Hazlitt had come out to Castle William," he said. "With so many *true* citizens of the Crown on the island, it was easy enough for anyone to conceal himself among them, which I suppose is what he counted on. He could have come upon Pentyre at any time, stabbed him, and disappeared into the crowd. He had this upon him." From the pocket of his cloak Coldstone took a long, thin-bladed knife, of the kind stationers sell, to cut open the pages of books. It had been sharpened to a razor keenness. Abigail turned her eyes from it, remembering not only Perdita Pentyre's mutilated body, but the fact that Hazlitt had also slaughtered Zulieka Fishwire's cats.

Such men will continue killing . . . Coldstone had said.

God made me what I am, but I chose to fight for our rights . . .

God spoke to Job out of the whirlwind and said, *Things are this way because I am the Lord*. There seemed nothing else to say.

"Miss Fluckner knew you were working with us?"

"Her father's butler wrote her," said Coldstone. "She came to me Thursday night, with her maid, soon after I got your note. They told me the maid had just seen the man who was pursuing her, there, on the island, in the fort. She pointed him out to me, but he was already making his way to the dock. I think he must have learned somehow that the game was up—"

Sons of Liberty on Castle Island, Orion had whispered feverishly to her. *Watching for me* . . .

Thank you, Sam. "So you followed him—"

"I knew that if he had killed his mother," said Coldstone, "the only place left for him to go, was back to this Gilead that you spoke of in your note to me. And he would lead us there."

Pattie came in with coffee, but Coldstone shook his head. "I will not stay, Mrs. Adams," he said, rising and taking up cloak and hat. "At the risk of sounding ungentlemanly, I fear you are still far from well, and will not further trespass. And, I must still visit Griffin's Wharf, and see what damage was done."

"None, I hear." There was a note of slightly triumphant malice in Rebecca's voice. "Not so much as a hatch cover broken. They were, I understand, quite well-mannered Indians." His face a mask, the British officer bowed over her hand, and over Abigail's in turn. "Nevertheless," he said, "the Governor has sent a complaint to Parliament. I fear there will be hell to pay."

Abigail said, "There always is."

FROM

BARBARA HAMILTON

SUP WITH THE DEVIL

AN ABIGAIL ADAMS MYSTERY

Divided loyalties can lead to deadly obsessions in the rebellious Massachusetts colony . . .

1774: Spring brings uncertainty to Boston as the entire city awaits the Crown's response to the infamous Tea Party. Urged on by the Sons of Liberty—and Abigail's husband, John—militias form and arm themselves. But when a Harvard Loyalist is murdered, the only side Abigail finds herself on is the side of justice . . .

After an attempt on the life of her scholarly young nephew Horace, Abigail travels to Harvard to investigate. A mysterious woman had hired Horace to translate some Arabic, only to leave him disoriented and frightened—and at the mercy of her henchmen. But Horace survived—with a tale of pirate treasure . . .

While Abigail and Horace try to unravel the strange circumstances, one of his fellow students—a young man loyal to the King—is murdered. And though the Sons of Liberty are desperate to find the rumored gold, Abigail is more interested in the truth. For the Devil's treasure comes with a curse that could bring down anyone, regardless of where their allegiance lies . . .

"An exciting new mystery series."
—Sharon Kay Penman, author of *Devil's Brood*

penguin.com

M899T0511